Wild Hunt

BLOOD OF THE ISIR
BOOK THREE

Erik Henry Vick

Ratatoskr Publishing

New York

Ratatoskr Publishing
2080 Nine Mile Point Road, Unit 106
Penfield, NY 14526

Publisher's Note: This is a work of fiction. Names, characters, places, and incidents are a product of the author's imagination. Locales and public names are sometimes used for atmospheric purposes. Any resemblance to actual people, living or dead, or to businesses, companies, events, institutions, or locales is completely coincidental.

Wild Hunt/ **Erik Henry Vick**. -- 1st ed.
ISBN 978-0-9990795-4-6

For my parents,
Patricia and Jerome Vick,
who always told me I could do anything.

A person did what a person could, whether it was setting up gravestones or trying to convince twenty-first century men and women that there were monsters in the world, and their greatest advantage was the unwillingness of rational people to believe.

—Stephen King

He who fights with monsters should look to it that he himself does not become a monster. And if you gaze long into the abyss, the abyss also gazes into you.

—Friedrich Nietzsche

I hope you enjoy *Wild Hunt*. If so, please consider joining my Readers Group—details can be found at the end of the last chapter.

ONE

I have said to the gods and the sons of the god,
The things that whetted my thoughts;
But before thee alone do I now go forth,
For thou fightest well, I ween

—The Lokasenna (The Poetic Edda)

The woman awoke at a wormlike pace, coming back to herself bit by bit as if she had slept for ages. Her tongue lay in her mouth like a dead slug and tasted of a bitter metal, or perhaps blood. Her ears rang with the silence that encircled her, entombed her. Her memory was foggy…incomplete.

She hung in an empty space surrounded by a kaleidoscopic horror of colors and abstract geometric shapes exploding around her. Time and space held no meaning for her, there was no up nor down, only the mysterious sensation of tides pulling at her from every direction. No solid ground existed beneath her feet, no liquid…nothing.

Named Hel, Queen of Osgarthr, rightful ruler of the Isir, her own people had betrayed her centuries ago, and, more recently, her allies—the *Plowir Medn*—had betrayed her, too. She remembered the foul blue creatures teleporting her away from the battle with that damn cop and his cohorts—she'd almost forgotten fighting with Hank Jensen, but she felt a vague tickle about battling a colossal bear, and then thousands of robots had come at her from out of nowhere. *Haymtatlr's guardians*! Her rage was a palpable thing, a beast, alive and clawing for dominance.

Luka was not with her—the *Plowir Medn* had left him behind as if he counted for nothing—but her mind ran in circles, first imagining Luka was with her, wondering where he was, cursing the *Plowir Medn*, wondering if Haymtatlr's guardians had killed the Isir. *Haymtatlr betrayed me, just like all the others—the Isir, my allies, even my so-called* "guides" *who abandoned me toward the end of the rebellion*!

She drifted in utter silence, lost, bereft—even the voices had abandoned her…those two voices—both unfamiliar, and yet, as intimate as lovers—had she imagined them? The *Plowir Medn* had named them

Mirkur and Owraythu. Hel had never heard those names before, not in all her travels, not from any of the peoples she had visited in her many years of life, and yet…and yet she seemed to know them, to recognize the sound of their voices.

Their names were jokes…Mirkur meant "darkness" in the *Gamla Toonkumowl* while Owraythu meant "chaos." The silly blue men claimed they were brother and sister, and worse yet, ancient gods of great power. It made sense that the *Plowir Medn* would worship deities who claimed to embody darkness and chaos. As a race, they embraced disorder…they seemed to *feed* off it.

How long Owraythu had kept her imprisoned, she couldn't say. An hour? A day? A year? She had no idea—time was meaningless in this eternally variegated changing pattern of colors and images.

The last thing she remembered was Owraythu saying, "You refused to play by the rules. For that, you will pay the price." And…

The pain had engulfed her, then. Wave after wave of nauseating agony seared her nerves and racked her body. Her muscles had refused to obey her, even her mouth and throat. She hadn't even been able to scream.

It had gone on and on, just her and the pain. Her senses had shut down one by one, her vision, her sense of smell, her hearing, her sense of touch, and even the taste of her tongue in her own mouth as it dried. Only the pain had been constant.

When the darkness had overtaken her mind, she had welcomed its release, but now she regretted the loss...of memory, of her sense of place in the universe. *What did they do to me while my mind rebelled and ran away from the pain? Where am I, and more importantly, how can I escape? How can I get back to my war?*

"*Lyows!*" she said into the dead space in which she hung. Nothing happened, and a tingle of fear rattled around her belly like dice in a gaming cup. Her memory of what had happened after Owraythu had told her she would pay the price was fuzzy. She thought something else had happened, but she couldn't pin it down. "*Luka!* Where are you, my Champion?" she yelled.

Nothing and no one answered her, not even the echo of her own voice. She was alone. A mere mote of sentience in a polychromatic nightmare.

She no longer felt any pain—she no longer felt *anything*. Her skin was neither hot nor cold—it was as though whatever surrounded her maintained the same temperature as her body. Even the air enwrapped her in stillness...no breeze...nothing.

Owraythu had mentioned something about Hel's refusal to play by the rules...but what did she mean by that? Was it a reference to breaking the *Ayn Loug*? Or did it have a more sinister meaning? Hel didn't know and was not sure she cared.

She drifted through the orgy of hues, the mad finger painting of Owraythu and Mirkur on the satin black canvas of the place in which they incarcerated her. Well, maybe Owraythu alone had created the superfluity of color, since the shades of soot accounted for every tincture on Mirkur's palette. Her eyelids drooped to half-cover her eyes, and her eyes unfocused. Her mind ran down, thoughts coming slower and slower until she drifted in a fugue of non-thought, of nothingness in stark contrast to the chaos of exploding colors she drowned in.

Time lost all meaning. One moment was indistinguishable from the next. Nothing *happened*, nothing marked the passage of time—no sun arcing through the sky, no pitter-patter of animal life, no people, no weather, no sounds of sea or wind or war. Nothing.

Just nothingness.

"This one senses you've awakened," said a voice like fingernails scratched across textured glass.

Owraythu, Hel thought.

"As good a cognomen as any other." The voice seemed to growl from the very air, from all around her, the rumbling staccato of a machine gun nest.

"Why… What do…"

"Cease!" snapped Owraythu. "The time for this one to talk has arrived, and with it, the time for you to listen."

"Wait a minute! I'm the rightful—"

"Desist in this irrelevant clangor!" Owraythu's voice thundered, adding artillery barrages to the persistent drumming of machine guns, painful to the ear and brain.

Hel's jaw and tongue worked, but no sound came out. She could breathe, but she could not speak. She couldn't even form coherent speech in her own mind.

"Sibling?"

Half the space around Hel dimmed as if someone had turned down the rheostat governing the saturation of the colors swirling around her. The colors leached out of the nothingness encircling her, and Hel understood the true meaning of nothingness. She tried to turn so that all she saw was the psychotic symphony of shades, but the umbral midnight murk moved with her. Either that, or the sensation of moving was hallucinatory, and she hung motionless instead of twisting like a fish on a line.

"This one does not savor the presence of this…this…this woman. *If* she can still be cleped thus."

"This one comprehends your distaste but abandon your disquiet. She will either assimilate, or she will suffer in this crucible of torment this one has created."

Hel wanted to say she would listen, she tried to nod, to kneel, to do *anything*, but Owraythu denied her all forms of communication. She hung, speechless, motionless, expressionless.

"She is…" said Mirkur, and his voice abraded Hel's nerves.

"Yes," said Owraythu. "She entreats us to reform her errancy."

"Affirmation. The small one demands correction."

The darkness seemed to pulse with the arrant lack of light, or perhaps it breathed. Hel couldn't stand to look at it.

"Her capacity to perceive our realm for what it is reeks of the lacking," said Owraythu. "Baseness and avarice are the *sui generis* roots of her psyche, in part—"

"Inconsequence," said Mirkur.

"Yes, yet her pattern of cognition resides at the root of her error. This small one conjectures her disgraceful creed protects her from—"

"She *shall* learn."

Owraythu said nothing, but the paroxysmal bursts of color shouted her pique at being interrupted. At least that's how it seemed to Hel.

"She *will* take correction."

"Agreement."

"This one requires that she dwell here in suffering until she grows submissive and—"

"This one assimilates, Mirkur. Leave the chore with this one. The task will consummate in success, or the task shall continue without end, without pause."

The categorical, tenebrous lack of everything related to light and life faded, replaced by a detonation of color that threatened to sear Hel's brain. In it, Hel thought she detected a sense of maleficent triumph in Owraythu's interruption of Mirkur's thoughts. Like called to like, after all.

"Alone at last," crooned Owraythu. "Allow this one to begin." The myriad hues and shades surrounding Hel pulsed faster and faster—like the heartbeat of a sprinting woman. "This one has such sublimities to share with you."

TWO

"I think it's now or never, Hank," said Yowtgayrr. Glancing down at the shimmering platform with a trace of distaste on his face, he stepped up and moved to stand next to Jane.

I glanced at Althyof. "I'm going with them," he said. "Sounds like fun." He tipped a wink and stepped up on the platform.

With a shrug, I called Keri and Fretyi to my side and stepped up next to the others. "Hit it, Haymtatlr." A nanosecond later, he did, and my next breath tasted of home.

The breath right after that tasted of dust, damnation, and death. Keri and Fretyi growled and took a few stiff-legged steps, fur standing on end along the ridge of their backs. "Weapons," I snapped, letting my arms do what they knew so well. Yowtgayrr sketched his silvery runes in the air and disappeared.

Kunknir and Krati in hand, I stepped clear of the others and peered into the stygian satin shadows. "*Lyows*," I said, and a warm golden light washed away the darkness.

We stood in an unknown yarl's old great hall. Three bodies lay in a small group in the center of the hall, and blood pooled around them, wafting the scent of coppery blood and the charnel smells of the slaughterhouse. At the far corner, a battered yew door flapped in the wind.

"What's that…Oh my God, Hank! That one in the middle…was he *butchered*?"

"Yeah," I breathed. "Leg's cut away. Chopped away, more like it."

While the pups sniffed around the edge of the blood, Althyof crept to the bodies, daggers out, cadmium red cartoon shapes jigging and jagging. "This one's dead by violence," he said, touching the foot of one body. "This one…the one missing the leg…he's an *oolfur*, Hank."

I raised my eyebrows. "A *dead oolfur*?"

"Yes, killed by an Isir using *saytr*, unless I miss my guess."

"Luka," I rasped.

The Tverkr shrugged. "Who else? This guy here, he died fighting this *oolfur*, I'd guess."

"What makes you say that?" asked Jane, gaze drilling into the dark corners of the room.

"Well, the *oolfur* has his bowels in his hand."

The puppies stood still, staring at the yew door and the shrieking storm beyond it. Keri had one foot up as though he were about to take a step. As I watched, Fretyi sank into a slinking crouch and edged toward the shadows at the edge of the room.

"Oh."

"It appears the disemboweled guy died trying to unsee something," I said. "This other guy...could they be brothers?"

Althyof peered at their faces. "I have no idea. All you Isir look alike." He smiled weakly and shrugged when no one joined him.

"Maybe the disemboweled guy tried to save this other one—his brother? Sacrificing his bowels so this other one could get away, but when the other saw what was happening, he turned and came back to stand and fight with his brother."

"No way to know," said Althyof with a shrug and a grim expression. "Not unless you can cause the dead to speak."

The door of the great hall snapped shut, and Yowtgayrr appeared, sheathing his longsword and dagger as he did so. He glanced at the bodies, then met my eye. "No threats," he said. "There is a faint trail in the snow, but a blizzard rages and the trail won't last."

"Then we'd better get after Luka," I said.

Jane approached the three bodies at the center of the room. "Shouldn't we…I mean, we're not going to leave them this way, are we?"

"Hon, there's no time. Snow obscures Luka's trail as we speak. We've got to get moving."

She tilted her head to the side. "Yeah. But are we so driven to find that inhuman bastard that we don't have time to act like humans?"

I rubbed my face. She was right, and she *knew* she was right. "Okay," I breathed.

"Freya?" a weak voice gasped, and we all jumped a little, even Althyof, and the pups barked, eyes riveted on the disemboweled man. His eyelids fluttered, and his gaze fixed on Jane's face. He opened his mouth to speak again but only gasped.

"Hank…" said Jane.

"What can we do?" I murmured.

Jane held up Sif's bag.

"You have no need of ointments and tonics, Jane," said Yowtgayrr in his understated way.

Jane shook her head, looking from me to Yowtgayrr to the dying man. "What else can I do?"

"Use the ring," said Althyof, his eyes on my face. "If you want to save him, Jane, use the ring."

"The ring?" Jane asked. "It can…" She looked down at the platinum band around her finger. "It can help something this…bad?"

Althyof nodded. "It can heal anything up to death." He glanced at the man dying at their feet. "So, if you want to save him, I'd recommend you do it now."

Jane handed me her shield and her spear and squatted next to the man—I should say "the kid" because he wasn't more than seventeen or eighteen unless my year in Osgarthr had robbed me of my common sense. She lay her hands on the boy's cheek, and he opened his eyes.

His gaze bounced across her face and then over her shoulder, and he saw me standing behind her and to the side, holding her golden spear and her shield with the raven enameled in black in its center. Althyof shifted his feet, and the boy's gaze darted first to him, then to Yowtgayrr, and finally back to Jane's face. "My lady…" he breathed. "Will it be Valhatla or Fowlkvankr?"

"Quiet, now," Jane murmured. "It is not your time, not if I have anything to say about it." Eyes squeezed shut, she extended her arm to hover over the ghastly wound in his abdomen. Her face tensed with concentration and her head tilted to the side as though she were listening to something far away or at the edge of her hearing. Her sable hair hung in the boy's face, but he didn't seem to mind.

The tableau stretched, and no one even drew breath for fear of interrupting the process. The boy's bowels twitched as though filled with baby snakes, and he screamed. Jane didn't move, didn't open her eyes, didn't comfort him. If anything, her face grew even more tense, and the twitching in the boy's exposed bowels became slithering wriggles as they worked their way back inside the torn skin and muscles of his gut.

His head thrashed back and forth, eyes squeezed shut, veins visible in his forehead and neck, mouth open in a soundless scream of suffering, but she kept going. Tears shimmered down his cheeks, and his lips trembled, but he didn't fight her, didn't push her away. The last of his exposed bowel retreated inside his abdomen, and the boy's muscles slackened all at once.

"Almost," Jane breathed. "The laceration next…" She constricted her eyes even tighter and pursed her lips, breathing fast as if she'd run a mile at top speed. The long gash in the boy's belly closed as though zippered shut from within, and Jane fell back on her butt and blew out a long breath. "That's it," she said and flopped over on her side, enervated and boneless.

"Jane!" I said, dropping her gear and going to her side.

"S'okay," she whispered. "He'll live now." Her eyes drifted closed, and her breathing settled into the familiar rhythm of her sleep.

I glanced up at Yowtgayrr. "So that's a 'no' on tracking Luka through the storm. Any other ideas?"

"You," he said.

"Me?"

"Your ravens."

"Oh, yeah… I almost forgot about them." The *triblinkr* I'd learned from my grimoire rolled from my lips, and I lay back on the floor next to Jane. "I'll take a look."

I pushed myself to my feet and popped a single, separated animus—which took a form the size and shape of a raven made from coal-black smoke—out through the ceiling of the great hall and into the swirling snow and freezing wind of the blizzard. The white wall of the winter storm hid everything farther away than ten or twenty feet, so I dropped to the ground in front of the yew door. The trail Yowtgayrr had mentioned was clear enough from there, but the falling snow had filled the knee-deep tracks more than three quarters of the way. I sent my animus to follow the trail, keeping half my mind on it, and focused on the room with my physical body. "I'm on their trail," I said. I took Jane in my arms and eased her away from the thickening pool of blood. "Can we move him, do you suppose?"

Althyof looked at the man Jane had healed and shrugged. "I've no idea. He looks…peaceful."

"I'm… I feel strange, weak," the man gasped. His eyes remained closed, but he lifted his head a little. "I *would* prefer to get out of this blood."

"Don't blame you," I said. "Althyof?"

The Tverkr gave me a sour look but bent and offered his hand. The young man grasped his hand with his eyes still closed. Althyof pulled him to his feet, and while the man groaned, he came upright with little fanfare. Standing, he kept Althyof's hand trapped in his grip and opened his eyes.

As he saw Althyof, he started and blushed to the roots of his hair. "My apologies," he said. "I've… I don't…"

"It's all right," I said. "Meet master *runeskowld* Althyof of the Tverkar, binder of Friner, slayer of the troll Fowrpauti in single combat."

The young man straightened from his bow, his wide eyes going even wider as his gaze darted from the distinctive triangular shape of his trapezoids, his strangely colored skin and hair, and traveled over the runed leather cloak. "A Tverkr?"

Althyof nodded his head once, a grave expression on his face.

"Am I dead? Have I arrived in Nitavetlir?"

Althyof scoffed. "No, boy. My homeland is a place of beauty—worked stone, fine metals, shining jewels. We would not live in a sty such as this hall. Besides, I've never seen a dead human walking around back home."

The man stood staring, mouth drooping open. His eyes drifted from Althyof to Yowtgayrr, and he shook his head. "I... I do not mean to offend, but your appearance is dissimilar to the Tverkar spoken of in the sagas."

Yowtgayrr shrugged. "I'm not a Tverkar. I'm an Alf. Yowtgayrr by name."

"Not a Svartalf?" asked the man.

Yowtgayrr stiffened and shook his head.

"That's a touchy subject for an Alf. Best to keep such comparisons to yourself," I said.

The man's eyes drifted to mine before coursing over my body, lingering on my gun belt and my two pistols. "This is a strange dream," he muttered. "My name is Krowkr."

"It's no meaningless dream, Krowkr," I said. "No *troymskrok*. No dream at all. You were nearly dead."

"Yes, I remember. Freya herself came to me and gave me back my life."

I chuckled. "My wife healed your injuries," I said, gesturing at Jane's prone form.

"Is she…" he said, eyes opening wide as he glanced at her.

"What? Dead? No, no. The effort exhausted her," I said. He wouldn't bring his gaze any higher than my knees.

Althyof grunted. "You were more dead than alive."

Krowkr glanced at him. "Yes. We fought Yarl Oolfreekr. My…my brother and I stood against him when he attacked us. He…" His voice broke.

"That's him beside the yarl?" I asked in a muted tone.

Krowkr nodded and sighed. "I…I suppose it was too late to save him."

"Why did you confront this *oolfur*—this Yarl Oolfreekr—with only the two of you?" asked Yowtgayrr. "You must have known what the result would be."

Krowkr gulped and squeezed his eyes shut. "There were three of us. We came here… Our friend, Skatlakrimr, convinced us to come."

"Whatever for?" asked Althyof, but the stormy expression on his face led me to believe he knew their purpose.

"I…that is, Skatlakrimr had, uh, heard the yarl grew sick and died. He…he wanted to come here and…and search for treasures. Yarl Oolfreekr was very rich."

Althyof made a disgusted noise deep in his throat. "Skatlakrimr wanted such and so. He said, he led. And you and your brother? Are you not men? What did *you* want?"

The man shrugged. "My brother, Owfastr, felt loyalty to Skatlakrimr, and the power the yarl held drew him—the respect, the prowess in battle. He…" His voice broke, and he glanced down at his brother's corpse. "He thought we might rise in stature after such a journey."

"And you?" demanded Althyof. "Didn't you have better sense than to come here and confront an *oolfur* with such weapons at that?" He pointed at the iron sword and axe lying in the clotting blood.

Krowkr blushed and dropped his eyes. "Master Tverkr, Owfastr is…*was*…the only family I had left. I couldn't…"

"Yes," said Yowtgayrr. "That is understandable, but couldn't you persuade your brother—"

"I *tried*," he wailed.

"Let's leave that for now," I said. "How did you kill the *oolfur*?"

"The *oolfhyethidn*? We tried, Lord, but failed, as you can see," he said. "Owfastr and I tried, that is. Skatlakrimr hid in the shadows after the first exchange of blows failed to injure the yarl."

"He sounds like a man to follow," scoffed Althyof.

Krowkr shrugged. "In the past, he was…different. Brave, confident."

"You tried to distract the beast so your brother could escape," said Yowtgayrr. "You stood alone?"

"Yes. I was already…" Krowkr's eyes widened, and his hand flew to his belly. "He had disemboweled me."

"Yes, she healed your wound," I said.

"Yes, Lord, and I thank both her and you for my life."

"You don't have to call—"

"Call him Hank," said Jane in a bleary voice. "Or it'll tie him up in knots, and he'll complain about it until I want to hit him."

Krowkr gulped. "*Hanki?*"

"Close enough," said Jane. "How do you feel?"

Hanki meant "the hanged one" in the *Gamla Toonkumowl*, and I grimaced. I'd only been back on Mithgarthr for a few minutes, and I already had a new nickname. Shaking my head, I sighed.

"I feel well, Lady Freya. I thank you." Krowkr bowed at the waist.

"Oh, I'm not Freya," said Jane. "She is much prettier than me."

"She is *not*," I said.

"Yeah, but you're required by law to say that in at least three states." I held out my hand to her, but she waved it away. "I'm good right here for now, but I need food."

"Spoken like the dainty wench you are," I said with a lilt in my voice.

"Where's my spear? I need to skewer you with it."

"And that is why I've got it tucked away by the wall. Out of reach."

"Don't make me shake you until you break, dear one."

Krowkr watched our exchange with widened eyes. He leaned closer to Althyof. "What are their true names?" he whispered.

"They told you what to call him, boy. These two do not lie."

"Call me Jane. No more of this 'Lady Freya' nonsense."

"Kefn?"

"No, Krowkr. It's not a name you are familiar with," I said.

He nodded his head once but didn't attempt her name again. "Yes, Lord Hanki."

Jane giggled.

"Why don't you call her 'Skyowlf.'"

"Hank, don't—"

"What's good for the goose," I said with a smile. "And you did threaten to shake me until I break. That's what it means: 'shaker.'"

She waggled her head side to side. "Not bad, I guess. Better than Aylootr, anyway." She arched an eyebrow at me. "Haven't you forgotten something?"

"No, not that—"

"Food. I need it."

"Right. I'll send Yowrnsaxa an email."

Jane sighed. "In my pack, knucklehead."

"I'll make a fire," said Yowtgayrr, hiding a smile by dipping his chin to his chest. "Is there wood?" he asked Krowkr.

"I'd only just arrived and when the yarl set upon us… We had no chance to search, Lord Alf."

"It's no matter. I'll find something." He turned and surveyed the room with sharp eyes.

"How did you kill the *oolfur*?" asked Althyof. "And what happened to his leg?"

"*Oolfur*? Do you mean *oolfhyethidn*, a wolf-warrior?"

"Yes, yes!" snapped Althyof. "How did you kill him?"

Krowkr blushed and hung his head. "We didn't kill Yarl Oolfreekr. When he… When I fell, I saw something in that corner," he said and pointed at where our *proo* now stood. His mouth dropped open. "That. That is what I saw."

"It's a—"

"The *Reknpokaprooin*, yes. I recognize it from the sagas. It appeared, and…and a man stood next to it. He was dressed in shadows so I couldn't see—"

"Luka," I said.

He glanced at my ankles. "Yes, my lord. Skatlakrimr ran to him and fell to his knees. After that, I… My memory gets blurry at that point, but at the end of the battle, Luka changed as Yarl Oolfreekr had before him. A huge, wolf-like creature. An *oolfhyethidn*."

"Yes," I said. "It's his favorite trick."

Krowkr's head bobbed. "Yes, Lord. Luka killed the yarl, and Owfastr charged over, thinking to save me from Luka." He waved his hand at his brother's corpse. "Luka did that."

"And the leg?" demanded Althyof.

"Skatlakrimr. Luka promised to teach him to become…to become an *oolfur*. He said Skatlakrimr must…must eat human flesh to…to…"

"That's how it works, Krowkr—how one becomes an *oolfur*, by breaking the *Ayn Loug*."

"The *Ayn Loug*, Lord?"

"'It is forbidden to eat the flesh of men,'" said Althyof.

"I… I've not heard that law, Lord Tverkr."

The Tverkr sighed. "Might as well call me Althyof, boy."

"Yes, Lord Althyof."

Althyof lifted his hands away from his sides and let them drop.

"Annoying, isn't it?" I asked him.

Fretyi came to my side, eyes glued to Krowkr, tail erect.

"You…you have a wolf, my lord?" Krowkr asked, unable to keep the awe from his voice.

"No. I have two."

"And they're not wolves," said Jane. "They are *varkr*. Dire wolves."

"Yes, my lady."

"You will have to relax around us, Krowkr," she mused. "We won't bite." She glanced around and blanched. "I'm sorry. That was in poor taste."

Yowtgayrr returned with an armload of old gray wood and dumped it into the firepit. "I have a flint and steel in my pack." He turned toward the *proo*, where he'd deposited his pack.

"Don't bother," I said. I pointed at the wood and said, "*Predna*." The old wood burst into warm, golden flames.

"Show off," said Jane.

"All men know women enjoy it when we do things like that." Jane rolled her eyes. "Oh, don't deny it, I know the truth."

"I may have to beat you with the truth. Give me my shield."

"Heck, no. Do you think I'm insane?"

She cocked her eyebrow. "Do you want me to answer that?"

"No, I don't think I do."

She snapped her fingers. "Food. Pack. Now."

"Yes, dear," I said.

"That's better. And you cook."

"Yes, dear." I got the food from her pack—a haunch of meat out of Yowrnsaxa's stores—and spitted it over the fire. I waved at Althyof. "Help me with these bodies."

"Yes, dear," he said with a mischievous smile.

As we dragged the bodies outside, my animus caught sight of Luka and his new disciple for the first time.

THREE

My animus hovered high in a Norwegian spruce, twenty feet above Luka's makeshift camp. Luka had also used the *strenkir af krafti* to start a fire in the gusting wind and low temperatures of the blizzard raging outside. Despite the fire, the man, who must have been Skatlakrimr, shivered with rough violence, even being wrapped in thick furs.

"Lord Luka, we must find shelter."

Luka waved his hand. "Eat, Skatlakrimr." He wore no furs and did not huddle next to the fire as Skatlakrimr did. After all, the cold couldn't hurt him.

Skatlakrimr's face stiffened, and his eyes cut to the leg lying next to the fire. "Raw, Lord?"

"Raw, cooked. Whatever. Just do it before I lose patience with you."

"Yes, Lord." The young man slid off the stump he had been sitting on and knee-walked to the haunch of meat that had been Yarl Oolfreekr's left leg until a few hours before. He pulled a long dagger from its sheath at his side and hesitated, his throat working and spasming. "I…"

"Boy," growled Luka. "*Eat*!"

Skatlakrimr bent to his task, and I flew higher in the tree, using the branches as a wind-and-snow break. I wanted to get an idea of the land surrounding us, but outside the reach of the trees, there was naught but the white wall of blown snow.

"Cut a piece and eat it!" snarled Luka. "You said you wanted this. Either do it, or I will leave you here."

"Yes, Lord Luka," said Skatlakrimr. He sliced into the amputated leg and carved away a palm-sized chunk of flesh.

"When you eat the flesh of men, your body changes, grows stronger, better. The more often and larger the volume of human flesh you eat, the faster your powers will develop." Luka shifted sideways to look at the younger man, and his eyes were cold. "Unless you are a thrall, in which case, nothing will happen."

"I'm not a thrall, Lord. I come from a long line of karls bound to—"

"I don't care, boy. The petty distinctions of Mithgarthr are meaningless. What matters is in your blood."

Skatlakrimr took a small bite from the hank of flesh he held, his face screwed up in a grimace of distaste. As he chewed, the grimace relaxed. "It's not as bad as I thought," he muttered.

"You will come to enjoy it. From this moment on, no other meat, no other plant, will do. Only human flesh will nourish your changed body. Likewise, you will not find relief for your thirst in anything but human blood. And, take it from me the hotter, the better." Luka's cold gaze crawled over Skatlakrimr, and he frowned at something he saw or failed to see. "Unless you have the wrong blood."

"Yes, Lord. What do you mean about my blood, Lord?"

"If you have enough of the blood of the Isir. I can't tell. It may be you have some Isir in your blood but diluted like water. We shall see."

"And…and if my blood is insufficient?"

"In that case, you will serve as the meal for the next disciple who *will* have a sufficient purity."

Skatlakrimr swallowed. "Yes, Lord. H-how will we know?"

"*I* will see how your body reacts to breaking the *Ayn Loug*. I will either kill you or not. That is how *you* will know."

Skatlakrimr looked down at the meat in his hand and took a large bite. He chewed quickly and took another bite, followed by yet another. "It's…"

"Good? Yes. Human flesh does not differ from an animal's in that regard. Each species has its own taste. I find the flesh of men tastes similar to the flesh of pigs."

"Yes, Lord. I was thinking that very thing."

Luka nodded. "Now, continue eating while I tell you a thing or two. When you finish that piece, carve another. I want at least half that thigh gone by morning."

"Yes, Lord."

"You may think you do this in my name—learning the *layth oolfsins*—the way of the wolf, breaking the *Ayn Loug*."

"Am I not, Lord Luka?"

"No, obviously you are not, or I would not be telling you this. Use your head, boy."

"Yes, Lord."

"You do this in the name of my queen. In her name, I instruct you in the *layth oolfsins*."

"Yes, Lord."

"'Yes, Lord,'" Luka mocked. "Do you even know her name? Do you understand anything about what we are fighting for?"

Skatlakrimr kept his gaze on the meat he was eating and said nothing.

"You are now in the service of Queen Hel, the true ruler of Osgarthr."

Skatlakrimr's head shot up. "Hel? But I thought Owthidn—"

"*Queen* Hel," snapped Luka. He glowered at the man across from him.

Skatlakrimr looked down at the meat in his hand, then away into the storm. "I..."

"Will this be a problem, boy?" Luka growled, but laughed and waved it all away. "It doesn't matter if it is a problem for you or not. It's too late to change your mind. You *are* in the service of Queen Hel, and you *are* her bondsman. You will do as I instruct, or you will become my next meal—blood of the Isir or no."

Skatlakrimr took a deep breath and took a large bite of the old yarl's flesh. "Yes, Lord."

"If you do well, I may permit you to meet her, to stand in her presence. She won't notice you, most likely, not for centuries, but you might gaze on her beautiful face."

"Yes, Lord." Skatlakrimr took another huge bite. "Is it true she is both black and white? Split down the middle?"

Luka scoffed and waved the question out into the blizzard. "The queen is engaged in a war against a pack of fools, and the fate of the entire universe may be at stake."

"*Ragnaruechkr*?"

"No!" sneered Luka. "Not that old yarn. This...this is a battle between dark, faceless forces where the distinction between good and evil do not apply. These mysterious forces manipulate the fools who fight her. Enigmatic figures who tried, and failed, to manipulate the queen and me in past ages."

Skatlakrimr nodded.

"These forces, these…these *things* in the outer darkness…what they want…"

"Yes, Lord?"

Luka sighed. "According to them, no light exists, no darkness, either—they desire to manipulate the state of things, to remake the universe in their own image."

"And you…Queen Hel, and the rest of the *Briethralak Oolfur*…you fight against these forces? These faceless ones…"

Luka nodded looking away to conceal the sly expression that stole over his face, but from my vantage, I could see it clearly. "What we do— breaking the *Ayn Loug*—isn't only an avenue to greater power. We discovered that it puts you outside the perception of those that would control things."

"I…I don't understand, Lord."

Luka shook his head. "Never mind that for now, and truth to tell, I don't understand what their ultimate goals are—neither does the queen—but we object to having our lives manipulated. We object to being positioned like pieces of a grand game. We stand outside their reach, we live our lives according to what *we* think, what *we* wish." Luka's glance at the other man's face was sharp, probing. "But don't concern yourself with things beyond your ken. The immediate threat I want you to focus on is the group of Isir standing in opposition to the queen's rightful rule." Luka jumped as though he'd heard something in the storm, and I couldn't tell if it was genuine or all an act for Skatlakrimr's benefit. He stared into the darkness around the makeshift camp, eyes darting from one set of shadows to another at a frantic pace.

"What is it, Lord?" asked Skatlakrimr, half-rising and putting his hand on the haft of his axe.

"Quiet! I...I feel as if we are being watched." Luka stared into the shadows of the trees. "But it's impossible," he murmured. "They have no access to the *preer*."

Skatlakrimr peered into the swirling wind. "An animal, Lord?"

"No."

The young man's eyes were no threat—he only thought in two dimensions—but Luka was looking up into the trees. I shrank back against the trunk of the tree and slipped inside its flesh. I could no longer see the men below me, but I could still hear their speech, though muffled by the boughs of the tree.

"See anything?" asked Skatlakrimr.

"No," said Luka. "But that means nothing."

"Yes, Lord."

"Go on eating. It doesn't matter if anyone overhears this."

"Yes, Lord."

"Stop saying that," growled Luka. "We are in a war, boy, and earlier today, we lost a battle, and I lost a great friend whom I've known for many times your lifetime. He was...cut down by the traitors, *murdered*, and now, I'm separated from the queen, and instead of having a thriving set of disciples, I have only you, thanks to that fool Oolfreekr. That is something we must rectify."

"Yes, Lo—Uh, how can I help, Lord?"

"We need converts, Skatlakrimr."

"Converts?"

"Yes. We must build a small cadre of *oolfur*. We must rebuild the *Briethralak Oolfur* in Mithgarthr."

"How will we make converts, Lord Luka?"

I edged out of the trunk of the tree and slid upward, away from the two men seated below. Luka glanced around but then relaxed with a visible effort.

"The way one always makes converts, Skatlakrimr, by showing what we can do and appealing to a man's avarice."

"And we show what we can do by…"

"Tell me, Skatlakrimr, do men still duel for property? For riches?"

Skatlakrimr cut another chunk of meat from the yarl's leg and took a bite, nodding. "Oh yes," he said around his mouthful. "All the time."

"That is what we will do. Who is the richest man in this area?"

"I'm from across the mountains, Lord. I knew of Yarl Oolfreekr from his legend, but…"

"Fine. How far to the richest man *you* know?"

Skatlakrimr shrugged. "A day? Two, maybe."

"Good," said Luka. "Your adaptation should be well on its way by that time. You will challenge this man as a man, and once the fool accepts, and the fight begins, you will change…you will become *oolfur*. I will play the fool hiding in the shadows, so I may bet on the outcome and increase our riches."

"This man… Lord, the outcome of such a duel is far from sure."

"As you are now, I've no doubt of that. As you will be after two days of my instruction? No man of Mithgarthr will stand a chance."

FOUR

I let my animus fade back into my conscious mind. It was too dangerous to stay so close when there was so little to distract Luka. "I found them," I said. "They have camped for the night."

"Where?" asked Althyof.

"Five miles to the west in a copse of spruce. Luka is…" I shook my head. "Luka is teaching Skatlakrimr and making plans. *Layth oolfsins.*"

Althyof made a disgusted noise in his throat. "We can overtake them."

The meat I'd spitted sizzled and popped over the warm golden flames. Jane slouched next to the fire, turning the spit now and again. She held a water skin in her other hand and took small sips every few seconds.

"We aren't ready to travel," I said, looking at Jane. "These two need rest and more food, I bet."

Krowkr sat up straighter. "I can go if that's necessary."

"No," I said. "I can track them as I just did. It won't be hard."

"And you'll have the energy to track them across large distances while you move your physical body?" asked Althyof.

"Yes. Each time I split my animus, it gets easier to do multiple things at once."

"We'll make a *runeskowld* of you yet, Isir."

"I think this meat is ready," said Jane with exhaustion dragging at her voice like a ship's anchor. "Who's hungry?" She pulled a sharp dagger from her belt and sawed off portions of the meat. Keri and Fretyi held a foot race to see who could get to Jane's side faster.

Fretyi won.

The aroma of the roasting meat was fantastic, but every time I looked at it, the memory of Skatlakrimr cutting larger and larger chunks out of Yarl Oolfreekr's thigh floated to the fore, and I lost my appetite. "Give mine to the pups," I said and stood.

I walked around the great hall while Jane doled out the meat to everyone who asked. The place was in a horrible condition. I couldn't image Meuhlnir or Veethar's estates falling into such disrepair—not while anyone in either family lived. Carvings of massive battles had been scored through as though someone had run a multi-bladed plow through the carvings. Or maybe a clawed hand.

"What are Luka's plans?" asked Yowtgayrr quietly.

"He's training a new disciple and wants more. The native, this Skatlakrimr, his blood may not be pure enough for the *layth oolfsins* to take hold. At least according to Luka. That may be one of Luka's tricks though, a technique to manipulate Skatlakrimr into trying harder." I shrugged. "I don't know."

"How does he plan to gather new recruits?"

"Dueling. He asked Skatlakrimr to take him to the closest wealthy man, and I gathered the plan will be to challenge the karl and usurp his lands and wealth."

Yowtgayrr pursed his lips. "We cannot allow that."

"No." I gestured at the old, gray carvings and the slashes through them. "How long since someone took care of this place?"

"Ten years? Perhaps more." Yowtgayrr shook his head. "Mithgarthr breeds such contempt for nature."

"You should see it in my time."

Yowtgayrr shook his head. "Somehow, I don't relish the prospect."

"What about Krowkr? Do you trust his account?"

Yowtgayrr glanced over his shoulder at the Viking. "I don't know. There is something in his tale…something that rings false."

I nodded. "I thought the same thing. He's hiding something." I tipped him a wink. "Cop radar."

"Is this a new power from your *puntidn stavsetninkarpowk*?" He glanced at the gilded scroll case hanging from my left shoulder.

"No," I said with a grin. "I was a cop before all this. I spent fifteen years building a skill set that allows me to judge whether someone is telling the truth."

"A good skill to have," said the Alf. "And it tells you in this case, that the boy is being less than honest?"

"About something," I said with a shrug. "It's not foolproof, but I trust the instinct."

"Can we *trust* him?"

I glanced at Krowkr. He squatted next to the fire, taking small, almost dainty bites from the slab of meat Jane had carved for him. His gaze tracked back and forth from Jane to the pups, lingering more on Jane when she wasn't looking. "I get the feeling that to him, we are gods. That's in our favor in this."

"Yes." Yowtgayrr's tone was matter-of-fact. "This is often the case when dealing with a more primitive society, but people are not always honest with their gods."

"Maybe," I said, "but he believes Jane is Freya, and he thinks I'm Odin—the ruler of the Isir according to the mythology of his people. I don't believe his dishonesty would extend to intentional dishonesty about anything that would impact us."

"Perhaps."

I glanced at Krowkr again and blew out a breath. "I don't like it, this god thing, but I don't think anything I say on the matter will change his mind."

"Perhaps not."

I turned my attention back to the desecrated carving. It depicted a one-sided battle—a large force of men on horseback against fourteen thin men who stood far apart from one another. In the carving's background stood a forest of spruce and yew and an *oolfur* sheltered in the trees. The beast seemed to stare at me. "Do you suppose those fourteen thin men are *oolfur*?"

"What else?" asked Yowtgayrr. "They bait the army into a charge, change and wreak their carnage."

"Luka plans to do something similar in the duel. He wants to use Skatlakrimr in human form as the bait, and when the duel begins…"

"Yes. We must not allow that to happen."

I sighed. "I'm not sure how we can stop it." I glanced around the hall. "To tell you the truth, now we are here, and I know where Luka is, I'm having a hard time coming up with reasons not to go back across the *proo* and rejoin the others."

Yowtgayrr starred at me for a moment, his face carefully slack. "That carries the real risk that Luka will disappear into the *stathur* of the universe."

"Yeah…but I have no idea what to do if we catch him. We don't have enough firepower here to kill him—it took all of us to put Vowli down."

"True, but it wouldn't please Meuhlnir if we killed Luka in any case."

"No, it wouldn't, but Luka might not give us a choice. Can we risk a confrontation before we can handle anything he throws at us?"

Yowtgayrr's eyes brushed across the scroll case at my side. "Perhaps…"

I put my hand on the case. "The two *triblinkr* I've learned so far have been helpful, it's true, but I have no idea what else is on the scroll. It seems a little too convenient that every *triblinkr* written in the scroll is tailored to our needs."

"Would it not be better to know?"

The scroll seemed to grow heavier as the Alf spoke, dragging at my shoulder. The gold filigree worked into the leather case grew warm against my palm, as though the scroll wanted me to get it out, to read it, to learn whatever *kaltrar* it contained. "I…"

"I know Althyof has counseled you to ignore the thing until you've mastered your art, but in less than twenty-four hours, you've gained the knowledge of two powerful *kaltrar* and have been able to employ them with a master *runeskowld's* grace."

"I'll consider it. That's all I can promise you for now."

Yowtgayrr nodded his head. "Fair enough."

"For now, let's assume there is nothing else to help us against Luka. How do we capture him? How can we contain him?"

"A difficult problem, no doubt. I shall think on it."

My gaze roved across the old carving one more time and then found the Alf's. "There was something else."

Yowtgayrr pursed his lips but crooked one eyebrow.

"Luka said—and this may be utter nonsense designed to trick his new disciple, but he said mysterious forces are trying to reshape the universe to their own design. He said these figures are manipulating all of us on a grand scale, and that by breaking the *Ayn Loug*, they put themselves outside the reach of these dark figures."

Yowtgayrr stroked his chin, an expression of puzzlement on his face. "I…" He cleared his throat and cocked his head to the side. "I've never heard that breaking the *Ayn Loug* has any effects other than granting one certain powers and twisting one's soul toward darkness."

"You've heard of these other forces? These faceless enigmas?"

Yowtgayrr glanced toward the carving. "Hank, there are…forces in the universe. That much is true. Tiwaz, to whom I dedicate my life, is one such being."

"Gods?" I smiled. "Gods of the gods?"

Yowtgayrr opened his mouth but hesitated, a thoughtful expression on his face. "Recall what I said moments ago, about primitive civilizations coming into contact with civilizations far advanced by comparison?"

"And so Tiwaz is merely another being, like yourself, but from a more advanced civilization?"

Yowtgayrr scratched the back of his neck. "I've never met him, nor seen him, nor known anyone who has, but it stands to reason that gods would have their own civilizations, their own motivations—other than our petty lives."

"Men rarely, if ever, manage to dream up a god superior to themselves. Most gods have the manners and morals of a spoiled child," I mused.

"What?"

"It's a quote by a famous writer on Mithgarthr. He didn't have much of a positive view of what humans have done in the name of their gods."

"Ah. Tiwaz provided us with a guide for living but made no other demands. Perhaps human gods are not as advanced."

"Perhaps they aren't." I smiled and tipped him a wink. "Certainly, Luka and Hel haven't reached that level."

"And perhaps Luka's imperfections skew his understanding of these 'dark, faceless figures.'"

"That's not a tough sell. Still, I'd like to know what he's referring to."

Yowtgayrr shrugged and smiled. "When we capture him, ask him."

"Not much else I can do." I clapped the Alf on the back. "Still, it shines a different light on Kuhntul's visits."

"The Tisir are anything but gods," said Yowtgayrr with a shake of his head.

We rejoined the others sitting around the firepit. Thankfully, they had finished eating, and Jane had taken the meat off the fire. "How are you two feeling?" I asked.

Jane shrugged. "I'm tired, but not out of the fight."

Krowkr nodded while gazing at my knees.

"Up to a bit of slogging around in the wind and snow?"

"Before we get to that, I've been thinking," said Jane. "If I can heal wounds such as Krowkr here had, I could heal Meuhlnir."

I searched her face for signs of exhaustion but found none. "Without knocking yourself out again?"

She shrugged. "Won't know until I try. I could pop back through, heal him, and come back."

"And if Haymtatlr turns off the *proo* while you are there? No, I don't think so."

"I can handle Haymtatlr."

"Yeah, a four-thousand-year-old insane A.I. has nothing on you."

She gave me her patented squinty-eyed look. "I'm too tired to smack you with my pretty shield, so count yourself lucky."

"How could I not?" I tossed her a wink. "At any rate, if any one of us goes across, Haymtatlr could trap us in Osgarthr, dropping whoever stays here into real trouble. It would be nice to have Veethar or

Meuhlnir along for the ride, but I'm not sure *we* could contain Luka even with all four of us."

Krowkr perked up, gaze finally drifting up to meet mine. "Did you say 'Veethar,' my lord?"

I nodded. "I did." Krowkr clasped a pendant around his neck. I waited for him to go on, but his gaze snapped back down to my knees, and his mouth closed in a tight line.

"None of us can risk taking the *proo* for the reason you already mentioned, so all this talk of having more Isir along is just so much wasted breath," said Althyof.

"Is it?" I asked.

"Oh, ho, he's got an idea," muttered the Tverkr. "How will I contain my surprise?"

"What if I sent an animus through?"

"Can you even do that?" asked Jane.

"Only one way to know the answer to that," I said.

"At what risk, Isir?" snapped Althyof. "What if Haymtatlr traps your animus on Osgarthr? What then? Had you considered that?"

I nodded. "When I'm done with my animus, I don't have to bring it back. I can dissolve it wherever it is, and I'm whole again. That should be true of Osgarthr, too."

"*Should* be," said Jane. "You may not be able to control your animus across such a gulf of time and space. And what if Hawking was right about the whole multiverse thing and Osgarthr isn't part of *this* universe? You are bad enough whole. I can't begin to imagine what a pain in the ass you'd be with half your mind trapped a cajillion light-years away."

"I will go," whispered Krowkr.

"No," I said. "Althyof is right. None of us can risk using the *proo*."

Krowkr's eyes drifted to the shimmering silver shape in the corner. "I could go, my lord. There's no risk to your party if I am trapped in Osgarthr."

"No," said Jane, her tone leaving no doubt as to the finality of her decision. "No one is going. The others will rejoin us when they can."

"We thank you for your offer, Krowkr, but it's too dangerous," I said. "In the meantime, we will follow Luka and capture him if we can. Or at least stop him from building another *Briethralak Oolfur* in Mithgarthr."

"So, it's settled," said Althyof.

Krowkr's eyes remained glued to the *proo*. I stepped over to where he was sitting and gracefully fell to the floor next to him. I put my hand on his shoulder. "Put it out of your mind, Krowkr. Danger lies on the other side, from the forces of Hel, or from the crazy guardian of the *preer*."

"Haymtatlr," he breathed.

"The very one. Going back—even with my animus—was a crazy thought. We are here to keep track of Luka, to capture him if we can. All other considerations are moot."

"Yes, my lord," he said, and the memory of Skatlakrimr saying the same came to mind unbidden and unwanted.

WILD HUNT ❈ 45

"Call me Hank," I said. "Not 'my lord.'"

In answer, Krowkr ducked his head and filled his mouth with food.

When the food was finished, Jane and Krowkr claimed to be ready. We stepped out of Yarl Oolfreekr's great hall and into the swirling maelstrom of the blizzard. We were wrapped up as best we could be, but the cold ate into my joints as though I were naked.

FIVE

"**H**urry," I said to my companions, being careful to speak only through my physical mouth. Luka and his new disciple had led us on a merry chase for two grueling days, but we had a weapon they didn't know about—my animus—which swam in the shadows near the peak of a wooden longhouse. In the square below me, Skatlakrimr stood, holding his axe in a grip that even I knew was weak, wrong.

Luka moved through the edge of the crowd, throwing his voice as he had during the confrontation at Piltsfetl, taunting the crowd, disparaging Skatlakrimr.

"What's happening, Hank?" asked Jane.

My physical body was miles away yet, slogging through hip-deep snow, along with the rest of my party. The pups acted like dolphins—burrowing through the snow, only surfacing now and again to check their bearings. I shook my head. "He's baiting them, pretending to be weak, untrained. Luka is slithering around the edge of the crowd trying to stir them up. We have to hurry." Keri and Fretyi barked to punctuate my urgency.

As soon as I'd said the words, a burly Viking stepped out of the crowd and laughed. "If you want a fight, boy, I'll give you one. But let's not make it a duel. Let's keep it friendly."

"Coward!" hissed Luka and ducked farther into the crowd.

"I'm no coward," said the burly man. "But where's the honor in killing one such as this in a duel?"

The crowd susurrated and muttered, but I couldn't make out if they agreed with the burly Viking or not.

"There is none!" I shouted with my animus.

Luka's gaze snapped up and around, looking for who'd spoken with eyes that burned with anger.

"That's right," said the big man. "I didn't earn my name only to dash it to pieces in a silly, dishonorable duel against one so unprepared."

"That's the right of it, Gunthistayn," said someone in the crowd.

"Gunthistayn, is it?" asked Skatlakrimr.

"Aye, it is. Gunthistayn Ryettlowtur."

"The Righteous, is it? More like the fat coward!" snapped Skatlakrimr.

"Boy," growled Gunthistayn.

"Oh, are you insulted, coward?" said Luka. He used the voice of a woman, but I still knew it was him.

"Who said that?" snapped the big warrior.

Trudging through the snow, I sighed. "I don't think I can delay them much longer. They've almost got their first victim mad enough to fight."

"We must run," said Althyof.

"This snow isn't helping."

"I've got just the thing." The Tverkr cleared his throat and began to sing a *trowba* while shuffling his feet through the snow. The power of the *kaltrar* whirled around us like snow in the wind.

The snowpack rarefied—it was like going from struggling through knee-deep mud to strolling along through fall leaves—and our pace picked up.

Below my animus in the village square, Gunthistayn's face came over brick red, and his hand strayed toward his belt, where his notched and well-worn axe hung. "Who is it that challenges me? You boy? Or your woman skulking about in the crowd?"

Skatlakrimr raised his axe over his head. "I challenge you. I have no woman, so whoever said it must be one of your neighbors, who no doubt knows the truth of her claim."

Gunthistayn took a step forward, his hand tightening on the head of his axe. "No. It is a trick," he growled. "My neighbors know me, it is true, and because of that, they know I am no coward."

"If you say so," jeered Skatlakrimr. "Either way, we all know you are full of talk and low on deeds. Either duel me or get away. I'm not here to bandy words, I'm here to *fight*."

Gunthistayn's eyes grew cold and a vein in his forehead engorged and pulsed. He tilted his head to the side and glared at Skatlakrimr but didn't speak.

"Does this little one scare you, big man?" Luka catcalled in the raspy voice of an old man.

Gunthistayn's eyes widened at the jibe, and his nostrils flared. "You want a duel, you great git? Fine. I'll duel you, but I'll not be held accountable. I've done my best to dissuade him, have I not?" His eyes swept the now silent crowd of villagers. "Can anyone say I should have done more? Can anyone say I was not provoked?"

I blew out a sigh and shook my head. "It's about to start. The first duel."

"How much farther?" asked Jane.

Krowkr pointed at a hill a quarter of a mile away. "It's beyond that hill, Lady Fr—er, Skyowlf."

"Then we can stop it," she said. "I can fly ahead, Hank. That should bring everything to a halt. Right?"

In the first exchange of blows, Gunthistayn came within a hair's breadth of cleaving Skatlakrimr's head down the middle. He moved with uncanny speed and grace that reminded me of Mothi. Skatlakrimr dodged to his right and Gunthistayn's axe head lodged in his left shoulder.

"There, boy," snapped Gunthistayn. "Let's end this foolishness at first blood. It's not as if you can give me a good fight with that wound in any case."

Skatlakrimr laughed and shook his head. "Not unless you cede your lands and possessions to me." With a quick, disgusted snort, he swatted at Gunthistayn's axe haft with his own axe, dislodging the head. A gaping gash bisected Skatlakrimr's trapezius and collar bone on his left side.

The Viking warrior scoffed and glanced around at the crowd. "This one is insane. Or god-touched."

If only he knew the truth of that! I thought.

The crowd fell silent, expecting a quick end to the battle, but they were to be disappointed.

"Hurry," I said to my companions sludging through the snow. "The Viking drew first blood, but it will not end well. Skatlakrimr's blood is pure enough—he's laughing at an axe lodged in his shoulder."

"I'm going to fly over there," said Jane. Krowkr's eyes lingered on her, awe and wonder settling on his face. My wife shrugged one shoulder free of her pack. "Someone take my pack, I want to be able to move easily."

The hill loomed closer but still too far away. "No, Jane. Luka is right there, and there's no telling what he will do."

"But I can—"

"No. Remember the sea dragon? The thing in the desert? There are *two oolfa* in that village."

Gunthistayn unleashed a fusillade of sweeping slashes and cunning chops that staggered Skatlakrimr and splattered more of the nascent *oolfur's* blood on the muddy ground. The Viking's expression was grim, his mouth set in a moue of distaste. "Yield, boy!" he rasped.

In answer, Skatlakrimr laughed and immediately hacked and coughed, blood trickling from the corner of his mouth. "Is that all, old man?" he asked. "I thought you'd be more fun."

Gunthistayn sighed, and it sounded as though he stood at his mother's own deathbed. "Lad…"

"Is that all you can muster? *Lad*? *Boy*? Shut up and fight!"

I shook my head. "It's getting bad. Skatlakrimr is about to begin, I think." The hill was close now, perhaps two hundred yards, but we still had to climb it, still had to make it the rest of the way to the village and push our way to the square.

"I should go, Hank," said Jane. "Your split personality is there. Surely between the two of us—"

"Not yet, Jane," I said. "We'll all be there soon."

Gunthistayn took a step away from Skatlakrimr. "I don't want to kill you, boy."

"Fool! As if an old man such as you *could*!" Skatlakrimr scoffed and shook his head.

The Viking warrior straightened but kept his axe ready. "Lad, I'm not sure what dream you are having, but if I hadn't held back on that last exchange, you'd be lying dead at my feet. Hear sense! Leave off, now."

Skatlakrimr laughed once more, a great, belly-shaking howl of amusement. His eyes lit up, and he threw back his head and howled like a wolf.

Gunthistayn took another step back, his gaze darting to various men standing in the square and watching. "This one *is* god-touched," he said. "We should restrain him."

"Coward!" shouted Luka in the voice of a young man.

Skatlakrimr's face twisted. "Mad, am I? God-touched?" he demanded, stepping toward Gunthistayn. "Insane? In need of restraint?" He threw back his head and laughed raucously. "If you only *knew* the god who touched me!" He took another menacing step toward the big warrior and hefted his own as yet unbloodied axe. "Tell me, old man…is it my turn yet? Is it?"

Gunthistayn shook his head as a sad expression settled onto his features, and he sank into a fighting crouch, axe head weaving and whirling through an intricate pattern in the air between them. "I've tried and tried to spare you, lad, but you seem intent on dying here today."

"Silly old man, I'm not the one who will die," hissed Skatlakrimr. He stood straight and threw down his axe. "I don't need sharpened steel to end your pathetic existence."

Gunthistayn took another step back, his axe slowing until it was still. "This is wrong," he muttered. Then, raising his voice to be heard over the muttering and murmuring of the crowd. "I can't kill an unarmed, insane boy!"

Skatlakrimr's lips peeled back to reveal his teeth in a ferocious grin. "Back to name calling? Well, here's a name that's correct. *Oolfhyethidn*!"

Gunthistayn shook his head and glanced around the square. "Is the yarl here?" he asked. "We must see to this boy. It's only right."

Jane crested the hill first, followed by Yowtgayrr. Her arm snapped up. "I can see it!"

"Go on," I said. "We'll be right behind you."

Jane tossed her pack at Krowkr even as her raven-black wings emerged from the slits hidden in her mail shirt. She strapped her raven-emblazoned shield to her arm and took up her golden spear. "Don't leave me hanging," she said.

"Never in life. Don't get in trouble until you can see us getting close."

She nodded and with two massive beats of her wings was airborne. Krowkr's gaze followed her, and his hand went to the pendant at his neck. His lips moved, but whatever he said was inaudible. Jane turned and raced toward the village, her golden spear twinkling in the morning sun.

"We should sprint," I said.

"Can you?" asked Yowtgayrr without malice.

"Maybe, but if I can't, leave me behind."

Althyof shook his head. "If we do, the snow will condense again."

"If it does, it does," I said. "Now let's go!" I set off at a run, not yet giving it my all, just testing the waters. Even with the far-from-pleasant jarring in my legs, hips, and back, it was far more than I'd have been able to do without Sif's magic medicine. I thought I could make it to the village at what remained of my top speed. It was downhill all the way. "I'm not going to be as fast as the rest of you. Don't wait for me."

"Give me your pack, Lord," said Krowkr, holding out his hand.

I shook my head. He already had Jane's pack and his own.

"Allow me to carry it for you, Lord," he said. "You should be free for battle. And I'm young, I can take the extra weight."

I grimaced but shrugged off my pack. I wanted to hand him my arms and armor, too, but I had to draw the line somewhere. "Thanks, Krowkr. When we get to the edge of the village, I will strip off the rest of my gear. I want you to stand guard over it. None of it should fall into the wrong hands."

"But, Lord, you'll be going into battle! You can't go unarmed and unarmored!"

I grinned at that. "You'll understand when we get there." Keri and Fretyi yipped from somewhere under the snow ahead, sounding like excited children.

In the square below me, Skatlakrimr danced around on the balls of his feet, throwing punches at Gunthistayn. The big Viking watched the younger man shuck and jive, uncertainty written across his face.

"Come on, old man," crooned Skatlakrimr. "Let's fight."

I shook my head even though it was still a football field away. I doubted Skatlakrimr had performed the change more than once as of yet, and already he displayed the bumptious arrogance of Luka and Hel.

Skatlakrimr leapt forward abruptly and slapped Gunthistayn across the face. "There, old man! Feel my wrath!"

"Finish it!" yelled Luka, this time in his own voice, and the command lashed the air, making both combatants jump. "Something is coming. I smell evil on the wind!"

Gunthistayn shook his head and raised his axe, and as he did so, Skatlakrimr stopped dancing around like a drunken fool and stood before the big man, arms held out to his sides at shoulder height. "Boy, you are a fool," said the big Viking, raising his axe high. His shoulders bunched and the muscles across his back flexed as he brought the axe whistling toward Skatlakrimr's head.

A small smile danced on Skatlakrimr's lips, and he winked up at the big man. "*Oolfur*!" he shouted, and the *prayteenk*—the change from man to *oolfur*—rippled through him to the sound of breaking bones and ripping skin. His left hand shot toward the axe whistling down at his head, knocking it out of its deadly trajectory as if it were a child's toy. Gunthistayn grunted in surprise as he struggled to recover from the massive swing. In a move too fast for the human eye to follow, Skatlakrimr was up close, inside the reach of the axe, and his hand was on Gunthistayn's neck.

"*Frist*!" I shouted.

Skatlakrimr stood frozen, as still as a stone, but the *prayteenk* continued—coarse brown fur that was so dark it bordered on black sprouted from the skin around his neck and shoulders. His jaw dislocated and stretched, fangs pushing his human teeth out of his head, his ears shifted and grew pointed as they traveled to the top of his skull. His eyes doubled in size, then tripled, even as he grew to loom over Gunthistayn, whose own eyes were wide as he struggled to free himself from the grip of the *oolfur*, muscles bunched, fingers fruitlessly prying at Skatlakrimr's hand.

Luka's voice boomed across the square. "Who hides in the shadows? Who is it that speaks the *Gamla Toonkumowl*? Who dares to use *saytr* on one of the *Briethralak Oolfur*?"

Outside of the hideous sounds that accompanied Skatlakrimr's *prayteenk*, silence reigned in the village. I kept my animus close to the peak of the roof, hidden deep in the shadows, while Luka's eyes swept first the crowd and then every doorway open to the square.

"*Kverfa*!" he snapped, pointing a long, graceful finger at his apprentice.

Skatlakrimr rolled his head and snarled—too far gone in his change for human speech—and clamped his hand around Gunthistayn's throat with bone-crunching strength. The big Viking didn't even have time to gasp before Skatlakrimr cut off his wind. Without apparent effort, Skatlakrimr lifted the burly chested Viking with one hand and straightened to his full height.

He wasn't as tall as Luka, nor as impressive, but his new form impressed the villagers, nonetheless. Many of the younger men stood staring with avarice in their eyes. The older men turned aside as if not looking at the *oolfur* could somehow rob him of his reality.

"On your knees!" snapped Luka, all pretenses of being anything but the Trickster dismissed. Even in his human form, Luka cut a tall and imposing figure. He wasn't muscular—quite the reverse, he appeared wasted, sickly—but large bones filled his broad frame and the arrogance of living for centuries virtually unchallenged filled his every move. Almost as one, the villagers dropped to their knees in the cold, muddy square. Luka strode to Skatlakrimr's side and beckoned the *oolfur* to bend his head down to the level of Luka's head. He whispered in Skatlakrimr's ear.

If human anatomy had limited me, I wouldn't have had a clue what he said, but as an animus, I had no anatomy at all. What he whispered in the wolf-like ear was this: "The time for showmanship has passed. There is an interloper in the village. Dispose of this twit quickly and be ready for a real fight when I flush the man out. If it is who I think it is, no matter how impossible it is that he is here, he will pose quite a danger to you."

"Not good!" I shouted to the men running toward the village with me. "Skatlakrimr has changed. I tried to stop him, but Luka dispelled my *kaltrar*. He knows someone is there, someone with the ability to *vefa strenki*. I get the feeling he knows it's me."

Just then, Jane swooped down from the sky and hurled her spear at Skatlakrimr. The golden spear leapt from her hand and transformed into a golden lightning bolt before crashing into the *oolfur's* furred chest.

Skatlakrimr convulsed as the lightning struck, coming up on the balls of his feet, clonic seizures racing up and down his muscles, jaw snapping open and closed. With a bright flash, the lightning was gone, and the head of Jane's golden spear protruded from his back, the shaft from his chest. The convulsions persisted for a moment and then became tonic. Guthistayn hung limply from the *oolfur's* hand, claws piercing his throat, eyes bulging, thick purple tongue between his lips, sclera awash with bright blood.

Luka whirled to face her, eyes blazing. "*You*!" he spat.

"Hey there, dog-face," said Jane without a hint of fear in her voice. "Did you miss me?" She held out her hand. "*Aftur*!" With the sickening sound of a butcher's cleaver leaving flesh, the spear returned to her hand.

"I suppose *he* is here, as well? I thought I smelled him. How did you get past Haymtatlr?" Luka demanded.

Jane shrugged and grinned crookedly. "Haymtatlr likes me better than you."

Luka hawked and spat half the distance separating them. "And I suppose my fool of a brother is somewhere in the shadows, too? Come out, *brother*. Let's finish our talk from yesterday." His eyes snapped back to Jane. "Where is he?"

"Where is who?"

"My brother. Your asshole husband. Veethar. Mothi. *Whoever*. I know you aren't here alone."

Jane shrugged and flapped her wings. "Float like a butterfly," she said.

"What?" His head jerked back, then recognition washed over his features. "Oh, Cassius Clay, yes, I remember him."

"That's kind of rude, no?"

"Rude?" Luka glanced around, confusion twitching in his eyes. "Are you talking to me?"

"Yes, dog-face. *Muhammad Ali* was his name. He changed it. You could at least use the name he called himself."

Luka cocked his head at Jane as though he couldn't quite follow the conversation. "I knew of him when he called himself Clay."

I took the opportunity to sink into the ground and cross to the other side of the square, being careful to avoid Luka and Skatlakrimr's feet. When I emerged and floated up to the shadows near the peak of another longhouse, a teenage boy's eyes tracked my progress; his mouth fell open. He tugged on the boy next to him—who was slightly older and bore a remarkable resemblance. "A magic raven!" he whispered.

Luka's head snapped around, eyes boring into the boy's face. "What did you say?"

The boy hung his head.

"Boy, you'd better answer me, or so help me I will eat your tongue while you watch."

"A…raven," he murmured. "A magic raven."

"A raven? Where?"

The boy pointed up at the roof of the longhouse. "It flew over the house."

Luka's eyes traversed the roof, squinting with suspicion. "Why do you say it was magical? Was it a flesh-and-blood raven or was it an *antafukl*? A bird made of black smoke? A *spirit* bird?"

"I don't know."

Jane brought her spear up and drew back her arm to hurl it at Luka. Skatlakrimr snarled and leapt toward her. Flapping her black wings hard, she sprang into the air and hovered, switched her target to Skatlakrimr and let the spear fly.

As we reached the edge of the village, I heard the crackle of lightning and Skatlakrimr's involuntary howl followed by the thud of his elongated body hitting the ground. I stopped and pointed at Krowkr. "Here," I said, and stripped off my cloak and armor, wincing at the sudden onslaught of my painful curse. Keri and Fretyi danced at my sides, then sprinted toward the village and turned back to look at me as if to ask if I were coming with them.

Luka tore his eyes away from the shadows where my animus hung like a spider in its web. "I wish you would stop doing that," he sighed. "Skatlakrimr is new to this. Quit picking on him, you bully."

"Oh, that's rich," laughed Jane. She recalled her spear and hovered thirty feet in the air, shield held ready in case Luka hurled fire at her.

Krowkr took my armor and my gun belt as I handed them to him. He tried for an impassive expression, but it was evident that the suspense was killing him. I grinned at him. "Now, you'll want to stand back." I chanted the Kuthbyuhrn *triblinkr* as I walked naked toward the village square. It took less effort than the last time I had made the change— maybe some function of fatigue had made it so hard in the battle with Hel. As I dropped forward to the now-familiar quadrupedal gait, I heard Krowkr gasp. *If he didn't think I was a god before, he will from now on*, I thought and made the distinctive sound bears used to express amusement.

I saw the shadow of my physical body in bear form edging closer to the village square and imagined my animus was bigger—as big as I'd been when I fought Vowli. The boy kneeling on the ground below me gasped, then clamped his hand over his mouth.

"Another raven?" asked Luka laconically. He glanced at the boy, and when he did, he saw me, now the size of a bird too large to fly but flying, nonetheless.

"Yes," I said and dove at him, talons extended, wings tucked for maximum acceleration. With my physical body, I stood on my hind legs, easily taller than the longhouses bordering the square, and roared a challenge. Ahead of me, Althyof entered the square with a dancer's flourish, singing a battle *trowba*, cadmium red cartoon daggers doing their stretch-shrink-stretch-shrink thing.

Skatlakrimr picked himself up, staggering as though drunk and shaking his head to clear it. He glanced at Luka, bleary eyed and drooling a little, and staggered to his side.

I dipped a wingtip and swerved in midair, switching targets from Luka to the *oolfur* swaying next to him. Skatlakrimr ducked his head, but it was too late, and my talons plowed furrows across the back of his neck and head. He yelped like a dog and threw up his arms, trying to ward me off, but I was already gone.

With a thought, I transported my animus to hover next to Jane. She glanced at me out of the corner of her eye. "Show off," she whispered.

I roared and shambled into the village square on all fours. Luka tore his gaze from my animus and sneered at my bear costume.

"Such a waste," he muttered. He shoved Skatlakrimr into my path, and the *oolfur* whined like a puppy.

I ducked my shoulder to barge the *oolfur* and dove for his eyes with my *antafukl*, my bird of smoke. Keri and Fretyi drove in low—at Skatlakrimr's ankles, as silent as a midnight snowfall.

"Hank, look out!" shouted Jane.

Two things happened at once: Luka said, "*Huent elti*," and lifted his hand above his head, and Skatlakrimr roared and leapt on my back. Luka's hand blossomed with flames the color of a canary's plumage, and he laughed. He whipped his hand in a half-circle, front to back, and the longhouses to his right burst into flames.

Villagers shrieked and screamed as though in counterpoint to Althyof's melody. Skatlakrimr straddled my neck like a cowboy on a bronco, talons ripping at my flesh. I dipped my shoulder and rolled across the square and slammed into the fool with my animus, which had grown to the size of a small car. Skatlakrimr flew off me and slammed into the flaming wall of a longhouse with a yelp that sounded more like a scream of agony, then rebounded—right into a sweeping strike from my massive front paw. He flew back into the flaming wall, head lolling. Yowtgayrr appeared next to me, sword and dagger held ready. He lifted his foot and planted it in the *oolfur's* midsection, pressing him into the flames and the wall they consumed. The Alf shoved hard, and the wall creaked and collapsed. Skatlakrimr fell inside the burning building with the screech of a scared child. Yowtgayrr stood in front of the opening in the fiery wall, staring into the flames with the intensity of a hunting predator.

Luka ran away from us, flinging fire helter-skelter, hammering at the screaming villagers who dared to get in his way. He glanced back over his shoulders, and his gaze, glowing with hatred, first washed over my physical form, and then strayed up to my animus. His lips twitched in a fulminating grimace.

"*Riknink*!" I boomed from the non-mouth of my animus, and dark storm clouds swirled into existence above us. Fat, bitterly-cold raindrops fell, sizzling into steam when they hit fire.

Luka ducked out of sight around the corner of a building.

"Hank! He's getting away! *Again*!" yelled Jane, frustration singing an aria in her voice.

Inside the building burning next to me, Skatlakrimr first whined in pain, then roared with anger. He burst out of the hole through which he'd fallen, bowling Yowtgayrr over, embers glowing and open flame dancing in the *oolfur's* fur. He screeched, head snapping this way and that, and beat at the flames consuming his flesh.

Althyof leapt with a natural-born dancer's grace, spinning in midair as his twin daggers flickered across the beast's throat and upper chest, the red auras of his blades lurching and stabbing as though they had minds of their own. Where the metal blades plowed through flesh, long lacerations appeared. Where the dancing, ethereal red auras touched, star-shaped marks of charred flesh appeared.

Skatlakrimr wailed and slashed blindly at the Tverkr, but Althyof was already gone. The *oolfur* forced his eyes open, head swinging this way and that, flickering from face to face—looking for Luka. When he didn't find his master, he howled, then craned his neck to listen for a reply.

Yowtgayrr rolled to his feet, eyes dancing to the fire spreading around us, despite the rain. With a flourish, he sheathed his blades and wrote silvery runes in the air, muttering as he did so. The fires flickered and died back a little. He glanced up at my animus. "I will control the fires, Hank. We must not allow Luka to disappear in the confusion."

"Right," I said. I thought about the last place I'd seen Luka and appeared above it, hovering in midair. Behind me, villagers cried out with fear and awe.

"Don't be afraid!" yelled Krowkr. "He is Hanki, and these are his servants."

Skatlakrimr roared in anger and slashed his talons through the air, expressing his anger at being abandoned rather than attacking anyone. His eyes narrowed and locked on mine.

I shook my shaggy head, trying to ward him off, but it was useless.

With a snarl, he pounced toward me. I sank low, my belly scraping the mud in the center of the square as I lunged upward, jaws spreading wide to catch his throat as I had caught Vowli a few days before. I plowed upward, springing toward the sky with my front paws, and pushing with my back legs. The *oolfur* fell into my waiting jaws and arms, and I crushed him close. This time, I didn't waste time holding him aloft, I spun on one hind paw and slammed him to the ground, piling my weight on top of him. His breath exploded out of him on impact.

Behind me, Jane sank to the ground, her eyes tracking from one burn victim to the next. "This will take time," she said.

I grunted.

"Okay. Here goes." She planted her golden spear next to her, and hung her shield from it, black-enameled raven looking down over her shoulder. She tucked her wings but didn't make them disappear to wherever they went when she wasn't flying around like a little bumble-bee.

Althyof danced around Skatlakrimr and me, his *trowba* shifting from one of battle to one of recovery and healing. As with the battle in the *Herperty af Rostrum*, I knew which rune he'd cast next, and I added my own runes, throwing them out in time with his.

"People," Jane called. "Bring your wounded to me. Bring the worst injuries first."

I scanned the empty lanes Luka had used to flee, casting more fire as he went. I called for rain as I zipped toward the edge of the village, thinking Luka would try to get away—that he was sacrificing Skatlakrimr to make his escape. He'd never viewed the people of Mithgarthr as any more than objects to be used and discarded at his convenience. I gained altitude as I flew, doing the equivalent of squinting my eyes against the smoke and rain. The more I squinted, the farther I could see.

Beneath me, Skatlakrimr kicked and scratched and punched, throwing his weight first to one side, then exploding in the other direction when he felt my weight shift. None of it mattered, though—I outweighed him by at least three times his mass. As a reward for his efforts, I put my front paws on his chest so even more of my weight would bear down on him. I locked the knees of my hind legs, pushing forward and down, grinding the *oolfur* into the mud, my jaws closed around his throat, but not to kill him—only to control him.

I didn't want to take his life. I didn't want that on my conscience.

A mother ran to Jane, cradling a small child—a boy—in her arms. Char scribbled over half the boy's face, and his little arm was desiccated, shrunken like a mummified arm. His chest hitched and froze, hitched and froze, and he coughed wretchedly, but other than that was silent—too far gone into what was likely terminal shock. Jane held out her arms like a faith healer from television and squeezed her eyes shut. Her hands glowed with the same cadmium red aura of Althyof's daggers, and a moment later, the aura expanded to encompass the small boy.

Luka ran from the village in long strides, his form convulsing into that of a heinous combination of a man and a diseased stag. He sprinted with incredible speed—he'd already covered most of the ground to the stony hills. I imagined myself over his head, and just like that, my animus soared above him, roaring with laughter. He flinched, lurching a few steps to the left and looking up. His eyes settled on my *antafukl,* and he scowled up at me for a moment before pouring on yet more speed.

The little boy gasped as the red aura washed the charred flesh away and slid into his mouth and nose. His mother cried out in awe as his breathing eased again. The boy smiled, his eyes filled with wonder, and he held out his arms to Jane. She bent and let him hug her neck while she kissed his cheek.

Skatlakrimr snarled and bit at Althyof every time the Tverkr passed by. I growled deep in my chest, and the sound pulsed against his throat. I tightened my jaw muscles, cutting off more of his air, and he went rigid beneath me.

Luka hissed over his shoulder at me. I flew behind him, not interfering with him in any way—I only wanted to know where he was going. He bore down and accelerated, but my animus weighed precisely nothing, so I had no problem keeping up. I didn't even know if I had to flap my wings to fly, or if I could float behind him like a Hollywood special effect, but the flapping felt *right.*

Yowtgayrr clapped Jane on the shoulder as he strode toward the other side of the square, fighting the rampaging fire with his skittery silver runes with his other hand. The villagers stood well away from the Alf, despite his smiles of reassurance.

There had to be a better way of containing Skatlakrimr. I couldn't pin him forever. I thought the *triblinkr* to spawn another animus, and the locals gasped as another *antafukl* burst into being above me. This one was much smaller—the size of an actual raven, instead of the size of a VW Beetle.

"Althyof," I said, using the raven.

He glanced up at me and nodded.

"We need a jail," I said. "Something to hold this one in."

Althyof nodded and pointed to the edge of the village. He danced that direction, keeping his supporting *trowba* going all the while. I rocked back, holding Skatlakrimr's throat between my jaws and scooped him up with my front paws. I bear-walked behind Althyof, squeezing the *oolfur* tight to my chest.

Jane stooped over a burned old woman, her glowing hands darting here and there across the woman's body. Her half-closed eyes flickered to the old woman's face, and Jane gasped, stumbling back on unsteady feet. The old woman's eyes fluttered open, and she smiled at Jane.

"My Lady Freya," the old woman whispered. "Come to carry me to Fowlkvankr?" Her breath rattled in her throat as she died.

Jane dashed her palm across her cheeks, wiping at the tears there. She already looked exhausted, and the line of waiting injured only got longer as word of her healings spread.

"Don't overdo," I said.

She waved me away. "Bear. Two birds. Talk to me when *you're* not overdoing it, and maybe I'll listen."

"Love you."

"Yeah, sure. Kiss up now," she said, but she winked, and a small smile had replaced the look of mourning on her face. "Go on, now. Do your own work."

I followed my own furry back toward the edge of town, and with one last, assessing look at Jane, Keri and Fretyi followed suit.

Luka scrambled into the rocks and treefalls of the mountains. The stag was undoubtedly a versatile form to take for traveling. He found an almost overgrown path and darted up it.

Althyof stopped almost a football field away from the edge of the small Norse village. He paced off a circle twenty-five yards in diameter. "Put him in there when I nod," he said.

Skatlakrimr craned his neck to see over his own shoulder and thrashed against me, fighting harder than ever to free himself from my hug. He howled and whined, but nothing he did made the slightest difference.

Luka raced up the mountain, bounding from place to place with a huge stride and the grace of a forest creature while I followed him, enjoying the chase through the beautiful scenery. When he stopped, his breath huffed in and out like an idling steam engine. His deer-like mouth twisted with effort. "*Mathur*," he croaked and began his change back to human form, staring at me with a sour expression as I hovered thirty feet above him.

Althyof scuffed the snow away and found eight head-sized stones. He walked around the circumference of the circle he described earlier, setting the rocks down at regular intervals. "Don't suppose you have that nifty chisel handy?" he asked.

I made negative bear noises but swooped with my animus to land on the rock nearest the Tverkr. I imagined the silver chisel, imagined I felt its pulsing warmth in my taloned foot, and the tool appeared on the stone, my foot displaced upward to rest on top of it.

"You are going to tell me about those dreams you had while staving off death, right?" Althyof asked.

I imagined my animus hovering in the air, and just like that, it was. The Tverkr stooped and picked up both the chisel and the stone. He chanted a *kaltrar*, slicing into the rock with sharp, confident stokes of the silver chisel. He repeated the process with all but the last stone, then beckoned me over.

"I'll enchant this last stone—all but the last stroke of the chisel. You stand here, and when I nod, throw the *oolfur* as far from you as you can. But, listen, you must not move forward, just throw him. Understand?"

"Yes," I said through my animus.

Luka gazed up at me, face twisted with anger and frustration. "Proud of your new toys, aren't you?" He shook his head, a puzzled look in his eyes. "How could... Did my brother teach you all this? A full change of shape? This...well, whatever it is you are doing right now?"

"No, but Meuhlnir taught me other things."

"Ah," he said, sounding satisfied—perhaps even relieved. "Why are you following me?"

"Why do you think, dummy?" I snapped.

He shook his head. "*That* again?"

"Give it up, Luka. You won't escape, and Hel has abandoned you."

He laughed, great booming cackles that echoed back and forth through the mountains. "Hardly," he gasped between breaths.

Althyof chanted his *kaltrar* and whipped the chisel across the face of the stone. He looked at me and nodded. I unclamped my jaws from Skatlakrimr's neck and hurled him away from me, stepping back at the same time so I could fall forward to a quadrupedal gait once again, Keri and Fretyi dancing back out of my way. Althyof carved the last mark into the stone and set it down as Skatlakrimr landed on his feet with a roar that the *varkr* pups felt obliged to answer with a symphony of snarls. The *oolfur* charged toward us, and I readied myself to grab him again if it came to that.

When the last echoes of his laugh died away, Luka wiped the mirthful tears from his eyes and shook his head. "No, Hank. Hel did not abandon me. She knew I could handle you and your friends as I easily did. She wouldn't have left at all, but for the disgusting little *Plowir Medn*. They don't always do as they are told."

"She should pick better friends."

Luka rolled his eyes and shook his head. "You don't know enough of how the universe works to be a judge of anything she does. You are puny—*puny*—compared to her."

"Yeah, yeah," I said, alighting on a nearby branch. "That's an old argument that wasn't true back there on Mithgarthr. You're quite insane, you know."

"Not that old lay again."

"Well, it's true, isn't it?"

Luka blew out a breath, shaking his head. "Follow me if you want. I've got a cabin at the end of this path. Come visit. Hell, bring your lovely wife. We'll make a night of it."

I stared down at him without speaking, content to let him think he'd had the last word. With a lift of his shoulders, he turned and strolled up the path. After a moment, I slipped into flight, insubstantial wings spread to catch what breeze there was.

Before Skatlakrimr reached the stone Althyof had just finished, the *runeskowld* chanted a *triblinkr* and a shimmering soap bubble of energy popped into existence. The *oolfur* slammed into the glistening bubble, and it stretched, absorbing his momentum, and Keri and Fretyi barked like mad. He hung there trapped in midair for the space of a breath before the bubble snapped back into shape, flinging him back across the circle. He landed on his ass past the center of the ring and skidded to a stop, staring at us with a forlorn expression twitching on his lupine face. The whole thing gave Keri and Fretyi a severe case of the head-tilts.

"There," said Althyof with an air of satisfaction.

"How long will it hold him?" I asked.

"Forever, unless I break the enchantment."

Skatlakrimr's eyes bounced back and forth between Althyof and my *antafukl* as though he were watching tennis. He slumped where he sat, his too-long hands resting on his legs. He was the picture of dejection.

"Bet he doesn't know how to change back," said Althyof. "It's '*mathur*,' in case your master forgot to tell you."

Skatlakrimr spun where he sat, so he no longer had to look at us. Althyof chuckled, tapping the chisel in his hand. "And you, Hank," he said. "Might as well become a man again."

I shook my shaggy head. "What about Luka? Can he break this over-sized soap bubble?"

Althyof laughed. "The day an Isir can break one of my enchantments is the day I'll shave off this masterpiece of a beard."

I chuffed through my nose and padded back toward the village square. I left my second animus hovering in midair, staring down at Skatlakrimr.

The path led through the rarified air near the top of the mountain. It reminded me of the *proo* we'd taken to the Darks of Kruyn the previous year. The thin air didn't affect my animus, of course, but Luka panted as he walked toward the cabin built from time-grayed logs. He pushed the door open and stood aside. "Well? Come the hell on in, Hank," he said with a nasty smile.

My mind raced back through time to that night at the safehouse when he'd said the same thing, inviting me to step in from the kitchen to the room where he'd displayed Jax's broken, gnawed-on body on the dining room table. Anger prickled the back of my mind.

"No? Fine by me." Luka walked into the cabin, pulling the door closed behind him.

I imagined myself inside the little building, hovering up near the peak of the roof, but unlike every other time I'd tried that trick, nothing happened. I tried it again and failed again. I drifted closer to the cabin, trying time and time again, but could not seem to get inside. As an experiment, I popped twenty feet back toward the path and instantly reappeared there. I slid up to the door and tried to swim through it as I could with most material things, but I could not.

My wife stood in the center of a ring of smiling people. She looked terrible—like a soldier who hadn't slept in seven days, like a punch-drunk prize fighter three sheets to the wind. The villagers reached toward her, never quite touching her. I ambled to her side, careful not to crush anyone, though they made plenty of room for me.

Jane looked up at me as if surprised I was there, and leaned into me, letting me bear the majority of her weight. She tilted her head back against the pillow of my furry shoulder. "Girl could get used to this," she murmured.

The villagers backed away, making twitchy little bows in our direction. The fires were out, smoke drifting toward the overcast sky. Of Yowtgayrr, there was no sign, but Krowkr stepped forward, carrying our packs, and my clothing.

"Is the danger over?" he asked.

I turned my furred head to look him in the eye and made the exaggerated nod my bear body limited me to. Jane sighed and pushed herself away from me. "Are there any more injured, Krowkr? Have we found them all?"

"We are still looking, Lady Fr—my lady."

I chuffed through my nose, but softly. There was no getting away from it. In my mind, I chanted the *triblinkr* that would make me a human again and began to shrink and shift back into the form of a man. We could do things they didn't understand, so it must be magic.

It didn't help that it seemed like magic to me as well.

I glided around the cabin on the mountaintop, shrinking ever smaller, looking for a break in the chinking or a hole in the eaves. But there was nothing. *Must be enchanted*, I thought. He could have a series of tunnels under that cabin—he could be running through them now, making good his escape.

Krowkr approached, holding out my mail in one hand and my gun belt in the other. I got dressed, sighing as the cloak settled around my shoulders and brushed away the aches that had settled into my joints when I left the bear form behind. I donned my floppy hat and smiled at the young man. "Thanks, Krowkr."

"It is my honor, Lord Hanki."

I shook my head but said nothing. I was already tired of trying to convince him to treat me as he would any other man.

"Luka?" asked Jane.

I nodded toward the mountains. "He's got a cabin, but I can't get inside."

"Rodent-proof?" she asked with an arched eyebrow and a teasing lilt.

"Raven-proof, at least."

She nodded wearily, leaning on her golden spear.

All around us, the villagers soaked up every word, their awe approaching worship with every second that passed.

SIX

Luka's visit cost the residents dearly—all told, five died, two of them young children. Jane healed half the village, it seemed, while the rest of us did what we could to shore up the damaged buildings. The villagers worked side-by-side with us, but with a quiet reverence that irritated my sensibilities, though Althyof and Yowtgayrr took it all in with an equable grace.

Late that afternoon, I led the others up the stony path Luka had taken earlier in the day. We climbed in silence—all except Keri and Fretyi, who kept up a kind of running version of their foot-attacking game, barking and yipping the entire time. Karls from the village followed us, armed for battle.

I'd tried, but I couldn't dissuade them. They were a proud bunch.

"I wish we could have done more," Jane whispered. She walked next to me on the path, her eyes on mine.

"We did what we could," said Yowtgayrr.

"More than anyone could expect," said Krowkr. "More than anyone could have hoped for." He had also refused to stay behind. He had listened to my arguments with a strange fervor burning in his eyes I didn't much like, and at the end of my little speech, he'd nodded but kept right on walking with us.

When we reached the clearing that held Luka's little cabin, the karls lined up at the edge of the clearing, strapping their shields to their arms and making their weapons ready. A small waterfall crashed into a rocky stream in the cabin's rear.

"If there is a fight, Krowkr, you and the karls stay back. Let us deal with Luka."

Eyes shining with a zealotry that made me nervous, he bowed his head, a forceful reminder of Yowtgayrr's comment about people lying to their gods.

The pups circled Althyof as the Tverkr approached the cabin, his daggers out but free, for once, of their red auras. He looked at the door and cocked his head to the side, and the puppies sat, one on either side, and emulated his head-cock, each going a different direction. With a shrug, he pushed the door open on squeaking iron hinges. He glanced inside and walked back over to us. "It's empty," he said. "Except for a *proo*."

Instead of following him, Fretyi nosed the door open a little more. Keri turned, nose to the ground and followed a trail around to the side of the cabin.

"Why would he leave it open? He must have known we'd come up here," I said.

"Yes." The Tverkr shrugged. "He may have set another trap." He hooked a thumb at Keri. "It could be that the *proo* inside leads to somewhere…uncomfortable."

I remembered where he'd left the first *proo* I'd traveled across. "Or it's another one of his deadly 'jokes.'"

"Or that." Althyof glanced at the top of the waterfall, barely visible over the peaked cabin roof. "There's something…"

"Yes?" I asked.

"I feel it, too," said Yowtgayrr.

"Feel what?" asked Jane.

"Perhaps a bird's-eye view?"

I nodded and muttered the *triblinkr* to split an animus away from my consciousness once again as Fretyi trotted to join his brother. Behind us, the karls gasped. I shook my head and sent my animus straight up. I couldn't seem to stop it from showing up in the form of a raven made from black smoke. *Maybe it's something in the* triblinkr.

"What am I looking for?" I asked.

My animus soared through the crisp, cold air above the clearing, the bright eyes of my *varkr* puppies following my flight. The karls stared up at it, shielding their eyes. Krowkr stood behind me, smiling like the cat that ate the canary.

"There's more here than meets the eye," said Yowtgayrr. "I'll be back." He traced a few silver runes in the air and disappeared. The karls gasped, and I shook my head. *How can we ever convince this bunch we are only men if we keep performing miracles?*

From my lofty perspective—or maybe it had more to do with the embodiment of my animus—I could see the disturbance in the air caused by Yowtgayrr's movements. He circled wide around the cabin, taking his time, never setting his foot down on something that would make noise.

I scoured the space between the cabin and the rock face from above. I couldn't discern anything out of the ordinary. The waterfall crashed into a small pool, feeding the creek that snaked away through the woods and down the mountainside. There were no buildings, no huts, nothing that could conceal Luka.

"I can't see anything back there," I said.

Still holding his daggers, Althyof grunted. "Be ready for anything."

Jane tightened the strap of her shield on her arm and hefted her golden spear. "Keri, Fretyi!" she called. "To me, now." The two pups turned and looked at her but didn't move a step in our direction. "Your puppies need better training, Hank."

"I'm telling you, there's nothing back there. Just the waterfall and the stream." I clicked my tongue, and the pups came on the run, not stopping until they sat by my side facing back and front like some weird *varkr*-Janus, one looking at the waterfall, one at the line of karls.

Althyof shook his head and stepped away from us, muttering a *triblinkr* of his own. The customary red auras snapped around the blades of his daggers and began their jagged, stretch-shrink-stretch dance. Jane moved to my left side and set her feet, peering over the edge of her shield and holding her spear up at shoulder height. Behind us, the karls from the village made a shieldwall.

I swooped over to hover above the waterfall to get an oblique view of the back of the cabin. It looked similar to the front—stacked logs with a single door in the middle. Yowtgayrr stood in the center of the cabin's backyard, turning in slow circles as if he couldn't decide where the threat would come from.

"This is silly," I said. "There's nothing—"

A rumbling crack ripped through the air. It sounded as though an iceberg had split and dropped a huge chunk into the waiting sea. Althyof crouched, holding one cartoon dagger in front of him, and one stuck out behind.

"Guns, dork," murmured Jane.

I pulled my pistols but stood with them pointed at the ground. "Nothing to shoot at," I said. "Noise." Both *varkr* were on their feet, growling deep in their chests, staring at the falling water.

"Puppies don't approve of it, though," muttered Jane. "Neither do I."

Yowtgayrr whirled to stare at the rock face beneath me. His sword and dagger came out with the whispered hiss of steel on steel. He moved to the side, eyes never leaving the cliff.

But there was nothing there. Nothing I could see from my animus at any rate. I walked over so I could see past the cabin and Jane followed, the puppies walking with us, but absently, never taking their eyes off the waterfall.

"What is it?" she asked.

"Can't see anything, but both Althyof and Yowtgayrr are staring at the cliff back there. No idea why."

Another rumbling crack assaulted the air. The water jetting down from the top of the cliff parted with a hiss of spray, and a massive chunk of ice fell to the pool below.

"Something's in the water," I said. "Behind the waterfall somehow."

Althyof began to sing a *trowba*, and the air crackled with power. He whirled into the area behind the cabin, spinning and leaping as he cast runes and the energy built until the air seemed charged with it.

I pointed at Krowkr and the karls from the village. "Stay here!" I commanded and followed the Tverkr, Jane at my left and one pup on either side of us, as if we needed chaperones.

A throaty, inarticulate shout boomed across the meadow, echoing from the stone face of the mountain, and reverberating off through the trees opposite. Keri and Fretyi added their barks to the auditory assault. A long, pale azure arm penetrated the falling water and hurled an ice boulder the size of a man's head at Althyof. The Tverkr avoided it easily, spinning away long before the ice struck the ground. He made a throwing motion with one of his daggers and a red bolt of power shot from its tip and sliced through the water, followed by a bellow of rage and pain.

"Come on," I said to Jane and started toward the waterfall. At the same time, I sent my animus diving into the foot-thick column of water pouring down the face of the cliff. I skimmed down through the rushing water and emerged in a hollow behind the waterfall. Against the back wall of the grotto stood another silvery *proo*, and between it and me stood a humongous blue-skinned giant of a man.

He stood on two legs, but his limbs were over-long, and his joints were bulbous and thick. Despite his muscular neck and shoulders, the creature's bald head seemed too big to support. White horns jutted from where a man's collarbones would be, and again from his elbows and knees. His eyes were a brilliant red and stared at my animus with baleful, threatening intensity.

"A blue-skinned troll or a demon or something," I said. I tried to make my animus as translucent as possible and moved to the side of the cavern, but those sinister red eyes followed me, nonetheless.

The thing reached toward the water, and where his hand intersected the stream, another ball of ice formed. With a guttural roar, he threw the ice boulder at my animus. I darted away, and the ice exploded when it hit the stone wall of the cavern.

Althyof threw another bolt of power through the waterfall. It slammed into the thing's abdomen with a hiss, and the creature screamed in rage. With one last glare at my animus, he grabbed another handful of quick-freezing water, and I let my animus fade— no sense getting him all riled up.

He erupted from the waterfall, ice shards as sharp as any dagger exploding into the clearing. The *varkr* snarled and paced, stiff-legged. Althyof whirled and danced, hurling bolts of power every few steps, but now that the blue-skinned creature could see them coming, he avoided them with the ease the Tverkr had avoided his ice boulder.

My guns came up as though my hands had minds of their own, but I checked my fire at the last instant—the big blue brute wasn't attacking—not yet, anyway. He stood staring at us, head moving ponderously from one face to the next: Althyof, Jane, me, back to Althyof again, as if trying to solve a complex math problem but having no idea of where to start.

"Is it me, or does he seem…*limited?*" asked Jane.

"It's not you."

At the sound of our voices, he growled, showing a mouth full of fangs and sharpened teeth. He took a giant step forward but kept his feet in the freezing water, and the puppies barked in earnest, hair standing up on their backs. His gaze bounced between the pups, and his lip curled with hatred. He bent and scooped up two handfuls of flash-frozen water and hurled them at the *varkr*.

Kunknir and Krati bucked in my hands, reports crashing against the cliff and bouncing back undiminished. The karls gasped at the noise the guns made. Jane hurled her golden spear, and the air crackled as it turned to lightning. The bullets hit first, slamming into the blue creature's chest, flinging pale green blood into the water behind him, and half spinning him around. The golden bolt of lightning hit him broadside, and for a moment, he convulsed where he stood.

With a shout of pure malice and rage, he scooped up more ice and hurled it at us, but two rounds from Kunknir's ever-diminishing supply shattered them in midair. Fretyi and Keri raced toward the stream, barking and snarling. Althyof spun between the blue giant and us, singing a *trowba* at the top of his lungs.

"We have to get it out of the water," Yowtgayrr said from somewhere off to my left. "Limit the frost giant's ammunition."

"Okay," I said. "We'll try." I whistled for the puppies, and they scampered back to my side. Jane and I backed away from the stream, putting the cabin at our backs. After a single pass, Althyof looped around behind us, singing and casting runes to magnify our agility. I took up his song, casting the runes along with him. Jane called her spear back and hunched behind her shield at my left.

The frost giant scowled at us and scooped two more handfuls of ice out of the stream. Jane barged her shield at him, and it pinged like a giant wind chime. A jagged black beam ripped the air between her and the frost giant, and the blue-skinned creature flew from his feet and landed on his back on the far bank. Chunks of ice clung to his feet like shoes.

The giant bellowed and slammed his fists into the earth on either side of him. He lurched into a sitting position and glared at Jane. Something splashed through the stream—Yowtgayrr, still invisible—and the giant's head snapped in that direction.

"He could see my animus, even as translucent as I could make it!" I shouted. The frost giant glanced at me, then back to track Yowtgayrr.

I snapped off two rounds from Krati, trying to draw the giant's attention, but he ignored me. Jane hurled her spear again, then held her hand out, as if beckoning the frost giant to take her hand. The giant's gaze drifted up to the sky and then back down to take in the water rushing past him at his feet. He shook his head like a drunk and glanced at me, bleary-eyed.

"Can we defeat it?" I asked.

As if in answer, Yowtgayrr appeared behind the giant, his longsword and long dagger held aloft, pointed downward at the giant. He plunged the blades down, piercing the giant's flesh near the horns at his shoulders. The giant lurched and shuddered as the blades bit deep into his chest.

Althyof shouted two discordant words in the space between two short lines of his *trowba*: "*Hyarta umsikyanti!*" Two red bolts shot from the tips of his daggers and ripped into the giant's chest above his heart.

The giant's muscles tensed all at once, arching his back, and as a result, ripping Yowtgayrr's blades from the Alf's hands. As if in a daze, the blue creature swept an arm in a flat arc to his side, slamming Yowtgayrr through the air. The Alf landed in a boneless heap.

I strode forward, muscle-memory from a thousand move-and-shoot drills taking over, pulling the triggers of my pistols as fast as I could. Rounds from Krati peppered the blue skin of the giant's torso while rounds from Kunknir hammered into the creature's face. Green blood flew, coating the giant's body. He bellowed, and more greenish blood erupted from his mouth. Jane barged at him with her shield again, ripping the hand she beckoned him with toward her as she did so.

The giant lurched forward as the air pinged and the black beam tore at the air. The beam slammed into the giant and drove him over backward, feet splayed in the air. Yowtgayrr's blades sank to their hilts into the giant's flesh.

"Help Yowtgayrr," I said, and Althyof nodded, whirling and dancing toward the Alf.

Jane recalled her spear and threw it again, hurling it as if she'd grown up throwing spears. She held out her hand again and beckoned, eyes boring into the frost giant's prone form. I fired off a few more rounds from Krati, but the giant never moved, except to twitch as the rounds bit into its flesh.

I continued moving toward the stream, both guns covering the giant, but I checked my fire. There was no sense wasting rounds shooting a dying (or dead) thing. Jane shuffled forward at my side, holding her shield ready. The *varkr* pups escorted us, walking stiff-legged, holding their tails out behind them as though they were hunting.

I stopped when we stood across the stream from the ever-increasing pool of pale green blood and the giant it came from. Muscles slack, eyes rolled up in his head, the creature didn't move. I stepped into the stream, wincing as the temperature of the water lanced through the joints in my feet and ankles. The puppies sniffed the water but didn't follow us.

"Not too close," murmured Jane.

"I think he's dead," I said.

"Still."

I nodded and changed directions, so we came out of the stream ten feet from the giant blue corpse. His blood steamed, boiling in the frigid mountain air, and his eyes turned black while they smoked and hissed. As we watched, the giant's flesh collapsed and decayed, releasing a sickly white smoke and the stench of putrefaction.

Althyof offered his hand to Yowtgayrr and pulled the Alf to his feet. "Are you all right?" Jane asked.

Yowtgayrr nodded and retrieved his weapons, grimacing at the gunk that stuck to the blades. He grabbed handfuls of the sparse grass and cleaned his sword and dagger as best he could.

A clamor came from behind us, and I turned to see the karls from the village below standing in the cabin's side yard. Mouths hung agape, and eyes were round and open wide.

"I don't suppose we can ask them not to tell stories about this."

"Doubt it," said Jane. "Why did that thing attack us?"

"Frost giant," grunted Althyof. "Nasty creatures. *Rude.*"

"What was it doing here?"

"There's another *proo* inside a grotto behind the waterfall," I said. "Maybe it wandered too close to the other end and got pulled through."

"Are they intelligent?" asked Jane.

"You could say that if you were feeling generous," said Althyof. "More than a troll, less than a Svartalf."

"Wouldn't it have known what a *proo* was?"

Althyof shrugged. "Perhaps Luka left this one as a guardian of that *proo*. Or perhaps it was another of his jokes."

I watched the outer layer of the frost giant's skin liquify, melting as if it were ice, giving off more noxious white smoke, as all but a few of the Viking karls crossed the stream to see the thing for themselves. "Why is it melting?

"They come from a strange *stathur*, one that is very, very cold by our standards. This *klith* is too hot for them, and they can't stay long. Even up here in the heights, the temperatures limit their stay to mercifully short periods," said Yowtgayrr.

"Did you notice how it stayed in the water?" asked Althyof. "Cooling."

"How long could it have been in the grotto?" Fretyi whined and yawned as widely as his jaws could move. "Well, come here, puppy," I said to him and held out my hand. Krowkr shooed the puppies toward me and stepped into the stream behind them.

Althyof pursed his lips. "Not long." His eyes strayed to the rear door of the cabin. "When I opened the door… What's that idiot doing?"

I turned in time to see one of the karls push the back door of the cabin open. "Hey! Get away—"

A searing thunderclap of color and light blinded me. The ground beneath my feet leapt out from under me, and a blast of hot wind knocked me ass-over-teakettle. A whump I associated with heavy explosives deafened me. I hit the ground in a reverse belly-flop, and the air burst from my lungs. A moment later, a cold wind blew from the other direction, filling the void created by the release of energy.

My ears rang to the exclusion of all other sound, and I had monstrous purple and green spots in the shape of the cabin floating in my gaze. *We should be dead*, I thought. Explosions didn't work like in the movies. The initial blast wave should have pulverized our organs, and if we somehow survived that, the high velocity shock wave—the hot wind—should have poured even more energy into our innards. The following cold wind should have hit with equal force next, what the bomb squad called a "blast wind," flipping us back toward the cabin until we hit something.

Jane was on the ground next to me, holding her head. She nodded when I put my hand on her shoulder. Althyof and Yowtgayrr had become entwined in a heap of limbs, but both were aware and moving around. Krowkr lay in the stream, face toward the sky, an oversized puppy in each arm. The karls on our side of the stream lay scattered about but seemed no worse off than we were. The other side of the stream, however, was as different from ours as night is to day.

I shook my head, trying to clear the purple and green outlines of the cabin out of my vision. The actual cabin was gone, and I don't mean blown to smithereens. It was *gone*, as in disappeared, vanished. There was no debris, no shrapnel, as there should have been in any explosion big enough to generate a blast equal to the one we'd experienced.

The karls who had stayed back near the cabin littered the ground, like so much thrown confetti after a parade. Blood and clear fluids streamed from their eyes and ears. None of them moved or groaned or, by the look of it, breathed.

Not even a smear of blood remained of the karl who had opened the door and entered the cabin. He was just gone.

On my hands and knees, I crawled to Krowkr and pulled him out of the icy stream. While dazed, he didn't appear to be seriously injured. The pups crawled up his torso to avoid the water, moving as if they were half-asleep.

"What was that?" asked Jane.

"Cabin's gone," I said.

She stared across the stream and rubbed her eyes. "Where did it go?"

"It's *gone*. No shrapnel, no debris, nothing left of it. Same with the idiot who went inside."

"The *proo's* still there, though," said Althyof, disentangling himself from Yowtgayrr and walking over to us. "I think those men are done for."

"Yeah," I sighed. "Still, we should check on them."

"I'll see to it."

"Thanks, Althyof."

"Is Krowkr okay?" asked Jane.

"Yes, my lady," he said, but he didn't move. "The Trickster left a trick for us to stumble upon."

Yowtgayrr walked over to the other karls on our side of the stream and helped them sit up, speaking softly, resting a hand on a shoulder here and there.

I got to my feet after a short struggle, the puppies watching me warily as though scared I'd fall on them. The *proo* shimmered where the cabin once stood. "Two *preer*," I murmured.

"Double the pleasure, double the fun," muttered Jane in a sour tone. "How do we choose?"

I sighed and lifted my shoulders for a moment before letting them drop. The movement made my upper back ache. "That was no explosion, though."

"No?"

"No. We'd all be dead if explosives had caused that blast wave."

Jane sighed. "Magic?"

"You've got me."

"Full of answers today, aren't you?"

I walked through the stream, intent on examining the *proo* and the space the cabin had occupied. Behind me, Keri and Fretyi whined. "Stay with your mommy," I said over my shoulder. As I walked, I changed the magazine in each pistol for a fresh, fully loaded one, and let my fingers reload the spent rounds on autopilot. I pawed through the pouches in Prokkr's fabulous gun belt, counting shells, and grimaced at the results. I only had twenty-four .45 caliber rounds left for Kunknir and thirty-one rounds for Krati. Three full magazines for each gun with a few spares for shits and giggles.

As if to remind me of its presence, the scroll case that held my grimoire bumped against the small of my back as I walked. *Wonder what Althyof will say if I start reading this thing again?* So far, his dire predictions of *kaltrar* that were too powerful for me to handle hadn't played out.

And the simple fact was that three magazines per pistol would not be enough to capture Luka. Not unless he surrendered without a fight.

Where the cabin had stood, there was only a spot of bare earth filled with holes at regular intervals where the foundation posts had been sunk. No other hint that a cabin had once stood there existed—no furniture, no household goods, no debris. The *proo* hung a few inches off the ground, shining in the morning light.

The *proo* that the cabin had hidden from sight looked no different from any other *proo* I'd seen. A million colors swirled and merged at such a speed that, when viewed as a whole, made the *proo* appear as a silver mirror missing its stand.

Jane had the right of it. How could we pick between the two *preer* without taking a wild-assed guess? And once we picked one, how would we know we were on the right track on the other side? I shook my head and sighed.

Althyof came to my side, his expression grim. "All dead," he said.

I groaned and shook my head. "What was this?" I asked, waving my hand at the empty space and the holes in the earth.

The Tverkr stroked his beard. "A *kaltrar*, obviously," he murmured. "But what kind?" He shook his head. "If I had to guess, I'd say Luka has devised a way to blur the lines between *stathur*."

I glanced at the *proo*.

"Yes," he said. "No doubt the *proo* played a role. I believe his trap opened the *proo* and sucked a piece of one of the wild *stathur* into this place. Because the laws of the *stathur* differ from the physical laws of this place, the nugget of foreign *stathur* obliterated itself, the cabin, and everything within reach when the *proo* snapped closed. The shock wave killed the other karls and knocked us about."

"How sure are you?"

"I'm guessing, of course. There's no way to be sure."

I grimaced and shook my head. "Is there another explanation?"

"None I can think of, but that means very little, Hank."

Frustration bubbled in my guts. "So how do we choose between the two *proo*?"

Althyof glanced at the *proo* nearby. "I, for one, am not going through this *proo*. Not for all the silver in Osgarthr."

We walked back to the stream. Jane saw to the injuries, which were mild compared to what we saw on the other side of the river. Yowtgayrr had his blades sheathed and helped the karls to their feet. Keri and Fretyi cavorted in the grass as if nothing had happened. I watched them for a moment, thinking of how they had acted when we'd first approached the cabin.

"He had someone's scent," I murmured.

"What was that?" asked Althyof.

Fretyi had been intent on what was inside the cabin, but Keri... Keri had run around the side of the cabin, nose to the ground. Keri had followed the *scent trail* of someone walking around the cabin. *But was it Luka's scent?*

"When we first arrived, Fretyi sniffed the air from inside the cabin, but Keri ran around the side of the cabin with his nose to the ground."

"Following a scent?"

I nodded. "I think so."

"Perhaps he can help us choose."

I walked through the water, not even noticing the chill. I scooped up Keri, feeling a twinge in my lower back as I straightened. They were growing faster than I could keep up with, and I kept underestimating their weight and size. Keri was marginally smaller than Fretyi, but he was already eighteen inches at the shoulder and must have weighed forty pounds. Keri lolled in my arms, looking back at his brother, and switched into full play mode and tried to eat my arm. "Come on, wolflet," I said. "I've got work for you to do."

At the sound of my voice, Keri broke off trying to rip my arm off and stared up at me, his gaze intent, as if he could almost understand me. He cocked his head to the side and yipped.

"Yeah, yeah," I said, turning and walking toward the spot where the cabin's front door had stood. "Remember when you followed a scent? Remember that?"

Keri lay in my arms, belly toward the sky, paws folded across his tummy, head cocked to the side.

"You are too cute, you know that?" I asked and scratched his belly. "I thought *varkr* were fierce."

He barked in my face.

I set him down on the ground, and he sat, looking up at me and wagging his tail. "Yes, *very* fierce, and I asked for it." I pointed at the ground and tapped his nose. "Can you find that scent again?"

He cocked his head to the side, one ear flopping across the top of his head. He lifted a paw and clawed at the air.

"Find that scent, Keri," I crooned.

He tilted his head the other direction, complete with more ear flopping, and looked at the ground between his front paws. He glanced up at me.

"Yes, find the scent on the ground, goober."

He stood and put his nose to the ground. He sniffed in a circle, lifting his head once to bark at the *proo* and watch it for a moment as if it might move at any second. With the *proo* chastised, he went back to sniffing the ground, walking in widening circles. After a minute or so, he yipped with excitement and looked up at me, wagging his tail.

"Got it? Follow it."

He wagged his tail, then put his nose back to the ground and raced around the cabin's empty footprint, avoiding the bodies of the dead karls, and beelined to the cliff, right at the edge of the waterfall. He looked at me and barked, as if to say, "Hurry up, slowpoke."

WILD HUNT ❉ 99

"It's as though he understands you," said Jane as I passed her.

"Maybe he does," I said with a laugh. "An old dog to a young pup."

"He's beginning to," said Yowtgayrr at the same time. "As he gets older, his understanding will grow."

I stopped, surprised, and looked at the Alf, scanning his face for signs he was pulling our legs. He returned my gaze, the picture of placid calm.

"You're kidding, right?" asked Jane.

"No. In time, Hank may grow to understand *him*...as with the bears."

Krowkr's eyes were about as big as I'd ever seen human eyes get.

"Next nickname will have something to do with bears, I'd bet my life-savings on it," I muttered.

"Yeah?" asked Jane with a twinkle in her eye. "Pooh-bear? Teddy-bear?"

"Prooni," murmured Krowkr.

I glowered at him, but he'd already turned away. It meant 'brown bear.'

"Don't give them any ideas." Keri barked his "quit your yapping and get over here" bark. "It's clear that Luka walked from the cabin to that grotto."

"Or someone did," said Althyof.

"He's the only one I saw here."

"And the frost giant?"

"Couldn't have fit inside the cabin, let alone fit through the door."

"The problems of the unnecessarily tall," said Althyof. "My people solved these problems long ago."

I couldn't tell if he was kidding or not. I rested my hand on the scroll case. With a glance at the karls, I motioned the others closer. "When we arrived, I suggested sending my animus across the *proo* to communicate with Meuhlnir and Veethar. You all convinced me it was too risky, and I agreed with you."

"I don't like where this is going," said Jane.

"Indeed," said Althyof. "Our arguments have not lessened in strength."

"Here's the thing," I said, holding up my hand for quiet. "We are now faced with a choice: use everything at our disposal or proceed on a guess." Jane opened her mouth to argue, but I shook my head. "No matter how well informed the guess is, it's still a guess. Isn't leaving a false trail to a deadly *proo* right up Luka's alley?" Her mouth closed with a snap. "Thanks to this scroll, I can have a tripartite consciousness. I have used this ability in battle, and we've relied on it to inform our decisions. I don't see a way around using it now, except to go ahead on the guess that the trail is real—something that seems ˙ infinitely more dangerous for all of you."

"And to you?" Jane demanded.

I shrugged. "We don't *know* it's dangerous for me to jump through a *proo* as a raven. We are—"

"But you want to proceed on a guess in that case," she said. "Why not in the choice of *preer*?"

I shook my head and held up my hands, palms up. "I have a feeling I can do this."

"A *feeling*?" Jane threw up her hands and looked at Althyof. "Will you beat some sense into my husband?"

Althyof's gaze bounced back and forth between us. "I'm…uh, that is…"

"There's something else pertinent to this discussion. I'm low on ammunition."

"Low?" asked Yowtgayrr. "Specifics?"

"Three magazines. Twenty-one shots from Kunknir, thirty from Krati."

"And this is too few?" asked Althyof.

I nodded. "Yes, it is. If I only shoot when I have a good target—no distracting shots, no warnings—I could stretch it to three small skirmishes that end quickly. Anything more than that…"

Althyof's eyes narrowed. "Did I not say this would happen? Did I not tell you to push that damn scroll from your thoughts?"

I blinked at his vehemence. "I'm not saying I have to use the scroll. But I can't use my guns exclusively, and we learned back in Osgarthr that the bear-form has limits we can't get around. I'm just saying I have to do *something* to augment my abilities with the pistols. I can't stand by while everyone else engages."

The Tverkr's face soured. "And what might that be?"

"I don't know," I said. "Perhaps I can augment what you do. You could teach me the red dancy thing your daggers do."

"'Dancy thing?'" His face scrunched up and turned red.

"Yeah. The stretching and shrinking, and the way you send the power blazing away from them—what we did against the spiders in the Great Forest of Suel before Ivalti arrived. I don't think there's enough time for me to learn a melee skill to the point I could stand against Luka."

Yowtgayrr pursed his lips and shook his head. "No."

"There seem to be four choices to remedy my lack of ammunition—and these are in addition to the decision we must make about sending a raven through the *preer*. One, I can try to use the *strenkir af krafti* alone—use *saytr* I mean. Two, I can try my hand supporting Althyof as a novice *runeskowld*. Three, I can travel back to Osgarthr and have Haymtatlr either open a *proo* to Nitavetlir and hope Prokkr has finished ammunition for me, or open one to Mithgarthr to visit a gun shop. Four, I can read the rest of the scroll. I can tell Althyof what the *kaltrar* are, and he can advise me on whether or not they will kill me."

Jane shook her head. "A little risky, risky, riskier, riskiest."

"Hon, I don't know what else to do." I bunched my shoulders and winced at the twinge of searing pain that accompanied the movement.

"How about standing back? How about staying out of fights?"

"And we've been married how long? You know I can't do that." My hands fidgeted with the belt Prokkr had made me, twiddling with the flaps over the ammo pouches, drifting across the butts of my pistols, fiddling with the ingenious clamps that held the magazines ready.

"You could if I knocked you out." She said it in a stern voice but couldn't keep her lips from twitching with a smile.

"You know my head is way too hard for that."

"Ain't that the truth," she said and gave up trying to keep a straight face.

"Let me see if I understand the choices you are giving us," said Althyof. "Either you do something foolhardy, or I do something foolhardy, or you do something else foolhardy, or we abandon the pursuit of Luka."

I frowned and looked down. "The way you say it makes it sound bad." I peeked at him from the corner of my eye and saw the grin he suppressed. "I think the scroll is the best of those options. I promise not to try anything without talking to you first."

"No. You will promise not to try any of them unless I give you tacit approval of the *kaltrar* you wish to try."

"Yeah, that's what I meant."

"Say what you mean, Hank Jensen," he said with a flinty expression. "Also, we will advance your training to cover more useful *lausaveesa* and *triblinkr*, and perhaps even a *trowba* or two, but—" He held up a warning finger. "—I will limit you to the *kaltrar* I choose for you, and you will perform them by rote. Do you hear, Aylootr? *No* improvisation."

"You are buying into this nonsense?" Jane asked him, but he neither looked at her nor responded.

"I promise not to attempt any of the *kaltrar* in the scroll without your prior approval," I said. "I promise to learn the *kaltrar* you teach me and perform them only by rote—no improvising, no experimentation."

The Tverkr *runeskowld* grunted and nodded once. "Break either promise and our relationship as master and apprentice is over."

"I understood that before I made the promise," I said.

Jane stepped in front of me, blocking my eye contact with Althyof. "You made a promise to me eighteen years ago, Hank." She held up her hand with the ring Althyof made glinting from her finger. "And we renewed those promises last year to my way of thinking. We're either partners in this or all this is worthless."

"We've always been partners, Jane. If you don't want me to use this stuff, I won't. I'll figure out something else." I rapped my knuckles against her shiny shield. "You could loan me this."

She blushed, knowing full well what I meant by that. She'd stay out of a battle I was in about as much as I would sit out the next one we faced. "That's different."

"Is it?" I asked.

"It is," she said firmly. "This shield can't kill me."

"Maybe not, but any battle you use it in could end badly."

She shook her head. "These 'choices' you are talking about—"

"Jane," I breathed. "I'm doing the best I can here."

She closed her eyes and gave a soft shake of her head.

"I'll tell you what, you decide what I do next."

Eyes still squeezed shut, she sighed. "Oh sure, play the reasonable card."

I gave her a one-armed hug and stepped away. I glanced at Althyof. "Should I read first or try to send my animus across one of these *preer* first?"

"The scroll," he said. "Perhaps you will find something that makes risking yourself by traveling the *preer* irrelevant."

I glanced at Jane and smiled. "Okay with you?"

"I so want to punch you right now," she said, shaking her fist under my nose. But she smiled as she did, and that made the world a better place.

"Come here, Keri!" I shouted, and the *varkr* pup bounded toward us and, at the last second, pounced on Fretyi, and they dissolved into a rolling, yipping dust cloud. I sat on the bank and pulled my *puntidn stavsetninkarpowk*—the idiomatic grimoire I'd found in Kuthbyuhrn and Kyellroona's room full of loot—out of its case.

Excitement bubbled in my veins, and nervousness roiled in the pit of my stomach. This would make the fourth time I'd read the scroll, but the first time had only bound the grimoire to me—and I didn't even remember the *kaltrar* that had done the work. The other two times had occurred on the same day, the day of the battle at the *Herperty af Roostum*—the Rooms of Ruin. Both readings on that fateful day had given me powers I'd never imagined possible. I was more than a little scared, but, for the most part, I burned with curiosity.

Jane knelt next to me and put her hand on my shoulder. "Try not to die," she said. "At least don't die more than you can handle." She smiled as she said both sentences, but I knew her more than well enough to hear the fear and worry in her voice.

"Will do. Have I mentioned that you are an insane person?"

"Only in passing, and I took it as a compliment coming from you." She smiled and kissed my cheek.

Althyof cleared his throat. "Stand away, Jane. I'll create a barrier that will mitigate runaway *kaltrar*."

"What?" She scowled at the Tverkr. "You said—"

He smiled. "Only kidding. This is…well, not *safe*, but at least not stupid."

"Thanks," she said. "That's reassuring."

"You really suck at this, Althyof," I said.

"At what?"

"Reassuring people."

"Is that what I'm doing?"

I gazed up at him for a moment and rolled my eye. "That's your answer to everything."

"Is it?"

"Yes," said Jane. "And you've taught the habit to the lunkhead here."

"Has he?" I asked.

"Are you sure I couldn't knock you out with my pretty shield? Just once?"

I grinned, trying not to let my impatience show on my face. The scroll felt like a brick in my hand rather than paper. Jane stood and walked a few paces away.

"Remember what I said," she whispered.

I bent over the scroll and opened it. The other times I'd read from it, I hadn't had time to savor the experience. I've always loved books—the smell of the binding, the feel of the paper beneath my fingertips—though my Personal Monster™ had stuck me with ebooks for the past several years. Peeling away layers of the scroll was similar to cracking open a cherished book—it *smelled* like an old book, and the feel of the paper on which it was written sent little jolts of excitement through my fingertips and into my brain.

When I'd opened it far enough to expose the pages of the *kaltrar* I'd already read, I bent my head and closed my eye for a moment, just breathing, drawing my concentration and blocking out the sounds of the puppies playing, the karls chatting and moving around, even the wind.

When I opened my eye, the writing on the page wriggled and crawled for a heartbeat before the squiggles resolved into runes I could read and understand. My gaze raced over the *kaltrar*, an intellectual lust rushing to the fore of my mind. The runes ran by faster and faster as I read and understood the intent of the first *kaltrar* easily—to manipulate molecules in a wide area. If only I understood how to use something like that.

I went to the next *kaltrar* without pause and raced through it. My stomach turned as I understood the *triblinkr* reanimated corpses, either to speak or to rise by changing a single word in the chant. Memories of the *truykar* from the Darks of Kruyn shambled through my mind.

As I came to the end of that *kaltrar,* I felt strange— as if parts of my mind were being changed by the act of reading the scroll. The *triblinkr* I learned while in the *Herperty af Roostum* had changed me in fundamental ways—I knew that much, and I was okay with those changes, but these new *kaltrar* seemed to be of a different sort all together. I thought about stopping, about rerolling the scroll, putting it in its case and shoving it to the bottom of my pack.

Instead, I kept right on reading, page after page, *kaltrar* after *kaltrar*, reading voraciously. My mind seemed to swell, to expand to contain all the new ideas, the new knowledge of how things *really* worked… I raced to the end of the scroll and let it slide from my fingers into my lap. I sighed, feeling anesthetized, enervated.

"Well, you're still alive," said Jane. "That's a plus."

I summoned the energy to nod, staring into the distance, eyes unfocused, brain filled with white noise. The *kaltrar* I'd read felt like a tumor, like a mass of pick-up sticks wedged into my head, and I needed time to unwind them, to sort them out.

"Well?" asked Althyof. "What have you learned?"

I held up my hand. "It's too much. What I read in the beginning—the first two or three *kaltrar*—they are still clear, but the rest…it's a rat's nest of ideas, runes, and…and…"

Althyof bent and put his hand on my shoulder. "Relax, Hank. There's time. Does anything stand out? Any way to avoid sending your animus through the *preer*?"

"The *preer*…" I murmured. "I… I…"

"Okay," said Althyof. "Relax a bit."

The karls had seen the ancient scroll and had come as close as they dared. They stood there, staring at me in perfect silence, with awe in their eyes, and I hated it. They didn't understand—to them, we were gods, and that onus was one more than I wanted. "Send them on their way," I said. "Send them home."

Althyof glanced over his shoulder before hunkering down in front of me. "There's nothing to do, Hank. They will believe what they want…what they *need* to believe."

I shook my head.

"Let's play a little game," he said, putting his hand on my shoulder. "You pretend not to notice those karls, and I'll ask you a few leading questions—see if we can't make sense out of what you read."

"Yeah," I muttered. "Okay."

"Was there anything on your scroll that might strengthen your animus?"

I rubbed my eye sockets with the heels of my hands. Even my eyeball felt stuffed with irritating, crawling things …ants, maybe. "I… No. Well, maybe. I don't know."

"Okay," he said with a shrug. "Was there anything that—"

"I think I learned a *triblinkr* similar to the Kuthbyuhrn one, but…but…it's different somehow. It feels…more malevolent… They all *feel* different from the first two."

"*Kaltrar* are neither good nor evil, Hank," said Yowtgayrr softly. "It's their use that gives them that quality."

"Yeah, I know," I sighed. "But—"

"There is risk in great power, Hank," said Althyof. "Power leads to arrogance, and arrogance leads to corruption."

"Power corrupts, and absolute power corrupts absolutely," I said.

"Yes, that's it." Althyof stroked his beard with a thoughtful expression on his face. "This new shapechanging *triblinkr* tempts you?"

"Well, no, not really. I can see its usefulness, but it seems…dishonest."

Althyof threw back his head and laughed. "In that case, it's perfect for a *runeskowld*, since it is a Tverkar art," he said. "Listen to me, novice. *Kaltrar* are neither good nor evil, honest nor dishonest. As our Alf friend has already said, it's the use of the power that defines them."

"I guess," I said.

"Hank, I do not guess. Not in this. The *kaltrar* you learned are not malevolent, and they are not good.

They are merely tools you may use or not use as you see fit. But I will say this: that it worries you indicates to me that those *kaltrar* are in good hands." Althyof squatted next to me. "Let's focus on whether they are *safe* for you to use."

"Okay."

"The shapechanging *triblinkr* seems safe since you already do something similar, although with a different target. Tell me of the other two you can make sense of."

"The first one…I understand it, but I don't understand what use it would be."

Althyof spun his index finger in a small circle.

"It lets me cast a field that manipulates things like the molecules of the air, or water in the sea."

"Manipulate how?"

"I can either suppress them or excite them."

"Ah," said Althyof. "The Alfar do similar things." He nodded at Yowtgayrr.

"Yes," said the Alf. "Remember being trapped by Hel inside our shield? I used a *kaltrar* to cool the air— with little success—by reducing the excitation of the molecules in the air."

"Ah. I see."

"You could also put out a flame or boil water."

"Melt frost giants," I said.

"An Alf would not do so, but it is possible," said Yowtgayrr.

"Yeah, you guys don't seem to use your gifts much. Why is that?"

Yowtgayrr looked up at the sky. "We prefer not to use the *strenkir af krafti* to act directly on living beings, except ourselves. Tiwaz granted our power to help us be better servants of nature, not to control nature."

"I can respect that," I said.

"Can you remember anything else?" asked Althyof.

"Yes," I sighed. "It's one of the worst things I can imagine, though." I looked down at the ground between my knees. "I can...I *think* I can create *truykar*."

The Alf and the Tverkr exchanged a quick glance without speaking.

"Worse yet," I said. "I can command them to speak to me, to answer my questions."

Althyof leaned closer. "That could be useful, if distasteful."

"How so?"

"I imagine you could ask the remains of the frost giant which *proo* Luka took."

I shuddered. "I don't want to do that."

"Safer than flinging your consciousness all over the cosmos," said Yowtgayrr. "But there isn't much time. His body has almost melted."

SEVEN

The frost giant was little more than lumps of smoking, melting flesh. I wished it was too far gone, too melted to be revived. "I'm not sure I should do this," I murmured to Jane.

"Better than becoming an idiot," she whispered back. "Well, more of an idiot."

"Thanks. I love you, too."

"It's as they said. It's not an evil act unless you make it one."

"One of those slippery slopes," I said.

She shrugged. "Welcome to life, sailor. It's nothing *but* slippery slopes."

I glanced at Yowtgayrr. The planes of his face seemed harsh, immobile, but when he caught me looking, his expression softened. "It is as you said, Hank. Distasteful. But it isn't *wrong* if you don't chain him to the place of his death, as with the *truykar*. Release the body afterward."

I took a deep breath and blew it out through numb lips. I took another to steady my nerves and chanted the *triblinkr* in nothing more than a whisper. The frost giant's body stopped smoking first, then reformed the more melted parts. I didn't dare look at the karls, but I heard the muttering and whispering.

The giant's first breath was ragged and raspy. When the fingers of his right hand twitched, the noise from the karls swelled. His eyelids fluttered open, and the karls gasped. He drew another breath, eyes rolling toward me. "It wasn't enough to kill me?" he rasped. "You find you must pull me from the grave as well?"

I glanced at Supergirl, standing at my side. Her face was drawn, pale. "Go on, Hank," she murmured.

"This won't take long," I said. "I need your help."

The giant shook his head and groaned. "Why…why should I help you?"

I shrugged. "Because you have no choice. But you have my word I will release you."

"Ask."

"Where did Luka go? Which of the two *proo* did he use?"

"Luka?" the giant rasped. "I know no Luka."

My cop radar pinged. He was lying.

"The Isir that was here before us," said Jane.

His monstrous black eyes drifted toward her face, then snapped back to glower at me.

"The man that asked you to stay in the grotto?" I asked. "You knew him. You know Luka."

"By another name, perhaps," grated the giant.

"Which *proo* did he travel through?" I asked again.

"In my lands, we know him as Kvethrunkr, though some call him Lochkemant because of his twisting nature."

"Very educational, but all we need to know is which *proo* he took."

The giant's eyes rolled up to the pale blue sky above our heads. "So ugly here," he murmured. "So hot."

"I will release you when you answer my question."

"The grotto," mused the frost giant. "Or the shack. One is a trap, one is a knack."

"What does that mean?" I asked.

The giant's black eyes rolled down to meet my gaze. "It's what you bade me say."

"What? I didn't tell you to say anything. I *asked* you to—"

"You *did*. The other one brought you to me in the realm beyond. You told me to speak the words I have spoken and to say no more. You said you would deny it."

I looked at Jane, my confusion echoed in her eyes. "I think you must be confused. Which *proo* did Kvethrunkr use?"

The giant snickered and shook his head. "This is a silly game. You know the answer already. You knew before you awakened this body."

"Althyof, do you have—"

"Release me! I have done as you asked."

"You *haven't*," I said. "You've done nothing but avoid doing what I asked."

"Bah!" The giant struggled to sit up, but most of his musculature was gone—melted away—and he sank back. "When I can, I will get up and set to breaking you puny Isir as I couldn't while life still flowed in these veins."

"Release him, Hank," said Yowtgayrr. "We will get no help from this one."

I glanced at the Alf, but he wouldn't meet my gaze. Exhaustion crept up my spine, and muddy thoughts swirled in my mind. "Last chance to speak in this world," I said to the giant.

"Kvethrunkr spoke the truth about you, Isir," he rasped. "Rapscallion. Rogue. Scapegrace."

I sighed as pain snaked over the back of my head and throbbed in my temples. "He's never spoken the truth," I said. "About me or anyone else." The light seemed to stab at my eye.

"*Release me*!" the giant boomed. "Oh and say hello to my father. Wish him well… Afterward, he will grind your bones to dust for what you have done."

I glanced at Althyof, and the Tverkr shrugged. "Go, then. I release you to your death." As soon as the words left my mouth, the giant spasmed once and collapsed and in gouts of whitish smoke, melted much more rapidly than before. Within minutes, his flesh disappeared, revealing smoking bones, and within another few minutes, they too melted away. In the end, all that remained of the frost giant was a discolored patch of grass and a few tendrils of white smoke.

"That was not what I expected," I said letting my shoulders slump and closing my eyelids against the brutal light. "I thought the binding would force him to tell the truth."

"Perhaps he was telling the truth," muttered Althyof. "If you can learn a *triblinkr* to assume another man's image, then others could as well."

"He said I came to him *after* he died."

Althyof shrugged. "There are more things in the cosmos than one man can understand."

"What do we do now?" asked Jane.

"Grotto or shack, trap and knack. What *is* a knack, anyway?"

"A trick for deceiving an enemy," said Yowtgayrr. "A stratagem."

"Well, if one is a trap, and the other is a trick, it sounds as if we shouldn't take either *proo*," said Jane.

"Yet Luka took one of them," said Althyof.

"Maybe we should—" I started but swooned before finishing, overcome with dizziness. In a heartbeat, Jane was there, an arm around my waist, taking my bulk as if I weighed nothing at all.

"Remember all those cracks about me overdoing it?" she asked. "When you've recovered, I'm definitely punching you with my pretty shield."

"All talk," I murmured. "Promises. No action."

"Move him away from the where the giant fell," said Yowtgayrr, moving to help. He arrived as my knees gave out and the world faded into the mist.

EIGHT

I soared above the mountaintops, reveling in the sensation of the cold, crisp air under my wings. Black feathers drank in the sun's warmth, keeping the frigid temperatures at bay.

I didn't remember how I'd gotten to the mountains—the last I remembered was flying over an ocean, with...something...chasing me. Another bird? I swayed to my wingtip, cutting a tight turn from the air, eyes hawkish.

But there was no threat. No kites, no...other things in pursuit. I sent a barbaric *crrruck echoing* from the rooftop of the world and would have smiled if I had lips.

A clearing in the trees widened below me. Icy water streamed through it, fed from a waterfall that came from even higher on the mountain. A crowd had gathered. Men, an Isir woman, a Tverkr, and even an Alf, stood around a big Isir man who lay on the ground.

He looked familiar, that one on the ground.

The woman turned her face up toward me and lifted her hand to point. It seemed I should recognize her, too.

A proo shimmered near them, and somehow, I knew there was another hidden behind the waterfall. A trail led down the mountainside.

Two varkr pups barked and yipped, spinning wildly beneath me. I sent a crrruck echoing down at them, a warm sentiment fluttering in my chest.

Can I be friends with varkr? I wondered. Surely not.

The shimmery proo that stood out in the open drew my gaze as if it hadn't a care in the world. It seemed to glow as though surrounded by a pale blue aura. I sent another crrruck warbling at it down through the cold air.

To my surprise, an answering crrruck floated up to me, coming from the…from the proo! I spun on a wingtip, tucked my wings, and dropped like a stone. The varkr puppies danced and leapt, yipping at me as I fell. At the last moment, I snapped my wings out, cupped the air, and arrested my plummeting fall.

Reflected in the mirror-like surface of the proo *was another raven. A* white *raven, and it seemed somehow familiar. I flew around the* proo*, scared to land lest the cavorting* varkr *puppies suddenly remember they liked bird meat. The reflection of the white raven followed me around to the back of the* proo*.*

I craned my neck, jigging and juking in the air to see behind me. No raven, white or otherwise, shared my sky.

"Oh, hurry up, Hank," said the reflection of the white raven.

Hank*!* Hank is my name*, I thought with a burble of excitement. I* crrrucked *a question at the white raven reflected in the* proo*, cocking my head and tilting my wings just so to make my question clear.*

The white bird shook its head as if annoyed. "You're not really a bird, bird-brain."

I knew that white bird. Somehow. I recognized—

"Hank! Hurry up. Fly into the proo*. Jane's fears are groundless."*

Jane? The woman! The Isir woman hovering over the fallen Isir man! *Supergirl*! Does that mean…

"Yes, nitwit. That 'Isir man' is you—your real body, anyway. Now, come on! There are things to see."

I made a noise in my throat, a strange cross between a crrruck *and a funny sounding collection of syllables: Kuhntul.*

"Finally, your mind is joining the conversation. You can speak, you know. You aren't limited to those silly raven calls."

Tired of the pedantic white bird, I flew at the proo, intending to veer away at the last moment, but an invisible something reached out and grabbed me, jerking me into the shiny surface. With a squawk, I was through and swimming in something thick and slimy—a viscous fluid that wasn't a fluid at all.

The white raven's feathers melted together, forming large fish-like scales. "It will be easier if you assume a better form for the environment."

Disparate forces seemed to tug at me from several directions at once, and a cacophony of colors swarmed in the distance. A woman screamed somewhere far away.

"Hurry," whispered the white fish, her voice brimming with impatience. "We don't want to be caught by the denizen of this place, Hank."

She stared at me for several heartbeats. "By the Maids! What are you doing, man? This shape isn't your only shape! Change!"

I shook my head, the viscous fluid or forces or whatever the hell it was making the movement feel slow, languid.

"Hank… What's the matter with you?"

I opened my beak to give her a good crrruck, but she reached out with a hand-like fin and snapped my beak shut.

"No! No sound!" she said.

Who knew fish could be simpletons? I thought.

She sighed with exasperation. "No, Hank. I'm not the simpleton in this tale." She shook her fishy head and muttered something too low for me to hear.

My feathers felt strange. Alarmed, I glanced down at my breast. My feathers were melting, becoming spade-like! My body was changing, too, losing its flight-optimized shape, becoming bullet-like and sleek. It is the shape of a...a... *I almost had it.* A yellow-fin tuna*! My wings twisted and slid down toward my centerline, my shoulders crumbling and reforming.*

What the hell is this*? Is this a dream? I thought.*

"No, silly. Birds can't dream."

In the distance, a woman screamed again. Torment filled her voice, but also exhaustion and hopelessness.

The white fish was staring at me intently. "Do you recognize her?" she asked.

I tried to shake my head, but I no longer had a neck. No, *I thought.*

"That's Hel. She's trapped here, and Owraythu is trying to break her mind."

None of this makes any sense.

"That's only because you are out like a light and believe you are dreaming," said Kuhntul.

Kuhntul*? Why do I know your name?*

"It'll come to you," she said.

What are we doing in this place*?*

"I grew tired of waiting for you to realize you can send your animus through a proo *as long as it is open. I grew tired of watching you flail about,*

reading your puntidn stavsetninkarpowk*, wasting time with that silly dead giant. And, you needed to see this place, to see what they are trying to do to Hel."*

I don't understand.

"Don't worry. You will. It'll all come to you as soon as you wake up."

So, this is just a dream*?* A…a *troymskrok?*

"Hardly a troymskrok*, Hank. This is the same as when you visited me at the base of Iktrasitl—a dreamslice."*

Oh. I don't understand what that means.

"It'll come back to you. Trust me on this."

I tried to shrug, but with no neck and no shoulders, the movement was lost in a shiver of black scales.

"If Owraythu succeeds in what she's attempting, Hel will become much more of a problem for you, Hank. She will be more powerful, and she will have the backing of Mirkur and Owraythu, though they will no doubt keep her on a tighter leash."

Okay. Am I supposed to rescue her*?*

"By the Maids, no! Owraythu would gobble you up like a cherry if you oppose her openly in her own realm as you are now. Even if you had all your wits about you. There are more things in the cosmos than a single man can understand. Even one as cute as you."

Uh…

"Don't worry, Hank. I know you love Jane and would never betray her."

126 ❀ ERIK HENRY VICK

That's right. Not in a million years.

"More's the pity."

I didn't know big, torpedo-shaped fish could look mischievous, but Kuhntul pulled it off. Tell me what you want—

Something gave me a jerk, pulling me away from Kuhntul, and I flew backward until...

NINE

I opened my eyelids, as Jane shook me a second time. Keri and Fretyi stared down at me, tongues lolling, drool splattering my cheeks. "What's going on?" I croaked.

"You passed out again," said Jane. "You and your grimoire."

"But no harm was done. And it wasn't the grimoire." I sat up and shook my head. "I think—"

"Ha!" said Jane.

"Funny. I… I dreamed…the bird-thing again."

"Where did you go this time?" asked Althyof.

"It's hard to remember, but I flew overhead, watching you guys." I glanced skyward. "But I didn't know who you were." Keri and Fretyi piled into my lap—which was an awesome experience given their weight and size—and let it be known their ears needed scratching. "I think Kuhntul was in it, but she was a fish or something."

"And what did the Tisir have to say this time?"

"It's fuzzy. But it annoyed her that I hadn't gone into the *proo* over there, yet. She said...something about the *preer* being safe as long as they stayed open. That I could send my animus across without fear."

"Ha!" said Jane. "Sounds more like a wish-fulfillment dream."

I shook my head. "I don't think so. She... I believe she took me somewhere...to a *stathur* that has different rules. She wanted me to do something..."

"Well, there's a shock," muttered Jane.

"Do you recall what?" asked Yowtgayrr.

I shook my head again. "No, but it had something to do with the place she took me."

"Which one?" asked Althyof, gaze switching back and forth between the waterfall and the *proo* glinting in the late afternoon sun.

"Which one what?"

"Which *proo* did she pull you into?"

"Oh. That one," I said pointing at the *proo* the cabin had hidden until it exploded into nothingness.

"And it took you to a strange *stathur*?"

"Yeah, I mean, she was a fish, right? Then she turned me into one, except we weren't quite fishes."

Jane rocked back on her heels. "The thing with the giant was a bust. This dream of yours wasn't much better from the sound of it. How do we decide between these two *preer*?"

"I'm going to send my animus across and explore."

Jane rolled her eyes, a scowl settling over her face. "You put a lot of faith in these dreams of yours, Henry Jensen."

"Yeah," I said. "But so far, they've all been correct."

She shrugged. "There's that."

"We can't hang around here forever, Hon. I either send my animus, or we risk going across in person. Which is more of a risk?"

She shrugged again and looked away.

"So I'll try it. It will be fine, though. Kuhntul hasn't led me wrong so far."

"Don't trust her too much," said Althyof.

"I've got you three to make sure I don't."

"Do it," said Jane. "But if you are simple after this, I won't get to say, 'I told you so.' That's hardly fair." She grinned as she said it.

"You've already gotten to say that particular phrase more than is fair, so it equals out." That earned me a raspberry. I gave the puppies a pat each and shooed them away. I lay down and winked at my wife. "Now you won't have to catch me if I pass out."

"I'd let you fall. It might jar a little sense into you."

"Nah. Might dent the ground, though." I muttered the *triblinkr* to split off an animus, and it appeared floating above me—in the shape of the weird fish-thing from my dream. "Well, that's weird," I mumbled. I focused on the shape of a raven, and my animus melted and reformed. The karls made annoying noises, and I shook my head. "Someone send the karls on their way. I've done enough religion-building today."

"Krowkr, can I speak with you?" called Jane.

I turned my attention to my animus and moved it to the *proo* shining in the afternoon light. I reached out, not with my talons or my wings, but with my mind, and touched the *proo*. Unlike when I moved across a *proo* physically, the change wasn't instantaneous. There was a sensation of being pulled, of movement. I could see nothing, hear nothing, but I could *sense* things slithering nearby, maintaining a discreet distance, but coming very close to touching me. The sense that these things had a kind of terrible intelligence, godlike and expansive, the sensation you expected to feel confronting Lovecraft's Great Old Ones, settled on me like a nightmare. I imagined great slithering things living in the void between the ends of the *proo*—vast, titanic beasts of unimaginable power.

I hoped they wouldn't notice me and kept my mental gaze averted.

And then it was over, and I drifted in a semi-fluidic space. I had no sense of gravity, no sense of up or down, no sense of relative motion. I no longer sensed the Great Old Ones from the *proo*, but I had the sense of large things surrounding me. They didn't seem like living things, however, just large masses of something.

When I tried to look at the things, it was as if I looked into a kaleidoscope of worlds, each overlapping the next. It hurt my head to look for too long, so I looked outward from them—toward whatever else was there.

I could perceive light, but not the way I could at home, not really. It wasn't that I could *see* the light with my little raven eyes—I couldn't—it was more like a sensation on my skin, like wind or waves at the beach. I had the sense that whatever existed in the opposite direction from the overlapping masses, it was akin to space at home, but it looked nothing like it.

My mind wandered in the nothingness I floated in. I found I could make ripples in the fabric of the semi-fluidic gunk around me, like a child slamming his hand into the water to splash waves around the bathtub. It fascinated me—I couldn't *see* these ripples, but I knew they were there, the way you know where your bedroom furniture is in the middle of a moonless night.

I stretched my senses for any sign of Luka—listening, feeling, looking, tasting, smelling—but if he'd been here, I was simply not equipped to sense his passage. I couldn't even detect my own boundaries, outside of the body my brain insisted I had. If he came this way, he'd succeeded in losing us.

Turning back toward the way I believed I'd come, I sensed something approaching me. It had a form, but I can't describe how my senses insisted on defining the thing. Whatever it looked like, it was immense, and it gave off a strong sensation of hunger.

Panic gripped me as the thing seemed to blot out what served as the sky. Was it flying? I had no idea. I searched for the terminus of the *proo* I'd traveled through, but there was no shimmering silver portal anywhere near me. The only thing close was that kaleidoscopic mass of twisting, slithering worlds.

I glanced over my shoulder and would have shouted in fear if I had a mouth or a voice. The vast, hungry entity had closed the distance while I looked behind me. It loomed over me, blocking the wave-like sensation of light radiating on my skin.

The entity—no, that's wrong, it wasn't a single entity, it was many, many entities, working together as one. Whatever it was, it lurched down at me, and I jetted away in fear, as a squid might, and I wished for all the world that I had a cloud of ink to release in my wake. The hungry...*colony*...of denizens from the *stathur* twisted away, as though surprised by my movement.

I drifted toward the kaleidoscope, not by any conscious intent, just the luck of the draw as it turned out. I gained speed, moving faster the closer I got to the thing. The twirling images of world upon world upon world blurred faster and faster as I drew close, the colors merging into the familiar shimmery silver of the *proo.*

I glanced over my shoulder as I approached the *proo.* The hungry colony-thing lurched toward me, reminding me of a striking snake. Before the thing struck me, the *proo* took hold, and I zipped away, back into that in-between space filled with the Great Old Ones.

Eyes closed, I rode the current of the *proo* back toward that chilly mountaintop somewhere in Scandinavia, trying not to think too loudly, trying not to wonder what the behemoths in the darkness were and whether they, also, were hungry.

I emerged into Mithgarthr and sighed with relief.

"That good, huh?" asked Jane.

"I don't recommend that *proo,*" I said through my physical mouth while I moved my animus to the grotto behind the waterfall. "It would mess up your hair. It leads to one of the *stathur* Meuhlnir warned us about. One with different physical laws. I'm not sure we would survive going there physically."

"The trap, then?" asked Althyof.

"I'd say so. Althyof, Yowtgayrr, what do the two of you know about the *preer?*"

"Not much, to be honest," said the Tverkr. "We never discovered how to create them and don't understand how the Isir manipulate them. We just use what's there."

"Yowtgayrr? How about the Alfar?"

"We understand them better than the Tverkar, at least on a conceptual level, but we can't create them either."

"Have either of you heard of things living in the *preer*?"

"No," said the Alfar. "The *preer* don't exist in the manner you are imagining. There is no physical bridge between the two endpoints and moving from one endpoint to the other is instantaneous. Only the ends are real. Think of them as a folded scrap of leather with a hole punched through both sides."

"I always believed so, too," I said. "But after traveling through one with my animus, I can categorically say that is not factual. There is a pathway, and things do live in the in-between."

"I do not doubt your word, Hank," said Yowtgayrr. "But perhaps traveling as an animus creates the illusion of this path."

"It seemed quite real."

"Maybe you shouldn't do it again," said Jane.

"You don't need to," said Althyof. "We know which *proo* to take by the process of elimination."

I let my animus go with a smile. "I hadn't considered that." I got to my feet. "The only thing is, that *proo* sitting out there in the open is dangerous. I'm sure that if you traveled it in physical form, you'd arrive dead."

"Too bad the cabin exploded," said Jane.

"We can't leave it like that. A curious Viking will try to use it, believing it's the *Reknpokaprooin* and get himself killed."

"If only someone knew a *kaltrar* to, I don't know, make a suppressive field around the thing," said Althyof.

"Yeah?"

"Got a better idea?"

"No, I don't," I said. I walked toward the *proo*, my step uncertain. "How big does it need to be?"

"Big enough no one can reach the surface of the *proo*," said Yowtgayrr.

"This one seems livelier than the others, as though it can reach out and grab a guy." I shrugged. "Here goes. Be ready to catch me if I pass out again."

Althyof shrugged. "The ground looks soft enough."

"Hey, this is your idea, Tverkr."

"Yes, but it's your *triblinkr*, Isir."

I sighed. "How do I give it a specific size? Do I need rune markers similar to the ones you used down in the village?"

"If you want it to remain after you leave, you do. I make them, you set them out."

He held out his hand, and I focused on the chisel Kuhntul had given me. When it appeared in my hand, I passed it to him, and he got to work chiseling runes into stones from the stream's bed. He made six of them each with three runes carved expertly into their tops, and I placed them in a rough circle, about four feet from the *proo*.

"How do I link the stones to the suppression field?"

"Add a stanza immediately before the last stanza. Use the runes I carved into each stone."

"Sounds easy enough."

Althyof scoffed and shook his head.

I chanted the *triblinkr,* focusing on slowing the air molecules as close to a zero-energy state as I could get them. One line before the conclusion, I added three lines using the runes he'd carved into the river stones and finished the *kaltrar*.

I picked up a stick and threw it at the dome that appeared around the *proo*, and Keri and Fretyi attacked my ankles. The stick bounced off the dome with a sound like a bell striking.

"Neat trick. Sig will hate it the next time he gets in trouble and loses his electronics."

"You better believe it," I said.

The karls stood at the edge of the clearing, at the head of the path that led down the mountain. Of course, they'd stayed to see the whole thing. When they saw me looking, they averted their eyes and shuffled down the trail.

Krowkr stood a few paces away but within earshot. He, too, kept his eyes averted. He stroked the amulet he wore around his neck with his thumb.

"Krowkr, stay with your people. Your part in this is finished."

"Lord, if…that is, I'd rather stay with you and Lady Fr—er, I'd prefer to stay with the four of you. I'm an able hand with both axe and sword. I'd very much like to meet Veethar, as I have met you." He swallowed hard. "Besides, I've no one left here."

"There is danger in what we do, lad," said Yowtgayrr. "It would be wise to stay."

Krowkr ducked his head. "That may be, Lord Alf, but I could help you. I'm a fair cook, and I have knowledge of hunting and trapping."

I arched an eyebrow at Yowtgayrr. "This isn't an audition, Krowkr. You don't have to prove your worth. It's just that there is every possibility you will die if you come with us."

Krowkr shrugged. "Lord, I was dying when you found me—when Lady Freya saved me. My life is already yours."

I glanced at Jane. Her expression matched how I felt. Neither one of us wanted worshippers. Neither one of us wanted to pretend to be gods from the Norse pantheon.

"Krowkr, you don't owe me anything," Jane said. "I could help, and so I did. There's nothing more to it."

"Yes, Lady Skyowlf," he said with perfect subservience. "I apologize for the slip of the tongue a moment ago."

Jane shook her head and glanced at me with a smile playing at her lips. "I don't think we can . dissuade him, Hanki."

I sighed and shook my head. "No, Skyowlf, it appears we can't." I scratched my beard and turned my gaze to Krowkr. "Here's the thing, Krowkr. I don't want your death on my conscience. There's enough there already."

He shrugged in a way that made me want to groan—that very stubborn Norwegian shrug that said "I will agree with you even though you are wrong." He nodded at Jane and said, "Your lady wife is correct, Lord. The two of you will not put me off. It is my duty to remain at your sides. I feel…*called*…to the task."

"Krowkr, we are not who you believe we are. Yes, we have capabilities that might seem magical to you, but they are—"

"Hank," said Yowtgayrr with a small shake of his head.

"If we tell you not to follow us, will you go home?" Jane asked.

"No, Lady. I will run the *Reknpokaprooin* after you've left. I will follow behind your party if you don't wish me to travel with you." He hung his head.

Jane looked at me and shrugged.

"That would be even more foolhardy and dangerous, Krowkr," I said with a sigh. "What can I say to convince you to go home?"

"With respect, Lord, there is nothing you can say." Krowkr stood still fingering the amulet around his neck.

"Oh, all right. But stop calling me 'lord.' My name is Hank." I hooked my thumb at Jane. "Her name is Jane."

"Yes, Lo—er…Hank."

"Marginally better. Keep working on it."

Krowkr nodded, still not meeting my gaze. "And since you won't *defer* to us, don't be *deferential*." I stood up and shouldered my pack. "Come on, puppies." I turned and walked toward the waterfall, escorted by the two silliest creatures in the world, trying to walk as they tried to attack my feet.

TEN

I emerged from the *proo,* and the water left on my clothes from the waterfall on Mithgarthr flash-froze in the searing cold. As far as I could see, a blanket of peculiar bluish-white ice and snow coated the ground, and a pale mist hung in the air like a bride's veil. No trees were visible, no animals, no life of any kind. Lumpy shapes stood in the distance, but whether they were natural rock formations or buildings was anyone's guess. A set of tracks still snaked toward one of the mounds, although almost obscured by snow and wind.

I stepped away from the *proo* and set my wriggling puppies down on the gelid ground. I put on my modern winter coat and my gloves, hoping they could withstand the temperatures.

Jane appeared next to the shimmering silver oval, and her face wrinkled at the cold. "Great. Cold. I so love the cold."

"You've got the cold weather gear Yowrnsaxa bought you?"

"Never leave home without it," she said in a cheesy voice.

The others came through, each dropping his pack at once and digging out extreme-weather gear. "Niflhaymr," said Althyof with a shudder. "I hate this place."

"Because of the frost giants?"

"No, because of the cold!" He glanced upward, and his eyes twitched away. "That sky."

I glanced up at the grim sky. From horizon to horizon, charcoal gray clouds tinged with bitter celestial blue gloomed down at us. A meager, blue-tinged light squeezed through the cloud-cover, but it was insubstantial, ineffective against the pale fog and the perpetual gloaming. "Where are they?"

"The frost giants? They huddle in their cities. Anything exposed to the air once night falls is dead by morning, even them." Althyof stomped his feet and blew into his already-blue-tinged hands. "Speaking of which, we need to find shelter. Best bet may be to follow Luka's trail. He's no doubt headed for the closest sanctuary."

"Hmm… Trust Luka?" Jane's tone made it clear she'd rather gargle with molten glass.

"I can send out my ravens. Do a little scout," I said with a smile.

"Your 'ravens?' Wow. That didn't take long," said Jane with a small smile on her lips.

"I'm tired of saying 'animus' every other minute."

"Whatever. If only we had Yowrnsaxa or Frikka along," she mused. "They could use the *Syown* or perform an augury or something *useful*—like map out our possible futures."

Something about that tickled in the back of my mind. *Why can I see into the future or past when I'm dreaming? Why* can't *I perform auguries if I have prophetic dreams?* That prickly mass of *kaltrar* in my head shuddered, and it was almost a physical sensation as though something inside my brain had juddered and rolled over.

"What's the matter? You look like you ate a rotten egg."

"Bet you say that to all the sailors," I murmured. I shook my head to get rid of the sensation but couldn't dislodge the feeling. Buzzing and bouncing, my thoughts skittered and skipped like a needle on a record during an earthquake. *Why can't I do it? Frikka seemed to think my dreams were a form of augury.*

My thoughts swirled in my head like the whirlwinds of dirt and dust that always followed Pigpen in the Peanuts comics.

"Hank?" asked Jane, a note of concern edging into her voice.

"Yeah, I'm fine. Just thinking…or trying to, in any case."

"Don't hurt yourself."

Yowtgayrr pointed at the slowly disappearing trail. "We'd better get moving before the snow makes our decision moot. Hank, you should send an animus along this trail, in case we lose it to the weather."

"Good idea." I muttered the *triblinkr* that split my consciousness into separate animuses, forming two ravens of black smoke. One I sent to the farthest point of Luka's trail I could see. From there, I looked out through smoky black raven eyes and hopped to the farthest point I could see. I kept on in that vein while I sent the other animus into a circular search pattern with my physical body as its center point. "I'm following the trail, but I'm also scanning the surrounding area, in case the trail is another of Luka's little tricks."

"The frost giant said this *proo* led to a knack," said Althyof. "Prudent to keep an eye out."

"So far, nothing on the circle," I said as that animus completed a circuit and moved farther away to begin again at a greater radius.

"Good work. Does Polly want a cracker?" asked Jane with a mischievous smile.

"Next time, I'll make them something else—like palmetto bugs."

"Do that, and I'll stop protecting you from spiders."

Althyof shook his bowed head, but I thought I glimpsed a smile on his face. "What else can we do about my scarcity of ammunition?" I asked him.

"You may discover other *kaltrar* as your brain assimilates everything from the scroll." He looked at me askance and shrugged. "You did well enough as a supporting *runeskowld* when we battled the spiders in the Great Forest of Suel. Don't improvise while I'm singing a *trowba*." His gaze turned stern. "That means no *saytr*, no improvised lyrics or steps. The same rules as the rote *trowba* I'm going to teach you."

"I understand. I would be interested in trying to combine a *lausaveesa* with *saytr*, but only with your approval and guidance. Something little and easy."

"I'll admit I am interested in the idea, but I won't allow it if you are going to be foolhardy at the slightest success."

"I won't," I said.

"Would someone be willing to teach me the *saytr*?" asked Krowkr in a timid voice.

He was such a quiet, unobtrusive man, it was easy to almost forget about him. "Our resident *vefari* are still on Osgarthr." His face fell.

"I understand," he said.

"I can teach you a thing or two but recognize that this is not my area of expertise."

He brightened and smiled. "Thank you, Hanki."

"Just 'Hank,'" I said.

"My apologies. I keep forgetting. It's such a strange name."

"Not as strange as 'Jane,' though."

Krowkr's grin widened. "No, not as strange as that."

"Keep it up, both of you," said Jane. "I can probably swat you both with one swing of my pretty raven bracelet." She thunked the edge of her shield with her thumb. "It would make a nice dent in your foreheads."

Krowkr looked so stricken, I couldn't help but laugh.

"Besides, everyone knows I am strange-*awesome*, not strange-weird."

Far ahead of us on the trail, I halted my animus before a vast depression. The snow and ice had been cleared, revealing azure rock and immense buildings carved from a glacier of pale blue ice. "Luka's trail ends at a city in a valley up ahead," I said to my companions as I turned my attention to my other *antafukl*. "The area around us is pristine, except for this trail.

"Let's follow the trail," said Yowtgayrr. "We can take precautions against ambush."

"I'll keep my *antafukl* circling ahead of us."

"Good idea. I will range ahead, but I will be close."

"Good enough," I said.

Yowtgayrr nodded and wrote silvery runes in the air before fading from sight.

"It's cold," said Jane. "Whatever we're doing, let's get on with it."

We moved off, following the trail. Every now and again, I darted a glance over my shoulder, to make sure the *proo* stayed put. I imagined my animus near the city in the same pale blue hue as the glacier-city and the mist that hung above it like a shroud.

I moved forward, skimming close to the surface, and as I drew closer, details became clear. The city seemed to have been carved in one giant piece, and the tailings from the interior of the buildings had been reused to make walls surrounding the city.

The strange architecture showed sweeping curves that looked not quite right. The scale was massive, but it wasn't the proper scale for giants or for humans. It was somewhere in between and inconstant to boot. It struck me as more of a vista H. R. Giger or H. P. Lovecraft might have imagined.

Domes atop towers were ridged with long, curve-hugging cylinders carved such that the leading point mimicked a giant's skull, and the domed roofs themselves eschewed pure hemispheres in favor of lopsided onion-shapes. Tall towers thrust toward the dirty, achromatic sky, but even they were not based on genuine circles but were instead crushed ovals in cross-section, and each was different from the next. A unique sculpture, the subject of which ranged from human heads to hideous scenes of torture and dismemberment, decorated the dome of each tower in bas-relief.

From the top of the wall encircling the city jutted huge bent spikes that seemed more organically grown than carved or built from bricks of ice. As I drew closer, I discerned thousands upon thousands of remains carved into the wall itself. At the bottom, they had depicted the remains as skeletons, while at the top, they seemed to be complete, undecayed bodies. Corpses arrayed in various states of decomposition made up the multitude of layers in between, and a hoary blue frost accented it all to hideous effect.

"It's like some Lovecraftian city of the dead," I muttered. "They carved the ice of the walls to imitate stacked bodies."

"Those aren't carvings," said Althyof. "The frost giants entomb their dead in the ice walls of their cities and their buildings. They consider it a great honor to be entombed in the walls of the homes of great or famous giants. There is even a lottery to be interred in the walls of the mayoral mansion once per cycle." Althyof shuddered, but whether from the cold or the subject matter, I couldn't say. "It's a disgusting practice, but there's no explaining these races that have drifted so far from the *Plauinn*."

"Sounds like a lovely spot for a vacation," Jane muttered.

As we walked on, I brought my pale blue animus closer to the city. Instead of gates set into the walls, there were wide tunnels with no barrier to entry. I hugged the top of the closest tunnel, which was ribbed with vertebral shapes, giving the act of passing through the tunnel a feeling of being swallowed alive.

Inside the wall, the city bustled with activity. An uncountable number of blue-skinned giants crowded and jostled through the street that the tunnel became. Almost as crowded as the cavern cities of Nitavetlir, it lacked the warmth—as strange as that may sound. They barked at each other in the street, even those that walked with one another. Constant scuffles and shoving matches occurred, but they didn't have that playful, joshing feeling of similar fights between the Tverkar. No, these fights seemed serious.

The giants themselves varied in height, as expected of any race, but also in general proportion and features. Some had horns jutting from various parts of their bodies, but not necessarily the *same* body parts. Others had massive, scale-like protuberances near their knees and elbows, creating organic armor. Still others had no boney protrusions at all but had soft, human-like skin instead. Some had jutting brows, some twisted ears, and others even had short tails that wrapped around their upper-thighs. Hair and body hair were as varied, with some having thick, lush blue or gray hair, and others being entirely hairless while a thick, coarse hair covered others all over their bodies. Some had asymmetrical facial features, yet others were akin to idealized projections of human beauty. Their skin tones ranged from azure to a blue-tinged paleness that made me think of Grecian statues.

As a race, they appeared to be in mid-mutation, but from which form to which, I had no idea. On the whole, it was disconcerting, to say the least. There was no "normal," no mold from which I could judge the race.

"What happened to these giants?" I asked Althyof as we walked toward the city.

"What do you mean?"

"Their physical forms are so different, so varied."

The Tverkr shrugged. "I've heard it said the language of the *Plauinn* has grown dim here, and that the frost giants are an example of nature gone wild. I have no idea. They are ugly and brutish. Like the trolls."

"Are they related to the trolls or vice versa?"

Again, the Tverkr bumped his shoulders toward the sky. "I'm not versed in racial genealogies."

The giants went about their business, glaring and snarling with what appeared to be real hatred for one another. Their clothing and manner of dress varied as much as their physical appearances, and I didn't spot one giant who appeared to be a guard, a policeman, or anyone who seemed to have an official role. I let my animus drift through the smoke and haze that hovered twenty feet above the street.

I glanced at Althyof. "How do they govern themselves? Do they have a culture?"

The Tverkr pursed his lips and shrugged. "They pay well."

"That's it? That's all you know?" asked Jane.

Althyof shrugged again. "I don't know *everything*. That's Meuhlnir's job."

Something formed in the air next to the animus I had circling ahead of us, looking for an ambush. It appeared to be smoke, and the color of it matched the snow and ice.

"Something ahead," I said.

Althyof pulled his daggers and squinted into the distance before us. "Where?"

"By my animus," I said.

The thing formed into the shape of a woman. "You're getting predictable, Tyeldnir," said Kuhntul.

"What?" I asked using my animus.

"Black birds…*again*."

"Jane said nearly the same thing."

"Did she?" A smile formed from the smoke making up Kuhntul's face. "You know you can make them take any shape, any color?"

"What do you have to tell me?" I said suppressing a sigh.

"Don't be that way, Tyeldnir. We have fun in our little journeys together, don't we?" Her form solidified and took the shape of a woman carrying a spear and flapping huge wings.

Jane. I snapped, "Don't do that!"

Kuhntul only shrugged, a smile playing on her face, but she let the form fade into a column of blueish smoke.

"What do you want, Kuhntul?" I asked.

"You mustn't go into the city ahead. Luka's already been there, and he's told lies about you to the frost giants. Your reception would be a cold one."

"Very punny," I muttered.

"So grumpy, today. You seemed much less so earlier."

"Why did you take me to Hel's prison?"

"Time enough for that later," said Kuhntul, glancing up at the darkening sky. "You must go into the city, donning Luka's skin, and undo what he's done."

"Donning his skin?"

Kuhntul shrugged. "Call it what you will."

"How do you even know I learned that *kaltrar*?"

She treated me to a stern look and a small shake of her head. "Time's a-wasting, Tyeldnir."

"Yeah, yeah," I grumbled as the column of smoke dissipated. "False alarm," I said to Althyof. "Kuhntul again."

"What did she want?"

"To tell me Luka has already turned the frost giants against us. To encourage me to use the *doppelgänger triblinkr*."

"*Doppelgänger*?" asked Althyof.

"Yeah. Body double, twin. Whatever."

"The new shapeshifting *triblinkr*?"

I nodded.

"Might as well call it that, yes?"

"She says I should 'take Luka's skin' and go into the town to undo his trickery."

"Alone, I bet," said Jane with a trace of sourness.

"It would have to be," I said.

"No, it wouldn't," said Yowtgayrr's disembodied voice. "And it will not be, though none will be the wiser."

"Good idea," said Jane. "What do the rest of us do?"

"Try to stay warm?" I asked.

She gave me the stink-eye. "Remind me to beat you later."

I chanted the new *triblinkr* holding Luka's image in my mind's eye, and as the *prayteenk* settled over me, Jane stepped back and then turned away. The *varkr* pups backed away with stiff-legged slowness, growling, but looking confused. I glanced down at my long, lanky frame. The ground seemed a lot farther away than it should, but I guess that goes with being ridiculously tall.

Althyof grimaced. "I'd say it worked."

"I don't feel different, except for the height. When I change into a bear, *everything* seems different, even my instincts."

"Makes sense," said Yowtgayrr. "After all, you are not a bear, but you *are* an Isir."

"Somehow I have a hard time thinking of Luka as anything but an *oolfur*."

"Me, too," murmured Jane before she continued in a louder voice. "I'm not going to kiss you goodbye, not with that face. Hurry and be done with it. And don't get killed wearing that skin."

ELEVEN

I walked through the tunnel carved in the body-strewn ice wall. I'd expected it to reek, but it didn't. The air was crisp and clean, akin to winter air after a snowstorm.

I'd left one animus with Jane, Krowkr, and Althyof. "I'm entering the city," I said to them.

"Hurry," said Jane. "It's already freezing, and the temperature is dropping fast."

I stood at the edge of the tunnel, looking at the sea of frost giants pushing and shoving their way along. "I've just realized I have no idea where to go," I muttered.

"Tell it to your mother," said a frost giant as he shoved past me.

Making sure I kept my mouth closed, I repeated the phrase to the others.

"Why am I not surprised?" asked Jane with a smile. "Are you willing to ask for directions?"

"Directions to where? 'Excuse me, sir, can you tell me where a man matching my appearance went to tell lies about me?'"

"Leave it to Kuhntul to tell you only part of the information you need," said Althyof. "*Tisir*!"

"Scout," said Jane. "With your other *parakeet*."

"Yes, dear." I brought my animus down out of the smoke and haze and hovered there without moving. "Er, scout for what?"

"I don't know! Luka-ness!"

"Well, I'm not exactly sure what that is, but I'll—"

"You going to stand there blocking the passage like an idiot, Isir?" demanded a frost giant behind me.

"Tricksy things. Wolf droppings," said Jane. "*Something*."

"Pardon me," I said and stepped aside.

"Remember who you are," whispered Yowtgayrr.

With a curt nod, I stepped into the crowded street, pushing frost giants from my path. When they accosted me, I glared at them with my best 'I'm a werewolf, so you'd better leave me alone' expression. I wandered, taking turns at random, spreading my attention between where I was walking and my animuses.

The throngs of giants seemed to wander almost as aimlessly as me. They pushed their way into a building, but then re-entered the stream of bodies after a few seconds, sometimes going the other direction. What they were doing mystified me. The city had no market squares, no community areas, no parks or fora—at least none that I could find. I couldn't even distinguish restaurants or taverns.

I thumped a giant who walked ahead of me in the endless flow of colossal blue figures. "You there!" I called.

He glared at me over his shoulder. "What do you want, little Isir?"

"I need an inn."

His expression darkened and twisted. "An inn? You?"

"Yes, me. Where is the closest inn?"

"The closest that will serve your kind, you mean," sneered the giant. A horn jutted out of his forehead, erupting from a section of skin that was so rough, it almost looked scaled. He caught me looking at it and shoved me.

I reeled into a giant on the other side who cursed and shoved me back. The horned giant balled his fists and squinted at me through narrowed eyelids.

"The inn?" I demanded.

"There is no inn on Niflhaymr that will serve your kind. You are repulsive." He swung his fist.

I ducked it and twisted away through the crowd, shoving and stepping on pale blue feet as I went. The giant with the horn in his forehead lurched after me but tripped and spilled face first into the street to the laughter and jeers of the other giants.

Yowtgayrr, I thought. "That's another one I owe you," I whispered. I kept running and twisting through the crowd, followed by a wave of angry jeering and catcalls. I glanced over my shoulder, searching for signs of more than vocal disapproval, and when I faced forward, I ran smack into the front of an enormous giant.

He didn't move at all, except to sneer down at me, arms akimbo. His nose wrinkled, and he shook his head. He was the biggest giant I'd seen, arms layered in thick thews, ringed in bony scales around his elbows and wrists. His eyes tracked up to mine and widened. "*You*," he muttered.

"My apologies," I said, climbing to my feet.

"What do you want? Why have you come back?" The giant glanced around. "And why are you running through the crowd like a child? And since when do you *apologize*?"

"I was… I wanted to find an inn, and I—"

The tall giant laughed and swatted one of his neighbors on the shoulder. "You make me laugh, Luka Oolfhyethidn. Always, you joke. But tell me, why have you returned? I said I would watch for these intruders you warned me about. Have you returned the *preer* you jumbled to their proper exits? After such a long time without them working, having them hidden has been quite inconvenient for the rest of the city, you know."

The other giants in the street cut a swath around us, glaring at the massive giant opposite me, but no one touched us, and no one said a word. "I was mistaken about the others. They mean you no harm." I'd have to figure out the mess about the *preer* later.

He looked at me askance, forehead wrinkled with suspicion. "You were quite sure before. What has changed?"

"I think—" I bit off my words as a giant shoved me to the side.

The big giant roared incoherently at the one who'd pushed me and hit him with one massive fist that sent him to the street on his back. Unconscious.

"Why did you do that, Vefsterkur?" demanded another giant standing to the side. "Do you take the side of an Isir over one of your own kind?"

The colossal giant—Vefsterkur, I guessed— laughed and pointed a thick finger at the crowd around him. "I did no such thing, you all saw it. I took offense at having my conversation with this little Isir interrupted." The giants looked away, and Vefsterkur put a large blue hand on my shoulder and guided me through the crowd. "You should know better than to walk in the thoroughfares, Luka," he muttered.

He led me to a narrow alley that barely looked wide enough for me, let alone Vefsterkur. The darkened lane smelled of refuse and bodily wastes and stretched away into the growing gloom, winding like a snake's path. He navigated the place as if he walked the alley often, never slowing, tapping me on the left shoulder when he wanted me to bear left, and on the right when he preferred that direction. At last, he grabbed my shoulder and dragged me to a halt. The giant pushed his hand under his clothing. He withdrew a thick wooden key, which he inserted into a crack in the ice wall to my left.

He turned the key, and with a clunk, a door opened onto the alley. "Welcome back to my hall once more, Luka, albeit approached from the back way. You no doubt recall the way to the front entrance." He pulled the hidden door closed behind us and re-locked it with a solid-sounding clunk. "Now, tell me what you want."

Though warmer than outside, I'd have guessed the internal temperature was just below freezing. There were no windows visible anywhere, and the interior had been carved from ice—there were still pick marks cut into every surface. The furniture, if it could be called that, was arranged without apparent thought or pattern. A block of ice here, a block of ice there—it seemed more like a scattering of toy blocks than furniture.

Vefsterkur sat on one of the blocks of ice and waved at another. "Make yourself comfortable, Luka. You know I don't require formality."

"Yes," I said, eyeing the ice block and trying to figure out how badly it would affect my hips to sit on it. "To tell you the truth, I'd rather stand."

"Suit yourself." Even seated, he had to look down to meet my gaze. "Let's get on with it." A harsh, impatient tone had crept into his voice.

"As I said in the street, more information has presented itself, and I was wrong about the nature of those following me."

"Hmmm." He narrowed his eyes. "And what is their true nature?"

"Harmless to those that leave them in peace."

Vefsterkur pursed his blueberry lips. "Is it so?"

Something is wrong here. But what? I kept my gaze firmly locked on his. "It isn't going well," I said through my animus outside the city. "He suspects something."

"Giants are a suspicious lot," said Althyof. "Remember to act the way Luka would. Brash, confident, irreverent, arrogant."

I turned my attention back to the giant. "Do you question my judgment?" I demanded in an imperious tone.

"I do not question the judgment of Luka Oolfhyethidn, not he who I have known for eons." He cocked his head to the side and squinted at me in the dim light. "I do, however, question whether you *are* Luka Oolfhyethidn."

"Of *course* I am he," I said with a curl of my lip. "Have you lost your wits? Do I not *look* like myself?"

The giant grunted and shifted his weight on the ice block that served him as a chair. "I'm sure I haven't, *Isir*, and you do *look* like Oolfhyethidn. Whether you *are* he is another question."

I scoffed and pasted a sneer on my face. "If you don't believe me, I'll take my leave."

The giant shook his head. "I think not. No, you won't leave this hall unless you have satisfied my suspicions."

I shook my head with scorn. "Tell me what you require of me," I snapped.

"Answer me this, *Luka*, if it is really you: what is the name of that which heralds the day from the east each morning?"

I thought furiously for a moment. "Shining sunlight."

"Sunlight, is it?" he asked with a scowl on his face. He shifted his weight forward as though making ready to pounce.

The Romans and Greeks had a myth about the Sun's path through the sky, and I thought the Norse did too, but I couldn't remember it. I wracked my mind. *Something about a horse?*

"Quick," I said through my animus. "He's asking me what heralds the day in the east each morning. I said sunlight, but that didn't satisfy him."

Jane and Althyof exchanged a bewildered look.

"Skinfaxi," said Krowkr.

Of course! The horse with the shining mane. "Yes," I said to the giant. "Sunlight shining from the mane of Skinfaxi."

The giant sat back a little, looking mollified to a degree. "And what brings about the darkness of night?"

Through my animus, I asked, "Krowkr, what is the name of the horse that brings the night sky?"

"Hrimfaxi," he said without pausing to think.

"Thanks," I said and returned my attention to Vefsterkur. "He of the frosty mane. Hrimfaxi."

"Where is it you go?" the giant asked.

"Go? I am right here."

"Yes, but your mind goes elsewhere before you answer. Where is it you go?"

I forced a laugh. "I go woolgathering."

"Woolgathering?" The big giant looked perplexed.

"Searching my memory. I haven't thought of these things in a long, long time."

He scratched his chin. "Very well. But tell me, what is it that separates my realm from yours?"

I had a vague memory that there was a river in Norse mythology that defined the boundary of the two realms, but I didn't think that was what he meant. I turned my attention to my comrades outside the city. "Althyof, this one is for you. He asked me what separates Niflhaymr from Osgarthr."

"The river Ifing," said Krowkr.

"You know the answer, Hank. A *proo*."

"Thanks." I looked up at Vefsterkur and grinned. "That one is tricksy."

"Woolgathering, again?" he asked with a hint of suspicion.

"Yes, but here's the answer to your trick question. A *proo*."

He nodded and relaxed back on his icy throne. "Welcome to my home, Luka."

"You're sure now?" I asked lacing my voice with irritation.

"Yes, I am satisfied."

Luka wouldn't have let it end there. "Then it's my turn."

"Your turn?" asked the giant.

"Yes, you asked me questions, now answer mine." It was precisely what Luka would insist on: tit for tat. "Answer my questions, if you can, Vefsterkur."

With a small, sour smile, the giant nodded.

"All the races, all the known *klith*, all the known *stathur*...where did they come from?"

Vefsterkur laughed derisively. "Such an easy one? Do you think me feeble?"

"That doesn't sound like an answer."

"All are descended from the *Plauinn*. The worlds split from each other in the Sundering."

I scowled. "Any child knows that."

"It was *your* question, Luka," said the giant in an amused tone. "Do you have one more suited for adults?"

"What is the real separation between our realms?"

Vefsterkur cast a confused glance my way. "A *proo* as you've already said."

"No." A sly smile spread on my lips. "The *preer* are bridges between the two worlds, but that isn't what I meant. What makes a giant a giant and an Isir an Isir?"

The giant brought a thick hand to his face and scratched a scaly growth under his chin. "A difficult question, but the answer must be the bits of the

Plauinn that have gone awry in the time since the First War."

I nodded grudgingly. "Yes, I suppose that will do."

"You are satisfied?"

"No," I snapped. "I've more."

The giant chuckled and shrugged as if he didn't care, but irritation rumbled in that chuckle, and the shrug twitched with the urge to smash my head in. "Ask your riddles."

"At the base of a tree, there are three. Do you know of what I speak?" I leaned forward and jutted out my jaw.

A small smile creased his face. "Your speech amuses me, Isir. But, yes, the Three Maids are known to me." He sniffed as if he'd caught a scent on the currents of the air.

"And the tree?"

"Iktrasitl, of course."

"Tell me, if you know. Is the tree real? Where does it lie?"

The giant's shoulders tensed, and his eyes narrowed. "Why do you ask this?"

"I *already* know. I want to know if you do."

He glared at me for the space of a minute or two before shrugging. "At the center, the meeting place. Where the world of the *Plauinn* once stood."

I shrugged. "Very good."

"You're satisfied?" he asked. His nostrils flared, and he sucked a long breath through his nose.

"I am." *Out of decent questions is what I am.*

"Let me ask you one more."

"I guess," I said. "If you must."

The giant nodded and shifted his weight forward to the edge of the ice block. "Is that the blood of a frost giant I discern on your skin, Isir?"

I stared at him, flummoxed. "What? No. I have no idea what you perceive, but it—"

"*Do not lie to me*!" he bellowed.

"What if it is? Perhaps from the fight in the street."

His eyelids squeezed to slits. "I don't think so, Isir. When you came to me before, you asked for a frost giant to wait in ambush for those that pursued you."

"Yes, I remember," I lied.

"I sent my lesser son."

"Yes." I wanted—*needed*—a way out of the conversation, but my mind refused to give me anything but single word answers. "You sent your son with me. He bids me tell you hello."

He grimaced and gave his head a slight shake. "I sent my lesser son…with *Luka*."

"This again?" I asked, mind racing a million miles a minute.

Vefsterkur stood, stretching up toward the ceiling, a redwood with tree-trunk legs. His hands curled into fists. "He was my lesser son, but he was still my son." His voice had gone cold.

"Uh-oh," I said through my animus outside the city.

"What?" asked Jane.

"He knows about the frost giant we killed. It was his son. That's what he meant by 'tell my father hello.'"

"Get out of there! Run!"

"Too late for that." I popped both of my *antafukl* to the air above Vefsterkur's head. "Now, wait a minute, Vefsterkur. I can explain."

"I think not," he spat.

"Move, Hank!" said Yowtgayrr, and I dove behind the block of ice that was to have been my seat.

"Who is it who stands before me?" roared Vefsterkur, but whether he addressed Yowtgayrr or me, I couldn't say.

I didn't have enough ammunition to kill the brute, not even with Yowtgayrr's help. In my mind's eye, golden runes appeared in the air in front of me. At first, I thought it was Yowtgayrr using one of the Alfar *kaltrar*, but a strange voice spoke in my head, speaking a *triblinkr* that seemed more than familiar. It felt more like a memory.

It was a *triblinkr*. One I had read in my grimoire. Crawling on my hands and knees back toward the door we'd come in, I chanted the *triblinkr*.

The giant took one huge stride and caught me up, but before he could do anything, I finished the *triblinkr* and felt the power of it snap out toward Vefsterkur. "What is this?" he demanded, standing as still as a stone, fear burning on his face. "Do you curse me, Isir?"

I crawled away from him, and his head snapped toward the sound, but his eyes looked at a point beyond me.

"You can't escape me, Isir." He chuckled. "Curse me with blindness all you want. I locked the doors, and I have the only key." He swept his arms in a huge circle around himself, fingers curled into claws. "I will tear you apart slowly, Isir. Your limbs, I'll peel from your body and beat you with them. I will grind your bones to dust and entomb them with the body of my son. I know this hall like my own hand." Two long slashes from Yowtgayrr's weapons appeared across his back, and he screamed in pain. "You must do more than that to end my existence, Isir."

My hands fell to the butts of my pistols, but they were the wrong weapons for this fight. Not only did I not have enough ammunition, but they were too loud, and who knew how many other giants would come running to investigate their thunder. I let Luka's form evaporate.

I dove on the giant from above, talons extended. With a *crrruck* to end all *crrrucks*, I raked my claws across his plane of a forehead. That was great as a distraction, but I needed more than ravens made of smoke to beat Vefsterkur.

"A scratch!" he boomed with a laugh. "You'll find I have more resilience than my son."

I could do more with my animus than be a bird— I knew from my dream-trip with Kuhntul. They could be anything I wanted them to be. I slid out of my armor and my pistols, tucking everything behind an ice block. I'd been a fish in the *stathur* that imprisoned Hel, maybe I could also form them into other animals.

"Here, giant," said Yowtgayrr, allowing his invisibility to fade—not that it mattered against a blind opponent.

Vefsterkur's head whipped to the side. "Who is it who speaks to me? Who has entered my hall unannounced, uninvited?"

In answer, another set of slashes appeared across his back.

He straightened, grimacing with pain. "Whoever you are, you shall not leave this hall breathing. That is a promise."

I brought both ravens to the ground, not bothering to fly down, just making them appear there in an instant. I thought about Keri and Fretyi's mother and reshaped one of my animuses in her image. The other I reformed in the image of a predator from Mithgarthr that always inspired fear—a magnificent lion of smoke.

I could move them without a sound, but I *wanted* them to make noise. I wanted them to draw Vefsterkur's attention away from Yowtgayrr and myself. In the *varkr* form, I leapt to one of the ice blocks and let loose a howl. In the lion form, I rushed forward in a thundering charge, roaring as loud as I could.

The giant's head whipped toward the *varkr* for a split-second but refocused on the sounds of the charging lion. He set his feet and spread his arms wide. At the last moment before impact, I shifted the animus back to where it had started from.

Vefsterkur stood waiting for a few moments, then shook his head and extended his arm to feel for the beast. Using the spirit-*varkr*, I bit his outstretched hand, willing my fangs to be as hard as diamonds, as sharp as edged-steel, and he shouted, jerking his hand to his chest.

I began the Kuthbyuhrn *triblinkr* once I'd removed the last of my gear. The frigid air clawed into my joints and bones. With a perfect understanding of my tactic, Yowtgayrr swept in from the giant's flank, stabbing with his longsword and slicing at the back of the giant's knee with his long dagger.

The giant whirled toward him, arms sweeping wide, but Yowtgayrr was already rolling away. I repeated my earlier charge with my animus, pounding paws made from smoke against the ice, making as much noise as I could. The giant whirled toward the sound and set himself to take the charge yet again. My *prayteenk* reached its conclusion, and I reared up on my hind legs and roared.

Vefsterkur wheeled toward me, but the sound of the charging animus drew his attention like a package store does a drunk. With the *varkr,* I leapt at the giant from the side, jaws gaping, and I stepped forward on my hind legs, arms held wide.

"Over here," said Yowtgayrr before leaping away.

The spirit-*varkr* collided with the giant, fangs sinking into the side of his neck. Vefsterkur grabbed for it, but I popped it away, leaving green blood streaming down the giant's throat without apparent cause. I wrapped my arms around him and snapped my ursine jaws around his neck. At the same time, I let the lion-shaped animus slam into him, striking him across the thighs.

The two of us were of a height, but I outweighed the giant, so when the animus slammed into him, he staggered to the side, and I shoved him hard. He sprawled over an ice block, and the *varkr* was there, jaws snapping chunks out of the giant's flesh, slinging pale green blood around like Jackson Pollack.

"Hold him," said Yowtgayrr, and I fell on the giant's exposed back, pinning him where he lay.

The giant struggled, elbowing, kicking, wriggling like a snake, but my instincts took over, and I snapped my jaws around the back of his head and ground my fangs into his skull. He howled in pain, and I mocked him by howling from the *varkr*'s jaws. Yowtgayrr stepped forward and stabbed the giant through the side. I pressed my weight on Vefsterkur's back and changed my animuses into the form of humongous crocodiles to help hold down the thrashing giant. I brought each to bear, snapping their jaws closed around the giant's upper arms.

The giant screamed and kicked his legs, flailing for purchase. Yowtgayrr stabbed him again, and Vefsterkur bellowed in pain and tried to arch his back. I sank lower, resting my broad bestial chest against his torso and pressed with my hind legs. I whipped my head back and forth, trying to crack his neck if I could.

Even with an alligator clamped onto each of his biceps, Vefsterkur put up a tremendous fight. He pummeled me with his fists, kicked at my hind legs—everything he could think of to impart harm.

I squeezed my jaws, and my fangs skidded across his temples and into the giant's ears. He thrashed his arms and legs in a blind panic. With a pop, my teeth punched into his brain, and all the fight left him. I continued to bear down until my jaws suddenly slammed together with a brutal, sickening crunch that left no doubt whether Vefsterkur still lived.

Retching, I performed the *triblinkr* to regain my own form, and when the *prayteenk* finished, I puked on the rimed floor. Shaking my head, I got my gear and put it back on. "That was…"

"Yes," said Yowtgayrr. "But we have no time to waste. We must get the others into the city and into this hall before the day dies."

"How can we get them here without some giant—"

"It seemed to me that when Vefsterkur made it clear you were with him; the other giants left you alone." Yowtgayrr gazed at me without blinking.

"Yes. Of *course*." I stared at the giant's corpse, fixing his image in my mind. I chanted the *triblinkr* to take his form, fighting a wave of sudden, debilitating exhaustion. My head pounded with each staccato beat of my heart.

I grew in herky-jerky spurts as the *prayteenk* worked toward its finish. "Running out of gas," I muttered.

"As in the last battle with Hel?"

"Yeah. This *prayteenk* is easier than the bear—I guess it's closer to my natural form—but it's taking more concentration than switching to the form of another Isir."

"Three changes in a short time frame," said Yowtgayrr. "That's a lot to ask of anyone."

I nodded. "Where do you suppose Luka hid the *proo*?"

The Alf shrugged. "Somewhere close. He wouldn't want it to be so far away as to be inconvenient in case he needed to return."

"Yeah, but Luka can move the *preer* around somehow. Same as Meuhlnir and Veethar."

The Alf shrugged once more, looking up at me before glancing at Vefsterkur's corpse. "An exact likeness, to my eye."

"Good. Let me tell the others to meet us near the city." I reshaped my animuses, turning one into the pale blue raven shape I'd used for reconnaissance earlier, and sending the other back to Althyof and Jane.

"Come meet us at the gate," I said. "I'm in an ice giant costume, so don't freak out."

"A giant? What happened with the giant you met?" asked Jane.

I grimaced at the memory of his brains squirting into my mouth. As a bear, my instinct had been to swallow—the high fat content was perfect for pre-hibernation—but my human soul had rebelled. "Long story, but he won't be bothering us anymore. Follow my raven to the city, I'll meet you there."

Yowtgayrr bent and went through Vefsterkur's clothing, looking for the key to the back entrance, and once he found it, we headed back out into the dark, twisting alleys.

TWELVE

lthyof chuckled when I told him about the fight with the giant. "Too bad the Alf was with you. You could have added a line such , as 'bested the troll Fowrpauti in single combat' to your list of deeds."

"Yeah," said Jane. "That's exactly what you need—a *bigger* head."

We sat close together under a shield bubble in one of Vefsterkur's frozen side rooms, hoping our body heat would warm the air trapped with us. So far, it seemed a daft plan.

"What if I use the new *triblinkr* to heat the air?"

"I'd rather you tried that for the first time on air that didn't contain my flesh," said Althyof in a wry tone.

Krowkr hadn't said a word when I'd met them at the gates, all dressed up in my Vefsterkur costume. He hadn't said a word when I'd led them past Vefsterkur's body. Krowkr had watched in silence as I performed the *triblinkr* to regain the form my mother gave me. He hadn't said anything, but the reverence in his eyes… I hoped it would not be a problem. I *wished* it wouldn't be a problem, but you know what they say about wishes and fishes.

We'd eaten a cold (and I mean *cold*) meal in the small side room and should have been brainstorming about where Luka had hidden the *preer*. My brain didn't want to work, and though the cold was part of the reason why, it was not the whole reason. I felt cotton-headed, tired. My thoughts slid around in my head slug-like and ponderous.

"Where would he put it?" I asked Althyof.

"You're asking me? You are the Isir. He's more similar to you than to me."

"He's nothing like Hank!" snapped Jane, taking my hand.

"Well, they *are* related, after all." Althyof shrugged and put his arms behind him so he could recline.

"You know how you and Yowtgayrr don't appreciate a reminder of your relationship to the Svartalfar?" I asked in a mild voice.

"Point taken. Tell me again what the giant said."

I had to suppress a sigh. "He asked if I would return the *preer* to normal functioning. He said it was an inconvenience."

"No, he said more than that." Althyof mimed pulling a rope.

"No, that's what he said. It was an inconvenience to the rest of the city."

"Yes! That's it." Althyof beamed at me. "And that's the clue."

"What are you going on about, Althyof?" asked Jane in a sleepy tone.

"He said it was an inconvenience for *the rest of the city*. Not an inconvenience for him."

"Maybe he didn't use the damn thing," I grumbled.

"No, I don't think that's it. I think Luka moved the city's *preer* from their usual public places to hidden places. *Private* places."

"Okay, fine. Say you're right. How does that help?"

"What private place would make it inconvenient for everyone else, but not for Vefsterkur?"

Jane glanced at me, wide-eyed. "Do you think…"

"What? Do I think what?" I groused. "Stop being all mysterious and say it plain, Althyof."

"They are here, Hank. The *preer* are somewhere in Vefsterkur's household."

"Yes, I suppose that makes sense." I rubbed my hand across my forehead and eyes. "We'd better get moving. We can split up, find it faster that way."

"You're not going anywhere, Mister," said Jane.

Althyof glanced at her before turning an assessing gaze on me. "That's right, Hank. You will stay here and rest while Yowtgayrr, Krowkr and I investigate."

"More people mean a faster search. Jane and I—"

"Will be right here," said Jane in a firm tone. "You will rest; I will babysit you to make sure you do."

"I don't need a—"

"So," she said, turning to Althyof as if I hadn't spoken. "Do you need me to do anything while I babysit?"

"No, that seems like a big enough job. Even for a woman of your capabilities."

She nodded and glared at me. "You. On your back, eyes closed."

With a sigh, I resigned myself to an uncomfortable nap on a floor made of ice.

THIRTEEN

I walked through the empty streets of the city, and that felt strangely wrong. The ice walls displayed a million decaying ravens, and the domes topping the buildings bore intricate carvings of another million birds in flight.

My head throbbed as if someone had packed the double-bass drums from a speed-metal concert into the middle of my head. My vision beclouded once again, almost to the point of blindness, and all I wanted to do was sit down and rest. But I couldn't, and I didn't understand why.

I needed to keep moving—the irresistible compulsion forced me to keep putting one massive blue foot in front of the other. I had to, but I didn't understand why.

"Such a nice day for a walk," said the blue-skinned giantess beside me. "Don't you think so, Tyeldnir?"

"What? Who are you? Where did you come from?"

The giantess pouted and raked her hands through her cobalt hair. "You've forgotten me again? What must I do to make an indelible mark in your memory?"

I relaxed. "Kuhntul."

"The very one."

"Why have you brought me here this time?"

"Me? I didn't bring you to this dreamslice, Tyeldnir. It was you who summoned me."

I frowned and scratched my blue head. "I did?"

"You did. I see you've learned to take a shape other than that silly bird. It's so much easier to talk with a humanoid body." She ran her hand down her side enticingly. "Among other things."

"You never quit."

"Are you sure you want me to?"

I waved my hand in dismissal. "Is this… Is this Niflhaymr?"

She laughed—a perfect imitation of glass bells tinkling in the wind. That meant something, but I couldn't guess what. "Where else? Did you know your Viking ancestors called this place Niflhel?"

I shook my head. "Why would they do that?"

"They believe this is where Hel's dead go. The dead who Owthidn or Freya don't claim."

"You've heard of Odin?"

She laughed again. "Of course I have. Hasn't everyone?"

"The Isir don't seem to recognize the name."

"I am Tisir," she said with a shrug.

"I wish I knew what that meant."

She glanced at me, laughter dancing in her eyes. "You haven't guessed? You haven't put two and two together?" The sound of glass bells rang in the air as she laughed again. "Though, I prefer one and one."

"Do you remember when I was…after my injuries in the cave…"

She shrugged and put an enormous, yet somehow dainty hand on my shoulder. "When you hung in Iktrasitl? Yes, I remember."

"Was it… There was another in the tree."

"Yes. Ratatoskr. He's cute."

"Don't tell him that. He gets quite offended."

Her eyes seemed to whirl with amusement. "Is it so?" She flipped her long white hair over her white-cloaked shoulder.

I nodded and blew out a breath. "But I meant someone else. Up there in the branches with me."

"Ah." She smiled, and it was a knowing, secretive smile. Her pale skin seemed…pristine, new.

"Who was that? Was that Odin?"

She laughed and did a little dance. "This is so much fun." She patted my cheek. "What name did he give you?"

"Owsakrimmr."

"Ha!" she said, smiling still. "And does this name mean nothing to you?" She stopped me with a hand on my arm and pulled me around to face her. The pale light of Niflhaymr's distant sun shone from her white breastplate.

"No," I said.

"Or perhaps Isakrim?"

"No, never heard of him, either."

"Oh."

"So…was it Odin?"

"Well," she said, drawing her finger down the side of my face and across my lower lip. "If you kiss me, I will tell you."

"That's not going to happen, Kuhntul."

"Jane wouldn't mind." Her ice-blue eyes danced.

"She would, but more to the point, I won't betray her trust."

She straightened and sighed. "More's the pity, Hrafnakuth." She flipped her long blonde hair to the other side of her back.

"Oh, no, not another one."

She smiled and twirled a finger in my hair. "Kiss me, and I'll tell you what it means."

"No kisses." I took her hand and pushed it away gently.

"You're no fun." She sighed but smiled through it. "Anyway, it means 'Raven God.' You know because you always—"

"Appear as a raven in these dreams. Yeah, I know, but I'm no god." I looked at her askance. "Won't you

tell me if it was Odin that gave me the Gamla Toonkumowl, *the runes?"*

"If you say 'pretty please.'"

"Pretty please."

"Okay." In a flash, she went on tiptoe and planted a kiss on my lips. "And there's my kiss, so…yes, you could say that Owsakrimmr was Odin."

I couldn't stop the sigh from escaping my lips. She would never quit with the flirting. "Why don't the Isir—"

"The Isir don't understand half as much as they assume they do," she said with a trace of irritation. "I told you that before, remember?"

"Yeah, I do. If only you could tell me which half."

She tilted her head back on her slim neck and laughed, and the sound of glass bells tickled my ears. "Oh, Tyeldnir, you can be so funny."

"Well, thanks." I turned and walked toward the end of the street, and she linked her arm through mine.

"Such a nice day for a walk," she said.

"Yes." But still, I felt there was something I should be doing. Something important.

"Why did you summon me to this place, Tyeldnir? As much as I don't mind, I don't want Mother Skult to register my absence."

"I wasn't even aware I summoned you, Kuhntul. I don't know how I did it, so your guess is as good as mine as to why." My gaze met hers askance. "Who is Mother Skult? I mean, she's one of the Nornir, but who is she in the general scheme of things?"

Kuhntul shrugged. "She is the one who watches what should occur."

"And the other Nornir?"

"Urthr watches over what has happened, and Verthanti watches what is happening."

"Past, Present, and Future?"

Again, she shrugged. "Not quite, but something close to that."

"And you, Kuhntul? Where do you fit in that?"

"I am Tisir."

"Yeah, but I don't understand what that means, remember?"

She favored me with a small smile. "Yes, you do."

"I wish I did," I said again.

She stopped and again drew me around to face her, but this time her face was serious, intense. "You keep saying that, but you must understand by now."

I sighed. "Kuhntul, I'm sorry if this upsets you."

She shook her head. "It is no matter."

"But, what does it mean to be Tisir? Oh, I know your fate is entwined with someone else's—a filkya of sorts."

"There is a bit of truth in that but consider the meanings of that word."

"Well, filkya means 'to accompany.'"

"Correct."

"Okay. How does that help me?"

"Tisir does not mean that, and with most things in this universe of ours, the name derives from our function. Tisir is simply the plural of the old word 'tis,' *variously used to mean 'lady,' 'matron,' and sometimes 'wife.'"*

"Jane is my wife," I said too quickly and with too sharp of a tone.

Kuhntul dropped her eyes. "Yes. And that is not the sense of the word from which the Tisir name comes. In our naming, the meaning is matron. People often associate us with uhrluhk, but that is a misconception."

"But you serve the Nornir."

She shrugged. "It is convenient for now, and it coincides with what my estimation of what my duties are. In truth, I serve another."

"Roonateer?"

She smiled, and her eyes regained a smattering of their customary mischievous twinkle. "Good guess."

"And what do the Nornir think of your split loyalties?"

"If they knew, they'd be cross."

I nodded, gazing into her ice-blue eyes. "So, it's a risk?"

She shrugged. "Perhaps. It isn't clear who would prevail if it came to open battle."

"And this Roonateer's power outweighs that of the Three?"

A half-smile cracked her face. "I meant between myself and the Nornir. But I'd say Roonateer's working on it. In the end, he will be."

"You make little sense, sometimes."

"Is it so?" she asked and tipped me a wink. "Do you have that chisel I gave you?"

"It seems like I always do, as long as I focus my mind on it."

"May I borrow it a moment?"

I focused on the chisel, and its warm weight filled my hand. "Even works in a dream. Nice." I handed it to her. "What are you going to do? Carve a bit of graffiti?"

She treated me to a sly look. "You could say that." Without warning, she swept my legs out from under me and straddled across my chest. "This may sting a little."

"What are you—" I struggled to push her off, to sit up, but she sank her weight onto my chest, pinning my upper arms with her knees.

"Trust me, Tyeldnir," she crooned. "I'm not out to hurt you."

"What the fuck do you think you're doing?"

She leaned close, her ice-blue eyes seeming to spin and twirl. With exaggerated care, she put the tip of the chisel on my forehead. "Stop twitching around, Tyeldnir. This is delicate work."

"Let me up! Don't you dare—"

She drew a deep breath and let it out as a sigh. She put her left index finger on my forehead, next to the freakish warmth of the silvery chisel. "Svepn," she said, and a dollop of icy cold appeared where her fingertip had been.

My struggles became weaker and less focused as the icy cold spread across my forehead, over the top of my head and down my neck. I felt a vague pressure on my forehead as she plied the chisel.

"There, there, Tyeldnir," said Kuhntul. "Trust me."

As if I had a choice.

FOURTEEN

My eye snapped open, and Kuhntul was holding my wrists, trying to hold me down. "Let me up, Kuhntul!"

"Hank," said Jane in an exasperated tone. "You're dreaming!"

My head felt as if someone had it in a vice and had cranked it as tight as it could go. I sank back to the bedroll that insulated me from the ice floor and let my eyelids droop closed.

"Bad one?"

"I… To tell you the truth, I don't know. Kuhntul was in it, and *we* were giants, walking around outside. She told me a few things, and then at the end there, she…well, I don't know what she did. Kuhntul put me out the way Sif did in Kuthbyuhrn's cave. She had the chisel she gave me and was doing something to my head."

Concern washed across Jane's face. "But you're okay now?"

"Headache." I sighed and pushed myself up. "Where are the others?"

"Still looking—it's only been about twenty minutes."

"Seems longer," I said, shaking my head. I stared down at my hand, focusing on the chisel Kuhntul had given me, wanting to see if I still "had" it or not. Its warm weight came first, then the pale light flickered off its surface.

"What did she do?"

"Nothing." I put the chisel in my pocket, knowing it would disappear as soon as I released it. "I don't know. God, my head hurts."

"Go back to sleep."

"Can't. Not after that dream. Who knows what I would dream about next."

"Me?" Jane batted her eyelids coquettishly.

"I don't need to dream about you, Supergirl. You're better in real life."

"Aw, you say the sweetest things."

"Plus, in my dreams, you never do the laundry."

She gave me a look and smacked her lips. "Guess I need to advance the beating schedule again."

"All talk, no tango."

"Tango? When *were* you born, Hank? 1918?"

"Just because you missed the fine experience of the seventies, doesn't mean—"

"Hey! I was alive in the late seventies."

I rolled my eye. "As if that counts."

Jane stuck out her tongue before looking away. "What did she do, do you think?" Her voice had taken on an arcadian quality, but the skin between her eyes wrinkled with tension.

"Maybe nothing. Maybe it was a *troymskrok*."

"You've never thought that before."

I shook my head. "She seemed... There was something that felt off—or possibly familiar—about her this time. She started out as a giant, changed to the all-white version, and ended up as a blue-eyed blonde."

"An Isir?" she asked.

"Yes, in the form of an Isir. She reminded me of Freya a little." I smacked my palm against my forehead. "That's it! Her laugh, her glass-bell-tinkling laugh!"

"Um, you know you sound like an insane person right now?"

"Yeah, yeah. In the dream, Kuhntul kept laughing, and it seemed so familiar, but I couldn't place it. But it reminded me of Freya's, that wind-chimes-in-a-light-breeze laugh she has."

"What does it mean?"

"I have no idea. It might be an Isir thing."

Jane shook her head. "Sif, Yowrnsaxa, and Frikka don't laugh like that."

I shrugged. "Perhaps Kuhntul is related to Freya somehow."

"*And* Hel."

I nodded grudgingly. "And Hel."

"But how could they be related? Hel and Freya are Isir—the only two sisters in their family, I thought. Kuhntul's a ghost…or whatever she is."

"She tried to tell me what being a Tisir means— she's always answering my questions with 'I am Tisir,' as if that explains anything."

'Well? Don't be stingy. What did she say?"

"She took great pains to distinguish Tisir from *filkya*, but I don't get why. She said their name comes from the *Gamla Toonkumowl* word for matron, but that it also means 'lady,' or…or 'woman.'"

"Matron, huh?"

"Yeah. Somehow the conversation shifted to the Nornir at that point, and she never elaborated."

"Matron can mean a bunch of different things. From 'mother' to 'the person in a women's restroom who hands out towels.'"

"Wow, you visit fancy-schmancy restrooms. But yeah, somehow I don't think it's that last one."

"It can also mean 'guard' or 'attendant,' the way it's used in a prison or a girls' school."

"Yeah, and I guess that definition matches best. After all, Kuhntul seems intent on guarding us against Hel's machinations."

Jane tilted her head to the side. "Does she?"

"Does she what?" asked Althyof from the doorway.

"Doesn't matter," I said with a glance at Jane. "Did you find anything?"

"Sure. Lots of things I can't mention in front of your lady-wife, but also…a *proo.*"

"Good. It's getting creepy in here," said Jane.

"Then keep your eyes shut as we walk to the room with the *proo* I found." The Tverkr made a show of looking around. "That Alf still out looking?"

"Both Yowtgayrr and Krowkr are still looking."

"Ah." He turned back to the hall. "Alf! Human! Come back!" he yelled.

Yowtgayrr turned the corner and smiled. "I found the first of the hidden *preer,*" he called.

"What? *I* found a *proo* first!" said Althyof.

Yowtgayrr tilted his head to the side, looking perplexed. "If this is a joke, I don't get the punch line."

"No joke." Althyof swept his hand in an arc in front of him. "At least not on my part. I found a *proo* and returned at once to tell of it. *Before* you arrived, blathering about being first."

Yowtgayrr walked toward us, shaking his head. At the other end of the hall, Krowkr appeared, wearing a broad smile. "I've found one!" he crowed.

Althyof shook his head and turned my way. "What now?"

"We should have known Luka wouldn't make it as easy as only having *two preer* to choose from. I guess I'll have to send ravens through all the *preer* until we find the right one."

"Uh, sure. You're not exhausted or anything," said Jane. "Why don't you carry everyone's pack, too?"

I smiled and blew her a kiss. "Laundry done, yet?"

She turned to Althyof. "Isn't there another way of testing these *preer*?"

"We could go through them, one at a time."

"That sounds safe," I said. Jane gave me a look I hadn't seen since the time I took a straw from the new box by mistake instead of using the last straw from the old box. What thin ice I walked on…

"What if I went through?" asked Jane. "Would the ring protect me?"

"If the *stathur's* physical laws are close to ours. If they are not…" The Tverkr shrugged. "Once you are dead, you can't heal."

"The animuses don't take much energy. It's not like a shape-change."

Jane shook her head and swept her pack onto her back. "How is it that the sick one of our group has to do everything?"

Althyof hitched his shoulders. "Isir are stubborn."

I laughed and got to my feet. "Take me to one of the hidden *preer.*"

Althyof led us to the *proo* he'd found. The second I saw the thing, I knew something was…*different.* On the surface, it looked the same as any other *proo* I'd seen: thousands or millions of colors swirling, overlapping, mixing to form a silvery, mirror-like surface, but when I looked at this *proo* there were…things hanging from the edges. They appeared as colored yarn or loose strings of whatever material made up the part of the *proo* visible to the eye. The string-like things moved as though caught in an ocean current, making me think of seaweed.

"What's the matter, Hank?" asked Jane.

"Something's different." The more I looked, the more things seemed to leap out at me. The *proo* had an aura of sorts, a shadow made of pure color—a light blue. I stared at it, trying to take the differences in. The whole thing seemed to twitch in time to the beat of some hidden conductor. "It's...it's moving."

"I think you need to rest, Hank," murmured Jane.

"No, the *proo* is fixed in place, but the part we can see is...twitching back and forth. And there are loose bits. They remind me of loose strings from a sweater or something."

Jane looked at the *proo* before turning her gaze on me. "If you say so."

"Take me to another one," I blurted. "I have to see if this is a onetime thing."

Yowtgayrr led us to the *proo* he'd found, and everyone walked in silence. I knew the minute we reached the door to the room that the *proo* inside the new room would be the same as the last—even before I saw it. There was a *feeling* to the *proo* that hadn't been there before.

The glowing ring shimmied and shook as the silvery part of the *proo* twitched. The stringy parts of it waved to a different rhythm, and the aura rippled between pale green to violent chartreuse and everything in between.

The *proo* was in the corner, shining like a beacon to a ship in storm-tossed seas. I left the others near the door and walked toward the *proo* slowly, almost mesmerized by the shifting colors, the twitchy circumference, the waving yarn-like extrusions.

Something was forming in my mind—a word on the tip of my mental tongue. It danced out of reach, but it had something to do with the parts of the *proo* that were now visible.

"What is it, Hank?"

"I don't know yet. There's something…"

Jane came to stand at my side, not speaking, but reassuring me by her presence.

"*Syow tyoopt*," I said. My remaining eye tingled the way it always did when enchanted for night vision, and indeed, I intended to charm my vision—but to see deep beneath the surface instead of in the dark.

The mirror-like surface of the *proo* sprang at me like the image from a pop-up book. The colors no longer seemed mixed—they seemed layered, one atop the other as though a part of some strange topographical map. Shapes lurked in that three-dimensional image, shapes that writhed and twisted to an unknown rhythm, perhaps fighting for dominance. Their forms brought to mind those cyclopean things I'd seen between the terminal ends of the *proo*—Lovecraftian Great Old Ones skittering around in the spaces between the realms.

"I can see them," I muttered.

"See who, Hank?" asked Jane in a worry-infused tone. "Is this because of what Kuhntul did with the chisel?"

"I don't know. Probably. Maybe not, though."

"Well, at least that's cleared up."

"They are…" The Great Old Ones became more organized, synchronizing their movements with one another. "Wait…something is changing."

"What?"

All at once, the *proo* cycled through all the colors of the spectrum in a heartbeat—a turbocharged hallucinogenic trip focused on rainbows. The Great Old Ones pulsed and fell still, and my eye went out of focus. Moving together, the undulating tendrils that ringed the edges of the *proo* curled inward, reaching, stretching, searching for something in the manner of sightless worms. One of them touched one of the Great Old Ones and twitched convulsively as though it had brushed against a live wire, then shriveled and darkened to an ashy gray—like a slug exposed to salt. The Great Old One it had come into contact with reared away from it and shook itself, like a dog shaking off snow, before settling back next to its neighbors. The remaining tendrils curled back toward the edge of the *proo* and seemed to cower there.

The colors cycled faster, and the Great Old Ones embedded in the *proo* twitched and pulsed in time. A sound similar to a strong wind whistling through an old keyhole invaded the room, and I got the sense that the noise issued from the mouths of the Great Old Ones. "What are you trying to tell me?" I murmured.

"Hank?" Jane put her hand on my forearm and gave it a little squeeze. "You're sort of freaking me out, jerkface."

"What? Oh." I patted her hand.

The Great Old Ones shuddered to a stop and, as one, swiveled toward Jane. They froze again, pointing at my wife like thick, blunt accusing fingers.

"Step back." I took a step in front of her, hand on Kunknir. The Great Old Ones shuddered as though laughing at me and squiggled and squirmed until they formed the shape of several runes. "*Raidho isaz thurisaz kaunan hagalaz*," I read.

"Loosely translated: 'Don't move. Danger, pain, destruction,'" said Althyof.

"Yeah," I breathed. "Not much room for doubt there."

"Where... Do you see those runes somewhere?" asked the Tverkr, peering into the depths of the *proo*.

"Yes. You don't?"

Althyof shook his head, a moue twisting his lips. "Where do you see these runes?"

"Right there... The Great Old Ones on the surface of the *proo*." Again, the thick, blunt shapes shuddered as though laughing.

Althyof gave me a critical, assessing look.

"I know how it sounds," I said. "Doesn't change the fact that I can see them. There are also tendrils all around the edge. When they brush against one of the Great Old Ones, they die."

Althyof cleared his throat and shrugged.

"It seems to me," began Yowtgayrr, "that if Hank sees danger in the surface of this *proo*, it would be pure folly to ignore it."

"Unless he's hallucinating," muttered Jane.

I turned and cocked my eyebrow at her, a small smile on my lips. "Okay, so dragons, elves, Norse gods, me turning into ravens and bears, growing wings from your shoulders, returning the guts of poor Krowkr here back to the inside of his body—all of that is okay, but me seeing something in the *proo* is one step too far?"

"Well, when you put it like that…I should have tied you down somewhere a long time ago, crazy-man."

"Again with the promises… All talk…"

Jane blushed and shook her head.

"Take me to the next one," I said as eager as a kid with a new toy.

With a start, Krowkr took the lead, traversing a twisting route of hallways that ended in a large, oval room. As with the large hall where we'd fought Vefsterkur, ice furniture was scattered about with no rhyme or reason I could detect, but I didn't care much about that. The *proo* pulsing in the center of the oval drew my gaze like a magnet draws iron filings.

The tendrils around its edge were longer and moved with a frenzied, convulsive quality. Great Old Ones twisted and swam about each other in the middle of the *proo*, playing and cavorting in the manner of kids in a pool. The vision of those Great Old Ones curling and winding in sinuous patterns disturbed me more than the thick, forbidding shapes in Yowtgayrr's *proo*.

"Any runes?" asked Althyof.

"No, nothing." As I watched, the Great Old Ones beckoned, though without arms or faces. I have no idea how they accomplished it, but I felt it, nonetheless. They moved as one, creating a circle in the exact center of the *proo* before beginning a swirling dance, drawing a circle with their bodies.

"Well?" asked Jane. "What do you see?"

"It's as if they are drawing me a picture. A circle." They broke apart, and as with the other *proo*, formed runes.

"Here we go. *Raidho ansuz fehu gebo othala algiz jera*."

Jane swatted me on the shoulder. "Well? What's it mean, bozo?"

"Could be: 'Prosperous travel, lucky gift: home, protection, peace.'"

"Yes, but it could also translate as: 'Travel Isir, expensive or valuable gifts: inheritance, protection, reward,'" said Althyof. "But either way, it's positive."

"An invitation?" asked Jane.

The Tverkr shrugged. "Could be. Or perhaps Luka left yet another trick."

"Let's go back to the first one," I said. "I want to see what it says." We traipsed back to the first *proo*, and as we entered the room, the Great Old Ones had already begun transmitting runes at us in a frenzy. "Eager this time," I muttered. "*Ansuz laguz uruz kaunan ansuz laguz…* It repeats after that."

"So: 'prosperity potential willfulness mortality.'"

Jane shook her head. "That doesn't make sense. Is it positive or negative?"

Althyof pulled a face. "This isn't as easy as it looks. Each rune can have many meanings, depending on context. It's not as cut and dried as you want it to be."

She shrugged, exasperated. "Then what else could it mean?"

"'Truth, fantasy, wisdom, knowledge.'"

"That makes even less sense."

I shrugged. "I can't change the runes they showed me." I glanced at the *proo* and twitched away a step.

"What?" Jane asked, glancing at the silvery thing.

"They are all right there—well, as many as can fit, I suppose."

"Who? The Great Old One things?"

I nodded. "They're packed in there like kids at a window."

She glanced at the *proo* again, a trifle more uneasily than before. "What are they doing?"

"Watching us. The question is: why?"

Althyof glared at the *proo* with a shrewd expression on his face. "Seems they have an interest in what we make of their runes."

Yowtgayrr had been standing there in silence the entire time, looking down at his feet. Without warning, he whooped and looked up at me, eyes burning. "You said the message was already going when we arrived?"

I nodded. "What does—"

"And that it repeated?"

"Yes."

"I think you have the order wrong." He grinned at me. "No offense meant."

I shook my head, confused.

Althyof smiled and nodded. "Not *ansuz laguz uruz kaunan*! *Laguz uruz kaunan ansuz*!"

"So: 'knowledge truth fantasy wisdom.' How does that help?" Jane looked from Althyof to Yowtgayrr to me. "How?"

I glanced at the *proo* to gauge the reaction of the Great Old Ones. After a momentary frenzy, they settled and flashed the same runes again, but this time the runes were all in reverse. "That's strange. They're showing me the same runes, but they are backward."

Yowtgayrr nodded. "That only confirms my thought. There is no ambiguity."

"No," said Althyof. "In this case, the runes mean: 'Chaos—'"

"Or perhaps: 'madness, obsession.'"

"No, Hank. As I said, in this case, the meaning is clear. 'Chaos, untamed potential, fire of transformation, and power.'"

Jane shook her head and opened her mouth, but Yowtgayrr put his hand on her shoulder, and she didn't speak.

"When their runes are written backward—as if viewed in a mirror—*laguz uruz kaunan ansuz* mean 'Madness, obsession, instability, manipulation.' With both sets of meanings in hand, the particular significance, in this case, becomes clear."

"Or in this case, who they mean," said Yowtgayrr.

I smacked myself in the forehead. "Of *course*! Using the runes as letters, it spells L-U-K-A. Luka!"

Yowtgayrr grimaced and nodded.

Realization dawned on Jane's face. "So, this is it? This is the one?"

"That would be my guess," I said. "But could Luka have manipulated the Great Old Ones somehow? Used them to trick us?"

Althyof shook his head. "No one knows anything about these Great Old Ones you keep blathering on about."

I glanced at Yowtgayrr, and he nodded. "No?"

"No," said Althyof. "But, we still have a choice to make. This *proo* which the Great Old Ones label 'Luka' or the last one which they called 'Travel Isir.' Either one seems just as likely to me."

Jane scoffed. "They as much as said this *proo* leads to Luka."

Althyof grinned. "Did they? I thought they said Luka manipulated this *proo*."

"The only thing we can agree on is that Yowtgayrr's *proo* is bad news." Jane shook her head. "Some superpower this turns out to be, Hank."

Something tickled the back of my mind, a vague memory of events barely remembered. "Superpower," I muttered. I pursued the thought, trying to force my mind to produce the information, but the more I did that, the farther away it seemed. I shook my head and shrugged. "So how do we decide? Should I send a raven through again?"

Jane scoffed and threw up her hands. "Ask your invisible friends in the *proo*."

"I don't know how to *ask* them anything. They do the rune dance when they want to—at least so far. Plus, we don't even know what these things are."

"Oh, for Christ's sake!" murmured Jane. She brushed past me, and, before I could stop her, reached out and touched the *proo*. The tendrils waving around the edge snapped around her hand and disappeared.

"Hank, sometimes your wife is—"

"*Awesome*," I said and touched the *proo*.

As though traveling as my animus—or perhaps the dream about Kuhntul chiseling away at my brain—had unlocked something within me, moving through the *proo* wasn't instantaneous, and this time, I could *see* inside the *proo*. It was as if I were falling, but *forward* instead of down. Wisps of light-infused dust surrounded me, streaking by out to the side, and behind them, huge, shadowy shapes writhed and braided, one with another. The Great Old Ones.

One of them twisted toward me, like a vast, blind worm, and I slowed to a stop, hanging in the middle of whatever made up the space between the *proo's* ends. After a moment, others joined the first, until I floated in the center of a ring of the colossal juggernauts.

A booming, oscillating shiver raced across my skin, leaving goose-flesh in its wake. It reminded me of how the sea dragon had assaulted us with those booming clicks, but without the auditory component, whether because of the nature of the *proo* or the nature of the Great Old Ones, I didn't know.

I opened my mouth to draw enough air into my lungs to speak, but there was no air to breathe, only a strange nothingness that wasn't the vacuum I'd expected. I shrugged and looked at the first Great Old One, motioning in the direction in which I had been traveling before it stopped me.

It shook its massive head and coated me in vibrations yet again. When I shrugged, it extruded a part of itself—a pseudopod of shadows—and stretched toward me. The memory of the tendril from the side of the proo touching the Great Old One and blackening and dying raced through me and I tried to lurch away. The Great Old One's advance was relentless, and I couldn't escape its touch.

Thoughts, images, ideas, and memories exploded through my mind, too fast for me to make any sense of them. The contact struck me as similar to a physical assault, like having my head shoved inside one of the massive horns of a concert sound system and cranking up the volume. I shuddered and writhed, but I couldn't pull away. The vibrations on my skin came again, burning me like flames. Had there been air, I would have been screaming, but things as they were reduced me to suffering in silence.

One of my favorite songs in the world was "One" by the heavy-metal behemoth, Metallica, and my predicament reminded me forcefully of that song and its music video of the wounded soldier thrashing in his bed, spelling out "kill me" in Morse code.

The barrage continued, images I couldn't understand slamming through me, and the vibrations continued to wash over me, to burn me the way cinnamon oil splashed over my skin would. The pseudopod morphed and stretched, moving with me as I thrashed around, protracting to encase the top of my head.

As its limb covered my eye, the swarm of thoughts and images congealed into coherence. The process reminded me of tuning in an AM station on an old radio, and as I tuned in, the pain fell away.

SMALL ONE, HEAR THIS ONE. TIME GROWS SHORT.

The words rang at the center of my mind, but they weren't words, that was how my mind interpreted what the Great Old One communicated to me. *Who are you?* I thought at it.

MEANINGLESS NON SEQUITUR. ATTEND! THIS ONE HAS MESSAGES TO IMPART. THIS ONE REQUIRES CONTACT FOR COMMUNION.

Well, you've got that already, don't you?

CEASE. CEASE. CEASE. YIELD TO THIS ONE.

I shook my head within its leathery grasp, the skin of my forehead rasping across the inner surface of its pseudopod. Rough bumps pebbled the membrane, as dry as desert sand. *I don't know what you are asking me to do.*

CEASE. YIELD. These last thoughts came with increasing pressure, increasing psionic emphasis. TIME SHORTENS, AND THE NEXUS LOOMS. THIS ONE DESIRES YOU TAKE ACTION. THE DESIRE FOR ACTION APPROACHES THE IMPERATIVE. YIELD UNTO THIS ONE.

I did not understand what it was going on about. We didn't appear to be moving within the space between the *proo*; instead we seemed mired in the nothingness that surrounded us.

IRRELEVANT. YOU HAVE BEEN MARKED BY THE AGENT, THE SELECTION HAS BEEN MADE. YOUR ACTION IS REQUIRED. YOUR ACTION IS INTEGRAL TO THE NEW PLAN.

New plan? What is this plan?

CEASE. BIFURCATED COMMUNICATION IS EXTRANEOUS, UNDESIRABLE...FRACTIOUS. ATTEND. UNDERSTAND. OBEY. YIELD TO THIS ONE.

Irrational anger seeped into my veins. *Sorry, chummy. I don't work that way, and to be frank, I'm full to the point of puking of this idea that I need to do what someone tells me without explanation, without my agreement. I've got news for you, big guy: I don't work that way.* There was a moment of silence before the cacophonous flood of images, thoughts, random words, and mental static began again, growing in volume until I wanted to scream, to gouge out whatever organ allowed me to hear these things. After what I experienced as an eternity, it stopped.

CEASE. YIELD.

The psychic pressure of his communication grew, and I hung there, not thinking, not looking, not curious about anything, just trying to recover from the onslaught.

YOU HAVE RECEIVED THE GIFTS. YOU BEAR THE MARK. CHOICE IS INSIGNIFICANT. PREFERENCE IS INSIGNIFICANT. YOUR LACK OF ACTION VERGES ON PEEVISHNESS. THIS ONE GROWS WEARY OF THE EFFORT. COMPULSION IS SATISFACTORY.

Something tickled the inside of my skull—ants crawling across its inner surface. One by one, parts of my mind that I'd never noticed before felt numb, as if disconnected from the whole. Ragged hallucinations plagued me—visions of depravity from my time as a cop who investigated gruesome crimes for the state of New York on Mithgarthr. Sounds that I couldn't actually hear assaulted my mind—screams, cries of pain and grief—the sickening symphony of psychic surgery. I struggled against it, but I was powerless in the face of the Great Old One's power.

After another eternity, the misplaced parts of my mind reconnected.

CULMINATION. CONSUMMATION OF PURPOSE. *TERMINOUS AD QUIEM*. HIGHEST LEVEL OF SUCCESS ACHIEVED.

If you say so, I thought, my mind still a-reel.

Without another thought, the pseudopod disengaged, snapping away from me with a ripping, tearing pop. For half a heartbeat, those terrible vibrations drummed around me, and then I was out of the *proo*, staggering to keep my balance.

FIFTEEN

I fought for balance in the hot sand that appeared beneath my feet. I sucked in a lungful of too-humid, too-hot afternoon air. Sweat prickled across my scalp in an instant, and I glanced up at the angry afternoon sun.

"Where have you been?" demanded Jane.

"I...uh..." I shook my head, my thoughts scattering. "I came through the *proo* the same as you. You traveled through a few seconds before I followed you."

"That was *twenty minutes* ago!"

"It seems longer," I muttered. "The Great Old Ones stopped me inside."

"What?" she asked.

The world tilted to the side, and I staggered a step or two, balance suddenly unreliable and hard to find.

Jane grabbed my arm to steady me, concern etched on her face. "What happened in there, Hank?"

"Travel across this *proo* wasn't instant as it always has been, similar to what happened when I went through with my animus. This time, I perceived the Great Old Ones floating around outside the path of the *proo*, and this time, they surrounded me, stopped me dead and…and *talked* to me, I guess."

"They talked to you?"

"More like talked at me. They weren't very interested in my side of the conversation."

"What did they say?" asked Jane.

"A lot of things such as: 'Cease. Obey. Yield.' Stuff in that vein. And it was only one of them. It grew an arm to grab my head and—"

"*Grew* an arm?"

"Yeah. They are like…I don't know, big amorphous slugs or something such as that. I guess it needed physical contact to make me understand it. Before it touched me, it reminded me of that sea dragon's clicks."

"The noise?"

"No, the feeling of it, the vibrations running through your body. It touched me, and my brain couldn't keep up with the thoughts. Eventually, the Great Old One got it right and told me that time was short, it required action, etc. It wouldn't give me any details, so I told it to go to hell, and it said it didn't have a problem forcing me to do what it wanted, and it did something to me."

"Alien examinations? Tickled your feet? What?" demanded Jane.

"I don't know, but if I had to guess, I'd say psychic surgery of some kind."

"Awesome," Jane spat. "Why do all these so-called 'gods' think you are their plaything?"

"If I had the answer to that question, they'd be abusing Althyof instead of me." That earned a small, short-lived grin from my wife. "There's not much I can do to stop any of them."

"Evidently."

I nodded. "Where are the others?

Jane shrugged and waved her hand at the maritime forest behind her. "I told them to go explore so I could kick your ass in private."

I smelled salt on the air and peered over my shoulder. Behind me was the *proo*, and behind it was a small expanse of sea water and another long, sheltering island. "Where do you suppose we are?"

She shook her head. "I didn't bring any sunblock, so wherever we are, I'm going to lobster."

"Let's get up by those trees and out of the sun."

We walked across the small shingle of sand, but before we reached the trees, Krowkr emerged and waved at us. "Come quick, Isir," he said. "We found a village like none other I've ever seen, but no people."

Jane and I followed him down an overgrown path, and as we walked, it dawned on me that there were tracks everywhere. Thousands upon thousands of glowing trails dotted the forest. "Do you see all the tracks?"

Jane looked at me sharply and shook her head.

"Strange," I said.

We emerged into a clearing, and into the remains of what looked to be an abandoned colonial village. More tracks—or maybe paths is a better description—saturated the walking spaces, leading from one door to another, or to the forest. The buildings were in the process of being reclaimed by the maritime forest that surrounded the place.

"Hank!" called Yowtgayrr. "We've found something over here."

In what had been the village square, the villagers had sunk a large post into the earth. Manacles hung from its top, and fire had charred its base. The tracks showed me where dozens of people had stood in a circle around the post, watching a spectacle. Lying a few feet from the stake were the skeletal remains of a man, bones charred by extreme heat, the ground beneath him blackened and seared into a hardened mass of ugly glass.

I could *see* things about the man. Perhaps 'see' wasn't precisely what was happening, but I had no better word.

I cleared my throat. "This man was named Jack Martin. Captain Martin, of the local militia. The villagers liked and respected…until… No, that's not right. Everyone liked and respected him but one couple—a woman he accused of witchcraft and her husband." I shook my head, images from the man's life flooding into my mind.

"How do you know?" asked Althyof.

"I…" I shook my head. "I can't explain it, but I can *sense* it."

"Sense it?" asked Yowtgayrr.

"Yes. It's as if…as if the information is tucked behind him, but it's not *actually* behind him… Oh, this is impossible to describe." I glanced back at the blackened skeleton. "He died in terror and in great pain. Burned to death, but the fire…"

"Yes, Hank?"

I jerked and took a step back, eyes scanning the woods and buildings around us.

"What is it?" asked Yowtgayrr, hands on his weapons.

"The fire…the fire was *green*."

"What else do you perceive?" asked Althyof.

I glanced around. "There was a gathering. Martin had shackled a woman to this post, but—"

"Burned at the stake," Jane murmured.

"What did she say?" asked Althyof.

"Burned at the stake," she repeated, louder. "It was the punishment for witchcraft in the good old days."

"Yes," I said. "There was a witch trial in that…church." I pointed at what remained of a building that had burned to the ground. "More green fire."

Althyof nodded. "The people of Mithgarthr have no access to the strings."

I shrugged. "It seems some do."

"Yes, but your blood is Isir. Most of the mundane people here can no more *vefa* than I can speak with modesty."

"I guess."

"The person convicted of witchcraft and sentenced to burn at the stake? This *woman*…she was Hel?"

With a sigh, I nodded and said, "The green fire gives it away, doesn't it?"

"Do you have any idea how long ago this was? Was Luka with her?"

"There is something strange here…" I walked around the square, paying close attention to the footprints that originated in the forest. "This…this happened three years ago." I waved my arm to encompass the entire town.

"Oh my God, Hank," said Jane, pointing at something on the opposite side of the stake.

I walked around it and looked where she was pointing. There was a single word carved into the post. "*Croatoan*," I said. "Well, at least now we know where we are."

"From that nonsense word?" scoffed Althyof.

"No, from history. There was a colony—we called it the Lost Colony—as Europeans first settled in the New World. It's famous because the colonists all disappeared without a trace, and the only clue was the word '*Croatoan*' carved into a post."

"Does this information help us?"

I shook my head. "Not at all. But now I understand what happened to the colonists. Hel and Luka happened to them."

"You don't think they *ate* the entire colony, do you?" asked Jane.

"From my experience with them, I do. Remember that cave where the Bristol Butchers laid out their victims like a vast smorgasbord for cannibals?"

Jane shuddered. "I'll never forget that place."

"A number of those bodies there were hundreds of years old. Some of them probably lived here before Hel and Luka took them."

"But...how? Why?"

I looked around, reading the signs, gathering the story. "Hel and Luka *lived* here. They were part of this colony. They came here from Europe, using mundane transportation instead of a *proo*. No idea why. They weren't using their Isir names, of course. He used the name Loke Estridsen, which shouldn't be much of a surprise since Loke is a younger variant of Loki. And the name she used was..."

SIXTEEN

Margaret Estridsen cried out as the militia pushed their way into her house. The man she called husband was away hunting, and events might have taken a different track had he been home. "Stop! You have no right to come into my home!"

"I beg to differ, Goody Estridsen," said Captain Martin as he strode through the door as if he were a bantam cock. His eyes swept the room, lingering on the shiny things lying around or set out on display. When his eyes met her own, as bold as you please, he grimaced. "Cover your hair, Madam."

"My hair would not lay exposed if you and your thugs had not barged in unannounced. My husband is away, as I think you must know, and it is unseemly for you to be here in his absence. I demand you leave this house! Speak with my husband on his return." She towered over the men of the militia as she walked to the cupboard and drew out a scarf to cover her hair.

"Alas, Margaret Estridsen, I cannot do as you ask. You must come with us."

"I shall do no such thing, *Jack* Martin."

"But you must," said the captain. "Goody Estridsen, I arrest you in the name of Her Majesty, Queen Elizabeth, sovereign of this colony."

Margaret laughed, but it wasn't a pleasant sound. "Arrest me? Whatever for?" She stood glaring at them, a twisted, angry grin plastered on her face.

Captain Martin's features stretched in a grin of his own. "Witchcraft."

Margaret laughed, and this time it seemed to be a real laugh, pressing her hand to her mouth. "Witchcraft," she mused. "The irony."

Nonplussed by her strange behavior, Jack Martin stared at her for a moment before snapping his fingers at his men. "Take her," he said. "Shackle her hands and loop the silver chain about her neck so she mayn't utter spells."

Standing on tiptoe, the militiaman still couldn't get the chain over her head. "Your pardon, Goody Estridsen, but could you please bend down?"

She glanced at the man, and for a moment, the air in the small house grew as cold as a mid-winter storm, and her eyes narrowed. But her cheeks stretched with a smile, and she ducked her head. "Of course."

"What kind of name is Estridsen?" demanded Captain Martin. "I've not encountered it, and I knew everyone aboard *The Lion*."

"Evidently not everyone," Margaret snapped, eyes dancing with either anger or mirth. "And the name is Norwegian, as are my husband and I."

"Well, no matter. I know you now." Again, Martin snapped his fingers at his men. "Take her to the church."

One of the men took Margaret by the arm in a rough grip, but she gave him such a look that he not only released her arm but took several steps back.

"For goodness' sake!" said the captain and grabbed the chain between her shackled wrists. He shoved the chain into the hands of his lieutenant and motioned toward the door.

"Are you not coming?" demanded Margaret.

"In my own time," he said with an avaricious smile.

Her eyes narrowed and bounced around the room, touching on all the brilliant objects in the room. "I know every item in this house, sir," she grated. "And will miss anything that is…*misplaced*…in my absence."

With a florid smile, Captain Martin waved the men out of the house. "Somehow, I doubt you will be able to complain."

They led her from her house on the edge of town through the streets of the colony, taking no pains with her comfort, nor with her modesty, without a thought for the potential of her dishabille—not that she cared in the least; it was a stupid concept that one's exposed hair was improper in public. As they yanked her one way, then another, she marked each of them, noting whether they acted with cruelty or simply without thinking.

The minister awaited them on the steps of the church. As the men brought her to him, he leaned forward and slapped her across the face. "Witch!" he scolded.

She smiled. "Convicted already, am I?"

He pulled his head back as though she'd spat in his face. "God knows your crimes, woman! Do not compound them with falsehoods!"

She sighed with weariness. "Were my husband at home, you would not speak in that tone."

"I speak with God's own wrath. Do you question it?"

"Doesn't your good book say: 'Let him who is without sin cast the first stone?'" she asked, smiling a bitter smile.

"*My* good book? Not *our* good book?" the minister snapped. "Do you admit your crime before we offer even the first bit of evidence?"

She sneered at him and rolled her eyes as she looked away. "Is all of your evidence as telling as a mere slip of the tongue?"

He treated her to an algid smile, a look of contempt in his eyes. "Fasten her chains to the ring set in the wall," he said to the men behind her. "Be sure to lock her chains. The trial will begin in two hours." With one last scowl at her, he walked past her, heading across the square toward the Widow Harrison's house where he ate his meals.

"If you remove these chains now, I will speak to my husband and tell him to pass over you and your families. I will instruct him to spare your lives."

One man forked a sign against evil at her and refused to meet her eye. "Into the church," he said in a shaky voice.

They had set the hook high up on the wall, designed to keep an accused witch on her toes during the time before and the proceedings of her farce of a trial. Margaret sniggered as the militiaman had to stand on tiptoe to slide her chain over the hook.

It wasn't comfortable, but her feet were flat against the floor, and her wrists rested against her collarbones. She sneered at the men staring at her. "Disappointed, boys? Were you hoping to see something…pop out?" She laughed at their red faces and scoffed as they threw more pathetic hand signs against evil in her direction.

After two hours, she was in a far fouler mood— her arms and wrists ached, and her feet throbbed from standing in one place. The minister's eyes crawled over her face as he came in, and a small, unpleasant smile shone on his face. "Did you have a pleasant lunch, Goody Estridsen?"

Anger stirred in her guts, and she scowled down at him. "You know good and well no one fed me, you pathetic little man. You arranged it that way."

He shrugged and winked at her. "Oh, I shall have a cross word with Captain Martin about this lack of courtesy."

"I bet you will," she growled. She shook her hands, rattling the chains that held her to the wall. "My husband should be home before dark. You don't want him to find me in this state. He will grow cross."

"Oh, don't I? And why ever not?"

"Because he will be cross," she said with a shrug. "And when he's cross, he can be most…*inventive*."

He treated her to a weak, craven smile. "Are you even married to the man in truth? You have enslaved his mind, no? That is the rumor around the village, but whether or not you have, I'm sure Master Estridsen will understand. Perhaps better than any other man could."

Her eyes grew cold, but her scowl grew hot. "Is it so?" she hissed.

The minister nodded. "To my mind, it is *definitely* so. But—"

"Why don't you get on with this farce?"

"—if he is in league with you as you say, Captain Martin and his militia will be more than his match."

She laughed, genuinely amused. "That, I would enjoy seeing. Perhaps I will before the sun sets."

"Alas, I find it doubtful you will still be alive when your husband returns. We have set the post; we have gathered the wood."

"Ah…so you will try to burn me?"

The minister shrugged. "It is the prescribed punishment for witchcraft."

The door opened, and people came into the church, sliding into the pews in silence, watching the exchange between the minister of the colony and the colony's strangest woman.

"And tell me, sir, if I *were* a witch, what makes you think these chains could hold me?"

He grinned and chuckled. "They seem to hold you."

"That's because I am no witch. Had you considered that possibility?"

His grin became condescending. "You are, by all reports, a disgusting slattern with strange powers and the ability to cast curses. There is no doubt in my mind you have consorted with Lucifer."

"Is it so?" she said in a tone that sounded almost bored. "And why haven't I used my abilities to rid the world of you?"

He laughed snidely. "Because, Wife of Satan, you stand in God's House now. You lost any chance you had to escape by use of your Satanic powers when you allowed the militiamen to lead you here."

She threw back her head and laughed as a man deep in his cups might. She glanced around the church with wild eyes. "Don't condemn yourselves as this pig of a man has."

"Do you admit you are a witch?" asked the minister.

"Hardly. But my husband—"

"Yes, yes," snapped Captain Martin from the door. "We will question your husband most sharply when he returns, and if he had knowledge of your foul conversations with the Father of Lies, he, too, will burn before next the sun sets." He turned his gaze to the minister. "Shall we proceed, Minister Hardy?"

"Yes, I do believe it's time." He ascended the pulpit and bowed his head as if in silent prayer. Hardy opened the large Bible on its stand before him. He held up his hands, palms toward the pews. "Dear Heavenly Father. Quieten our minds and still our hearts, for thy ways are what we seek, and we have an unpleasant task to perform this day. Lord, give us thine strength, inspire our intelligence, for, in thine own name, we do battle with thy Adversary and one of his chosen. Grant us thy grace, O Lord. Amen."

The congregation echoed his amen and lifted their heads.

"Brothers and sisters, I have called you here today to bear witness to the interrogations of one accused of witchcraft. This woman…" He flung his hand toward Margaret. "This woman has walked among us, has *lived* among us, and yet we know her not. Not the true being which resides in her heart."

Some of the women in the congregation nodded their heads and Margaret scoffed, a small smile playing on her lips.

"This woman calls herself Margaret Estridsen and claims a marriage before God to Loke Estridsen, whom we all know. They claim to have sailed with us from England, but do any have a memory of the Estridsens aboard *The Lion*?" Hardy paused, scanning the faces of his congregation. No one nodded. Hardy nodded his head. "It is as I thought."

The minister folded his hands behind his back and paced away from the pulpit, his face grave. "My cousin writes me that many ways to obtain the confession of a witch exist, but by His blessed grace, those methods are unnecessary in this case." He stopped and glared at Margaret. "No, in this case, we have enough testimony to convict this foul creature without such debasing methods." He nodded to Martin. "You may begin, Captain."

Captain Martin stood and smiled at the women in the congregation. "There is no reason to fear, sisters. We know this woman has sinned in the silence of the night and without accomplices. We will call on your testimony only to illustrate the truth. But first, we the brethren will give witness." His gaze swept the room and stopped on the militiaman who had grabbed her roughly. "You there, John Barnes. Step forward and remember that the eyes of our Lord are upon you as you give witness in his house."

Barnes swallowed hard and stood, hat in hand. He reached the pulpit in ten mincing strides. He nodded at Captain Martin. "I'm ready, sir."

"Very well, Barnes. You accompanied me to the Estridsen home earlier this morning?"

"Yes, sir. I had that honor."

"And when we arrived, what was *Goody* Estridsen's manner?"

"Her mood was dark, I'd say, Captain. She ordered us out of her home and refused your lawful command that she come with us."

Martin nodded. "And did anything strange happen during our visit?"

"You could say that, sir."

"Yes, yes, Barnes, but the question is: do *you* say so?"

"Oh. Yes, sir. She was overly familiar with yourself, sir, and if I may say so, in what appeared to be a wanton manner."

"Yes. Anything else?"

"Well, yes, sir. When you ordered us to remove her from her home by force and to convey her to this very church, I took her by the arm. When I did so, she gave me a look of pure evil, and I grew cold in an instant, despite the heat. Her eyes seemed to dance, such that I feared she was about to hurl a curse at me."

"And did she?" asked the minister.

"Not that I heard, Minister Hardy. But, still, I fear she may have."

Margaret scoffed and laughed, but with bitterness few could miss.

"Come to me after we've dealt with her, Brother Barnes," said Hardy. "We will pray to our Father to overcome her foul magic."

"Yes, Minister."

"What happened next, Barnes?" asked Martin.

The militiaman gulped. "Displaying great courage, if I may be so bold, Captain Martin stood forward and grasped the chain that binds her, disrupting her spells. In my belief, it was your faith, sir, that kept her magic still while we conveyed her here."

"Oh, this is ridiculous," said Margaret. "How convenient that I *could* have used my so-called powers to escape but for the *faith* of a lecherous, avaricious man."

In two strides, Captain Martin reached her and slapped her hard across the cheek. Her ears rang with the force of it, and her cheek burned with both anger and affront.

"Do not speak!" he commanded. "If we need your input, slattern of the Evil One, we will ask you directly."

"Do that again, and I *will* speak, Martin. And if I do, you will not enjoy what I may say."

With a small, crooked smile on his face, he winked at her, then plastered a fearful expression on his face and turned toward the congregation. "You witnessed it! She threatened to curse me!"

"Be at ease, Captain Martin," said Minister Hardy. "She has no power here."

"Do I not?" Margaret asked, turning a hateful stare on the minister. "Do I, the *witch*, the consort of Satan, not have power anywhere? Why am I accused? Since I have no power to do evil anywhere, what does it matter if I am a witch?"

"As the Lord sayeth in Exodus 22:18, 'Thou shalt not suffer a witch to live.'" The minister's voice rang with conviction.

"You fool," snapped Margaret. "That is a mistranslation! In the original Hebrew, the word is *mekhashepha*, and it means '*poisoner*,' not 'witch.'"

"Go on," said Minister Hardy with deceptive calm. "Correct the Good Book, but before you do, explain to us how you come to such knowledge?"

Margaret shook her head and kept her mouth shut.

Captain Martin smiled. "As we thought. You have no basis for your wild claims, do you, witch?" When she didn't answer, he turned to Minister Hardy. "Is more testimony required?"

Hardy squinted at Margaret, his head cocked to the side. "Will you confess?" When she again refused to answer, Hardy shook his head. "If you confess your sins, sister, the Lord shall allow you to repent."

Her head snapped up, and her eyes blazed with an almost physical force. Hardy lurched back, his hands up as if to ward off a blow. "*Sins*?" she demanded. "You *dare* to remove me from my home by force, by the threat of violence. You bind me and treat me as no better than an already condemned criminal, and you dare accuse *me* of sin?" She shook her head savagely. "If you knew to whom you spoke, you would show me the proper respect!"

With a metallic shriek, Martin drew his sword and laid it against her throat. "Speak again, witch," he hissed.

She turned her baleful gaze on him. "And you will learn the lesson first."

"Again, you threaten me?" He applied slightly more force to his blade, and a trickle of blood ran from her neck though she didn't react.

"Do any of the congregation need more proof?" asked the minister.

The silence in the church was absolute. Martin stared at Margaret with angry eyes, and she stared back with hatred burning in hers.

"By the power of the Lord our God, I hereby condemn the woman known as Margaret Estridsen as a foul Wife of Satan, a witch, in plain speech, and I sentence her to death. This witch shall burn in God's purifying fire until dead, this very afternoon."

Margaret laughed. She drew herself up and stared at the minister as if she would as soon eat him as speak to him. "*Shall* I?" She laughed again. "I think *not*."

"If any harbor doubts as to this slattern's guilt, let them think on her response to her sentence." Martin sank the edge of his blade deeper into her skin. "Once the fire has rendered your flesh to ash and bone, I will have your bones gathered and taken to the mill where they will be ground to dust and remixed with your ashes. Then we will cast the mixture upon the sea and distribute it to the four corners of the Earth, so you may never rise from your grave."

"Oh?" Her modest guise had disappeared, and an imperious shrew stood in its place. "Is that how it will be?"

"Oh, yes," said Martin with a grin. "Fire shall rid us of you, Mistress of Darkness. We will be here, and you will be in Hell."

Again, she laughed, and her eyes twinkled with hidden knowledge. "Do you even know the origin of that word?"

"Of course. It is the domain of the Evil One."

"Is it? Is it, indeed?"

Martin was nonplussed, but bravado surged to the fore. "And I will find your husband, and, wizard or not, he will suffer your fate," he whispered.

Without warning, Margaret lurched toward the militia captain with her mouth open wide as though to bite his face and cackled as he staggered away, stumbling for balance.

"For this, too, you will pay," he muttered. "Take this witch to the place of execution."

Her gaze tracked to the minister's. "*Kvul*," she said, and Hardy slapped his hands to his head and screamed.

"Hold her!" commanded Martin, stripping off his wide leather belt. Militiamen rushed forward, some grabbing her arms and two others holding her head. She opened her mouth to speak, and as she did, Martin shoved the leather strap into her mouth and cinched it tight. "Be sure this stays on," he said, cutting his eyes toward the minister who had collapsed against the pulpit moaning.

Martin snapped his fingers at his wife and motioned at Hardy. She sprang to her feet and rushed to the minister's side, leading him into the room behind the pulpit.

"Take her out," Martin commanded. He made sweeping motions at the congregation.

Outside, Martin cleared his throat. "Citizens of Roanoke. Brothers and sisters. We are gathered here this afternoon to witness God's own justice on this woman calling herself Margaret Estridsen. You've witnessed her trial, her condemnation, and her sentencing as a witch, a consort of Satan, a malefactor, and a priestess of Evil."

Margaret thrashed against the militiamen as they looped a chain around her, securing her to the post. Her eyes blazed with maleficence, but she stopped and grinned around her gag as a telltale grunt from the woods opposite her reached her ears.

Martin gazed at her with uncertain fear for a moment but turned his back and walked to the fire burning nearby. He retrieved a torch and set it in the flame. "Stack the wood around her and douse it with lamp oil."

His gaze met hers. "Harlot, are you prepared to meet the wrath of God Almighty?"

She winked at him and nodded.

Confusion at her utter lack of terror clouded his face, but he shook his head and forced a smile onto his lips. "Good, for you will soon face it."

The brush in the woods rustled as though a large animal sprinted through it, and Margaret smiled savagely.

Martin paused, then made a "hurry up" gesture at his men. He snatched up his torch and started toward her as his man poured the lamp oil around her feet. Behind her, a wolf snarled, and Captain Martin's eyes leapt past her and widened with fear. He lurched forward, trying to get close enough to light the wood piled at her feet.

A savage roar split the afternoon as her husband broke from the trees. The women of the village screamed as one and tried to gather their children. The men stumbled back, holding up crosses or making warding gestures against evil.

Around her gag, Margaret laughed.

Captain Martin's wide-eyed gaze locked on her own, fear dancing there. He pulled back his arm to throw the torch, and Luka roared again, rushing forward at inhuman speed.

Martin tried to dodge, tried to move fast enough, but it was too late. It had been too late when he forced his way into their home that morning, and now, he knew it.

The torch Martin held disappeared, along with his hand and forearm, in an explosion of red mist. He glanced around as if he couldn't understand what had happened, and Luka roared again.

Margaret enjoyed Martin's expression as his gaze crawled from the torch clutched by his severed forearm lying at his feet to what she knew loomed behind her. The captain's gaze darted from point to point, and she imagined what he was looking at: Luka as an *oolfur*, long limbs, impossible height, suppurating sores, coarse brown fur standing in clumps…and the head of a wolf, of course.

Insanity reigned in Martin's eyes, and he tried to teeter away, but shock and blood loss had done their work, and he stumbled to one knee, his gaze never leaving Luka.

Her champion, her lover, stepped from behind her and gazed into her face. She jangled the chains that bound her hands and held her to the stake that was to be her place of execution.

Rage that bordered on insanity blossomed in Luka's eyes, and he snapped his head around to roar and snarl, rooting the villagers to the spots where they stood—like rabbits gone tharn in the face of a predator. Many of the women and children screamed, and the odor of piss filled the air.

He turned back to Margaret and, with infinite gentleness, he took the chains that bound her and snapped them as easily as a child might rip a sheet of paper. He swept up one of the oil-soaked logs at her feet and whipped it into the crowd, knocking man, woman, and child spinning through the air.

Margaret patted his furry arm and removed the wide leather belt that gagged her. She threw the belt at Martin with disdain.

Luka stepped toward the man, snarling.

"No, my Champion. I will deal with the captain myself."

She stepped to the man's side and smiled down at him. "I don't think I shall burn today, Captain, but thank you for the invitation."

His eyes filled with tears, his face as white as a ghost.

"And as for meeting your puny god's wrath, I also decline. And you were right, my name is not Margaret Estridsen, though I knew Margaret the First of Denmark rather well. She was such a sweet child. My name is Hel." She laughed at the terror writ on his face. "Yes. Your pathetic myth of punishment owes its origin to *my* deeds. Allow me to introduce you to a goddess' wrath. Alas, I fear you won't survive it." She winked at him and raised a hand to point down at his face. "*Predna*," she said, and emerald green fire poured down on Martin's face and neck.

Captain Martin shrieked as the green flames engulfed his face and head. Fat sizzled and popped as his skin melted and curled. He screamed once, and the green blaze raced down his throat as if alive and greedy for his death, burning away his lungs.

The stunned crowd reacted, and panicked screams filled the village square. Mothers scooped up children and bolted toward their homes—as if wooden doors could keep Luka or Hel out.

Margaret kicked Martin in the side. "Do you see what you've wrought, you small little man? Do you feel the wrath of your Goddess?" But when she looked down into his face, his eyes had already burst from the heat, and death had freed him.

Luka roared as he chased people down and knocked them to the ground. He threw glances at her with each person he drove into the dirt as if seeking her permission to eat, to drink, to kill.

"My Champion," she purred, walking to his side. She stroked the coarse fur around his muzzle, stretching upward on tiptoe to reach. "You may kill a few, dear one, if you'd like, but I want most of them alive. Instruct them to pack their things. We shall undertake a long journey into the interior, and they will need supplies." She glanced at the church. "And that nasty man from the church. I want him along, so I may make him suffer every single day...until he begs me for death." She smirked. "And even after that."

Luka glanced down at her as she grinned with a malevolence so pure it could have peeled the paint from the church's doors.

"We must punish him. We must punish them *all*, but him most of all. We shall take our time."

Luka grinned a lupine grin and grunted. "Yes, my Queen," he grated.

SEVENTEEN

"After that, Luka rounded up all the villagers he didn't kill outright and herded them into the church, where Hel stood in judgment."

"What did they do with all those people?" asked Jane. "Or don't I want to know?"

I glanced around, reading the signs. "Most of them came out of the church, and Luka led them toward the mainland side of the island. Hel walked with them."

"And the ones that didn't come out of the church?"

"Some were dead when Hel blasted it with her green fire."

"But some weren't." It wasn't a question, so I didn't bother to answer.

"Most survived. At least that day."

Jane looked at up me with wide eyes. "How do you know all this stuff?"

"I have no idea. Something that the Great Old One did, or maybe whatever it was Kuhntul did to me with her magic chisel."

"Aren't you getting tired of being everybody's sandbox?"

"Now that you mention it, yeah, I am." I shrugged and frowned. "But it's not as if I have much choice in the matter, is it?"

Jane sighed. "I guess not. Next time ask to speak with someone's supervisor. Or at least get a case number for customer support." She put her hand on her hip and smiled at me, and suddenly, none of it seemed to matter.

"We need to find the mainland side of the island," said Althyof.

"I believe a path exists over this direction," said Yowtgayrr. "I believe the island is safe enough now."

"Yes," I said with a nod. "All of this happened years ago. But I don't think we need to go to the other side of the island. Luka and Hel are years gone, and the villagers with them. Besides, the version of Hel and Luka who were here are not the versions we want."

"Do you even speak English anymore?" asked Jane.

"You tell me, hon."

"It's getting hard to tell. You are becoming fluent in gobbledygook though."

"I'm glad you noticed. I've been studying at night after you go to sleep."

Jane stuck her tongue out at me and blew a raspberry. "Well, it's good you're putting your time to productive use."

"Someone must."

Althyof sighed and shook his head. "Not to break up all this flirting, but—"

"Flirting? You call this flirting?"

"In his defense, it does sound similar to Tverkar flirting," said Yowtgayrr.

Althyof cleared his throat. "Whatever you two call it, if we can simply get past it for a moment… Hank, you said something cryptic about Luka and Hel. Something about wrong versions?"

"Yes, I did. These two…they aren't… They don't *feel* right."

"Good thing you've learned to speak gobbledygook," muttered Jane.

"What do you mean, Hank?" asked Yowtgayrr.

"It's as though they don't…I don't know… They don't *know* me."

"Wait a minute. I thought you were getting this information from mysterious, magical tracks that only you can see with your magic eyeball."

"Eloquently put, Jane, and you're right. But they are more than simple tracks."

"What do you mean?"

"I can see more than only where they walked if I study them deeply enough. I can see what they did, but more than that, I can see their emotional state, their mental state. It's as if I can almost access their memories. Or maybe I *am* accessing their memories, and that's all these tracks are."

"Ah," said Yowtgayrr. "We call them *slowthar*."

"I'm telling you, Hank, you've got a future in the gobbledygook industry." She glanced at Yowtgayrr. "You, too."

"And you've got a career in the laundry industry."

Althyof smiled at that one. "So, what you're really saying, Hank, is that we are in the wrong place."

"Yeah."

"So why did the Great Old Ones lead us across this particular *proo*?"

I shrugged and let out a long breath. "Maybe the Great Old One who needed to mess around inside my head couldn't get a connecting flight to the other *proo*. It appears they were waiting for me in the *proo*. Maybe they needed to know the precise *proo* I'd travel across. Or maybe they needed me to come here and see all this."

"Are we done here, then?" asked Jane.

I glanced around the village square, looking for anything new, anything I might've missed. It was a sad tableau, both in the present and a few years past.

"Yes. There's nothing else here; a mystery for the next colonization mission Sir Walter Raleigh sends."

Jane turned and walked toward the forest. "If that's the case, let's get out of here."

We all traipsed along behind her, content to walk in silence. Other than our passage through the woods, every sound I heard was natural, expected. Birds. Small animals. The wind soughing through the boughs above us. Even so, I sensed eyes on me from somewhere. I sidled over next to Yowtgayrr and tapped his wrist with the back of my hand, trying to seem nonchalant.

The Alf glanced at me and flashed a small smile my way.

"Do you... Is there someone watching us?"

Yowtgayrr glanced around. "I sense nothing. No animals, no humans."

"Okay," I said. I looked around, trying to use my newfound ability to track people around me, and while the signs of a native population surrounded us, none of them were recent. "It's nothing."

We emerged from the woods onto the narrow strand of beach with the *proo* glimmering in the sun. "It's strange that this *proo* was left out here in the open," I mused.

"Yes," said Althyof. "Careless." The Tverkr strode toward the *proo*, hand already outstretched to make his passage.

But something snagged at my attention, something that seemed off. I stopped walking and stared at the *proo*, and as I did so, the sensation I had while we walked through the woods—the feeling of being watched—intensified.

At first glance, the *proo* matched all the others I'd seen since Kuhntul did whatever she'd done inside my head with her magic chisel. But as I stared at it, I recognized three things: the tendrils around the outside edge were actively reaching toward Althyof, trying to make contact as soon as possible; the massive, blind-worm shapes of the Great Old Ones were missing from its silvery surface; and if I looked at it in a certain way and with enough mental effort, I could see where the *proo* led. "Wait!" I yelled, lurching toward Althyof to yank him back, to pull his hand away from the reaching tendrils.

He pulled his hand back, avoiding contact with the most ambitious tendril by a hair's breadth. He turned toward me, his expression cross, eyes not quite blazing, but far from peaceful. "What is it? What is it *now*?"

"The *proo* has been…manipulated. Or moved. Or glamored, I don't know."

Althyof threw a sharp glance over his shoulder. "Seems normal."

"Trust me on this one, Althyof. It's far from *right*."

Yowtgayrr peered at me through concerned eyes. "Hank, is this—"

"Look," I said. "How this looks, how it *sounds*—it seems crazy—but I'm telling you: something's not right here."

Althyof lifted his shoulders and let them fall with a harsh gust of breath. "Then what?"

"Give me a minute to study it. Let me see what I can figure out."

Althyof waved his hand toward the *proo* in a be-my-guest gesture.

I crept around the *proo*, peering into its reflective depths. The tendrils lurched toward me as I moved, fluttering as though in a soft current. The surface was flat, glassy. When I'd walked in a full circle, I stopped.

"Well?" asked Jane. "Has someone rearranged the furniture or not?"

I shook my head, not willing to give in to distraction yet. "*Syow kaltur*," I breathed.

"That will not work, Hank," said Yowtgayrr. "The whole thing is made of the stuff that makes up the *strenkir af krafti*—magic, in other words."

My eye burned and tingled, watering to beat all. When I blinked the tears away, I gasped at the thing before me.

The *proo* glowed like a thousand suns—how I imagined the core of a thermonuclear explosion would flash blindingly-white. The tendrils, or what I'd *taken* for tendrils, reminded me of the reaching arms of *truykar*—blackened flesh dripping from decaying musculatures. The hands clenched and released, fingers stretching toward us with desperation.

I stared at the center of the *proo*, no longer trying to see the differences between this *proo* and the others

I'd seen that day, just taking it all in. Something tickled my mind, and the image of a kid tugging my shirt sleeve to get my attention flashed through my brain. "What is it you want me to see?" I muttered. "*Seentu myer!*"

As soon as the words left my lips, color and shapes exploded from the *proo*, a barrage of fractal psychedelic images that swirled and swooped and swam in my vision. After a moment of that, the images coalesced, painting a picture of a vast plain of burnt sienna sand under an azure sky. The desert stretched as far as I could see with no clusters of rocks, no cacti, no shantytowns, no trees, nothing. I stood there, gaping at the image, and as I did, a huge bright blue sun jumped skyward from below the horizon, so large it filled close to half the sky. The blue sun flashed through the heavens as if racing from one horizon to the other. After mere minutes, the massive sun set with as much alacrity as it had risen, but darkness didn't fall. The plain was lifeless, still. I turned in a circle, but everything was the same—lifeless, empty, burnt.

"Someone has moved the other end," I said. "This *proo* no longer connects with Niflhaymr—unless the place has suffered a massive, planet-rending catastrophe."

"Should we investigate?" said Althyof, but his tone made it clear he didn't relish the idea.

"No," I said, shaking my head. "No, that place is lifeless. Burnt, more like it. It's close to a blue star, and I have an idea the temperature there would bake us in an instant if we were to set foot there."

"Blue?"

I nodded. "Hot. If Siggy were here, he could tell you the sun's temperature." I waved up at Sol's yellow disc. "This star is almost ten times cooler than a blue."

Yowtgayrr whistled.

"Who moved it? And why?" demanded Jane. "The Great Old Ones, messing with us again?"

That didn't *feel* right. They could have sent us to our dooms at any time if they had the ability to control more than the start and end points of the *preer* as I suspected they did. "Luka or Hel would be my guess."

"But you said these were the wrong versions of our favorite couple."

"We should have them over for a cook-out," I said with a grin. "But, no, not…well, this is going to get confusing in a hurry, ain't it? Not the Roanoke versions, the 2017 versions."

"You know my rule, Hank. No cook-outs with cannibals." She glanced at the *proo* and shrugged in exasperation. "So, what? Are we trapped?"

"I don't have all the answers, hon."

"Ah! Finally, you admit it. Too bad I don't have a working video camera to preserve this moment for all time."

"That *is* too bad, isn't it," I said with a grin. I got that "pay attention to me" sensation again and glanced at the *proo*. The tendrils looked like harmless tendrils again, but perhaps the zombie-arms image was only a metaphor for how dangerous the things were. As I watched, the blind-worm shape of a Great Old One moseyed to the surface of the *proo*, as if looking for us. It came toward the surface, its body undulating like an eel swimming toward sunlight. *So, they* do *move*, I thought.

The Great Old One stopped its eeling movement and hung there motionless as though it needed to catch its breath. But, of course, there was no air inside the space between the *proo* ends for it to breathe. It hung there in front of me as though waiting for me to do something. Then, with a wriggle I took for impatience, it thrust its head toward me, as if it could reach out of the *proo*.

SMALL ONE. YOU WASTE PRECIOUS TIME. AND FOR LITTLE GAIN.

I scoffed at that. "Yeah, well, if you gave me a bit of instruction, I wouldn't have to waste so much time trying to figure out whatever it was you did to me."

INCONSEQUENCE. CEASE. GRASP THE HOOK.

"What's going on?" asked Jane.

"*What* hook? What the hell are you talking about?"

The Great Old One drifted closer, vying for a better look at me. ANNOYANCE. MATTER INTERFERES. It jerked forward the way a kid blowing out birthday candles would, and the floppy hat Althyof had enchanted after I lost my left eye flew off my head. NOW YOU CAN PERCEIVE.

I wasn't sure if it was a question or a statement, but nothing changed, except I lost depth perception. "What do you expect me to see? Let's start there."

VEXATION. DISTURBANCE OF TRANQUILITY. BOTHERATION. EXASPERATION.

"No need to curse… What do I call you, anyway?"

TIME DRIFTS AWAY. EXTRANEOUS QUERY IGNORED. THE HOOK…GRASP THE HOOK.

"It's not extraneous. How am I to recognize if you are the same…*thing*…next time?"

INSIGNIFICANCE.

"How am I to know the next blind *proo*-worm to approach me isn't trying to undo everything you are trying to get me to do?"

The thing hung in front of me for a few heartbeats, as still as if it were dead. If it had had eyes, I'd have expected them to stare at me without blinking.

THIS ONE IS NONPAREIL. NO OTHER WOULD DARE. YOU KNOW THIS ONE, IN ANY CASE.

"Yield," I said. "And I don't know you from Adam."

CAPRICE.

"It will help my small mind deal with you, okay?"

ACCEPTANCE. THIS ONE MAY BE THOUGHT OF AS "BIKKIR."

"Bikkir?"

AFFIRMATION. THE WORD MEANS—

"I recognize the word. 'Builder.' I'm fluent in the *Gamla Toonkumowl*."

IT IS SO.

I couldn't tell if that was irony or not—so much was lost without facial expression—but I thought it was. "Okay, Bikkir. Tell me what I'm supposed to be doing to avoid wasting time."

CEASE. YIELD.

"Oh, not back to that again. If you want—"

Bikkir lunged forward again, and intense pain blossomed in my empty left eye socket. I staggered back, Yowtgayrr's steady grasp keeping me on my feet in the loose sand.

"That's it!" snapped Jane. "We're getting away from this damn *proo*. Hel and Luka had one hidden near our home in Western New York in 2017, it's probably there now." She snapped at Althyof. "Don't just stand there gaping! Get a move on!"

ASPIRATION ACHIEVED. INSTRUCT THE LOUD ONE TO CEASE.

"No," I murmured. "It's okay, Jane, he's finished."

"Yeah?" she said with heat in her voice. "*I'm* not finished, and if that bastard expects to go on with his merry little life between the stars, you tell him to keep his damn hands off you."

AMUSEMENT.

"Not smart."

"Well, excuse me all to hell!" she snapped.

"No, honey, I mean Bikkir isn't all that smart. He seems to find this amusing."

Moving in sharp jerks, Jane found a rock and heaved it at the *proo*. The rock smacked into the mirrored surface with a bonging noise and disappeared.

NEGLIGIBLE EFFECT. POINTLESS ACTION.

"Get on with it. What do you *want*?" I yelled the last word, and it echoed up and down the beach.

Undeterred, Bikkir hung motionless. GRASP THE HOOK.

"I already told you! I don't see any goddamn..." But then I did.

The "hook" as Bikkir called it, appeared to be a tumorous growth in the upper arc of the *proo's* surface—almost like a knurl in an old tree. It bore bumps and indentations, as though it were a fancy machined knob in an airplane cockpit.

WONDEROUS PHENOMENON. YOU PERCEIVE IT AT LONG LAST. IN THE FUTURE, CLOSURE OF YOUR OCULAR CAVITY WILL PRECIPITATE ACTION.

I closed my eyeless socket, and the vision of the hook disappeared. "So much for that theory."

EXASPERATION. THE OTHER OCULAR CAVITY, SMALL ONE.

I switched eyes, and the hook was back. "Oh."

GRASP THE HOOK. GRASP IT.

I reached toward the *proo.*

CEASE. CEASE.

"You said to grab it! How do you expect me to do that without reaching for it?"

THINK, SMALL ONE. CLENCH THE HOOK WITH YOUR DREAMSLICE REFLECTION, NOT WITH THE MEANINGLESS MATTERSTREAM MANIFESTATION THAT ENTOMBS IT.

"I don't suppose you can explain how I'm to do that?"

FRIVOLOUS ORATION. CEASE. PERFORMANCE IS DESIRED.

I sighed. The Great Old Ones weren't turning out to be all that great. I focused on the knob-like hook and imagined grabbing it with an invisible arm. A tingle swept through me, like a mild electric shock.

SATISFACTORY, THOUGH PLETHORIC TIME HAS ELAPSED. KEEPING A FIRM GRASP ON THE HOOK, MANIPULATE THE APPENDAGE UNTIL ACHIEVING THE DESIRED OUTCOME.

I imagined turning the knob clockwise, and as the hook moved, I felt a tremor rumble through the space between the *proo* and myself. It wasn't a physical sensation, more of a psychic one.

SATISFACTORY. EXAMINE THE RESULT.

The *proo* appeared to be the same, and yet different in a subtle way. After a few moments, it dawned on me. "It's as if the colors that make up the shiny part have shifted in hue. Is that what I'm looking for?"

SATISFACTORY. THE SMALL ONE'S PREVIOUS ACTION WAS TAKEN WITHOUT DIRECTIVE FOCUS, AND THUS, COROLLARY COLOCATION IS ARBITRARY.

"All I need do is focus my mind on the destination?"

AGREEMENT.

"What if I've never been to the place I want to go?"

IRRELEVANCE.

"But how do I picture the place, in that case?"

VISUAL IDEATION NOT REQUIRED. FOCUS IS ALL THAT IS REQUIRED.

"Is this how the Isir move the *proo*?"

INSIGNIFICANT QUERY. IMPLEMENTATION OF FOCUSED-CHANGE IS DESIRED.

I shrugged wearily. "I wish, just once, you idiots would provide me with an instruction manual."

INAPPOSITE. IMPLEMENTATION OF—

"Yeah, yeah. Can it, Bikkir." I decided to start with something easy. Near our house in New York, there was a tract of land the locals called "The Thousand Acre Swamp," despite the fact that except for a small bog, a perfectly good forest made up most of the thousand acres. I fixed the image of the thickest, darkest part of that forest in my mind and twisted the hook. The psychic tremor rumbled through me again, and again, the *proo* looked unchanged, other than another one of those shifts in hue.

SATISFACTORY.

"You Great Old Ones are a laugh a minute," I muttered.

GREAT OLD ONES?

"Yeah. That's what I've been calling you. It comes from a writer on my *klith*—"

IRRELEVANT. GREAT OLD ONES. APT.

I had the distinct impression that Bikkir was laughing at me. "Is the *proo* where I pictured?"

TERMINOUS AD QUEM.

"You understand that's not actually an answer, right?" I asked, but Bikkir had already turned and was undulating away from the entrance to the *proo*.

"Well?" asked Jane. "Do I have to figure out a way to kill the damn thing or is everything okay?"

"Better than okay. I think Bikkir taught me how to control the *preer*."

"You mean you might finally serve a purpose," said Jane with a smile.

"Might as well ask if a bee makes honey. Honey."

"Don't try to be sweet."

"Boo," said Althyof.

"So where does this thing point now?" asked Jane.

"Thousand Acre Swamp."

Jane's eyebrows twitched skyward. "Yeah?"

"At least I think so. Bikkir was a little less than forthcoming."

Althyof grunted and rubbed his eyes. "No point wasting time with more chatter about how we can find out." He lifted his hand and touched the *proo*.

"So…should we wait around and see if he survived?"

"In for a penny," I said and ran the rainbow.

The air in the Thousand Acre Swamp snapped with a fall chill and my skin prickled at the change in humidity. There had been no sensation of traveling across the *proo*, no telltale psychic surgery performed by blind worms. Boring, really.

Althyof leaned against a tree, stroking his beard. "Well? Are we where you expected us to be?"

I nodded. "Yeah." I glanced up at the sun and pointed south. "Our house is that way."

Althyof nodded. "Are we sightseeing or is there a purpose to coming here?"

"For one thing," I said, patting Kunknir, "there is more ammunition here."

"Okay."

The others appeared, and Jane was already smiling.

EIGHTEEN

We stood a few paces back from the woods' edge, watching our house. Someone was inside, but by all rights, the house should have been empty. The way we'd left it…

"Who *is* that?" asked Jane. "She looks familiar."

"Looks a bit like…"

"Like who?"

"It's just a silhouette through a dark screen, but it looks a lot like you."

"Me?" she asked.

"Yeah, a little."

"My butt's not that big."

"You are perfect in every way, as I am contractually obligated to say."

"That's right, and you better mean it, too."

"What do we do now? I take it that is where you've hidden your ammunition?" asked Althyof.

I shook my head. "No, I brought all the ammo I had at the house. That, my friend, is where I've hidden my truck."

"Truck?"

"You'll enjoy it. Prokkr would go nuts over it."

"Take me to see it."

Jane shook her head. "Men are all alike. Cars, cars, girls, guns, cars… We have to find out who is in our house first. We can't walk in there like we own the place…even though we do."

"She's right. I'll go around to the front and ring the bell. Maybe the bank repossessed the place and resold it."

"You can't go, Hank. What if someone is looking for you? For us?"

I shrugged. "We can't send Althyof or Yowtgayrr." All eyes turned to Krowkr.

"I'd be honored," he said, and his eyes shone with reverence.

"No, we can't send you, either. None of you know anything about this time, this place."

"But Krowkr *can* go to the door…in a way." I fixed him in my gaze and began the *triblinkr* to assume his form. As the *prayteenk* began, something in his *slowthar* caught my attention…a memory or a thought. The images were insistent…they snagged my mind and sucked me in as though I were a leaf caught in a strong wind. I glanced up at the man himself and saw horror shining in his eyes. He shook his head as if refusing the memory…

NINETEEN

A blizzard raged, and still, the three young men walked on. The wind shrieked, flinging stinging ice crystals in their exposed faces. Skatlakrimr, the biggest of the three men, led the way, breaking a path through the knee-high snow. Two brothers, Owfastr and Krowkr, followed close in his footsteps, hoping the big man's bulk would offer them respite from the biting wind.

"Skatlakrimr, we should stop. Make a fire and get warm," said Owfastr. Beside him, his brother nodded.

Skatlakrimr shrugged without stopping. "Stop if you prefer. Make a fire if you want. I'm going on."

"Be reasonable, Skatlakrimr. Yarl Oolfreekr will still be there after the storm."

"Will he?" asked Skatlakrimr. "Come on. We are close. Hoos Oolfsins is just beyond that little hill."

The "little hill" was more mountain than hill. With a sigh and a glance at his brother, Owfastr shifted his weapons to a more comfortable position and kept walking. Behind him, Krowkr grimaced and trudged on.

None of the men wore mail—not in a blizzard such as this one. Furs wrapped each man, but each held a tightly wrapped wolf skin in his pack, protected from the weather. The legend said they needed a pristine pelt for the ceremony that Skatlakrimr desired more than life itself.

The three climbed the steep hill, Skatlakrimr outpacing the other two. At the crest of the hill, he stopped and looked back at his companions. He waved them on with the impatience for which he was known.

A thick, low-hanging mist filled the valley below. Krowkr shook his head. "That mist is an evil omen," he murmured. He sometimes spoke above a whisper, though not often, a fact which led many of the villagers to believe he was an aspect of mighty Veethar, the god of silence and vengeance. When he spoke, many of the men in the village listened to him, his young age notwithstanding.

With Skatlakrimr, however, his quiet ways didn't count for much. The big man scoffed. "Hoos Oolfsins is where we must go. Mist or no mist. He is the last one. You know this, Krowkr."

"Besides," said Owfastr, "we have sacrificed to Owthidn, patron of the berserks. Yarl Oolfreekr will welcome us!"

"Somehow, I do not think so," murmured Krowkr.

"Come, Brother, it's only a mist," said Owfastr.

"I sense evil on the wind."

"It's only the wind, you fool. And snow. And cold. And mist." Skatlakrimr turned his back to Krowkr.

"Omens and portents should not be—"

"Owfastr, your brother is talking as a coward would. Speak sense to him. I cannot." Skatlakrimr climbed down the hill toward the mist shrouded valley.

Krowkr shook his head but said no more.

"He didn't mean it as an insult, Krowkr. It's his way." Owfastr patted his brother on the shoulder. "Let's go get warm inside Hoos Oolfsins."

"Yes, warm," muttered Krowkr.

With a smile, Owfastr set off down the slope after their friend.

"Veethar, grant me strength," Krowkr breathed. After a moment, he followed the other two down into the mist, eyes tracking ill-seeming eddies and foul-swirlings in the gray mist. "Only the wind," he sneered. "Only the mist." Krowkr fingered the silver wolf's-head pendant Skatlakrimr had insisted each of them buy and wear. He slipped his thumb around to the back side of the silver disc, running the ball of his thumb across the rune he'd carved there. Veethar's rune.

The three men left the crown of the hill behind them, slipping and sliding down the ice-ridden slope, mouths stretched in rictus grins of discomfort, ice and snow crawling inside their clothes and down into their boots. The sun teetered on the horizon, promising a cold night if the three couldn't make it to Hoos Oolfsins before darkness fell.

A large cairn of stacked nepheline syenite rocks, each easily as big as Krowkr's head, loomed out of the mist. The cairn stretched toward the darkening sky, marking the boundaries of Hoos Oolfsins.

Krowkr's eyes crawled over the ancient rocks, creeping across the swirling patterns in the rock faces—patterns that all mimicked wolves: wolves fighting, wolves eating, wolves mating, wolves hunting. Krowkr slowed to a stop. "It's not too late, Owfastr. We need not intrude on Yarl Oolfreekr's lands. We can turn back, make camp until morning, and return home. We can—"

Owfastr cast a glance at his younger brother. "No, Krowkr. This is no time for nerves. Gird your courage, Brother. We're almost there!"

Skatlakrimr scoffed and spat into the snow swirling at Krowkr's feet. "Enough of this."

"Can't you feel it, Krowkr?" asked Owfastr. "This is our last night as mortals."

"Perhaps," said Krowkr, not taking his eyes off the stones that made up the cairn. It seemed—for an instant—that some of the wolves had moved.

Perhaps, but probably not as you mean it, Brother, he thought.

Skatlakrimr shook his head and rolled his eyes. "Can we get out of this wind? Eh, Krowkr? Can we go sit by a fire in the great hall of Hoos Oolfsins? Can we meet the man we came to meet and speak what we came to speak?"

Krowkr shrugged and nodded, resigning himself to what might await them at the end of their foolhardy quest. "Lead on, Skatlakrimr."

Skatlakrimr smiled. "That's the spirit. That's the Krowkr I know."

As an answer, Krowkr nodded, face set in grim lines, and pulled his furs closer around his face. He followed the other two as they made their way through the swirling snow and screeching wind. He stood behind them as Skatlakrimr drew his axe, reversed it, and pounded three times on the thick yew door of Hoos Oolfsins. Neither his brother, nor his friend, seemed to notice that the mighty Hoos Oolfsins lay in disused disorder, but Krowkr marked it and fingered the rune of Veethar again.

There was no answer to Skatlakrimr's thumping on the door. No pretty thralls bustled to open the door, to hand them warmed mulled wine, to take their skins. Hoos Oolfsins dwelled in deliberate darkness, swathed in studied silence.

"Should we go in?" asked Owfastr.

To Krowkr, his brother sounded uneasy, maybe even outright scared. "We don't have to," he murmured.

"And why not?" asked Skatlakrimr. "Owthidn received our sacrifices, Yarl Oolfreekr will—"

"Who disturbs my rest?" boomed a basso voice from beyond the yew door.

Skatlakrimr stood stone still for a moment, mouth agape, a certain wildness in his eyes. He closed his mouth with a click and swallowed hard. He glanced at Owfastr and pushed the thick yew door open.

Hoos Oolfsins huddled in shadows inside and out. No fires burned in the fire pits that ran the length of the room. No karls sat at the long tables, no thralls served food or poured mead and wine. A single torch guttered from one of the posts near the center of the long hall.

"Come in, fools, and close the door," snapped a voice out of the darkness. "I cannot die, but I can feel the cold."

Skatlakrimr's throat spasmed as he struggled to swallow. He forced a smile on his lips and strode into the room, shoulders thrown back, axe held in his fist, but without strength.

Krowkr grabbed his brother's elbow. "We should not be here," he hissed.

"You could be right," Owfastr whispered. "But we are, and Skatlakrimr is our friend. We can't abandon him." He shook Krowkr's hand off his arm and followed their lifelong friend into Yarl Oolfreekr's inhospitable hall.

With a sigh, Krowkr thumbed Veethar's sigil and stepped over the threshold.

"The door!" grated Oolfreekr.

With a half-bow, Krowkr turned and pushed the door closed, fighting the wind for every inch. Once closed, the door blocked the worst of the cold, the worst of the shrieking voices that danced in the wind.

"Are you three too stupid to stay at home in a storm such as the one roaring outside?" demanded the yarl.

"My lord, we have traveled far, and the storm was nothing more than a dark smudge on the horizon when we set out. We—"

"So, your answer is yes? Is it not winter? Don't all winter storms on this side of the mountains start the same way?"

Skatlakrimr cleared his throat and darted a glance at Owfastr. "Uh…"

"Well-said!" snapped the voice from the darkness. "Well? What do you want?"

Skatlakrimr set his jaw and squared his shoulders. He took a deep breath. "My lord yarl, men say you are the last of the *oolfur streethsmathur*."

"Is it so?" asked the yarl in a harsh tone.

"Um, yes, Yarl. The legend goes that, in the time of my grandfather's grandfather, you appeared a young man, but were already older than any could remember. They say you—"

"Who is this 'they' of whom you speak?"

Krowkr could have sworn the man in the shadows was moving around the room. Speaking from first one place, then the next.

"Well, er, the elders of our village. Our own yarl. Others we met while a-viking."

"And so it must all be true, with so many swearing to its veracity."

"Yarl, if it pleases you, the reputation of Hoos Oolfsins has spread far and wide. In your many duels, you have received many blows that would have killed another man."

The yarl laughed—great, booming roars that seemed fit to drown out the wind outside.

"Yarl, we came to learn from you. We want to study your ways, to rebuild the *Briethralak Oolfur*. Our sacrifice to Owthidn has been made. We carry the required reagents for the ceremony. We shall swear fealty to you, to serve Hoos Oolfsins, to build your reputation until even the Danes have heard your name." Skatlakrimr stopped, breathing a trifle hard, eyes blazing.

The hall stood steeped in silence, and it seemed that even the wind outside had stopped howling in the wake of Skatlakrimr's impassioned speech. Krowkr felt a shiver race down his spine. *This is a mistake*! a voice wailed deep inside his mind. *Run*! One glance at his brother told him that Owfastr had drawn the same conclusion, but the same glance told him Owfastr would stand by Skatlakrimr, come what may. *It is no matter*, he thought. *Owthidn wove our fates long ago*. Besides, everyone knew you couldn't outrun one of the *Briethralak Oolfur*.

When the voice came from the darkness again, it was mild. "All that? My, oh my!"

"Yes, Yarl," said Skatlakrimr in a shaking voice.

"And do all those others—the village elders, the others you met a-viking, your yarl—do they also tell you my full name?"

Skatlakrimr gulped like a gilled fish. "Yes, Yarl," he croaked.

"Yes, Yarl," mocked the voice from the darkness. "Tell me!"

Skatlakrimr, Owfastr, and Krowkr all jumped at the snap of command in the old yarl's voice. Skatlakrimr swallowed hard and said, "Yarl Oolfreekr Berserk-Morthinki, Lord."

'That's right!" snapped the yarl. A large form moved in the shadows at the end of the hall. Far larger than the largest man Krowkr had ever seen. "You understand those old words?"

"Wolf-warrior the Berserk-killer," muttered Skatlakrimr. "We know, Yarl."

"Is it so? Do these others also tell how I earned the name?"

"In your duels, Yarl," murmured Owfastr.

"What's that? Speak as a man if you are one."

"In your duels, Yarl," repeated Owfastr, his tone firm.

"Yes, yes, that much is obvious. Why?"

"Because," said Krowkr, "of who you dueled at the end."

"Ah, he speaks! Obviously, the brains of the bunch, which bodes well for the others, since stones or firewood won't best you in a test of intelligence."

Krowkr's cheeks burned, and Skatlakrimr's face settled in hard, angry lines. "Because you dueled the other members of the *Briethralak Oolfur*, Yarl. Because you killed your brothers."

"Yes," hissed the yarl. "And you came anyway." The last seemed to amuse the hulking figure swaddled in shadows. "Tell me: are all the men in your village so stupid?"

Skatlakrimr's shoulders tensed, muscles bunching and leaping under the furs he still wore against the chill. His hand tightened on the haft of his axe.

"Good," crooned the yarl. "You've spirit, that is good. Perhaps it will carry you on to Valhatla."

The words bore the discernable edge of challenge, and Skatlakrimr jerked his head back as if the old yarl had slapped him. "Old man, watch what you say."

"Ah, I've pricked your pride, at last." The man in the shadows lurched to his feet, a darker swatch against a backdrop of flickering shadows cast by the single torch. He stepped around the table and strode to the edge of the light.

Krowkr's heart leapt in his chest. The yarl's dimensions surpassed big. His form was immense, though thin to the point of death.

"Tell me, boy," said the yarl, jerking his chin at Krowkr. "You've more sense than this braggart here with the naked axe. Why have you let this man lead you to your doom?"

Krowkr shrugged. "These men are my friend and my brother. Should I not stand with them?" His hand went to the wolf's-head insignia around his throat, and his thumb stroked the rune of Veethar on its back.

"Not if you prefer your guts on the inside of your skin, no," grated the yarl.

"We three are standing here, in the light, in your hall, speaking to you as men would. There seems to be only one person here skulking in the shadows, bragging, trying to intimidate us," said Krowkr.

Skatlakrimr looked at him as though he'd grown a third limb.

The yarl burst into raucous, ill-mannered laughter. "So, you'd look on the visage of Yarl Oolfreekr Berserk-Morthinki, would you?"

"We've come to—" began Skatlakrimr.

"Shut up!" snapped the yarl, waving his hand at Skatlakrimr without looking at him. "I spoke to the little bird."

The ligaments in Skatlakrimr's axe-hand creaked with strain, and his knuckles blanched, yet his face suffused with angry blood.

Little bird, thought Krowkr. *How does he know the nickname Grandfather called me?* Maybe the yarl didn't—his name meant "rook," after all. "Yes, Lord," he said.

"*Lyows!*" said the yarl and a bright white light washed the shadows from the dark hall.

The yarl stood straight, and the top of his head was close to seven feet from the floor. His greasy hair hung limply across his back and shoulders. He smiled, and his lower lip split, dripping pus and blood down his chest. "Does what you see make an impression?" he crooned, a smile playing at his lips.

"Does my sallow, waxy skin attract you? Do these boils and weeping pustules mark me as healthy?"

"Not particularly," said Krowkr. "You appear to be in ill health, Yarl."

"But I am not. This has been the state of my body for a very long time, and I'll tell you a secret." He leaned forward, a parody of intimacy. "I cannot die."

"Yes, Yarl, that is why—" began Skatlakrimr.

"Hold your tongue!" snapped the yarl. "Or I will cut it from your head and eat it for my dinner." His eyes seemed to whirl in his anger, and Krowkr would have sworn they changed color. He glared at Skatlakrimr for a moment longer before his face relaxed, and his eyes drifted back toward Krowkr. "Have you nothing to say, little bird? No questions itching the back of your throat?"

Krowkr shook his head.

"And tell me, little bird, does this body of mine appeal to you? Do you want another such as this?"

Krowkr swallowed hard. The last thing he wanted was a pox-ridden, disease-riddled body. "Yarl, we've come to study the *layth oolfsins*. To become your apprentices. Either you will teach us, or you will not."

The emaciated yarl threw back his head and laughed. "Is that all there is to it, little bird? Either I will teach you or not?" He dashed a tear from his cheek, a sardonic twinkle in his eye. "Do you imagine that I will allow you to leave this hall? Are you that naïve?"

"Yarl, there is nothing I can do that will force you to behave in one way or another. All I can do—all we can do—is to rely on your sense of honor, on guest-right, and on the stories of your character, ancient though they may be."

"Is it so?" asked the suddenly somber yarl.

Krowkr wriggled out of his pack and set it on the floor at his feet. With a nod toward the yarl, he flipped open the bag and withdrew the perfect, preserved skin of a white wolf and unrolled it. "The elders say we each needed a skin from a wolf, and that you, as leader of the pack, would judge us based on the quality of the skin, and the quality of the animal from which the skin was cut. I hunted a white wolf, high in the mountains, above the ice-line. He led me on a merry chase, filled with guile and exhaustion, but in the end, I shot him in the eye with a single arrow, and he died."

"Is it so?" repeated the yarl. "Quite a deed, little bird, but you don't know what you are asking of me."

"Yarl, with your permission?" asked Owfastr.

The yarl nodded, but his steely eyes fastened on Skatlakrimr's in warning or challenge, Krowkr couldn't begin to guess.

"Lord Yarl," said Owfastr. "Please soften your heart, and hear our honest, respectful entreaties. The three of us have traveled a long way, we've followed the forms dictated to us by the village elders and from an old man dressed in wolf pelts that we met on the way here. We come to you on bended knee, out of respect. We come to you begging for the ancient knowledge you alone have. We want to become *oolfhyethidn*, *oolfur streethsmathur*, Yarl."

"Is it so?" asked the yarl for the third time.

"It is, Yarl," said Krowkr. "It has been all that we worked for, all that we've striven for, these many years. We come hoping you will find us worthy."

"More's the pity, lad," said the yarl, seeming morose. "It was a pretty speech, both of you." The tall man leaned against the table behind him. "You said you knew how I earned the name Berserk-Morthinki, but I don't believe you've taken the story to heart. You haven't asked yourselves why I slew all my so-called brothers of the wolf."

The three young men looked at each other, and, as one, met the yarl's gaze. "We assumed it was to gain leadership of the—"

"Stupid!" snapped the yarl, coming to his feet. "How can you look upon my body and not know? How can you stand in this long-abandoned hall and not know?"

"Know what, Lord?" asked Owfastr.

"That the *Briethralak Oolfur* is an abomination, for pity's sake! I killed all the other *oolfhyethidn* because they became drunk on their power! They became a blight on these lands, challenging land owners to duels in which the land owner stood no chance. No chance! We can't be killed! How do you expect anyone to win a duel against one of us?"

"And yet, Lord," said Skatlakrimr, a smile creasing his face, "you killed the others."

The yarl waved it away and sighed from the depths of his soul. "I had help, of course—from the gods themselves. But I speak to you plainly, and you do not see."

"Tell us, Lord. Help us see," said Krowkr, leaning forward, still holding the white wolf's skin.

"If I teach you the *layth oolfsins*, it will destroy you, little bird. It will destroy everything that makes you a good man. It will leave you filled with lust— lust for the life forever denied you from that moment onward, lust for the death you will never see, lust for yet more power until nothing has meaning for you, not brotherhood, not family, not kinship or country, nothing! You will watch everyone you've ever known wither and die. Do you know the village in which I was born isn't even a wide spot in the road anymore? You wouldn't even recognize its name!"

Skatlakrimr motioned to Owfastr, and both men dropped their packs and removed the skins of the wolves they had hunted. Skatlakrimr's was a beautiful sable that shone in the magical light. Owfastr's was that of a massive gray timber wolf.

Again, the yarl sighed and sat back against the table. "I cannot dissuade you?"

Skatlakrimr shook his head.

The yarl's eyes dismissed him and bored into Krowkr's. "And you, little bird?"

Krowkr pursed his lips. "Yarl, I hear what you say, and I take it to heart. But know these two men are all I have left in the world. If it is as you say—and I do not doubt your word, Lord—and my brother and friend follow the way of the wolf, and I do not, what will remain for me?"

"Your life! A woman! Children! A pure life!"

Krowkr nodded, face grim. "But I can have those things and keep my brother and friend too, can I not?"

The yarl stared at him, eyes hardening, tears shining in the white light that filled the hall. He shook his head, the picture of bitter remorse. "Then watch on, boys. Examine what you will become!" With a savage thrust of his arms, he propelled the table away from him and lurched to his feet. "*Oolfur*!" he screeched, and the air thrummed and crackled with power. "Feast your eyes on what it is to follow the *layth oolfsins*!" His voice had dropped several registers and had grown in volume. It sounded as if gravel filled his mouth and throat.

His arms and legs jerked and twitched, while his jaw elongated with a horrible pop. His eyes changed to an animal golden-yellow and coarse gray fur burst from his skin. His arms and legs stretched as taffy would on a summer's day, and his back hunched as though he wanted to hide his face from the three men. His ears melted and shifted upward, almost to the top of his skull, and then peaked and erupted with gray fur. He shook as a dog shakes water from his pelt before standing tall.

His head brushed the beams that supported the roof fifteen feet off the ground. He stretched his impossibly long arms wide and clicked his claws together as if he were snapping his fingers. His eyes narrowed, and he pointed one long finger at Skatlakrimr.

"Yes, Lord," breathed Skatlakrimr. "You are magnificent!"

The *oolfhyethidn* made a disgusted noise and jerked his finger at the axe hanging at Skatlakrimr's side. He tapped his chest, right in the middle.

"I think he wants you to attack him," breathed Owfastr. "To teach you…" He shrugged. "Something?"

"I have no wish to harm you, Yarl," said Skatlakrimr.

The…thing…the yarl had become made a rude noise and again pointed first at Skatlakrimr's axe and at his own chest. He opened his mouth and made a mocking, crooning sound.

Skatlakrimr shook his head. "Why do you goad me? Have I been anything other than respectful, Lord?"

The beast made a humming sound, punctuated by repeated spasms in his torso—as though he was about to be violently ill. It reminded Krowkr of laughter, but laughter that hurt to produce. Again, the *oolfhyethidn* beckoned Skatlakrimr.

The warrior shrugged and withdrew his mail shirt from his pack and set about knocking the ice out of it. Owfastr helped him get the heavy shirt over his head and settled across his shoulders. The yarl looked on with a decidedly snide twist to his facial expression.

When he was ready, Skatlakrimr glanced around. "Do you have a rope so we can mark out the square?" he asked.

In half a heartbeat, Yarl Oolfreekr rushed forward to tower over Skatlakrimr. With slow precision, he curled back his lips and exposed his fangs, growling all the while.

Skatlakrimr nodded to himself. "So be it." He looked away, and made as if to walk away, but threw his weight to the side at the last moment, spinning on his heel, and swung his axe at the *oolfhyethidn's* long neck.

The yarl must have seen the swing coming, must have known Skatlakrimr held nothing back, must have known it was a killing blow, but the beast did nothing—he didn't even twitch. If anything, he seemed to tilt his head away from the strike to expose more of his neck to the oncoming steel.

A hoarse roar burst from Skatlakrimr as the axe struck true and blood belched from the old yarl's neck. He jerked the weapon back, concern dawning on his face, and a great gout of gore gushed from the yarl's neck as the axe head pulled free. "I'm sorry, Lord... I—I thought you were ready... I thought... I thought..."

The yarl stood stone still, a small smile playing at his lupine lips. His eyes darted from man to man, first Krowkr, then Owfastr, and last, Skatlakrimr. He tilted his head to the side and spat a wad of bloody phlegm at Skatlakrimr's feet. Again, he beckoned the younger man forward. Again, he pointed at the axe and his chest.

Wide-eyed, Skatlakrimr glanced at Owfastr and shrugged as though asking what he should do.

The yarl growled deep in his chest and loosed a peculiar yipping bark, like a playful puppy.

Owfastr looked at his friend, arched his eyebrow and shrugged.

Skatlakrimr took a deep breath and set his feet in a firm stance. He adjusted his grip on the axe and lifted it high over his head.

The *oolfhyethidn* barked and waved his finger as if scolding a recalcitrant child. He tapped a long, clawed finger on the center of his own chest.

Skatlakrimr glanced at Owfastr again, and this time, Krowkr recognized the fear in his expression. He took a deep breath and lunged forward, putting his weight into his swing. The axe thumped into Oolfreekr's chest, making the same noise it would have made slamming into a hundred-year-old yew in the prime of its life.

The force of the blow must have been great, but the yarl didn't even sway as Skatlakrimr struck. He stood there, looking at the three men with an equable expression. He nodded at Skatlakrimr and motioned for him to remove the axe from the his chest.

When Skatlakrimr had done so, the yarl again pointed at his axe and tapped his chest, his claw sinking into the massive, gaping wound that was, even then, closing. Next, he pointed to Owfastr and the sword that hung at his side.

With a gulp and a glance at Krowkr, Owfastr repeated Skatlakrimr's preparations of his own mail shirt and shrugged into it. He strapped his shield to his arm and drew his sword with a metallic hiss. After saluting the yarl with the blade, Owfastr stepped forward and pointed at the *oolfhyethidn's* lanky thigh.

The yarl grunted and nodded in an exaggerated manner. He held up his finger, pointed at Skatlakrimr, touched his chest, pointed at Owfastr, and slapped the inside of his thigh, above the femoral artery.

When he nodded, both young men struck like snakes, each striking true, each embedding his own blade into the yarl's flesh. Blood sprayed the air and splattered the ground beneath them—the yarl's blood, but it didn't seem to matter to the *oolfhyethidn* in the least.

Oolfreekr nodded and made a burbling sound that Krowkr took to be praise. The colossal beast turned to Krowkr and at last something sparkled in his eye. The side of his face twitched in a gross parody of a crooked smile. He pointed at Krowkr, then at the small axe on his left hip and the sword on his right. He beckoned Krowkr to step forward.

Krowkr nodded and donned his armor. He freed his weapons from his belt. He strode forward as if he felt no nervousness at the thought of facing the immense creature.

Yarl Oolfreekr nodded once, expression brash. He went through the pantomime of assigning each warrior a body part to strike. To Krowkr, he assigned the sides of his abdomen and neck and motioned the man to go around behind him. He raised his hand and dropped it as though he was doing nothing more than starting a foot race.

The three men struck as one, each inflicting mortal wounds, but for the third time, the killing blows had no effect, and the yarl stood there gazing at them. He seemed to wait for something.

Skatlakrimr cleared his throat. "With your permission, Lord?"

The *oolfhyethidn* nodded.

"We understand this lesson, Great Wolf. As we are, we can't harm you, let alone kill you. This is the power we seek, Lord!"

The yarl blew through his nose, making it sound derisive, dismissive. Again, he pantomimed who would attack where, but this time, he pointed to his own chest and marked each of his young opponents in turn, Krowkr first, Owfastr second, and Skatlakrimr last.

Krowkr saw his friend bristle at the insult of being left last. Skatlakrimr was a vain man, and this meeting was not going well for him.

The yarl lifted his hand and let it drop.

Krowkr leapt high in the air, sweeping axe and sword toward the great beast's neck, but his blades whistled through empty air. Neither his brother's nor his friend's attacks landed either, and they ended the exchange staring at one another, only empty space between them.

Krowkr had seen the yarl move, but only just. The thing the yarl had become moved like lightning across the sky and with as little warning. From the darkness behind them, the yarl made his singular laughing sound.

"Lord, begging your pardon, but these exhibitions are unnecessary. We know what you can do, and we wish to learn to do it, too," said Skatlakrimr.

The yarl's freakish laugh stopped, and after a moment, a growl took its place.

"What must we do, Yarl Oolfreekr? What must we do to prove ourselves?" asked Owfastr.

The *oolfhyethidn* stalked from the shadows opposite from where Krowkr thought the sounds had originated. Eyes affixing Skatlakrimr, the yarl took two too-long steps and was in their midst. Without pausing, he snarled and pounced on Owfastr, claws rending his steel mail as though it were made from mist and sinking deep into the flesh of his chest and gut.

Skatlakrimr shrieked a war cry and launched himself at the *oolfhyethidn*, his ferocious swing making his axe whistle in a wide, disemboweling arc. Without taking his eyes off Owfastr's, the yarl shot his hand out and knocked the axe away.

Krowkr had always preferred guile to direct, brute force, and he edged into the shadows, circling toward his brother and the *oolfhyethidn's* exposed back.

Skatlakrimr stood for a moment, looking down at his hand as if he couldn't comprehend where his axe had gone. When he looked up, fear was written on his face in large, capital letters.

Owfastr made a gurgling noise, deep in his throat, and along with the sound came a fountain of bright red blood. The yarl leaned close to the younger man's face and crooned. Owfastr tried to lurch away but couldn't seem to get his feet moving. Oolfreekr put his hand on the man's chest, almost gently, and pushed.

As Owfastr toppled backward, two things happened at the same time. Skatlakrimr screamed and darted toward the shadows. Krowkr leapt out of the darkness, his sword opening a long, fruitless furrow across the *oolfhyethidn's* kidneys. At the same time, Krowkr chopped downward with his axe, trying to split the yarl's skull.

Oolfreekr lashed out, claws ripping through Krowkr's mail, requiring as little effort as they had to rupture his brother's. Krowkr felt the sticky-hot sensation of four wounds shredding across his upper chest and left bicep and cried out—more from anger than pain.

With a streak of gray fur, the *oolfhyethidn* ducked and spun away, arms thrown out, claws bared. His eyes darted toward the shadows—no doubt picking Skatlakrimr out of the darkness—and snapped to Krowkr's. "Little bird," he rumbled, his voice distorted and wrecked.

Krowkr nodded and dipped into a crouch. Guile would no longer serve him, he'd used it for all it was worth, and now there was nothing to do but stand guarding his brother and die well. He spun the sword in his hand and beckoned the yarl with his axe.

Oolfreekr's head tilted away, and he stared at Krowkr with appraising eyes for the space of a deep breath. When he came, he came with blistering, blinding speed and a savage howl. He came in low, almost on his knees, angling his jaws upward to knock Krowkr's head back and expose his throat.

Krowkr threw himself to the side, chopping at the yarl's neck with his axe on one side and his blade on the other. The yarl altered his approach in mid-stride, taking the axe blow on the shoulder and batting the sword down with arm-numbing force. Krowkr scrambled to keep his feet and his weapons, but his head snapped back with stunning force as the *oolfhyethidn* butted him, and stars exploded in his vision, and his ears rang with the sound of a thousand gongs. He fell, almost senseless, to the ground, but he kept hold of his weapons out of instinct.

The yarl loomed over him, gazing down at him without remorse, but also without anger or hatred. The yarl looked...bored. He made a strange, chin-jerking motion and curled back his lips to expose his fangs. He bent, and Krowkr readied himself to die.

Is that pity? Do I see compassion in this beast's eyes? he wondered. Krowkr turned his head, looking for the Valkyries, longing for the glorious sight of the goddess Freya. *Which will it be? Valhatla or Fowlkvankr?* In the corner of the hall, an oval filled with the colors of the rainbow swirled into existence. *I will soon see.*

A harsh shout filled the hall followed by the sound of a cleaver striking meat, and Krowkr no longer sensed the yarl standing over him. Fascinated by the emergence of the *Reknpokaprooin*—the Rainbow Bridge that linked Mithgarthr to Osgarthr, he didn't even look. A dark form emerged from the *Reknpokaprooin*, but its shape confused Krowkr. It was male, not female. Neither Freya nor a Valkyrie. Not even Hel herself, come to claim his soul for a slight to the gods. As he watched, a man ran to this new figure and fell to his knees.

The sound of a frantic battle crashed through the hall, accompanied by snarls and growls from the *oolfhyethidn*. Krowkr tore his eyes away from the *Reknpokaprooin*, almost swooning from the motion of his head.

His brother, Owfastr, stood between him and the beast, blood flooding down to pool at his feet. Krowkr struggled to believe his eyes—that his brother not only still clung to the thread of life but had somehow found his feet and faced the great *oolfhyethidn,* driving the beast back, giving Krowkr a chance to gather his wits.

Krowkr's gaze darted toward the corner, but the beautiful pool of molten color had disappeared, and only shadows reigned. He peered into the darkness, demanding that his eyes discern the two man-like shapes, but he could see nothing.

He shook his head and glanced down at his wounds. They didn't look fatal though the massive blow to the head he'd taken might limit his chances of surviving the night. He drew a huge breath, willing the sweet air to fuel his muscles, to clear his thinking.

Owfastr kept his feet and with wild swings of his sword and judicious use of his shield was holding his own for the moment. *Where is Skatlakrimr?* Krowkr wondered. *He's no coward. He's seen battle, seen poor odds before, and still he has stood with us.*

Krowkr lurched to his feet, and his mind reeled. His stomach rebelled at the abrupt movement, but he kept his feet, and his hands tightened around the hilts of his weapons. He knew what his brother expected of him, and he slipped away into the shadows, leaving Owfastr to draw the beast's attacks. It was time for more cagey fighting.

Once in the cloaking shadows, Krowkr sprinted around the edges of the room. The *oolfhyethidn's* eyes remained locked on his brother's, and Krowkr dared to hope.

The yarl lunged toward Owfastr, quicker than the eye could follow, and slapped the Viking's shield away into the darkness at the edges of the room.

Owfastr glanced down before shaking the broken leather strap from his arm and taking his sword in a two-handed grip. The yarl laughed his preternatural laugh and lunged forward, one clawed hand high, one low, and his jaws gaping wide.

With a roar, Krowkr charged out of the darkness, chopping his axe into the yarl's ankle, and ramming his sword between the beast's ribs, burying it to the hilt.

The yarl looked at him in surprise and cried out, this time from pain rather than to mock their paltry efforts. He tried to side-step on the ankle Krowkr had maimed and howled in agony as he teetered and fell. Even as he fell, he lashed out at Krowkr.

Pain exploded across his belly, and it felt as though something was snaking out of his stomach, hooked like a fish on a line. He let go of the sword, leaving it buried in the beast's chest and clamped his hand to his gut. When his hand sank into a hot mush, he understood there was no hope. He would die that foul night, disemboweled by the immortal *oolfhyethidn*.

Owfastr cried out, and Krowkr met his gaze. Anguish etched his brother's face, but Krowkr smiled, calm, accepting. He jerked his chin toward the door.

Owfastr shook his head wildly.

Krowkr made the gesture a second time and spared his brother one last, long glance. He looked down at the snarling beast who was pulling his guts out and smiled as he imagined Veethar might smile at a foe. He took his axe in both hands and lifted it high over his head.

The yarl's eyes widened with fear, and Krowkr smiled. He swept the axe down with all his remaining might, praying to Owthidn that Owfastr was running for the hills. As the axe slammed into the dome of the *oolfhyethidn's* skull, he realized that the yarl wasn't afraid of him.

Oolfreekr's wide eyes were not on Krowkr, nor on Krowkr's axe. His gaze traced to something behind Krowkr.

His axe stuck fast in the yarl's skull, and with a weak shrug, Krowkr released his grip on it and half-turned, half-fell to the side. Agony screamed through him as more of his bowel snaked into the open air, but he didn't cry out. He couldn't—amazement had stolen his voice.

The yarl stared at another *oolfhyethidn*, this one covered in coarse brown fur. At the new beast's side stood Skatlakrimr, smiling an evil smile and holding his axe.

With a cry, Owfastr stumbled back into the fray, sword arcing toward this new *oolfhyethidn*. The beast barely glanced at him before he ripped Owfastr's throat out with a single swipe of his claws.

"No!" screamed Krowkr, but it was no use. Owfastr fell lifeless to the floor.

His brother was dead!

The brown *oolfhyethidn* spared him a second's glance and spoke a garbled word. His bones snapped as he shrank, his coarse, disgusting fur fell out in pustulant clumps. When human teeth had pushed the lupine fangs from his mouth, and his palate was human enough, the man spoke, "Oolfreekr, is what this karl tells me true?" He was tall and as thin as the yarl had been, and though pustules and sores also covered his skin, he looked healthier than the yarl.

The yarl turned his head away, the axe embedded in the crown of his head making the movement comical.

"Revert! Speak to me as a man, Oolfreekr."

The yarl made the same garbled noise as the other *oolfhyethidn* and began to change back to his human guise. The axe clattered from his skull as it shrank and the yarl kicked at it as would a petulant child.

"Did you, Oolfreekr, kill the others of the *Briethralak Oolfur*? Did you break your vows?"

"Yes!" croaked the yarl. "You lied to us, Luka. The *layth oolfsins* did not make us gods. It only made us petty, avaricious. It made us demons, not gods."

Luka shook his head and sucked his teeth. "You were always the philosopher. I knew I should have killed you at the start." The tall, blond man began to pace. "Now, when I need the *Briethralak Oolfur*, I find only you. Now, when I could use the support of my brother *oolfa*, I find only a broken old fool, a dead boy…" Luka's gaze tracked over to Krowkr and followed the ruins of his bowel as it snaked across the floor with his eyes. "Make that two dead boys, and an eager young whelp who knows only that he wants what I offer." Luka's gaze crawled back to the yarl's, and his disgust and displeasure were evident in the gaze. "I should have killed you and eaten your heart."

"We tried, Lord Luka," said Skatlakrimr. "We came prepared for the ritual. We asked Yarl Oolfreekr to teach us, but he attacked us instead. He—"

Luka's lips twitched into a mean smile. "Ritual? Who told you there was a ritual?" Luka threw back his head and laughed. "If you have the blood, lad, all you need to do is eat!"

"Eat, Lord?" asked Skatlakrimr, a worried expression dancing on his face.

"Yes! Begin with this one," said Luka, kicking Owfastr's dead foot.

Skatlakrimr's face became a writhing mask of emotions: terror, disgust, avarice, wonder. "But...but Owfastr... I've known him since we were boys, Lord."

Luka shrugged. "He's not using his flesh any longer, surely he wouldn't begrudge you a meal." When Skatlakrimr's face twitched into a grimace, Luka's expression darkened. "What was it you said minutes ago? Oh, yes! 'Anything, Lord Luka! I will do anything you ask to learn *layth oolfsins*! Let me serve you, Lord.' That was what you said, no?"

Skatlakrimr nodded, but his expression didn't change.

"Oh, very well," snapped Luka. "Start with this one, then." This time he kicked Krowkr's foot. "He's not even dead, yet. Can't get any fresher than that!"

"Lord, I..."

"You begin to annoy me... What did you say your name was?"

"Skatlakrimr, Lord. Forgive me. This is all so...it's so much to take in."

Luka squinted at him but shrugged. "Yes, I guess it must be. Did you grow up with this old wretch, too?" he asked, kicking Oolfreekr's foot.

Skatlakrimr sighed with relief. "No, Lord Luka. For him, I have nothing but contempt. To give up such a gift is…is—"

"Yes, yes," said Luka.

Oolfreekr snarled up at him. "Am I to be an endless smorgasbord? A walking dinner?"

"Who said anything about immortality, Oolfreekr?" crooned Luka.

"Am I not *oolfur*?"

Luka shook his head. "You gave up the right to that title when you turned on your brothers. Now, you are nothing but cattle." He pointed a long finger at Oolfreekr. "*Tayia*!" he commanded, and the old yarl gasped and died.

Luka slapped Skatlakrimr on the back. "Take a haunch from his old corpse," he said. "No time like the present."

As Skatlakrimr strode forward, his hand wrapping his axe in a tight grip, Krowkr closed his eyes and pretended he couldn't hear his boyhood friend butchering the dead old man beside him.

"What about him?" asked Luka. "Shall I dispatch him, as well?"

"Lord, if… Lord Luka, I'd rather you didn't. I'd prefer to think that Krowkr may survive, no matter the state of his wounds."

"Such a compassionate soul," Luka mocked. "We must rid you of that if you are to become the new leader of the *Briethralak Oolfur*."

"Yes, Lord," said Skatlakrimr, and Krowkr could have sworn he was gloating. Krowkr shuddered and gave up his grip on consciousness.

TWENTY

The memory faded from my mind. Krowkr took one glance at my expression and averted his gaze. I shook my head. "Seems you might have left out a few salient points about what brought you to Yarl Oolfreekr's place, Krowkr."

His throat worked, and he nodded, but he didn't raise his eyes, and he didn't speak.

"What do you mean?" asked Jane. "What happened?"

"We'll get into it later...after we get indoors, but let's say it didn't happen *exactly* as Krowkr told the tale." Behind me, the garage door opener whirred to life, and a black SUV backed out into the circle. "We might have missed our chance." I turned to walk through the backyard, meaning to flag the SUV down, but Jane grabbed my arm.

"No, Hank. Let the car go. It's better if the house is empty."

"Okay, but I don't know how I feel about breaking into my own house."

"If it's still ours, it's hardly breaking in, is it?" Once the SUV had burbled off down the street, Jane nodded. "Now, go to the door and ring the bell. If no one answers, we'll go in."

"Okay," I said. "Everyone stays here. If no one answers, and if my key still fits the lock, I'll let you in from the deck." I turned and fixed the puppies with my sternest stare. "You two, *stay here*."

They wagged their tails and tilted their heads to opposite sides.

I walked out of the woods and skirted around to the front of the house. It was early morning, so there wasn't much activity in the *cul-de-sac*. The *slowthar* of several people meshed and intertwined on the driveway and front walk, and I recognized that one of them was Sig's without thinking about it. Another was Jane's. At the same time, though, something felt off.

None of the *slowthar* were mine.

The planting beds were different, and someone had added a flagstone walk between the driveway and the front porch. I walked up, bold and brash, and rang the bell.

I don't know what I was expecting, but I wasn't expecting Sig to answer the door. A taller and more filled out version of Sig. An *older* Sig.

"Can I help you?" he asked in an adult-sounding voice.

"Uh… Yes. Er, is your father home?"

He looked me over with a critical eye. "Excuse me for being blunt, but are you a salesman?"

"No."

"Political activist? Missionary?"

"No, neither of those."

"Hmm," he said, crossing his arms and leaning against the door frame. "Maybe you should tell me what you really want."

"I need to speak with your father. That's all."

He shook his head. "I don't think so."

I had to hide a grin. His voice sounded like a good imitation of what I called my Cop-voice. I glanced around, peering past him into the house. "I…"

"No, I don't think so," he repeated. "You should move on. My dad was with the NYSP, and you'd better believe we still have friends there. You know, at the barracks over by the library."

I nodded. "Yes. I'm not here to cause trouble, S—" I bit off his name, but by the way his eyes sharped on mine, he knew what I'd been about to say.

"Do I know you?" he asked.

"No, we've never met." '*Was*' he'd said. *My dad was with the NYSP.* A chill ran down my spine. Even so, the curse Hel laid on me had disabled me and ruined my career with the same agency. "I didn't mean to cause trouble. Sorry to have bothered you." I turned and walked back down the walk.

Sig watched me go, his face flinty, eyes sharp.

When I reached the driveway, he turned and went back inside, closing the door with a thump. I waited a moment, then walked to the other side of the drive where I couldn't be seen from any of the windows along the front of the house.

I walked back toward the house and alongside the garage to where there were two windows. Inside the garage was a dust-covered truck that appeared not to have moved in ages, but it wasn't *my* truck. It was the wrong color.

I turned and walked back to the street and headed up the block. Once I turned the corner, I snaked through one of the neighbor's yards and into the woods. I made my way back to the others, letting the image of Krowkr slough from my body.

"What's wrong?" asked Jane the second she could see my face.

"Turns out that in this *klith*, your butt *is* that big."

She paled a little, but both Keri and Fretyi's ears perked up, and they came to their feet, staring into the woods behind me with their ears perked and twitching.

"Oh, no," I murmured.

"*Dad?*" The bigger, older version of our son burst into the clearing, his eyes wide with shock. "Is that really you?"

My back was to him. *Too late for a disguise*, I thought.

Jane's eyes were wide, and she took a step toward the boy.

"Mom? What are you doing here? You said you had a meeting at work?"

Her mouth opened, then closed, and she shook her head.

"Dad?" he asked again, his voice plaintive.

I sighed and turned to face him.

"*Where have you been?*" He was suddenly furious, and tears streamed down his cheeks.

"Listen, Sig—"

"Sig? Why are you calling me Sig? No one has called me Sig since I was eight! Have you forgotten?"

I glanced at Jane sidelong, but she only shook her head, her eyes glued to the boy's face. "What should I call you?"

"Has it been so long you've forgotten my name?"

How could I have missed that before? How could I have missed that little fact in his *slowth*? Then again, I hadn't given it more than a cursory glance. I fought to keep the sigh in but failed. "There's something I have to explain."

"More than one thing!" he snapped.

"Lad," said Althyof, gently. "This isn't your father."

The boy's gaze zipped to the Tverkr's strangely shaped body, then to Yowtgayrr, then to me, then to Jane. "Get away from them, Mom."

"Listen," she said. "Just listen for a second."

His gaze slipped back to Althyof. "Why did you say he isn't my father?"

The Tverkr shrugged. "Because he isn't. He has a son that looks exactly like you, although younger by a few years. His son is named Sigurd."

His eyes traveled the group, pausing on our arms and armor, tracking to the pistol belt Prokkr had designed for me, up to my face, lingering on my empty left eye socket, to the floppy hat, back to Jane, and then down at Keri and Fretyi, where his gaze froze. The pups stood wagging their tails, heads cocked to the side. Keri yipped at him and took a step forward. "What are those?" the boy demanded.

"Those are *varkr* puppies. They are very fond of my son," I said with a calmness I didn't feel.

"*I'm* your son!" His eyes snapped up to mine, filled with confusion and anger.

"No," I said. "I'm not your father, though I must look an awful lot like the man."

He shook his head and turned to Jane. "Why's he doing this, Mom?"

Tears filled Jane's eyes. "Your mother is at work. This isn't a trick. This isn't a lie. We are not who you think we are."

"Well, who the fuh—who are you?" he demanded.

"My name is Hank Jensen, and this is my wife, Jane."

"Hank? *Jensen*?" The boy turned to Jane. "*Jane*? That's mom's middle name, and you never went by Hank. You used *your* middle name: Sigurd. *Our* middle name."

"What's your name?" I asked.

He smiled sourly. "*My* name is Henry. Henry Sigurd Vasvik."

I nodded. "That's the name of the town my paternal great-grandfather came from. Vasvik, Norway."

"Norway? Don't you mean Daneland?"

I shook my head. "Not where I'm from. When Napoleon suffered defeat, the Congress of Vienna dictated the Dano-Norwegian union."

"When was Emperor Bonaparte defeated?"

"Early eighteen-hundreds."

Henry shook his head. "No. The Danes defeated the Prussians that year, and Napoleon drove the British out of France."

"Not where I'm from," I said again.

"You keep saying that! *This* is where you are from!" He swept his arms wide. "You know…Penfield, New Avignon!"

"New Avignon," Jane mused. "France."

I smiled. "In my home, Penfield is in a state called New York. The British settled the whole area."

"The *British*?" he scoffed. "Emperor Bonaparte ended their aspirations of colonization in 1823 when he drove King George into the North Sea."

I shook my head. "So much is different, yet so much is the same," I said, staring at Henry.

"What year is it?" Jane asked.

"What year…" Henry let a breath gust out of him. "Has everyone gone insane?"

"We left our home in 2017," I said.

"2017? You disappeared in 2010 while you were working on a case. Your partner, Jack, was—"

"Is Jax alive?" I blurted.

Jane rested her hand on my arm. "Not *Jax*. He said Jack."

Henry watched the exchange through narrowed eyelids. "It's November 12th, 2020," he said at last. He stared me in the eye. "Do you know where *my* father is?"

"I'm sorry, Henry, but I don't."

"Maybe the same people that…that did whatever they did to you, did the same thing to him."

"It's possible," I said. "In 2010, I worked a serial case. The perps were cannibals, and…and more than that. They were… This will sound crazy, okay, but it's true."

"Yeah, because the rest of it sounds so sane."

"Got me there. The perps were the people that inspired the Loki and Hel mythologies in Norse sagas. We've spent the last year fighting them in Osgarthr, and—"

"Yeah, you were right. It sounds crazy."

I nodded, smiling. "It does. Hel cursed me back in 2010, and the curse disabled me while they made their getaway. In 2017, they came back and kidnapped Jane here, and our son—"

"On Halloween."

"—on Halloween." I glanced at Jane and winked. "You owe me a coke." I turned back to Henry. "They left me a message that I had to follow them, and I did."

"They could've tricked my dad into doing the same thing."

I shrugged. "I can't say for sure, but I doubt it was the same people."

"Maybe not. Maybe it was my universe's version of Hel and Loki."

"*Your* universe?"

"Hey," he said. "I read science fiction as much as the next guy."

I scratched my head and shrugged. "I don't know the answer, this is the first time I've seen…well, *doubles* of people. I've never given the possibility of multiple versions of Hel or Luka any thought."

"And none of it matters," said Jane. "Henry, look at me."

He turned his gaze to her. "You *could* be our son, and we *could* be your parents, and if we were, we would love you to the ends of the earth, same as your *real* parents do. But we are not your parents. And we have to leave, never to return."

His eyes found mine, and they filled with tears. "But…"

"Listen, Henry. Your dad would want you to take care of your mother, to always do your best, and to live an honorable life. He'd want you to succeed, to fall in love with a pretty girl or handsome guy, settle down, and have a family. He'd want you to go on with living your life."

"How…how do you know? You're not him."

"No, I'm not him, but those are things I want for Sig. And if I *were* your dad, and something happened to me, that's what I would want for you." He sobbed, standing there looking forlorn, and my heart broke for him. "It's okay, Henry," I said. "It's okay to grieve for your dad, and there's hope—as long as there is no body, there is hope that he's still alive."

"After all this time?" He sniffled and rubbed a hand across his eyes. "If you were a trooper, same as my dad, you know the probabilities of that."

"Yes, even after all this time," I said firmly. "We met a guy a few days ago who was taken from the 1790s. Over there, we live a long time, and since your dad and I may share the same genes, it could be true for him as well."

"Okay. I want to go with you."

I shook my head. "Think about what I said to you, Sig—"

"Henry."

"—and consider your mother. What would she think?"

"I could call her. I could get her to come home, and she could go with us!"

"Henry, if I knew where your father was, I'd go get him and bring him to you, but—"

"Henry," said Jane. "Your place is here, with your mother."

"Would you say that if I were *your* son and I could bring this guy back to you?" he asked, hooking his thumb at me.

"Yes," she said firmly. "This guy can take care of himself. Were you grown, maybe I'd answer differently, but you aren't."

His face reddened. "Can you stop me from following you?"

"Yes, I *can*," I said. "But I wouldn't want to. I'd rather convince you to stay."

He shook his head and wouldn't meet my eye.

"I know you miss him, Henry. You want to save him, to rescue him, but believe me when I say you are out of your depth here. *I'm* out of my depth, but I have no choice, I'm already in it up to my neck. I'll make you a deal, though: if you stay here, help your mom, and do all those things your dad would want you to do, if I can find him, I will bring your dad home to you. Deal?"

"That sounds like something *he* would say."

"Yeah, well… Great minds and all that."

He glanced at the others before meeting my eye. "How long?"

I lifted my shoulders and let them fall. "How long for what?"

"How long do I have to wait? Before I can go looking myself?"

"There's no way you'll be—"

"Until we come back," said Jane. "I don't know how long it will be, but Hank here seems to be able to do some pretty fireworks with the *preer* now. Once we've finished what we have to do, if we haven't already come across your father, we will look into his disappearance and come back to tell you what we've found."

I looked at her askance, eyebrows arched. She nodded, but at Henry, not at me.

"You can believe me, Henry, same as you would trust your own mom."

"Okay," he said in a quiet voice.

"Then it's time to head back home," I said. "I hope our son is as level-headed as you are when he reaches seventeen."

He nodded and turned but didn't walk away. Instead, he spun back and rushed over to envelop me in a huge hug. After the initial shock, I hugged him back.

Hard, the way Sig always wanted to be hugged.

As we stood there hugging one another, golden runes skittered across my vision, and that strange, yet familiar, voice spoke in my head again. I knew what I had to do.

When he stepped back, tears streaming down his face, I held him by the shoulders. "Want to see a magic trick?"

"Yeah," he said, trying for a smile, coming up with a grimace, instead.

I lifted my hand and put my index finger in the center of his forehead. "*Svepn*," I said, and he sagged into my arms.

"What are you doing?" demanded Jane.

"I can make him forget us."

"Steal his memory?"

I shrugged. "Yes. Isn't it better that way?"

"I…" She shook her head and made a helpless gesture. "Were you going to do this no matter what he said?"

"Isn't it for the best? But no, I just remembered the *triblinkr* for this."

"Isn't that convenient… Is what you want to do to him any different than what the Great Old Ones and Kuhntul have been doing to you?"

That barb sank home, and something turned over in my guts. "He doesn't deserve to live his life wondering when we will come back. What if we never can? What if I can't find our way back here?"

"For his own good, is it? Bet the Great Old Ones say the same thing about you." She released her breath in a gust and looked down at Henry's sleeping face. "Just do it," she said and turned away, "but leave him some of the hope."

"If I might?" said Yowtgayrr.

I nodded.

"A dream might offer hope, and yet not interfere with the young man's life."

"Do it that way," mumbled Jane in a teary voice.

And I did, though it felt as if I was betraying Sig every second it took to complete the job.

TWENTY-
ONE

W e traipsed back to the *proo*, no one speaking. I tried to keep my mind occupied by looking at all the psychic tracks—the *slowthar*—that romped through the woods. Most of them were teenagers in search of the perfect make-out spot.

"Do you see him?" asked Althyof.

"Who? Henry?"

"No, Luka."

I lifted my gaze and peered into the distance, turning a full circle. "No, but that means nothing. Maybe distance is a factor. It could be that in the years since—"

"The boy's pain is deep. It's a tragedy to lose a father so early in life," said Althyof.

"But…"

"But we have a job to do. Is it sad? Yes. Do I empathize with the lad? Yes, I do. Is there anything I can do for him? No."

Jane looked behind us wistfully.

"He has his own you," I whispered to her.

"Yeah," she breathed. "Doesn't help much, does it?"

I shook my head. "Not at all."

"We've lost Luka, haven't we?"

"He's lost us," I said, with a shake of my head. "If I can track him in any given *klith*, I should be able to track him between, right?" I looked at Althyof and Yowtgayrr in turn, but both Tverkr and Alf shrugged.

"You can try," said Jane.

"What if more than one of him exists in the multiverse? Or what if I can't distinguish between the timeline versions of him?"

"Then the search will be a long one," said Yowtgayrr with a subtle grin.

"We should go back to Niflhaymr, the last place we *know* the right Luka has been."

Jane waved her hand at the *proo*. "Do your thing. But make sure you move this *proo* when you're done. I don't want Henry waking up and stumbling across it."

I reached for the *proo's* hook, as Bikkir called the knobby projection, and fixed the room containing the *proo* we'd used in Vefsterkur's hall in my mind, and this time, I included the image of us leaving moments before. *If these damn things can bend time, I've got to learn how to use that feature.* When the psychic disturbance that went with moving the *proo* had subsided, I nodded at the others and touched the *proo's* surface.

Again, there was no sense of travel time. That's another thing I need to work out, I thought. I need the ability to contact the Great Old Ones when I need to, not just when they want me.

The room was as we'd left it, and I even detected Jane's scent in the cold air. I stepped away from the *proo* and took a moment to move the other end of the *proo* back to the beach near Roanoke. I examined the *slowthar* that covered the floor like a psychedelic carpet.

My *slowth* was easy to pick out, as was Jane's, but when I looked at another person's *slowth,* I had to fight the urge to follow the memories floating in them. It felt…well, it felt like an invasion of privacy, but more than that, the power of it…the power of sifting through someone's mind had a certain…*addictive*…appeal.

But still, without examining the *slowthar* in detail, I'd never understand who they belonged to. But getting a sense of the physicality of the individual: height and weight was easy. Their self-image, perhaps.

That helped—at least I didn't spend a bunch of time trying to track Yowtgayrr or a random female frost giant. Gazing around, focusing on racial type and height alone, I found the *slowthar* of another male Isir.

"I think I have him," I said. "I've got to look deeper to make sure it's the *right* Luka, though."

"Are you sure this is the right Niflhaymr?" asked Jane.

"Yes. I cut the *proo* back through time to the point right after we departed. I could still catch a whiff of your hair when I arrived."

"Oh. Well, I hope that's a good thing."

"As I am contractually obligated to say, you are perfect, dear, and so is your hair's scent."

"Aren't you also contractually obligated to wash my dirty socks?"

"Let's not get all crazy. Let's not get all carried away with the joy of my success as a psychic bloodhound."

"Speaking of that," said Althyof. "Can we get back to it?"

"Yeah." I turned back to the *slowthar* and focused on the one that belonged to an Isir male that wasn't me. I skimmed its surface, and without meaning to, I thought about the events that had taken place on Roanoke Island, about how easy it had been to *be* there as the events unrolled. Luka was always so devoted to Hel... He seemed oblivious to how she used him, how she treated him. Everyone knew love was blind, but even so, his devotion to her had always struck me as so…excessive.

I dipped into the *slowthar*—and that was the sensation of it: dipping my cupped hand into a stream of running water—and tasted the first memory I encountered.

I grimaced. "It's Luka, all right."

"You can track him?" asked Jane.

I meant to answer her, but a set of images in the stream drew my complete attention—images depicting Hel in a rage…

TWENTY-
TWO

The queen fumed, fury wafting off her like the shimmer of heat from desert sand. She paced back and forth—a tigress testing the limits of her cage.

"My Queen," he said. "Come and rest. There's nothing we can do—"

"Don't you think I *know* that, Luka?" she snapped, whirling to face him. "Hadn't you considered that I *know* we've lost this war?" She flung her hands up and out, toward the besieged city gates. "Can I not hear the assault on my gates? Do I not know my army lies broken on the plains beyond?"

"I didn't mean to—"

"No," she sneered. "No one ever does, and yet here we are." She stomped her foot. "Where is the damn smith? Has he overcome his natural stupidity?"

"I'll go see, my Queen," said Luka. He left the throne room, barely keeping his sigh a quiet one. Unhappy bitterness seemed to govern Suel's moods these days—ever since Meuhlnir and his ilk had split away in open rebellion. *That would upset anyone*, he thought. *But she seems upset by more than that*. He strode through the halls, his long legs carrying him at a rapid pace to the smithy he'd had built near the dungeons.

Vuhluntr was a proud man, but the queen would have her bespoke sword, and Luka was going to get it for her, even it if meant Vuhluntr died on its completion.

He reached Vuhluntr's cell and rattled the bars with both hands. The smith was *sleeping*! Anger burned in Luka's veins akin to Greek fire atop water: unquenchable, unstoppable. "*Get up*!" he screamed.

Vuhluntr rolled to face him, his face slack, serene. "What is it?"

"The sword! Have you finished it?"

Vuhluntr yawned and blew a raspberry. "My marriage? Has it happened?"

Luka scoffed. "That ship has sailed, *Master* Smith. Around the same time I hamstrung you and gifted you with those scars on your back for your . impertinence."

Vuhluntr shrugged. "And yet you demand what I was to give you as if the deal is still in force." He swung his legs out of bed and sat up, glaring at Luka. "It *isn't*!" he hissed. "I will fulfill no part of the previous deal, but remember you and *she* broke the terms!"

"Is it so?" asked Luka in a deceptively mild voice. "You would have us wed Freya to you against her wishes? You would have a wedding night by rape?"

Vuhluntr scoffed. "She would have done her duty if her sister *truly* desired it. But the queen didn't, did she? She promised whatever I asked, hoping I would complete the sword before I discovered her deception."

Luka smiled, but it felt ugly on his lips. He snapped his fingers at the guard, and with the cell door unlocked, swept inside and grabbed Vuhluntr by the jaw, lifting the brute of a man off his small cot without effort. "Banter." Luka spat onto the filthy floor. "Negotiations have ended."

"Is that what we were doing?" mused Vuhluntr.

"Now is the time for *work*, Smith. She will have her sword. You *will* forge that sword, and you will finish it *tonight*."

Vuhluntr hung limply from Luka's one-handed grip. "No, I don't think I will."

Luka pulled the man's face close to his. "There are worse things than being hamstrung and jilted."

"Many, I'm sure," murmured Vuhluntr. "But none of them will force me to forge a great work for your queen."

"*My* queen? She's *your* queen as well, worm!" Luka's anger took hold of him, and he dashed the smith to the cobbled floor. His boot arced out and connected with Vuhluntr's belly. "You will forge the sword," he hissed. "You will do it tonight, or I will serve you to the queen for breakfast."

The icy calm had burned off Vuhluntr's face, and fear crept into its place. "You… You wouldn't dare break the *Ayn Loug*."

Luka grinned a lupine grin. "Have you not heard, Vuhluntr?"

"Huh-heard what?"

"*Oolfur*," whispered Luka, and his grin stretched wider. The *prayteenk* dug its claws into his flesh, but it was almost pleasurable now. He arched his back against the pain caused by the rapid growth of his bones. He grimaced as fangs pushed his human teeth from his jaw, and he slurped his own blood as if it were a fine wine. His perspective changed: Vuhluntr was smaller, farther away; he had to bend forward and still his back scraped against the cell's ceiling, his arms felt long and spindly, but the claws at the ends of his fingers felt perfect. He traced the edge of Vuhluntr's jaw with one cold talon, leaving a slick trail of blood in its wake.

The feeling of the *oolfur* form struck him as tantamount to godhood—*real* godhood. Powerful beyond measure, an unstoppable force dedicated to the queen's service. With a bark-like grunt, he snatched Vuhluntr's ankle and dragged him to the smithy, flinging him toward the anvil. One-handed, he scooped up what would be a double-shovelful of fuel for the forge and slapped it into the combustion chamber.

With a snarl, he jerked Vuhluntr to his feet and shoved him toward his Tverkar-forged smithing tools. Luka pointed at the mound of coal and forced the word "*predna*" through his tortured throat. Flame leapt toward the ceiling but died back almost before the sound of the word had faded from the air.

Vuhluntr wiped his hand across his bloody face, wincing when he brushed against his nose. "Why do you do this?" he asked. "Why do you go to such lengths?"

Luka growled deep in his chest. He didn't want to answer such questions, especially not when asked by a peasant such as Vuhluntr. He didn't even want to *remember* what he'd already done for her, let alone what he *would* do. What he felt for Queen Suel…the power of his feelings overshadowed everything else in his life. Her happiness defined his life now, everything else was inconsequential.

Vuhluntr shrugged and picked up a lump of iron, scrutinizing it. He slid the metal into the hottest part of the fire. "Not much to do until that gets hot," he muttered, darting a glance up at Luka's mongrel face. He flopped a hand in Luka's direction. "You've made your point. You could at least offer me some conversation."

Luka snarled, but truth to tell, being fifteen feet tall inside a place built for humans lacked certain comforts. "*Mathur*," he growled and prepared himself to suffer through the *prayteenk* for the second time in ten minutes.

Vuhluntr watched him change, his eyes darting back and forth from Luka's face to his snapping joints, to the pile of wolf fangs accumulating at his feet. "How can you stand that?" he asked.

Luka grunted. "Each change takes a significant amount of energy. I grow hungry, Smith." He cast a baleful, meaningful glance at Vuhluntr. "If I have to make another change soon, I might not wish to control my hunger."

Vuhluntr blenched and took a half-step back, but an expression of bravado settled onto his features in place of the blanch. "You can't kill me, sir. Who would make your precious sword if you did?"

Luka let a wolfish smile crack his face and a ferocious light burn in his eyes. "I don't have to kill when I dine." He chuckled as Vuhluntr paled even more and pointed at the man's left thigh. "For example, it strikes me that with a stool, you could work metal without the benefit of that leg."

Vuhluntr turned away and made a show of checking the fire and the lump of iron inside it. He strode around to the opposite side of the forge and pumped one of the twin bellows-bags with each hand in an alternating rhythm. "I'm rather fond of my limbs," he said without meeting Luka's gaze.

"And I'm rather found of Queen Suel's happiness," grated Luka. "See to it we are both pleased with your results."

"Did you know the attack on the city would happen with such speed?"

Luka shook his head. "She misled us—the woman you wanted to marry."

"And how is the beautiful Freya?"

"Suffering for her deception."

Vuhluntr met his gaze at last. "I hope you will not allow the marring of her beauty?"

Luka smiled crookedly. "Still interested? After all this?"

Vuhluntr shrugged. "I've never begrudged forging the queen a sword as she describes. I love the work. This is a payment dispute, and that's all."

"A payment dispute," chuckled Luka. "Make sure your work pleases us and perhaps something will be worked out. The queen is less...*interested*...in what her sister wants at this time."

Vuhluntr nodded and checked the lump of now glowing iron again. "Almost ready to begin," he said.

Luka nodded, but his mind had already turned from the conversation. It didn't interest him much, outside of being a way to add a touch of happiness to the queen's life. He tried to recall the point when Suel's mood had changed for the worst. Her personality had taken on a darker cast, ever since the initial conversations between Luka, Suel, and Vowli that had led to the breaking of the *Ayn Loug*, but her mood had remained positive until sometime during the war.

At the start of the war, she'd been the same mischievous, fun woman. The pranks they'd played—on Vowli, on Meuhlnir, on the rebels...they had shown the queen's underlying happiness in a lousy situation. But those teasing moments had grown fewer and fewer and had stopped altogether at some point, and Luka had missed the reason.

"...does she want it that way? The design seems so...so *specific.*"

"What?" Luka shook his head. "Oh. A Svartalf *runekastari* named Ivalti provided the description. He will enchant the blade after you've finished. She told him what she wanted, and he told her what it would take."

"And what was it she wanted this blade to do?"

Luka narrowed his eyes at the smith and pursed his lips. "Why should I discuss the queen's wants with you?"

Vuhluntr shrugged. "You needn't. But as a craftsman, it might help me ensure the success of the blade if I understand its intended uses."

Luka grinned and glanced down at the flames. "This war tears our land apart. Divides our people. Over what? Over an ancient law the purpose—the very *meaning*—of which has been lost over the centuries. The two armies equal one another in all essential aspects, being as they are, made up of close to equal numbers of Isir and complementary armies of the other races." Luka looked at the man shrewdly.

"I'll tell you something only the queen's most trusted advisors know. But I warn you, Vuhluntr! No one knows this, so if it gets out, I will know where the leak is, and I will plug that leak."

Vuhluntr nodded.

"We can't beat them." Luka laughed at Vuhluntr's expression. "It's okay, though. They can't beat us, either. It's a stalemate, but a stalemate that will drive this culture to ruins, exhausting Osgarthr's resources, driving the Isir race to near extinction." Luka paused and sucked in a breath. *Could that be it? Could the moment Suel realized we were dooming the Isir by fighting this war be the moment where the dark bitterness began to fester?*

"Ah," said Vuhluntr. "It's ready." He withdrew the lump of glowing iron from the fire using long silvery tongs that almost glowed in the firelight. Holding the lump still, he thwacked it with a hammer made from the same shiny metal as the tongs. Sparks flew, and the iron morphed, to take on a smoother, more blade-like shape. Even after only one blow of the smith's hammer, the lump was less of a lump and more of a rough blade shape. "You were saying?"

"A dilemma faces the queen—one that has no answer: allow the dissidents to do as they please, lock the Isir into a pointless conflict that will only culminate when no more Isir remain to fight, or abdicate her throne and allow everything she's built to fall to ruin."

"Yes," muttered Vuhluntr as he drove the silvery hammer into the iron once more. "But how will the sword help?"

Luka chuckled. "I'd thought that part would be obvious."

The smith shrugged.

"Here's a hint: we will name the sword Kramr."

Again, the smith shrugged.

"Ah," breathed Luka. "Sometimes I forget you karls don't learn the *Gamla Toonkumowl*. The name means 'wrath.'"

"I see," said Vuhluntr as he rained hammer blows down on the iron, whose shape was becoming that of a fine longsword with a rapidity that amazed Luka.

"I will use it to decapitate the rebel snake. With it, I will kill my brother, Meuhlnir."

Vuhluntr's gaze darted up to Luka's face before slipping back down to his work.

"That should upset me?" snarled Luka.

"No. I care nothing about such things, Lord. I'm here to forge a sword, not to comment on its use."

"Is that so?" snapped Luka. Why does this man infuriate me? he asked himself. Why should I care what he thinks? He's a karl for Isi's sake, and a mercenary one at that...selling his skills to whoever will pay him the most.

"Yarl Luka," said the smith between hammer blows, "I make weapons of war. Weapons for taking lives. I've made weapons for assassins, for generals, for kings and queens. I *know* what my work facilitates. If it bothered me, I'd make jewelry."

Luka scoffed and turned away, but the man's words made sense. *Why does it seem everyone is judging me in this? Am I to live forever in the shadow of Paltr's death? Forever known as no better than a fratricide?* He shook his head. *Does anyone think that except me?*

Behind him, the hammer blows continued to ring on the iron lump. Vuhluntr's breath rasped in his throat. "You work fast, once you start," said Luka.

"Indeed," gasped the smith. "I must work while the ore is suitably malleable. That's a secret few master smiths will utter." The hammer blows stopped, and the iron rasped as it slid back into the grate holding the fire. "Many smiths of lesser quality push the limits of malleability, but the Tverkar taught me it's better to reheat more often than to gain a few extra hammer blows on increasingly brittle metal."

"Indeed?"

"Yes. The trick to evaluating a smith—even before you've seen his finished product—is to assess the color of the glow left in the ore when he returns it to the fire. It should be the color of old blood. Anything else and the smith is less than a master to my eye. Red, the metal is still hot enough to work. No glow left, and the metal is far too cool and will yield a more brittle product."

"What color was the iron when you returned it to the fire?"

"Blood red, of course."

"Of course," murmured Luka. "How long?"

"Until I'm finished?" asked the smith.

"Yes, until you finish your work." Luka turned back to the smith so he could watch his expression.

The smith shrugged. "It goes well. I will finish the rough shape of the blade with this subsequent heating. I will form the tang, as well. The heating after that will yield a folded, sharper blade. Do you have the material for the crossbar? If I heat it now, I can work it while the blade regains color."

Luka grunted. "You make it sound as if you will finish this tonight."

Vuhluntr nodded. "I will, except for polishing the blade and adding the gold inlays."

"Why lay up in the dungeon for weeks if you could have finished the sword in a day or two?"

The smith smiled. "My Tverkr master taught me to never work if the payment was in dispute. It's a policy that has served me well in the past."

Luka turned cold, merciless eyes on the smith's face. "Do we need to discuss that again?"

"No, Yarl," said Vuhluntr. "We will proceed knowing that the Lady Freya is again within these walls and that the queen is less…*tolerant*…of her sister's views on marriage."

"Very well," said Luka. "Finish your work." He motioned for a guard to take his place and left the smithy behind, long legs consuming the distance between the dungeon and the palace proper in the space of a few breaths. *This will please Suel,* he thought.

TWENTY-
THREE

The memory left me a little shaken, to be honest. I wasn't used to thinking of Luka as a man swayed by his emotions—except maybe his rage. That worry about Hel would so consume Luka shocked me a little. That he felt pangs of guilt about the murder of Paltr, and about the plan to murder Meuhlnir. "Strange," I muttered.

"What's that, Hank?" asked Jane. "You woolgathering again?"

"No, I got… One of Luka's memories swept me away there for a minute, as one of Krowkr's did back in the other Penfield."

"Speaking of which…" said Althyof.

"Krowkr will explain what he left out of the tale he told us back at Hoos Oolfsins." My eye burned as it tracked to Krowkr's gaze. "Isn't that correct?"

Krowkr gulped and nodded. "I didn't mean to…to…"

"And yet you told us a lie by omission, did you not?" I demanded, using the tone I reserved for getting the truth from Sig.

"I…" Krowkr drew himself up and pushed his shoulders back. "I did, Lord Hanki—Hank." He turned and bowed to Jane, then Yowtgayrr, and finally to Althyof. "I am not proud of our reasons for seeking Yarl Oolfreekr out. The idea of becoming *oolfur streethsmathur* attracted Skatlakrimr and my brother. They wanted to rekindle the *Briethralak Oolfur*."

Althyof's face scrunched in on itself. "Indeed?"

Krowkr blushed at the scorn in the Tverkr's voice but nodded and turned his head away.

"Yes," said Yowtgayrr in a soft voice. "Mistakes are easy to make under such circumstances."

Althyof grumbled something into his beard.

"We can talk about each other's mistakes later," said Jane.

Krowkr flashed her a look of gratitude—of *worshipful* gratitude. "Thank you, my lady," he said and bowed.

"Yes, well, I hope you realize the depth of your stupidity," said Althyof.

Jane glared at the Tverkr. "Right now, our focus is making sure my son and our friends are safe from Luka."

An awkward moment stretched itself out, and I cleared my throat. "This *is* the *slowth* of the right Luka. *Our* Luka."

"Good. Can you track him through the *preer*?" asked Althyof, turning away from Krowkr.

"I haven't tried that yet. I got…" I shook my head. "I got caught in one of Luka's memories."

Althyof's lips twisted in a moue, and he looked at me through narrowed eyes. "Is that so?"

"Yeah. It was… Have you heard of a man named Vuhluntr? A karl, I think."

"*Him*," sneered Althyof. "Yes, I've run across the bastard. Gives good Tverkar a bad name."

"I thought he was a karl? From Osgarthr."

"He was, but he learned his craft from the Tverkar, and his actions reflect badly."

I waved that away. "And this sword he made for Hel? Kramr, Luka called it? Have you heard of it, too?"

Althyof made a disgusted noise, and Yowtgayrr's expression wrinkled.

"I guess you have. The memory I experienced was of Luka forcing Vuhluntr to work on the sword. The sword the Dark Queen commissioned to kill Meuhlnir."

"Yes," said Yowtgayrr softly. "They never used it for its intended purpose."

"Obviously!" snapped Althyof.

"What happened to it?"

Yowtgayrr shrugged. "No one knows. Well, I suppose one person knows, but no one knows who that person is. It disappeared in the Battle of Suelhaym after Vuhluntr used it to rend the North Gate."

"Wait… *Vuhluntr* opened the gates?"

Althyof shook his head. "Vuhluntr merely held the hilt. Kramr sliced through the massive hinge at the top of the right gate. The bastard used the friction of the blade's passage through the hinge to slow his leap from the top of the wall. The damage caused that gate to slam into the ground, and to buckle the hinges of the other gate. After that, it was only a matter of pouring power into those hinges and ripping the gate out of the way."

"I'm confused," said Jane. "You seem to dislike this Vuhluntr guy—more than a little—but it sounds as though he handed you Suelhaym."

Althyof nodded. "Both ideas are accurate."

"His reasons for doing what he did are the distasteful part," said Yowtgayrr.

"The coward was running from Luka when he destroyed the hinge," said Althyof. "He didn't care a whit about the war. He didn't care which side won out. He only cared about being paid for his services, and everything else be damned."

"Yeah, I got that feeling about him from Luka's memory."

"We should speak on this newfound ability to sift through another's memories," muttered Althyof.

"Yeah, but later. After we've solved the problems we have to solve."

"Fair enough, but we have many such tabled topics. At some point, the tabled topics will outweigh everything, and that will force our discussion, circumstances notwithstanding."

I nodded. "From his *slowth*, Luka set this *proo* to take us back to Roanoke, and he's been back since…after laying the trap there." I shook my head. "He's a strange one."

"Who? Luka?"

"Let's review… Cannibal, check. Shapeshifter, check. Hangs out with the foulest bitch in the history of the universe, check. Yeah, that qualifies as strange." Jane's eyes danced as she ribbed me, and it made her even more beautiful.

"Well, if you put it *that* way…"

"What do you mean, Hank?" asked Yowtgayrr.

"He's not… I had this idea that he was nothing but an ice-cold killer. Especially after I heard the tale of Paltr and Huthr's cold-hearted murders—his own brothers. But… He's not… It's more complicated than that. He's not cold at all, not on the inside."

"He's still an asshole, cold or hot or lukewarm," said Jane.

"Yeah, I'm not saying he's a good person. He's just… He loves Hel. And I do mean *loves*. All he thinks about is making her happy, about getting her back to how she was before everything fell apart. At least at the time of that memory, but his dedication to her seems unchanged."

"Interesting," said Althyof.

"And it appears he truly regrets having taken part in the murders of his brothers. As if he thinks of it as something he had no choice in, but if he *had* had a choice, they wouldn't be dead."

"It may be," said Yowtgayrr with a shrug.

"And he might wear a pink tutu under his clothes," said Jane. "But he still did all those things."

"Yes," I said, "and he still has to *pay* for doing those things. It's only that…well…"

"You imagine a way in which he might *redeem* himself," spat Althyof. "You Isir! You never seem to realize when someone has earned their death."

I shrugged. "I'm not saying Luka might redeem himself, Althyof. All I'm saying is that his character isn't as cut and dried as it appears."

Silence fell amongst us, brittle and cold.

"We don't have to make any decisions," said Jane in a placating tone.

"No, and I'm not even advocating we change our minds," I said. "He caught me by surprise is all."

Althyof shrugged. "None of it matters if you can't track him."

"True. Let's figure out if I can, but before we go after him, I still want to go home and get ammunition."

"*Or* we can go to Nitavetlir and check if Prokkr has learned the art of making these bullets you set such store by."

"Or that. But first…" I stared down at the *slowthar* twisting over the floor of the chamber. I could pick out Luka's as quickly as any of my friends. *Maybe it has to do with how well I know them?*

I did not understand how to track Luka or anyone else, but I knew I *could*, so it was a matter of persistence and trying everything I could imagine. I focused on Luka's *slowth* and imagined myself standing next to him.

Nothing happened.

I imagined following his *slowth* in my mind's eye.

Again, nothing happened. "This may take a while."

"We have all the time in the universe, evidently," said Althyof.

I grinned at him and tipped him a wink. I ran through all the ideas I could think of: looking at the *slowth's* surface for clues as I would a *proo*, peering into it without allowing myself to get sucked along into memory, trying to pick through Luka's mind in the present rather than in memory, and reaching out with my mind to grasp its hook as Bikkir had taught me to do with the *preer*. None of it worked. None of it seemed to make any difference at all.

"I have no idea how to do this," I murmured.

"Well, don't look at us mortals," said Jane with a twist to her lips.

"Perhaps you can summon Bikkir?" said Yowtgayrr.

"I'm not sure Bikkir knows I can do this, and I'd rather keep it from him if he doesn't."

"Sensible."

"Can you choose what you… Which memories you…view?" asked Krowkr.

"What do you mean?"

"I think I get it," said Althyof. "Can you pick-and-choose between Luka's memories? Can you selectively view the memory of his travel out of here?"

I shrugged. "Both instances so far have been random memories. Or at least that's how it seems to me."

"Try it," said Jane with a shrug. "It's that or cook us dinner."

"In that case, I'll get back to work." I smiled at her and turned back to Luka's *slowth*. All the *slowthar* seemed the same on the surface. A sheath or a wrapper of some kind *segregated* all the streams of memory—similar to the insulation covering a copper wire. Both times memories had swept me away, it had been as if there was a tear in the insulation exposing the copper beneath.

I'm missing something about this whole thing. Something crucial. But what is it? If these slowthar *mimic wires, then the memories are…what? Something akin to electricity? Signals moving from one place to the next? Bits of data? But connected to what? If my* slowth *terminates at my present-self on one end, what's on the other end?*

I turned to my *slowth* and peered down at it. *I already have all these memories, so it should be easier to resist the temptation to watch one.* I began to trace it backward, shivering at the strange sensation that it produced inside my head—as if someone with very cold fingers was rummaging around in my mind. I could zip back along the memories, skipping whatever I wanted, by focusing on any scene from my past.

Skipping backward faster and faster, taking larger and larger leaps between orientation points, I zipped through my life with Jane, backward through my college days, high school, my childhood. I expected to stop at my birth, but with a start, I realized I was *past* that and still moving. For a time, there was nothing but darkness. *The darkness of the womb?* I wondered.

Then the path bifurcated, and I floated at the nexus of two separate routes. One track was my father's, and the other was my mother's. I looked at each path in turn, feeling like an intruder, like a voyeur peeking in their bedroom windows.

"Hank! Hank, stop it!"

I let the vision slide away and looked into Jane's worried face. "What? What is it?"

"You disappeared for a moment," said Althyof as if it happened every day.

"More than that," said Yowtgayrr. "You were drifting out of phase."

"I'll pretend I have the slightest idea what that even means," I said with a smile. "I was trying something—following my own *slowth* backward, trying to find where the path started, but it's as if… It doesn't start at my birth, instead it's—"

"Woven from the paths of your parents."

I nodded. "But their paths didn't end at my birth. My path is still here, despite having a son, so it's not a trunk-branch kind of thing."

"Yes," said Yowtgayrr. "Think of it in terms of weaving cloth. Or, more appropriately perhaps, weaving the tapestry of life. Your parents were yarns already present in the tapestry, and your conception added a new weft thread to the tapestry. Both of your parents' threads continue until the moment their lives leave the tapestry."

"And when parents and children are separated?" I asked, thinking of Henry.

Yowtgayrr shrugged. "If both lives continue in the tapestry, then other threads separate them. Or by their distance in the tapestry, if that makes more sense."

"But all this weaving talk feels… *wrong* somehow. These *slowthar* are not threads in some tapestry. They resemble *wires* conducting something from point A to point B."

Yowtgayrr shrugged again with a small smile. "I have no more claim on the answers to life's mysteries than any other, Hank."

"No, I suppose not, but this is really cramping your 'Wise Alf' quotient."

"Why does this twaddle matter?" asked Althyof.

"I can't figure out how to find out where Luka is," I said. "If I knew how the *slowthar* worked, I could figure out how to start figuring out a way to find where he is now."

"Isn't wherever he is now at the end of his *slowth*?" asked Althyof with a lopsided grin. "I certainly hope that's where I am."

I glanced at Yowtgayrr. "See what you've done? Now we've got to add a place on the board for 'Wise Tverkr.'"

"Oh, the horror," said the Alf with a broad grin.

"So, all he has to do is follow this *slowth* to wherever Luka is now? Why does that sound dangerous?"

"He doesn't have to go all the way to where Luka is at this moment, only close enough to determine where we must go."

"All this is assuming I have any choice in the matter. Yeah, I could move down my path backward, but that's because I have all the memories in the path already. I could use them as targets, so to speak."

"Is that how it works?" asked Althyof with a twitch of his eyebrows.

"Yeah, that's enough from the 'Wise Tverkr' to last a lifetime."

"Is it?"

I shook my head in mock-severity but spoiled it by grinning. "Okay, I can try it."

Althyof spread his hands. "If you think it might work…"

I glanced at Yowtgayrr again. "Do you get what you've done? He will be insufferable from now on."

"And that will be different…how?" asked the Alf with a grin and a wink.

"Good point." I closed my eyelids for a moment. "Okay, here goes." I imagined wrapping my arms around a giant wire—Luka's *slowth*—and dragging myself forward along its length.

Unlike traveling backward along my *slowth*, I moved against a kind of resistance—as though walking against the outgoing tide at the beach. Once I got comfortable with the method, I tried to move faster as though fast-forwarding a video.

I couldn't quite make out the events as I zipped by but felt that if I stopped and focused my will, I'd be sucked into the moment as I had been with both Krowkr's and Luka's memories previously.

Moving along the *slowthar* wasn't akin to traversing a physical space, nor was it like sliding along the inside of a *proo*. I could discern an infinite horizon stretching away in any direction I cared to look, and it felt less like I moved through the space than the space moved around me. To the front, everything faded into total darkness, but the view to the rear was like a million frames of video all overlapped—millions on millions of shapes and colors of every imaginable kind mixing in a hodge-podge of nonsense images. It made me a little sick to my stomach.

In a sense, I'd left my own *slowth* behind, but having Luka's *slowth* firmly in my grasp gave me a feeling of being tethered to something *real*, of being able to find my way back to myself. Even so, the disconnected sensation disconcerted me, much as I imagined clinging to a piece of flotsam adrift far out to sea might perturb me.

Something flickered in the stark darkness ahead. Similar to sunlight twinkling off the windshield of an oncoming car in my lane, the flashing, blinding light filled me with unreasonable fear. I imagined clamping down on the *slowth* I held in my arms, and I slowed—almost to the point of having no forward motion.

Peering ahead, I tried to discern movement or form associated with the blinding, blinking light. An imposing…*something*…stood there, still as a statue, watching—no, *guarding*—the way forward. I brought myself to a stop, unsure what to do next, wary of being discovered. I glanced down at the *slowth*, looking past the insulating layer at the stream of cognizance contained within.

I could make out pale walls and had the sense Luka had walked down a long, non-descript hallway. As I watched, he came to a blue door that was familiar.

I reversed direction and sped back along Luka's *slowth* until I found myself again. I let go and snapped my eye open wide. "He's doubled back! The bastard's back on Osgarthr! He's in the *Herperty af Roostum*! In the Rooms of Ruin!"

"Sig!" said Jane, alarm spreading red wings across her cheeks. "We have to get back there!"

"It's okay, both of you," said Althyof. "We have time."

"Time? That madman could be with our *friends and son!*" she snapped.

"You forget that Hank can wrap a *proo* to whatever time frame he desires."

He was right…I'd forgotten that, too.

TWENTY-
FOUR

I stepped out of the *proo* and into Veethar's Vault of *Preer* and breathed a sigh of relief. I hadn't been sure I had a firm enough fix on the place to dial the *proo* to the right place, but even the air smelled right.

If I'd gotten it right, we'd traveled backward in time to the hour after we'd left the *Herperty af Roostum* in pursuit of Luka. It was a small jump in time—a few days. Easy.

I'd wanted to go back further—to the hour after the party had embarked on our journey to the Rooms of Ruin, but the *preer* had been disabled during that time, and I didn't know if I could override Haymtatlr's control. The memories of the trip flooded my mind: Jane killing the sea dragon, learning to cast the runes, meeting Kuhntul for the first time, hanging from Iktrasitl with the enigmatic Owsakrimmr, meeting Kuthbyuhrn and Kyellroona, the Great Forest of Suel, the raven dreams, meeting John Calvin Black, Isi's Fast Track Transfer Network, the lava tubes, the battles in the Rooms of Ruin, Haymtatlr…all of it, and even though the trip had been difficult, the memories suffused me with a warmth I didn't expect.

The others popped in behind me, and I smiled when I met Althyof's gaze. I'd grown closer to the Tverkr on that trip—I'd grown closer to *all* my companions, but especially to him. I'd learned so much. It had been hard, but I wouldn't trade the experiences for anything.

Althyof nodded as if he could read my thoughts. "Would you change any of it?"

I shook my head. "No. We didn't do too badly."

"We did *well*, Hank," said Yowtgayrr. "Perhaps better than we had a right to expect."

I nodded. I'd been thinking the same thing since we embarked on the trip.

"What is this place?" asked Krowkr, his awe evident in his voice.

"Never you mind," snapped Althyof. "Sometimes it's better to accept what you don't know."

I stared at the runes inscribed in the stone walls. Now that I could read them, the organization of the place made more sense. Runes that seemed to point to different spots on the various *klith* filled one wall— the places similar enough to our homes that they were almost indistinguishable—as with Henry's Penfield or Osgarthr and Mithgarthr. One wall contained the *preer* for various other realms— Nitavetlir, Muspetlshaymr, Alfhaym, and the like. Another wall held runes that indicated danger: hot, cold, heavy, underwater, things such as that, and after each such rune, was the name of a place I'd never heard of before. Stathur, I thought. *Those places in the multiverse where the physical laws differ greatly from those we expect. Environments such as the place I visited as my animus.* The runes on the final wall seemed tied to both a time and a place.

I touched the rune for Nitavetlir, and the *proo* swirled into existence in the center of the room. "Here we go," I said.

"This is just a visit to the smithy to get ammo, right? We go to Sig the second you have it."

"Yes, honey," I said. "If Prokkr doesn't have my ammunition finished, I'll pop into our basement and go buy one or two hundred boxes at the gun shop in Walworth."

"You could get more methotrexate, too, if we went there instead of Nitavetlir."

"This stuff Sif made works just as well—maybe better—and I don't want to risk getting picked up for questioning or something unless we have to."

Jane shrugged as if it didn't matter, but I could tell she'd rather have a taste of home, no matter how brief.

I put my hand on her shoulder and squeezed. "We'll get there."

She nodded. "I know."

"Enough talk," said Althyof, and he reached out to touch the *proo*.

We followed him, and I immediately bumped my head. "You'd think someone would raise the ceiling in this little closet," I said.

Althyof shrugged in the near-darkness. "Seems fine to me."

The memory of my first trip to Nitavetlir was fragmented and foggy. When we'd emerged back at Veethar and Frikka's estate, there'd been a battle raging, and in that battle, I'd lost my left eye and *then* helped Althyof kill a white dragon. "Don't remember much about the place," I said.

Althyof threw open the door to the subterranean hall outside, and the clatter and cries of the Tverkar home realm filled the air. "It's no matter," he said. "I might know someone who could serve as our guide." He smiled and winked.

"Krowkr, keep close," I said.

"Yes, lad, stay with us, and, by all means, watch where you step. The last thing we want is to get into a brawl over your clumsiness." Althyof smiled at

Krowkr's unease and tipped me another wink before he swirled out into the hall. He threw back his head and roared, "I have returned! Never fear, Nitavetlir, Althyof has returned!"

"So?"

"Shut your trap, Tverkr!"

"Oh ho! Althyof is back! Hide your women!"

"How much would it cost to have you leave again?"

The catcalls echoed up the hall, and Althyof's smile grew wider at each one. Krowkr looked at me in confusion, and I smiled. "Don't worry. It's all part of the show."

"Follow me," said Althyof. "I know a shortcut to Prokkr's smithy." He turned at the first intersection of halls and led us to a nondescript door. He rapped on it twice and pushed it open. Behind it, two Tverkar napped in chairs tipped back against the room's walls. "Lazy louts!" yelled Althyof.

The two Tverkar snorted but didn't wake.

"Ah, well," murmured Althyof. "Down these stairs back here."

We descended on a wide spiral staircase carved from living rock. Althyof skipped down the steps, whistling a tune.

I nudged Jane's arm. "I've never seen him *whistle*. Think he's happy about something?"

"I think it means he has a slow leak."

"Heard that," said Althyof. "Heard both of you."

We climbed down the steps without pause until my thigh muscles were shrieking with exhaustion. "Tverkar need to learn about elevators," I said.

"What makes you think we don't know about them?"

"Stairs and ramps…"

Althyof shrugged. "Keeps one fit."

After that, I didn't have the breath to tease him. We spiraled down and down and down before we finally reached the bottom.

"This way," said the Tverkr, opening another door onto yet another stone hall.

The air in the hall was hot and stuffy, and I thought I could see an orange glow at the other end. It had been faster than Meuhlnir's route, I thought, but I wanted to collapse.

Althyof led us out onto the smithy's floor. He turned to Jane and pointed at a canal filled with creeping magma. "Do you see, Jane? If we have time, I'll make you a pendant from one of those channels of lava."

"Fine," she said, turning to me and rolling her eyes. "I said I believed you, right?"

Althyof smiled. "It never hurts to belabor a point."

"Master Jensen!" boomed Prokkr from across the work floor. "Does the belt I made you work in practice?"

I smiled at his eager tone. "Master Prokkr!" I called. "This belt is a work of pure genius!"

"Good, good!" He strode toward us, shoving his underlings out of the way when they ventured into his path. "And the armor? The bucklers?"

"Excellent."

He strode up to us, giving a terse nod to Althyof. His eyes lingered on Jane for a moment, then bored into Krowkr's for the space of ten breaths before turning back to me and smiling. "And Kunknir? Krati? I can't speak to the enchantments, mind, but how have they held up?"

"Very well. They were instrumental in helping Althyof to slay that white dragon and have seen a lot of action since."

His eyes brightened. "Might I…"

I smiled. "Any time, Master Prokkr." I drew Kunknir, cleared the chamber, and handed the big, enchanted Kimber .45 to him. As with the first time he saw it, his eyes crawled over every cranny, every feature of the pistol. It was almost as if he'd forgotten we were there, or where he was. Lesser smiths crowded behind him, vying for a look.

"Ah, yes," he breathed. "Such craftsmanship. But it appears to collect grime in these crevices."

"Residue from the propellants," I said. "An unavoidable consequence of firing them."

"Ah. One day, I'd like…that is, with your permission, Master Jensen, I'd enjoy firing these myself."

I smiled at his enthusiasm for new experiences—at least where engineering was concerned. "That can be arranged."

"If you've finished?" groused Althyof. "Our time is valuable, smith."

Prokkr's face soured. "I think I preferred our previous relationship, *enchanter*. The one where you were subservient to my will."

Althyof shrugged. "Things change, Tverkr. Adapt."

"Come," said Prokkr, whirling on his heel and striding away without returning Kunknir and without checking to see that we followed.

I grinned and shook my head, noticing the scowls on the faces of the Tverkr smiths as they watched their master trek to his private office. Inside, he turned, still holding Kunknir in both hands. "And what might I do for you today, Master Jensen."

"Let me introduce you to my wife, Jane," I said.

"Charmed," he said, barely glancing at her.

"And this is Krowkr."

"Yes, yes." He didn't bother looking at the Viking.

"I'm here to check on your experiments with the ammunition. I hope you've made progress."

"Of course!" he grunted. "It was a simple matter when we got down to it. A press, a few molds, quality checks at every step." He looked disappointed. "Is that all you came for today?"

"I'm afraid so."

He shook his head, but his eyes caught on the golden spear Jane carried. "Curious," he said. "Old craftsmanship in that."

"Yes," I said. "It was a gift from a pair of cave bears."

He turned to me slowly, eyebrows arched. "Is it so?"

"It is."

"Interesting." He reached out and flicked his thumb against her shield. "And this is quite nice."

"I like it," said Jane. "It goes with my wings."

Prokkr glanced at me uncertainly before meeting Jane's gaze. "I see. Extraordinary."

"She is," I said, taking her hand. "I wish we had more time, Prokkr, but—"

"Yes, time is as elusive as ever." He said it with such irritation in his voice that I was hard pressed not to smile. "I wish there were a way to control it, but in all my studies, I have found no principles by which to manipulate it."

Althyof grinned at me and shook his head. "The ammunition, Master Prokkr?"

"Yes, yes," said the master smith in a disinterested tone. He stooped and opened a cabinet under his work table, then withdrew two metal boxes close to a foot long, six inches wide, and six inches tall. Each box had a handle that folded flat into the hinged lid. "Thirteen hundred rounds for Kunknir, one thousand seven hundred and fifty rounds for Krati. Will you require more?"

Relief coursed through me. I hadn't wanted to face Luka crippled by a lack of ammunition, despite all the things I'd learned since the last time I'd fought him. "Let's make this a standing order," I said. "I'll take a can of each, every time I visit Nitavetlir."

"Hmm," said Prokkr. "I can do that with ease—as long as you don't return on subsequent days."

"Excellent. You don't know how good it is to hear you say that."

"The only matter to settle on is the price."

"Ah. Yes, about that—"

"My account," said Althyof. "Make the price reasonable, Prokkr, and we need never discuss it. Make the price egregious, and…well, sometimes it's best to remember how I defeated Fowrpauti in single combat."

The master smith rolled his eyes toward the ceiling. "Yes, yes. Each can will be a quarter bag, but that price is contingent on an agreement, Master Jensen."

"And what agreement is that?"

"I wish to learn more about the crafting techniques from your *klith*."

"Well… I'm not a smith—"

"Yes, yes. If you travel to your home, find me materials describing the processes used to create such a fine weapon. Find me material that describes the principles behind other, more exotic weapons."

I shrugged. "I guess I can do that, but the language spoken on Mithgarthr—"

He waved his big hands. "I understand I'll have to do the groundwork to understand the runes of that realm. It's settled."

"No," said Althyof. "If Hank is to *educate* you, these cans of ammunition are the least you can do for him."

Prokkr glowered at the Tverkr, using his height to loom over Althyof. "I don't recall you being part of the negotiation."

"Is it so?" said the *runeskowld*. "You don't recall that I'm the party *paying*?"

Prokkr harrumphed and rolled his eyes. "Or *not paying* if you get your way."

Althyof took a step closer to Prokkr and glared up into the master smith's face. "Should we discuss it outside?" Menace dripped from his voice, and a small, crazy smile flitted on his lips. "I throw you, I pay nothing per can. You throw me, we negotiate further."

"Ha! You throw me, and the cans are yours, but if I throw you, you pay one quarter bag."

"Acceptable," said Althyof.

"Fellas, listen—"

"Shh, Hank. We're negotiating," said Althyof with a secret smile. "Smith? After you?"

The wrestling match was short, and I left Nitavetlir with free ammo for life.

TWENTY-
FIVE

Weᵉ didn't want to risk taking one of Meuhlnir or Veethar's existing *proo* to the *Herperty af Roostum* and emerging outside in the middle of Hel's army, or somewhere far away from the parts we knew—or being accosted by more Great Old Ones—so I grabbed the hook of the *proo* we'd used to get there and spun it so it terminated in the room we'd slept in the first night before the battle with Vowli, except focused on the time right after I'd seen Luka traipsing through the halls of the place. I felt confident I had a grasp on that room, and as I twisted the *proo* to my purposes, only the doubt that I might inadvertently get the time scale wrong nagged me. But there was nothing I could do about it—I lacked a meaningful understanding of the mechanics of the damn things. *Are they wormholes? Warp tunnels right out of Star Trek? Magic doors similar to those in the Dark Tower series from Sai King? Or giant wardrobes with secret ways hidden behind the clothes?* I had no answers to those questions, and only two ways of educating myself were open to me—Bikkir and his pompous sesquipedalian nature or asking Kuhntul and hoping she'd give me not only a straight answer, but a *serviceable* one.

The silvery light splashed on the walls of Veethar's Vault of the *Preer*, and I glanced at my diminished party. "We could take the long way."

"What, go back through to Vefsterkur's place in Niflhaymr, sneak out of the city and traipse across that icy desert, take Luka's *proo* back to the cabin on the mountaintop, spend a few days walking back to Yarl Oolfreekr's place, and finally back through *that proo* to the Rooms of Ruin? Are you kidding?" Jane asked with a smile twitching on her lips.

"Well, when you put it that way, it sounds a little silly."

"Only a little?"

I grinned and waved my hand at the *proo* I'd manipulated. "Your chariot, m'lady."

"Looks more like a bunch of spilled silver paint, but whatever. I'm not going first, bozo. That's your job."

"How did I know you'd say that?"

She treated me to the full, ten-thousand-watt "Jane's so great" smile. "It's because I'm so wonderful. Plus, I trained you well."

"Yes, dear," I said and laughed. Out of the corner of my eye, I caught Krowkr's expression as he watched us flirt. It was a strange mix of jealousy and awe until he caught me watching him—at which point it all turned into a blush, and he found something interesting to look at on the ground. "It's okay, kid. She's awesome, and everyone knows it."

Krowkr nodded but kept his eyes down.

"But…I'll tell you the same thing I told Mothi Strongheart."

"Yes, Yarl Hanki?"

I fought a sigh. *Will I ever be just a man to him?* "Don't make me break your legs."

He looked at me askance, a troubled expression creeping over his features. "Yarl Hanki, I would *never*—"

"He's kidding, Krowkr," said Jane, turning her ten-thousand-watt smile on him.

His eyes bounced between us as if at a tennis match, me pretending to glare at him, her smiling.

"Before we go," said Yowtgayrr, "I'd hear the tale of Krowkr's reasons for visiting Yarl Oolfreekr."

With a grunt, Althyof nodded. "I agree."

Just like that, the light atmosphere dissipated. I nodded to the Viking. "Do you want to tell them, or should I?"

"Gentlemen, I really think—" began Jane.

"No, I should tell it." Blood blazed in the young man's cheeks. "I…I'm not *proud* of—"

"No, let's start with what you did, and then move on to the justifications," said Althyof.

"We—my brother and our lifelong friend— wanted to… Yarl Oolfreekr had a reputation as a berserker, as an *oolfhyethidn*, a wolf-warrior—"

"Yes, yes," snapped the *runeskowld*. "We do speak the language. It's ours, after all."

I put my hand on Althyof's shoulder. "Let him tell it in his own way," I said.

Krowkr gulped a breath. "We were… We weren't successful. Owfastr and I, we came from…er…from modest beginnings. Our father died a few short years after my birth, and our mother never married again. Her heart was forever our father's. Our friend, Skatlakrimr, he was better off, but with him, it was never enough. He craved respect, he wanted to be *important*."

Althyof grunted.

"We'd been a-viking, more than once, in fact, but things didn't go our way. It was nothing as bad as you might expect. We weren't cowards, it was more poor luck than anything. We'd be in the wrong boat and get blown off course, only to arrive *after* the battle. Or we'd search for plunder on the wrong side of the village first. Things like that."

"And that led you to decide to become *oolfa*?" asked Yowtgayrr in a flat, emotionless voice.

"No, it wasn't like that. Skatlakrimr began to speak of it last summer, at the end of our raiding season. He went on and on about the amount of respect paid to Yarl Oolfreekr. Skatlakrimr told us stories about Oolfreekr challenging rich landowners and other yarls to duels. The yarl fought for years, up and down the coast. He made so much money from his schemes that he hadn't been a-viking for years and years. No one dared challenge him, no other yarl dared attack him, though he had fewer and fewer karls and thralls each year. Skatlakrimr idolized this man he'd never met, and I fear now that the tales told of Oolfreekr may have been aggrandized."

"And? After Skatlakrimr told you these tales, you *still* sought the man out?"

"Truth be told, Oolfreekr and the *Briethralak Oolfur* never held *my* interest. But Skatlakrimr was our friend, and we listened to his tales. My brother, Owfastr, the one Luka murdered, he saw the romance of it—the mystery of it all excited him."

"Didn't you fools heed the stories? About the duels?"

"Yes, we knew he earned the name by dueling, and by killing all the other *oolfa*. Oolfreekr killed his brothers in the order, in the *Briethralak Oolfur*."

"He betrayed his own. The yarl lived by crookery, by fighting duels against opponents who had no chance."

"Yes," said Krowkr with a shrug. "And yet the men of the villages respected him."

"*Feared him!*" roared Althyof. "Fear and respect are not the same thing."

Krowkr nodded sheepishly. "Yes, I know that now."

"Krowkr, if you weren't interested in all this, why were you there? Why did you stand and fight him?" asked Jane.

Krowkr shrugged. "Owfastr was my brother, my only living relative. Skatlakrimr was our friend." Diamonds made of tears glittered in his eyes.

"Well spoken, lad," said Yowtgayrr in a kind voice.

"Yes, I don't suppose I can fault you for supporting your kin, but there comes a point in every folly where a man has to choose for himself."

Krowkr straightened and looked Althyof proudly in the eye. "I chose to support my brother and my friend."

"But what you would have sacrificed for them… Lad, do you know what fate would have been yours? Do you understand that you would have no longer been wholly human?"

Krowkr's proud gaze slithered away from the Tverkr's. "My people believe the Allfather writes our lives in the skein of fate." He darted a glance at me. "We made our sacrifices to Owthidn, we put our trust in him, and in…in others." His gaze crawled across my features.

It struck me how much he reminded me of Veethar in his quiet confidence, his sparse words. *He talks more than Veethar, though*, I thought. *Uses more words, says less*.

"We trusted in our sacrifices to the patron of berserkers, to…" Again, his gaze locked on mine for the briefest of moments before darting away. "We believed Owthidn would protect us. He would… Whatever happened, it would be the fate he'd written for us."

"Remind me to tell you of *uhrluhk*," I said.

"Oh lord, not that again," whispered Jane.

"Krowkr, I am not Odin—Owthidn. I'm only a man. A husband." I put my hand on Jane's arm. "We're not your deities. We're—"

"It's no use, Hank," murmured Yowtgayrr. "When a man believes something—*truly believes it*, mind—no amount of words will change that belief."

"But—"

"The only thing you can do is *show* him who you are by your actions."

"Oy," said Jane with a chuckle. "That's bad news."

Yowtgayrr smiled politely, but there was little humor in it. "And who's to say you don't embody the characteristics of this Owthidn?"

"But I don't want to be… I'm not… I don't want *worship*."

Yowtgayrr shrugged, and a small smile splashed across his visage. "And I don't want to be friends with a Tverkr."

"*Friends*?" scoffed Althyof. "At best we're—"

"What you did for Skowvithr," said the Alf with all trace of humor gone, "telling him of his brother's last moments, and treating *both* Alfar with such respect…that's when I began counting you my friend."

"Yes, well," grunted Althyof, and he cleared his throat. "Let's get back to the matter at hand…unless there's more complaining," he glanced at me, "flirting," he glanced at Jane, "or excessive Tverkr worship, that is." His gaze rested on Yowtgayrr's for a moment before both men smiled.

"Yes," I said. "I've seen his memories—*lived* them. Krowkr, left to his own devices, would never have come within a hundred miles of Hoos Oolfsins. The man doesn't suffer from the vagaries of the soul that Luka does."

Althyof looked at Krowkr hard for a drawn-out moment. "Do you hear who speaks for you? Do you hear his words?"

Krowkr swallowed and nodded, and his gaze crawled to mine. In it was everything I didn't want, but also more than mere worship—the beginnings of real trust.

"Don't let the words be false. Never in life."

"I… I swear it." His eyes burned with passion and met my gaze directly and without reservation.

It was a promise he would keep or die trying. I nodded. "Then it's done." I gestured at the *proo*. "Let's go see if we can find the others, and after that, find Luka."

Althyof nodded and touched the *proo*. One by one my companions touched it and disappeared, and I brushed the surface of the *proo* with my fingertips.

TWENTY-SIX

The *proo* twisted and warped around me, whipping to and fro like a snake in its death throes. The fabric of the universe seemed to shudder, to ripple with the power being exerted on it. Colors and smells flashed through my mind in nanosecond bursts of pure terror. Blackness entombed me—utter darkness, no sound, no sensory input of any kind—except for those brief respites of terrible color.

KANKARI.

The mental voice boomed in and around me as though a physical assault, vibrations crawled across my skin like maggots on a corpse. I tried to cringe away from it, but there was nowhere to go, nothing on which to gain traction, nothing to push against. I couldn't escape, couldn't flee, couldn't even move.

KANKARI, boomed the voice again.

It reminded me of talking to Bikkir, but a...*greasy*...aftertaste lingered after the words faded from my mind.

YOU MISSPEND THIS CONTINUANCE.

Bikkir? I thought and sensed an immediate rumble of amusement laced with annoyance.

NEGATION. DOES THIS ONE APPEAR AS A PERSEVERATING, PRETENTIOUS POMP? AMUSEMENT.

No matter how many times the Great Old One said I amused it, it was anything but amused. *Who are you*?

COGNOMINA ARE INAPPOSITE, BUT THIS ONE RECOGNIZES THE NEED OF LESSER BEINGS TO CATEGORIZE ENTITIES. RESEMBLANT COGNITIVE BOUNDS GOVERN THE PLOWIR MEDN. THIS ONE MAY BE IDEATED AS MIRKUR.

Mirkur? Darkness? What do you want? Where is Bikkir? My thoughts buzzed and ripped around inside my head like so many out-of-control windup toys.

BANISH COGNIZANCE OF THE LESSER OF MY KIND. CEASE. YIELD COGITATION OF WHAT IS NOT AND TURN YOUR EXECUTIVE PROCESSES TO WHAT IS.

What the hell does that even mean? I thought, but I tried to keep it to myself.

AMUSEMENT.

What do you want, Mirkur?

THIS ONE HAS DIVERTED KANKARI. THIS ONE—

Kankari? You called me that before. I thought you big-brained Great Old Ones had no need for…how did you put it…inapposite cognomina?

CEASE. YOU MISSPEND THE TIMESLICE. YOU CATALYZE BRUME WHERE LUCIDITY IS JUDICIOUS.

You know what? I don't give a fuck. You assholes are all the same. Cease this, yield to me that. I'll tell you what, Mirkur. You drop me back into the right proo and leave me alone. How's that for clarity? Agony burned through me, searing my nerves, boiling my blood. Pain wracked my physical body, but agony abraded against and abided within the dead center of my being. I felt my limbs thrashing in the non-corporeal *proo.* I opened my mouth to scream, but there was no air, no vacuum…only a squirming nothingness that marauded into my mouth and trespassed in my throat before I snapped my jaws shut.

THIS ONE IS NOT THE SAME AS BIKKIR. The voice hissed and sizzled in my mind like molten metal and burning stone. DISCOURTESY AND IMPERTINENCY ARE TO BE CASTIGATED. INDOCTRINATE THIS TRUTH AND ALLOW IT TO EDUCE DECOROUS DEMEANOR.

The agony dissipated as abruptly as it had begun. I didn't think, didn't speak—I lay there in the grip of whatever non-material made up the interior of the *preer* and waited.

OTHERS BEFORE YOU HAVE REBELLED. OTHERS WERE PUNISHED—ARE *BEING* PUNISHED—WITH PREJUDICE. DO YOU DESIRE SUCH TRIBULATION? WOE UNTO YOU. THERE WILL BE WEEPING AND GNASHING OF TEETH.

I apologize, I thought, working hard to keep my mind quiet, to prevent my feelings from leaking across whatever transmission conveyed my thoughts to Mirkur.

AEONIC TRIBULATIONS MINGLED AMONGST PROTRACTED TORTURES AND TRIALS! WOE!

I said nothing, thought nothing. If I just played along, maybe Mirkur would let me go, and I could join the others in the *Herperty af Roostum*. Most of all, I tried to keep the memory of Owraythu's domain and Hel's terrible screams out of my head.

YOUR EXISTENCE IS COROLLARY TO OUR OWN PASSAGE THROUGH SPACETIME. YOU ARE AS REFLUX, A WASTE PRODUCT OF OUR EVOLUTION. THIS ONE IS MASTER HERE!

Mirkur's rage palpitated inside the confines of the *proo*, surging like the surf of a storm-ridden sea. Whitecaps of anger slashed at me, breakers of bedlam battered me, but I kept silent and weathered the storm.

What may I do? I asked after a time.

THIS ONE IS MASTER HERE!

Yes, Mirkur. What may I do? I had the sense of something immense pulling away, of a large animal withdrawing its attacks to look upon its prey.

KANKARI…*WANDERER*…THUS THIS ONE CLEPES YOU BECAUSE IT IS YOUR NATURE TO TRAVEL THE VEINS OF THE UNDERVERSE.

The ire had departed from his mental voice and it no longer ripped through the air like a rag subject to the whims of a raging child. *As apt a description as any.*

AMUSEMENT. DECOMPRESSION AND REPOSE RETURN.

Good. Sorry about my behavior. What can I do for you?

REPLACEMENTS ARE REQUIRED TO FACILITATE THIS ONE'S DESIGNS. YOU SHALL PROVIDE THEM.

Replacements? Replacements for what?

PROXIES. ARBITERS OF OUR WILL. EMISSARIES TO THE LESSER REALMS.

Okay… You say there were others?

AFFIRMATION. THROUGHOUT THE CONTINUITY, THE *PLAUINN* HAVE STRIVEN TO GUIDE OUR CHILDREN, TO EDUCATE AND ELEVATE THEM FROM THEIR PETTY CONCERNS.

The Plauinn*? You are one of the* Plauinn?

IS THIS NOT COGNOSCIBLE? DO ALL SMALL ONES SUFFER IN SUCH PURBLINDNESS?

But…I thought… The Alfar believe themselves to be the close representatives to the Plauinn.

NUGATORY CONCEPTUALIZATIONS OF LESSER BEINGS CAUSE THIS ONE LITTLE AGITATION OF

THE SPIRIT. ADOPT TRANQUILITY, THIS ONE SHALL ELUCIDATE YOUR FUNCTION.

Mirkur? Does this function you speak of coincide with all that Bikkir taught me, demanded of me?

THAT ONE REEKS OF THE GLOAMING. DISREGARD HIS UTTERANCES.

Fair enough.

FROM THIS TIMESLICE ONWARD, YOU ARE THIS ONE'S CREATURE, AND THIS ONE'S CREATURE ALONE. YOU ANSWER ONLY TO THIS ONE.

That sounded about as good as being in a cell in Helhaym, but I kept that to myself.

THIS ONE SEEKS TO CORRECT ERRANT *UHRLUHK,* TO REFOCUS THE TIMEFLOWS AND THE MATTERSTREAMS. YOU WILL ASSIST THIS ONE. YOU WILL DISDAIN ALL OTHERS IN THIS. YOU WILL DO AS THIS ONE INSTRUCTS YOU.

Okay, I said, imagining my fingers crossed one over the other.

DECEPTION?

No, no deception.

THIS ONE SHALL SEE. YOU WILL TRAVEL TO THE CONFLUX AND ONCE THERE, YOU SHALL ALTER WHAT NEEDS BE ALTERED. BEGIN WITH THE THREE THAT HAVE BETRAYED THIS ONE. THEIR COGNOMINA ARE KNOWN TO YOU. HEL, LUKA, VOWLI. STRIKE THEM FROM THE TIMEFLOW. ERASE THEM FROM THE MATTERSTREAM. THUS IS THE FATE OF THOSE WHO BETRAY THIS ONE.

Vowli is dead. I...we...killed him.

CORPOREAL CESSATION IS *INSUFFICIENT.* NONEXISTENCE IS REQUIRED. NOTHINGNESS CONSIGNED TO THE OUTER DARKNESS IS REQUIRED. THE THREE ARE TO HAVE NEVER EXISTED.

When I'd met Hel and Luka, they'd appeared as gods to my eye—their powers insurmountable—but as time passed, and I learned the truth and the limits of their abilities, it had seemed less…divine. But Mirkur's power was…it was as the sun to Hel's single LED bulb. His hatred snapped and crackled in his mental voice, as did his unimaginable power. But even so, couldn't his power be the result of another step in the ladder of the unknown? I remembered the look of awe in Krowkr's eyes…did I appear to him as Mirkur did to me?

YOUR MIND SWIMS WITH QUERIES.

Yeah, sorry. It's my nature, I guess.

CATECHIZE.

I couldn't ask him the real questions, but I had to ask him something. *Why can't you make these changes yourself? Why do you need me to do it?*

AMUSEMENT. THIS ONE IS CONSIGNED TO THE UNDERVERSE, AS ARE ALL THE *PLAUINN.* WE SOUGHT A PEARL OF WISDOM…A PEARL OF GREAT PRICE…AND THE DISBURSEMENT CHANGED THE *PLAUINN.*

Are the Nornir Plauinn?

AMUSEMENT. THE *NORNIR* ARE MERELY DREAMSLICE REFLECTIONS OF LESSER *PLAUINN,* CONSIGNED TO MAINTAIN *UHRLUHK* ON THE

BEHALF AND TO THE SPECIFICATION OF THEIR BETTERS WHERE POSSIBLE. ELUCIDATE YOUR KNOWLEDGE OF THE *NORNIR*.

I was... A while ago, an undead bear almost killed me. While my friends fought to save my life, I had these dreams. In some of them, I was at the base of Iktrasitl—

THE CONFLUX.

—and the Three Maids were nearby, trying to decide what to do with me, I think.

AFFIRMATION.

In another part of the dream, I hung from the branches of Iktrasitl—

THE CONFLUX.

—and there was another behind me. Owsakrimmr he said his name was. He gave me knowledge of the Gamla Toonkumowl *and the runes. Was he a* Plauinn*?*

NEGATION. THIS BEING IS UNKNOWN TO ME.

Mirkur's voice sounded confident, but there was subtle hesitation in his answer. He was hiding something. *But who was—*

ADDITIONAL QUERIES? His voice carried a distinct edge.

What about the Tisir?

WHAT OF THEM?

Are they Plauinn?

NO. THE *PLAUINN* ARE THE *PLAUINN* AND NONE OTHER.

That sounded an awful lot like Kuhntul saying, "I am Tisir." I kept that thought tightly wrapped. *But the Nornir—*

CEASE. THIS ONE GROWS ENERVATED. PREPARE FOR TRAVEL TO THE CONFLUX.

Why do you call it the Conflux? The sense of something looming close made me shudder.

CEASE. BRACE FOR PEREGRINATION.

Wait! How do I make the changes? How do I get out of there when I'm done?

INSIGNIFICANCE.

Without another word, Mirkur flung me away.

TWENTY-SEVEN

I fell from a great height; the wind whistling in my ears as I shrieked. I'd never liked the sensation of falling—not since the age of five when I fell out of a tree onto its gnarled roots and lost my breath. Below me a great forest stretched from horizon to horizon. Each tree in the forest was immense, yet the grand tree standing in their midst dwarfed them all. I blinked the wind-born tears from my eye and focused on Iktrasitl, scouring its branches for Owsakrimmr and Ratatoskr. As I fell toward the crown of the great tree, my gaze fell on a huge bird—an eagle—that sat regally in the crown of the tree.

It was the size of a small plane if I could trust my sense of scale next to the huge World Tree. Its plumage ranged in hue from a pitch black on his breast, head, and tail to burnt sienna on the back of his neck and the front edges of his wings—almost similar to highlights in a woman's hair. Bright yellow down frosted his great beak, and his eyes matched his lighter feathers perfectly. Atop his hooked beak, and right between his eyes, sat a normal-sized hawk dressed in pale brown and ivory feathers. The eagle watched me fall, as still as a statue, but the hawk cracked her beak and emitted a sound that imitated a laughing child with a high degree of accuracy.

Why would a hawk sit on a giant eagle's beak like that? I wondered and laughed that a *giant eagle* sitting atop Iktrasitl seemed normal until I saw the hawk.

She is my friend, said a voice in my head.

I don't mind saying that by that point I was sick to death of things talking inside my head.

I apologize. Are you aware you are about to die? it asked.

Die?

The eagle twitched its head toward the ground. *You know...when you hit the ground.*

Oh. Yeah, but there's not much I can do about that.

The eagle twitched his head, dislodging the hawk who squawked and flapped her wings in a way that communicated her irritation in a clear enough manner. With a great leap that left the top of Iktrasitl swaying, the eagle was aloft. He beat his wings twice and had me in his curiously tender grip. *There you are, my friend. How did you get way up in the sky? How did you come to Iktrasitl?*

Do you know about the Plauinn?

The eagle let loose a pained-sounding cry and dipped his wings, gliding in a descending spiral. *Don't mention them*!

Well, that's how I came to be falling from the sky.

Ah. The eagle swooped toward the lower branches of the tree. *I apologize, but I can take you no farther. The wyrm at the base of the tr*ee…

Say no more, I said, thinking of the alternating roars I'd heard in my dreams of the Tree. *Are you aware Ratatoskr is perpetuating your fight with the dragon?*

The eagle deposited me on a lower branch and glided away, arching his neck to shoot a glance my way. *No, you've got that wrong, friend. He carries messages, no more.*

Well, that's kind of what I mean. Are the messages worthwhile?

The eagle beat his massive wings and gained altitude. *Ignoring the dispute won't solve it.*

No, I guess not. Before you go, can you tell me your name? Is it Owsakrimmr?

The eagle squawked, and I got the impression it was a sound of amusement. *No, that is not my name—it's yours. You may call me Tindur.*

Thanks, Tindur. But you've got that wrong. My name is Hank Jensen. I was here before—at least in a dream—and someone was in the tree behind me, out of sight. He said his name was Owsakrimmr.

You are sometimes quite strange. Did you know that?

So people have told me. The eagle was winging his way toward the top of the tree, his massive shape casting me in shadow. *Thanks, Tindur, for saving me.*

My pleasure, Hrafnakuth. We birds have to stick together.

I shook my head at that. It reminded me so much of something Kuthbyuhrn would say that for a moment loneliness overwhelmed me.

The hawk settled herself on the branch above my head and made the sound of a child's laughter again. "Go away," I said. "The last thing I need is a bird laughing at me." The hawk jumped from foot to foot, staring me in the eye and bobbing her head from side to side in perfect mimicry of a bobble-head.

"Yep, you're cool, but I'm going to be busy climbing, so…"

The hawk whistled in a high-pitched, plaintive tone.

I shrugged and uttered the *triblinkr* that summoned an animus, shaping it in the form of a raven. I sent it winging away over the trees, hoping the hawk would follow suit, but it only made the laughter sound again. "Suit yourself."

I slid to the trunk of the enormous tree. Iktrasitl's bark seemed to have been grown specifically for me to climb. The bark grew in large crenulated diamonds—each just large enough to make a good hand- or foot-hold.

I leaned toward the center of the trunk, putting one hand and one foot into a likely hold and shifting my weight. Behind me, the hawk dropped down to the branch I'd vacated and laughed at me yet again. "If you're not going to be helpful…"

The hawk squawked—almost as if insulted.

Far below, the dragon roared its earth-shaking cry, and the sound of Ratatoskr scaling the tree trunk rasped through the air. I climbed toward the foot of the tree, hoping the squirrel would watch where he was going.

I had no intention of doing anything for Mirkur, but there was no reason to hang out on a tree branch. Plus, I'd found Kuhntul at the base of Iktrasitl many times, and I hoped she'd be around.

Above me, the hawk screamed and sprang off the branch, whirled around the tree in a tight circle a few times, then swooped back to land on the branch again. Strange behavior for a hunting kite—well, for a bird in general.

I paused in my climb and glanced back up at the hawk. The sun glinted off the hawk's brilliant white feathers as the bird hopped from foot to foot, doing the bobble-head dance again, this time adding a peculiar open-beak, close-beak move to the rest.

It almost seemed like someone in a costume taunting me to guess who it was.

Kuhntul. Of course.

The hawk made the sound of children laughing again and morphed, stretching her wings out to the side and shaking her shoulders like a jazz dancer.

"Okay, okay," I said. "I get it now."

She laughed again. "Hello, bird-brain," she gurgled.

At that moment, the sound of a thousand chainsaws ripped up the trunk beneath my feet, and the hot wind of Ratatoskr's approach wafted up the trunk. "Clear off, there! Clear! Make way!" the squirrel rasped.

There was no place for me to go—I'd already climbed too low to return to the branch without a major effort, and there were no other suitable branches within reach. I did the next best thing: leaned into the trunk, hugging it with my arms, and squeezed my remaining eye shut.

"Watch out there!" yelled Ratatoskr. There was a flurry of claws on bark and a suspiciously dog-like yelp. "What are you doing? Don't you know this trunk is reserved for official business? Do you have a permit to be here? Where are your climbing spikes? Do you realize how *far* from the ground you are, Isir? Aren't you familiar with the rules of the trunk?" A pregnant pause followed, then the squirrel said, "Oh, it's you again."

"Hello, Ratatoskr," I said, daring to crack my one eye open.

"Yes, hello." He scampered up to eye level and peered around my shoulders. "No spear today?"

I chuckled. "It wasn't me who said he'd stab you with a spear. We've been through this."

"Oh! It's *you*."

"Yep. In the flesh."

"Well, okay. But this climbing about on the trunk is dangerous! Don't you realize how fast I can climb on this bark? How hard it is for me to stop at full-scamper?"

"I was trapped on the branch up there. Tindur carried me—"

"Tindur? *Tindur*? What was he doing out of the tree top?"

"Saving me. I was falling from a great height—don't ask me how I—"

"Yes, yes. No time for long stories. Important business with Tindur, you see."

"Yes, I know. More insults from the dragon?"

"Must keep the lines of communication open." He cocked his head and twitched his tail. "Uh, if it's not too rude to ask, why are you *climbing* down the trunk? Shouldn't you be hanging from a branch or something?"

"No, that was last time."

"Oh." He twitched his head to the side. "Well, if you say so."

"I do."

"Oh." This time, his head twitched the other way. "Okay. But *climbing*?"

"What would you have me do, Ratatoskr? Fly?"

Ratatoskr tittered his squirrelly laugh. "Fly! Oh, that's funny." He sobered and peered into my face. "But, yes. Why aren't you flying?"

"Human. No wings."

Ratatoskr cocked his head to the other side yet again and blinked at me rapidly. "You are sometimes quite strange. Do you know that?"

I fought a grin. "I have heard that before."

"Oh. Okay, then," said the squirrel. "Why aren't you flying again?"

"Human. No wings."

"*Riiiight*." His bushy tail twitched twice in rapid succession, and his lower jaw moved from one side to the other. "You know you can fly down, right?"

I sighed and shook one of my arms without letting go of the tree. "No wings, remember? Human."

Ratatoskr shook his head decisively. "Sure, sure. No wings. Human. Got it, got it. But climbing is dangerous. Why not fly?"

"Because I can't?"

"Right, right. You're human, blah-blah, no wings. But *she* can fly you down, certainly?" Ratatoskr jerked his head toward the branch above me.

I looked up, and Kuhntul reclined on the branch as if it were a chaise lounge, one leg on the bough, the other off and kicking in the wind. She grinned at me and tossed her white hair. "Hello again, bird-brain."

"Hello, Kuhntul." I glanced at Ratatoskr, who gave me an exaggerated wink. "Ratatoskr says I don't need to climb down the trunk, that you could fly me to the bottom."

Kuhntul smiled, then laughed her glass-bell laugh. "Have you forgotten already, bird-brain?"

"Forgotten?" I shook my head as best I could while clinging to the side of a huge tree with a squirrel crouched next to my face. "What... Oh. Duh. *Plyowta*." My feet left the stirrups in the giant ash tree's bark, and I laughed, letting go of the trunk altogether.

Ratatoskr winked his exaggerated wink at me again. "Don't climb," he mouthed without making a sound. "Fly."

"Yeah, fly."

"Try to stay out of the travel lane in the future," he chided. "Dangerous for non-squirrels."

"You got it, Ratatoskr."

"And...well, if it's not too much to ask...or rude...could you perhaps wear a name tag, so I can tell the two of you apart?"

I glanced at Kuhntul and shook my head. "We don't look very much alike."

"Well, of *course* you and Kuhntul don't look alike! Do you think I'm stupid? I mean the two of you who *do* look alike."

"You've lost me, Ratatoskr."

"Oh, never mind. I'll continue to ask you about the spear-thing. That's worked well so far."

I nodded, doing my best not to smile. "Thanks for not knocking me off the tree before I remembered I could float down."

"Pleasure, pleasure. Now, I really must be off. Important discussions afoot today. I really sense we're making progress!" Without another word, Ratatoskr turned his nose toward the top of the tree and sped off, accompanied by the sound of chainsaws ripping through soft wood.

"He's a funny little guy," I said.

"Indeed," said Kuhntul, still lying across the branch.

"Well? Are you coming?"

"Coming where, Tyeldnir? Didn't you come here looking for me?"

"Yeah, I guess I did. Still, wouldn't we be more comfortable—"

"The Nornir are down there. You don't want them to overhear your questions, do you?"

I nodded. "Oh. No, I guess not." I glanced at the branch. "Slide over."

She rubbed her hand down her side and smiled. "Are you sure you wouldn't rather cuddle here with me?"

"You know better, Kuhntul. Shove over."

With a sigh, she sat up and slid close to the trunk. "There. Happy now?"

"It's a start." I settled onto the branch next to her, looking out over the vast forest. "Sure is beautiful for a conflux."

Kuhntul sat up, eyes intent on my own. "What did you say?"

I shrugged and waved my hand at the view. "It's beautiful."

"Yes, yes. What *else* did you say?"

"I said, 'it sure is beautiful for a conflux.'"

"Why do you call it that?" Her eyes blazed, and blood colored the peaks of her cheeks.

"I ran into someone… Actually, I got hijacked by someone. He called this place 'The Conflux.'"

"One of…*them*…hijacked you?"

I nodded. "We needed to get back to the *Herperty af Roostum* to get back on Luka's trail. I set up a *proo* to take us there, but when I took it, I ended up in limbo, and not for the first time. But this time—"

"Again? You must tell me of this, Hank."

I raised my eyebrows at her, a smile dancing on my lips. "Hank? I don't think you've—"

"*Enough*!" she snapped. "Tell me of these trips to limbo."

I looked at her askance. "It's happened twice, now. Three times if you count the trip through the *proo* I took as my animus, but no one spoke to me at that time. This—"

"Who spoke to you?"

"This will be easier if you stop interrupting me."

She nodded, a false smile on her face.

"The first time, the time I traveled as my animus, I could sense these Great Old Ones in the fabric of what lies between the *preer*. They were huge, shapeless chunks of…of *essence*, I guess, but they didn't seem to notice me on that trip. The next time, we were in Niflhaymr, and—"

"The space between the *preer*? What *exactly* do you mean by that?"

"When you travel the *preer*, does it feel as if it happens in an instant?"

"Yes, to most people who use them."

I shook my head, noting the careful phrasing. She hadn't answered my question, not really. "It doesn't. I think the trip happens outside of time, and that we don't—or maybe can't—interpret the lack of linear time so the—"

"None of that makes any sense, Tyeldnir."

"Yeah, well, I never claimed to be Stephen Hawking."

"Who?"

I waved the question away. "It doesn't matter. I'm just a cop, remember?"

She arched an eyebrow. "Perhaps, but I doubt it."

"Anyway," I said with an exaggerated sigh. "I experienced the…the translation that time I went as an animus. It was like…like sliding through a giant tube that had a current like a river."

"And these essences were in the current with you? These Great Old Ones?"

I shook my head, looking up at the sky. "No… At least I don't think so. It was as though they existed outside the current, as if they did as they pleased." I shrugged. "Like I said, that first time they ignored me."

"Okay. Then tell me of the second time."

I nodded. "Luka trapped us on Niflhaymr—or is it *in* Niflhaymr? Anyway, Luka set another trap using *preer*, but this time there were three of them. This was after you visited me—"

"I visited you in Niflhaymr?" she asked, sounding incredulous.

"Well, in a dream that occurred in Niflhaymr while I slept in this frost giant's hall. His name was—"

"No matter. Tell me of this dream."

"You don't remember it?"

She shook her head, avoiding my gaze.

"You did something to me. You used the chisel you gave me and did something inside my head."

She shrugged, shaking her head slowly.

"Yeah, and about that… I'd appreciate you asking my permission before you do any more spiritual brain-surgery."

"I'll bear that in mind," she said with a wry grin.

"After that dream, when I looked at the *preer*, I could sense something more than what I could see. After I enchanted my vision, I could see things under the surface of the *proo*."

"More essences?"

"Yeah. I call them Great Old Ones—or at least I did before I met Mirkur inside the last *proo*—what he called the veins of the underverse."

Her lips ground into a thin, razor-sharp line.

"Yeah. But I'm getting this out of order. The Great Old Ones made the shape of runes in the surfaces of the three *preer* Luka left for us, helping us to avoid another deadly trap. They led us to choose a certain *proo,* and we traveled across it. That was the second time I experienced the interior of a *proo*, and that time, I met a cat who called himself Bikkir. He—"

"Why was there a cat inside the *proo?*"

"It's an expression. Bikkir did more brain-surgery after yelling at me for wasting time." I pursed my lips. "They are very strange."

She nodded.

"When he let me go, I arrived on Mithgarthr, but a few hundred years ago. We were near this place historians call the Lost Colony. It's on—"

"Roanoke Island," she breathed, eyes misty with intense thought or memories.

"Yeah, how'd you know?"

"I… I've heard of it in my travels." She looked away, and the wind ruffled her white hair.

"Oh." It was such an obvious lie…but getting into an argument with a Tisir several hundred feet in the air seemed like a bad idea. "Yeah, so anyway… It was a place where Hel and Luka had spent time, and…and I think this is a side-effect of whatever you did to me, but I can see *slowthar* now. I could pick out Luka and Hel's *slowthar* from the rest, and when I concentrated on them, I could *see* what had happened there."

"Yes." Kuhntul kept her face averted and dropped her head so that her long white hair fell like a curtain over the side of her face.

"When we returned to the *proo*, intent on going back to Niflhaymr, I saw that someone had manipulated it. Its terminus had been shifted and had we traveled across it, we would have all died. Bikkir appeared in the surface of the *proo* and yammered at me again, but this time, he actually taught me something *useful*."

"How to control the *preer*," she said in a dull, lifeless voice.

"Guessed it in one."

"And the last time? When you met Mirkur?"

"That happened right before I dropped in. These Great Old Ones, these essences that live in the *preer*..."

"Yes?"

"Mirkur claims they are the *Plauinn*."

"Yes." Her bland tone of voice rang about as far from the tone of surprise as I could imagine.

"He said...he said the *Plauinn* need agents in these 'lesser' realms, that the *Plauinn* can't exist here anymore."

"Only as reflections," she murmured.

"Yeah, but he called them 'dreamslice reflections,' whatever that means."

"Yes." Her voice was flat, dead.

"He said I am to be his agent in correcting *uhrluhk*."

"Tyeldnir," she said in a voice that quavered and shook, as suddenly full of emotion as it had lacked it a moment before, "This you must not do."

"Oh, I know. I went along with him, but I'll be damned if I will be ordered around like a peon by some giant slugs, rulers of the underverse or not."

She nodded, but the gesture seemed depressed, enervated.

"He also sent me to punish Hel, Luka, and Vowli. He said death was insufficient, that I am to erase them from the skein of fate."

She turned to me, and her eyes brimmed with enraged tears. "This…" She rocked her head, dashing away her tears. "We cannot allow these *manipulators* to succeed, Tyeldnir."

"Well, I'm not sure what I can do to—"

"You must… Tyeldnir, attend me now. Have I not served your interests? Have I not guided you as would a true friend?"

I nodded, moved by the passion in her gaze.

"And have I…have I lied to you or led you astray as you once believed I might?"

"No. No, you've been a true friend, I'd say."

"Then listen to me now. You *must* resist the *Plauinn*. You must not allow anyone to manipulate you, to *coerce you* into adopting their beliefs, their plans."

"I thought the *Plauinn* would be…I don't know, a force for good in the universe. Sounds stupid."

She put her hand on my shoulder and gave it a squeeze. "Many people—many *races* of Man—believe the same, Tyeldnir. It isn't stupid and were the *Plauinn* worthy of our respect, they would be forces for good." Her eyes blazed, seeming to leap out at me. "And yet, they *are not*! They are power-mad fools, toying with the underlayment of the universe, and despite the harsh lessons such actions have already taught them, they continue."

"Are you…" I shook my head. "Mirkur said the Nornir are lesser *Plauinn*—slaves to the others essentially—but he denied that the Tisir are—"

"No, we are not *Plauinn*." She lifted her shoulders and let them drop. "Have I never explained what we are?"

"Not really. You told me your people are matrons, protectors, but most of the time you shrug and say, 'I am Tisir,' if I ask you."

She threw back her head and laughed. "Is that not answer enough?"

I chuckled and shook my head. "It's not very elucidating."

She laughed again, and it pleased me to hear it. "Perhaps I'll explain it to you in a future dream." Her face grew sober, still. "Tyeldnir, Mirkur is dangerous. A being of great power. There are no…*constraints*…on what he does, what he can do. His very name—"

"Means 'darkness.' I know."

"Yes. And do you remember Owraythu and her realm of chaos?"

I nodded, thinking first of Hel's anguished screams.

"She is his sister. Between the two, it's unknown who is the most avaricious, the most tyrannous. They are named the *Tveeburar af Tikifiri*—the Twins of Chance—by those that worship them, but they are never content to leave things to chance. Together, they rule the *Plauinn*—at least the biggest faction. The Nornir…they *cower* like weaklings in the face of the *Tveeburar* demands, but they don't always... *Uhrluhk* has its own ways of resisting their manipulations."

"Then—"

"But the danger lies in how they manipulate others to take up their cause. They may tell you of actions they portray as evil—"

"No one needs to tell me about Hel's actions. They *are* evil."

Kuhntul turned to face me, her expression blank. For a moment, she almost seemed angry. "No. No one argues for a different interpretation. But...have you considered her motivations?"

"Her motivations don't—"

"Do they not? What *drove* her to make the choices she has? What led her down this path of bitterness, of fury...of *hatred*?"

"Look, Kuhntul, I don't know about—"

"Shouldn't you, though?" she demanded. "Shouldn't you consider that which drives someone to do what they do? How can you judge her actions without..." With a visible effort, she calmed herself and shook her head. "You've tasted Mirkur's techniques, seen the torments Owraythu is subjecting Hel to—or at least you've heard the results of those techniques. You've seen how we 'lesser beings' are thought of by these *Plauinn*—objects fit only for manipulation. Not *people* in their eyes, we are less than insects. We are *nothing*."

I looked down at the ground so far below us. "Does that make it okay? Are you even aware of what she's done?"

"I'm intimately aware of what she's done," she said so softly I almost missed it. "Perhaps more so than you."

"Oh, so she killed thousands and thousands of people on your *klith*?" I scoffed, trying to make it a chuckle but failing.

"Yes. Many, many more, actually."

"And I suppose she kidnapped *your* family? Cursed you, ruined your life?"

"The actions undertaken by the woman known as Hel have affected me in ways you can't imagine, and to say she ruined my life…well, at times, there aren't words to express the depths of my anger, my rage at how Hel's actions have impacted me over the course of my lifetime… But you know what, Tyeldnir? It isn't a competition between the two of us. She's done evil things. She's done monstrous, horrible things, and that can't be denied—not by anyone, me least of all. But still, she, like everyone, deserves compassion and an attempt at understanding. No one deserves to be tortured without pause for eternity."

An algid silence descended between us. I didn't look up at her, but I felt her eyes crawling over my face. "Why are you *defending* her?" I hissed.

Kuhntul sighed and shook her head. "I'm not… I'm…" She sighed again, and the sound of it was bitter, cold. "Oh, I don't know what I'm doing! But there's more to it than you understand, Tyeldnir. More to it than you *can* understand."

The wind gusted around us, and the sun sank lower in the sky. "What she's done…" She shook her head. "I'm not saying she's made good choices, Tyeldnir. But perhaps you can—"

"What does Hel's behavior have to do with Mirkur?"

"Do you truly not know? Have you not guessed?" Kuhntul sighed. "There is more going on here than you realize."

"You've said that."

"What about Luka? Do you have easier feelings—"

"Are you kidding?" I glared at her. "He killed my partner—no, he *ate* my partner."

"Yes," she said, hanging her head. "I'd forgotten." The last came as a whisper floating on the wind.

"I wish I could forget. He…Luka left him there, on the table between us when I caught up to him. Jax was—" Suddenly, it was all too much. The pain had scabbed over in the intervening years, but thinking about it, *talking* about it again, ripped that scab away, burned out the stops that I'd grown to keep the pain at bay.

"He, too, has made atrocious decisions, but even with that said, there were reasons he became what he is—"

"What?" I nearly shouted. "What *reasons*? What could possibly mitigate what he's done? To my family? To *his own family*?"

Her expression was grim, but she nodded.

I sucked in a long breath and let it out through my nose, going for a bit of Zen, trying to rein in my emotions; not only because the name of unfettered emotions was spelled P-A-I-N in the parlance of my Personal Monster™, but because I'd grown to *like* Kuhntul in the few weeks I'd known her, to respect her, and I didn't want to let the wedge that was swelling in the space between us solidify.

I nodded once, curtly. "Based on what Mirkur wants...*demands* I do to Hel, Luka, and Vowli, in conjunction with what you've alluded to tonight, I'm going to go out on a limb here. Did Mirkur recruit Hel as one of his agents? Is that where her depravity started?"

Kuhntul grimaced and shook her head.

"Or Luka, maybe? Vowli?"

"Mirkur..." She sighed, and her shoulders slumped. "The story is long and complex. It isn't as simple as saying Mirkur influenced their thinking, that he brought them all together and they went their own way. No. It was more than that. It was more than recruiting them..."

"Then what?"

She sighed. "Perhaps it is not the time. Maybe it is too soon, too fresh. Or perhaps you haven't seen enough of the *Plauinn* and how they operate."

I nodded and held out my hand, palm up. "Out of respect for you, and for Meuhlnir, I will *try* to keep my mind open. I will try to be open to...to whatever these mitigating circumstances might be."

"That's all I can ask. Watch the *Plauinn*. Watch the Isir. Watch *everything*, withhold your judgment if you can."

"Okay, I'll try."

She looked at me, and I read the depth of her passion in the set of her jaw, the twitching muscles around her eyes, her flared nostrils. "Tyeldnir, there are things I can't tell you, things I...I...things you should..."

"Kuhntul, listen. I understand how important this is to you, and for that reason alone, I would give all this my best effort, my best...uh...whatever it is. My best."

"Thank you, Hank Jensen."

I grinned and bumped her with my shoulder. "Aw, shucks, Kuhntul. I didn't know you even knew my full name, let alone could use it."

"I know many things about you, Tyeldnir. For one, it is apparent how much you enjoy it when I call you Tyeldnir, or Aylootr, or—"

"Um, I think you might have that one backward."

She winked at me and flashed a crooked smile. "No, I think not."

"If you say so." We sat next to one another for a time, legs dangling off the branch hundreds of feet off the ground, swinging our feet like children. I swept my hand at the horizon. "I thought this place was a dream."

"You mean it isn't?"

"We're here in the flesh this time, right?"

Kuhntul shrugged. "I am Tisir."

"Back to that?" I grinned at her. "No, I mean last time I was here, it was a...I don't know, a brink-of-death dream, right?"

"And what is different this time?"

"Mirkur sent me this time."

"You've said."

"I mean, I'm *actually* here this time. Not in spirit—"

"Dreamslice reflection," she said.

"—or whatever." I cocked my eyebrow at her. "So, last time, I was here the way the Three Maids are here?"

Kuhntul shrugged. "Who do you think I am, Stephen Hawkman?"

I grinned. "Hawking. Stephen Hawking."

"Him, too."

"Is that your way of admitting you don't know?"

"I am Tisir," she said with a shrug.

"Is this place *real*? Is it an actual place? A *physical* place?"

Kuhntul patted the branch we sat on, then rapped her knuckles on the trunk. "Seems so."

"Could a *proo* reach this place?"

"If you understood how to direct it here." She shrugged.

"Bikkir taught me how to put the end of a *proo* where I want it."

"Ah, so you've been traveling through the same *proo*?"

"We thought about trying one of Meuhlnir and Veethar's *preer*, but we didn't have any knowledge of where they ended up and—"

"That's how Mirkur found you."

"What?"

"Because you've been using the same *proo*, only switching its terminus."

"I don't understand."

"When you use the same *proo* every time you travel, or even if you use one more than any other, the *Plauinn* can sense it. If they are interested in you and sense your passage along a certain *proo* frequently, they will move into that *proo* and lie in wait."

"Why would they…" I shook my head and waved it all away. "Never mind that question for now. How do you know this?"

"I am Tisir."

"Yeah, but how do you know? Has it happened to you?"

Kuhntul lifted her chin and let it drop as she exhaled. "It is difficult to explain."

"Try," I said.

"My existence is…complicated. What has happened to another sometimes feels as if it has happened to me. Sometimes I… Sometimes I am confused by the memories—confused whether the memories are mine, those of the ones I am charged to watch over, or…or belonging to someone else entirely."

"Ah. You are Tisir."

"*Exactly*. Regardless, I have a memory of being accosted inside the *preer*. I don't think I knew it was there until you told me of your experiences, but it is a true memory, nonetheless." She gazed at the horizon for a moment, a thousand-yard stare wiping her features clean of expression. "I remember…"

"What?" I asked softly.

"I remember learning that my use of the same few *preer* was allowing the *Plauinn* to trace my movements, to follow what I was doing…" She shook her head. "Eventually, I learned that if I wanted to act with subterfuge, I needed to call a fresh *proo*—either to create one, or to call one at random and reset its terminus points to my liking."

"I don't know how to call a *proo*, let alone to *create* one from out of thin air."

She nodded once. "This thing, I can teach you."

"Bearing in mind I'm not Tisir, will I be able to do it?"

She turned slowly and locked gazes with me. "I wasn't always Tisir, Tyeldnir. I learned this trick before I…" She shook her head. "Before I transitioned from what I was into what I am."

Her manner had grown strange, her speech halting, broken. "How did you—"

She made a chopping gesture with her hand. "No. I will speak no more of it." She slid off the branch and hung in midair, arching an eyebrow at me. "Come."

"*Plyowta*," I said and slid off the branch. "Lead on, O Sage." I grinned, but Kuhntul didn't return it—she flipped her hair and held out her hand, instead. I grasped her hand, and she pulled me out over the forest, heading away from Iktrasitl.

"Too many prying eyes back there," she called over the wind-noise of our flight. After a few minutes' flight filled with course corrections that seemed random, Kuhntul swooped through the trees to land on the rich forest loam.

As soon as my feet touched the ground, I released her hand and took a step away. She turned and flashed a long-suffering grin at me.

"Tell me how this Bikkir taught you to manipulate the *preer*," she said.

"There's something he called 'the hook' on every *preer*, and I have to reach out and grab it with my mind. Once I have it, it twists the way a dial or a knob twists, and if I am picturing the destination with enough clarity, the *proo* snaps to it."

She made a face. "That's a strange method. I've never heard of anyone using a method such as that."

I shrugged. "Seems to work for me. How do other people do it? I know the Alfar and Tverkar don't even try."

"Ha! They *try* all right, they just can't do it very well."

"Oh. They led me to believe something else."

"By the Alfar? Or by your Tverkr pet?"

I nodded.

"Consider the source." Her voice had taken on an imperious tone that made my skin crawl.

"How do the Tisir do it?"

She turned away from me, presenting her profile, and gazed into the woods. "Tisir methods are for Tisir."

"Fine. How did you do it *before* you became a Tisir?"

"You know of the *strenkir af krafti* already, and know *vefari* have the ability to weave these strings of power, but has anyone explained to you that the strings vibrate at specific frequencies?"

"When Meuhlnir told me about Haymtatlr and the *Kyatlarhodn*, he mentioned something about the skein of fate vibrating once Haymtatlr blew the horn, but, between you and me, that all sounded like myth."

She bobbed her head from side to side. "As did the tales of the Isir, no? Did you believe Osgarthr existed before you came to be there? Did you believe Luka when he claimed to be a god the Norse named Loki?"

"Well, no, but he never actually—"

"Exactly. What that old fool calls the 'skein of fate' is nothing more than a representation of the *strenkir af krafti* combined with all the *slowthar* of all beings in the universe, living and dead."

"What about *uhrluhk*?"

She shrugged. "*Uhrluhk* isn't what most people think it is, as you've already learned. It isn't a fixed fate or a fixed destiny at all, but rather can be expressed as the sum of probabilities of what will happen. What *might be*, in other words. There is no single future, no absolute path that the universe must take."

"Yeah."

"All that's neither here nor there," she said, flapping a hand. "What we are interested in are the *strenkir* themselves."

I spread my hands. "Okay."

A half grin played on her lips. "What do you think the *proo* actually are?"

"I don't have any idea, really, but I've always thought they might be wormholes through space."

"Wormholes?"

"Tunnels. Short-cuts that skip the intervening physical distance between two points."

She chuckled. "And you are sure all such points have a distance between them?"

I held up my hands in surrender. "Cop, remember? Not Stephen Hawking. Or Stephen Hawkman, either."

"I've come to understand the *strenkir af krafti* in the time since my…since my transition. The strings connect everything in the universe. Either directly or as chains of strings. One connects you and me, for example. Another connects you and Jane. Yet another connects a point in spacetime on Mithgarthr to a point on Osgarthr. Do you see?"

"I guess, but that seems like an uncountably infinite number of strings to keep track of. It sounds a bit clunky."

She shrugged. "Who needs to keep track of them all? Surely not you or me."

"What about Mirkur?"

She made a face and flapped her hand. "He's not as all-knowing as he thinks. Nor as powerful. At most, one would need to keep track of the *strenkir* linked to oneself, and even that would be overkill."

"I'll take your word for it."

"Do you see how to create a *proo*?"

I shook my head. "Not really."

"Tyeldnir, the *strenkir af krafti* and the *preer*...they are different sides of the same coin."

I thought about that for a moment. If the *preer* and the *strenkir* were related to one another, then... No. She said they were two sides of the same coin. The *strenkir af krafti* and the *preer* are not merely related to one another, they are aspects of the same thing.

Her eyes were on mine, intense, burning with focus. "You begin to see it."

"I think so. This skein of fate, this tapestry..."

"Yes?"

"Do the *strenkir af krafti* form a mesh? A mesh that links everything to everything else?"

She nodded. "And more than that, but for now, it's enough. Can you see how to create a *proo* based on that idea?"

"No, but grabbing a *proo* at random would be as simple as co-opting a string from between two points in the general vicinity."

"Ye-e-e-s," she said. "But that would cause discontinuities in the density matrix."

"The *what*?"

She shrugged. "The phase-space probability measure." I shook my head, and she frowned. "Think of these discontinuities as decoherences in spacetime."

"A 'bad thing' in other words?"

"Well, in terms of the two points connected by the *strenkir* that had enjoyed a certain phase relation between each other, yes. But such decoherences occur naturally at every given moment. It's part of the probabilistic nature of the universal underlayment as we know it."

I waved my hands. "I'll just take your word for it."

"I should note that these discontinuities can be mended with closed timelike curves in other *strenkir*."

"Do I really need to understand all this?"

Her eyes popped open a bit wider, and she twitched as if waking from a dream. "What?"

"You were explaining what I assume to be the quantum physics of the *preer*."

"I…" She looked around. "I was? That's strange."

"Sister, you don't know the half of it."

She shook her head.

"I'd suggested that I could grab one of the *strenkir* from the surrounding area and co-opt it as a *proo*."

She shook her head. "No, you mustn't do that. The *strenkir af krafti* and the *preer* are two sides of the same coin—they are not the *same* side of the coin."

I shook my head and shrugged. "That doesn't do much to clarify the situation, I'm afraid."

She pursed her lips. "The Three Maids exist in this place as dreamslice reflections of their true selves, located somewhere in the underverse. Same as you were when you visited Iktrasitl while you lay dying in that cave on Osgarthr. Your body was there, yet your dreamslice reflection was here. You see? Two sides of the same coin."

I shrugged and blew out a breath. "Which was the real me?"

She flashed a crooked smile. "Neither. Two sides of the same coin, remember? Can one side of a coin exist without the other?"

"Oh…" I inclined my head. "I think I get it. The dreamslice reflections and the…what do you call the physical counterpart?"

"Matterstream manifestation."

"Right. So, this dreamslice reflection and this matterstream manifestation walk into a bar…"

She gave me a strange look. "I don't follow."

"That's how a bunch of bad jokes start back on Mithgarthr. Never mind."

"I don't remember jokes like that," she muttered.

"You've been to Mithgarthr?"

She started and looked away. "What? Oh, who hasn't been there?"

"As a Tisir or before?"

She shook her head. "You were saying something about dreamslice reflections?"

"Yeah." I couldn't see how talking about her pre-Tisir past would make her uncomfortable, but she gave off the vibe in waves. "The dreamslice reflection and the matterstream manifestation, together they define the person?"

"Or thing. Or place."

"Oh. I hadn't thought of that. What do you call the coin? The whole?"

She lifted her shoulders and abruptly let them drop. "The concinnity."

I swept my hand around us. "Is this the dreamslice reflection, the matterstream manifestation, or the concinnity of the Conflux?"

She raised her eyes and looked at the surrounding forest. "I'm... I don't know. Sometimes, it doesn't matter."

"So what is this place? The Conflux, I mean?"

Again, her shoulders hitched up and dropped. "It's the remains of the home realm of the *Plauinn*, and, as such, it's the point of unification for the timeflows."

"Oh, boy. I'm not going to ask."

"Think of it as the opposite of Owraythu's realm, where the timeflows have been forced into divergence."

"Yeah, that doesn't help. Thanks anyway."

"The distinction being that here there are an uncountably infinite number of potential *preer* to choose from in this place, while in Owraythu's realm, there are almost none."

"That seems like it would be particularly dangerous to open a *proo* to her realm, in that case."

Kuhntul nodded, her shoulders slumped and her eyes glistening. "Yes," she whispered. "And for that reason alone, a direct rescue of Hel would be very difficult."

"Let's get back to the *preer*," I said, not willing to open the subject of saving Hel from her torment again.

"Yes," she said dully. "Here, it is easy. Reach out your hand, and there is a *proo* beneath it. But other places are different and finding a *proo* can be too difficult. The *strenkir af krafti* is the matterstream manifestation while the concurrent *proo* is the dreamslice reflection. A concinnity is what we must create to bring a new *proo* into existence."

"I don't even understand what a concinnity is in this case."

Kuhntul's smile was a faint one. "But you do, you just don't *know* you know. What is a *proo,* in your own words?"

"A wormhole," I said with a shrug.

"And where does a wormhole exist?"

"In spacetime."

"No, that's too general. Where, *exactly*, does a wormhole exist?"

"What do you want me to say. A wormhole connects two points in spacetime with one another."

"Yes! A wormhole exists between two points."

"Ah," I breathed. "And the *strenkir af krafti*? The physical part? What is that? Where does it exist?"

"Very astute questions, Tyeldnir. The *strenkir* are expressions of the matterstream in widths that approach zero, depending on the size of the internal compact dimensions of the universe-slice it exists in."

"Oh, boy."

"They are thin, with a width smaller than the smallest bit of matter, but they can have infinite length."

"Okay. Extremely skinny, yet super-long streams of matter. What's a stream of matter look like?"

"I said, 'can have infinite length,' not 'do have.' They can be as short as they are wide, which is an important part of calling a *proo* into existence."

"I think I'm getting it. To create a *proo*, I need to connect two points that aren't already connected, and once that has happened, move one end of the *proo* to where I want it."

Kuhntul smiled and nodded. "That's it. That's right."

"How do I do it?"

"It's an act of creation, the same as when you *vefa strenki* or when you *stayba runana*. I bet none of your teachers taught you that aspect of the arts, did they?"

"No," I said, scratching my beard. "But it makes sense. I'd never thought of it that way. Meuhlnir creates a path for the lightning to follow. Mothi creates a path for the cells of his muscles to transform—to grow or shrink. Sif's healing creates a path for a wave of healing energy, creates the building blocks of life."

"Just so."

"Tell me how to do this!" I said, excitement bubbling in my voice.

"The first step is to create two small bits of something—almost unimaginably small. And you must create them within a field of power you maintain control of—at least at first. Attend me."

I enchanted my vision, so I could follow what she was doing. She held her hands in certain ways that reminded me of something I'd seen before, but which I couldn't place.

"*Akneer ayka syer stath*," she said, and with a tiny flash of light and an almost inaudible pop, twin points of brightness appeared between her out-thrust hands. "There, do you see?"

I nodded.

"And now the linkage." She took a deep breath and an expression of deep concentration settled on her features. "*Akneer hlechkur.*"

A vibration I almost heard occurred, and the two points of light hovering between her palms linked with a slash of light that was so thin it appeared to be a glint of sunlight on the edge of a finely sharpened blade.

"Now, the *proo*." The lines of concentration etched in her features deepened. "*Hlyowthu strenkidn*," she hissed. With a high frequency twang that I felt more than heard, another glinting line appeared between the flashing points of lights hovering between her palms. "Ah, that's fine," she said. "Can you see this hook Bikkir taught you to manipulate?"

"No," I said. "It's different from…" I peered at the symphony of light hovering between her palms. "Wait. I *can* see the hook even though the *proo* is as different from any *proo* I've seen as air is to water."

She chuckled. "That's because you are seeing it from the side rather than gazing into it from either end. *Snooa*," she crooned, and the lights rotated around their center point, when it was end-on, I saw the familiar silvery oval, but unlike the others I'd seen, there was another oval right behind the first.

"Ah, I see."

"And you can manipulate it as the *Plauinn* taught you?"

I grasped the hook and gave it a spin, focusing on the base of a tree twenty steps away. Immediately the far end of the *proo* disappeared and reappeared next to the tree's trunk.

"Interesting," she breathed. "If our roles were reversed, I doubt I could manipulate your *proo* while you held it in a field of control."

"Oh?"

"No," she said with a firm shake of her head. "Observe." She changed the configuration of her left hand and whispered, "*Fira*." The word meant 'move' in the *Gamla Toonkumowl*, and as she uttered it, the end of the *proo* slid toward us as though she pulled it on a string. "You see?"

"Yes," I said. "You move the particle, and the *proo* follows. I move the *proo,* and the particle follows."

"Yes." With a sigh of fatigue, she dropped her hands.

I thought the particles, the *strenki*, and the *proo*, would fade from existence, but they didn't. They began a frenetic dance—orbiting each other like the midair hijinks of two hummingbirds, the *strenki* and the *proo* stretching and snapping between them. "Beautiful," I breathed.

"Can you do this?" she asked.

"Yes," I said without pausing for thought. "I thought the particles would disappear when you released them, but they don't."

She shook her head. "No. Creation is the process of converting energy back to matter, just as destruction converts matter into energy. Once converted, in either direction, an object must live out its natural course in the timeflows."

I nodded as if I understood that perfectly. "What does striking off a series of events from the bark of Iktrasitl do?"

She tilted her head to the side and squinted. "That depends on the extent of the changes, I suppose."

"What if I did to Mirkur what he wants me to do to Hel?"

"I have never seen one of the *Plauinn* mentioned in the skein of fate."

"But they must be there!"

She shrugged. "Perhaps, but I've never seen them."

"Are there parts of the skein that the Nornir forbid you to look at?"

She shook her head. "Even if they did, there would be no real way to stop me from reading whatever I liked. All I'd have to do is wait for their absence. No, if the *Plauinn* are subject to *uhrluhk*, they must have their own tapestry somewhere else."

"Hmm. That seems...convenient. Wouldn't there need to be another conflux of timeflows as well?"

Her shoulders made their inevitable rise and fall. "Perhaps the *Plauinn* are not subject to temporal constraint since they live outside the timeflows. Or maybe there is another version of this conflux in the place of limbo you see between the ends of the *preer*."

I rubbed a hand across my eye sockets and forehead. "That's cheating."

"Maybe so."

"Is there no way to beat them?"

She turned away and looked at me from the corner of her eyes. "Hel avoided their machinations for a long time."

"How did she do that?"

"In addition to abstaining from travel by *preer*, she absconded to Mithgarthr."

I nodded slowly. "So that's why they came...why they stayed for so long."

Kuhntul sighed. "Yes."

"But why did she *want* to avoid them?"

Another sigh gusted out of Kuhntul. "The *Plauinn* manipulated her. They wanted a change to the flows, and Suel was an instrument of theirs. Maybe she proved unsuitable to perform the changes, or she may have refused, fought against them, but whatever the reason, they abandoned her during her war against the rebels. The *Plauinn* manipulated Suel, Luka, and Vowli into breaking the *Ayn Loug*, and in the original timeflow that led to—"

"The *original* timeflow?"

Kuhntul's mouth snapped shut with a click of her teeth. She shook her head and turned back toward Iktrasitl, so I couldn't see her face. "Never mind."

"No, it sounds pretty important."

"Those events never happened from your perspective."

"Even so, I'd like to hear what happened."

She shook her head. "No, it would only cloud the issues. Suffice it to say that the outcome of the *Plauinn* manipulation of the timeflow was...undesirable, to say the least. The resulting flows were dark and filled with misery."

"For who?"

Kuhntul sliced the air with her hand. "It doesn't matter. An intervention was planned and executed, and this timeflow has a much better potential outcome."

"I don't like this, Kuhntul."

She sighed and took a step away from me. "It is how it has to be."

"How was the original timeflow altered? Tell me that much."

Her shoulders slumped, and she hung her head. "Hel was told of the treachery of the *Plauinn*. Hel...she..." She shook her head. "Suel was lied to by the *Plauinn*. They poured bitterness and unrest into her ears at every opportunity. They turned her reign from its proper course. Perverting what would have been eons of peace and prosperity into a time of darkness, of despicable deeds done in the dark."

"I've heard about Suel's fall from grace."

"From Meuhlnir's perspective, no doubt."

"Yes."

"Then you only have heard half the story. He wasn't privy to—she'd been told he couldn't be trusted, that, in time, he would foster and lead a rebellion to depose her. It was part of how the *Plauinn* manipulated her into accepting the course they planned for her and for her empire." Her voice warbled with emotion. "She should have known better," she whispered.

"I've only known Meuhlnir for a short time in the cosmic scale of things, but I can't imagine him betraying anyone."

"Yes," she whispered. "But they were convincing. They manipulated events to underscore their dire prophecies. These 'advisors' created situations in which Meuhlnir acted in ways they predicted. They'd instructed her to watch for certain behaviors—from Meuhlnir, from Sif and Yowrnsaxa, from all the Isir close to her except for Luka and Vowli. Unwittingly, the Isir reinforced the poison the *Plauinn* dribbled in Suel's ear." She turned back to face me, high color on her cheeks and a glisten of wetness in her eyes. "She should have trusted her friends, but it was all so… The lies she was told, the behaviors she was told to watch for, the unrest in the karl caste, the complaints about taxation, all of it had been 'predicted' by the *Plauinn*. They played her like a lute, and Luka and Vowli danced to the tune."

"Still. I don't see how she could lose her faith in Meuhlnir—in her lifelong friends."

Kuhntul grunted sourly. "You don't understand what it takes to rule, the personal cost of it. The court intrigues, the constant gossip."

"No, I don't know what that's like, but I know what it is to put my life in another's hands and to trust that person. Meuhlnir almost died to save her life from assassins, and—"

"Even that was used to turn her from her path."

"What? How could that possibly be used *against* Meuhlnir?"

Kuhntul shook her head. "It had started by that time, of course. The manipulation, the fracture of her psyche, teaching her a dark, twisted form of *saytr* that focused on life and death. A horrible, despicable thing."

I shook my head. "When we first met, you seemed to hate Hel, but now—"

"No," she said, shaking her head. "You mistook hating the path she'd chosen for hating the woman herself. I do not hate her. What she became—both as a result of the manipulations, and as a result of rejecting them—I hate that, but the person she was is still there. Buried. Smothered." She shrugged. "But still there."

"Who are you, Kuhntul?" I whispered.

She glanced at my face, eyes seeking mine. "I am Kuhntul of the Tisir. No more, no less."

"That doesn't seem like a whole answer."

"Nevertheless, it is all the answer I can give you."

"There are times…times when you remind me of someone, but I can't place who."

She shrugged, a smile on her lips. "I am Kuhntul."

"Yes," I said and sighed.

The silence stretched the moment between us as we stood regarding one another. She tilted her head to the side. "You've heard Meuhlnir's tales. Hear a short one of mine."

"Sure."

"It was a time of great stress in Suel's life. She'd taken to walking late into the night, sometimes with Meuhlnir, but less and less so as the *Plauinn* poisoned her thoughts against him. After that, she walked with Luka or Vowli, whose motives the *Plauinn* vouched for. One night, she walked alone in her gardens. She came to the spot where Meuhlnir had fought against the two assassins and almost died to save her. She was in a melancholy mood, and her mind turned back to those events, replaying the night in her mind's eye…"

TWENTY-
EIGHT

uel strolled through the garden, following the
path she and Meuhlnir had taken on the night
of the assassination attempt. Her hand drifted
up to massage her throat, which had not yet healed
in fullness.

Things had taken a turn that night. If nothing else,
the brazen attempt on her life had made it impossible
to ignore the depths of unrest in her empire, and it
had underscored how futile her actions had been to

relieve the political pressure. *Damn those fools*, she thought, scalding anger pouring into her mind. *What more do they want from me?*

How could it be possible that Meuhlnir is against me? He fought for me; he saved *me from the assassin's arrows!* She shook her head and took a sweeping slice at the air with her hand. It couldn't be possible. She stopped walking and gazed up into the dark night sky. She released a heavy sigh.

Shadows thickened around her, and she let her eyes slide shut. The shadows felt like velvet as they caressed her skin. It reminded her of one her father's encompassing bearhugs.

Your mind is a tempest, small one, whispered a voice in her mind. *Her* voice, the woman who warned her about the plots within plots that grew unbounded across the empire.

"Yes," said Suel. "I can't believe my friend Meuhlnir would betray me."

Ah, that. He is but a male.

"Yes," breathed Suel.

Males are...complicated. You know this.

Suel nodded, but there was a still, small voice deep inside her that rejected the very idea that Meuhlnir would betray her.

The sound of laughter filled her mind. *Ah, small one, did I not explain his jealousy of your throne? Your power? Even as he lay dying before you, you reached into the void and drew such energy to your use that it filled him with jealousy, with rage against your natural talents. He could not save you, the way you saved him, and in his twisted way of viewing the universe, that is a betrayal.*

"But he's never—"

And why would he? Why do you expect him to be honest with you about his feelings? Men think emotions are a weakness! Surely, you know this. He is but a man, and that, above all else, dictates who he is.

Suel shook her head.

Yes, small one. The time you spend with the brother compounds his jealousy. This, too, counts as a betrayal in his eyes, and perhaps the more important of the two.

"No, you do him a disservice. Meuhlnir is not the same as other men. He's—"

Do not presume to tell me what he is, small one. I have the ability to reach inside him, to see his thoughts. It is you who do me the disservice. What do I gain by turning you against this man?

"I...I don't know," she finished lamely.

Nothing. My existence is far beyond your wildest imaginings, and as you are now, you can't understand my motivations. But I will tell you, if you will listen.

Suel nodded. "Yes, please," she breathed.

Your potential intrigues us. It has been so long since one such as you has graced the universe. Do you not feel your potential? Do you not sense how different you are from these puny beings who surround you? You and the brother, and perhaps one other...you three alone bear the potential to go beyond the petty trappings of this realm, of this plane of existence. I am here to serve as a guide, small one. I visit you to help you rise above your lowly beginnings, to surpass the constraints these petty beings place on you.

"But…aren't I one of them? My sister—"

Yes. Your sister might have the potential, being from the same genetic stock, but the necessary mindset eludes her—the ambition, the single-mindedness—that such a directed evolution requires. No, your sister will remain where she is, tied forever to this realm, to its insignificant events. You, my dear, will outgrow this place.

Suel shook her head. She always found the arguments convincing, and there was a part of her that already believed it all. The part of her that wasn't sure grew weaker and weaker every day—as the predictions proved accurate. "But what if I *told* Freya? What if I mentored her as you mentor me?"

No matter. Do so if you wish, but I tell you now she will never be a true sister to you, small one. She will never step from your shadow and stand shoulder to shoulder with you against your enemies. In fact, before events here conclude, she will betray you. They will all betray you. All but the brother and the other one.

Luka and Vowli, she thought.

The brother and the other, confirmed the voice in her head.

She meandered down the garden path, her mind reeling with what-ifs and maybes.

Did your childhood companion not act as I told you she would this day? Did she not sneer in secret? Did she not judge you, disapprove of you? Did she not display her hatred of you for all present to see?

Suel's mind replayed the events in her throne room that afternoon: her conversation with Vowli and Luka into which Sif had so rudely interjected herself. The scorn in Sif's voice, the look in her eye, they still rankled. *Who is she to judge me?*

Yes, crooned the voice in her head. *Who is she, indeed? You saw her true face this day. Remember it.*

"I will remember," she promised.

The thing she still hides from you, however, is her lust for the brother.

"What? She seems much more interested in Paltr."

Mere camouflage. In the darkness, when her secret heart beats true, she lusts after the one you call Luka. The one that will champion your cause, the one who will always stand at your side, ensuring your safety, your comfort before he even considers his own. This one with the 'cow's mouth' seeks to steal him away from you.

Suel's mind twisted back on itself. "That conniving little bitch!" she hissed.

You have little to worry about in that regard. My auguries show he will be forever by your side. It is naught but another example of how much these petty beings resent you, how they plot against your happiness, your very life. In the days that follow, she will join forces with this Paltr to discredit the brother, to drive him from your service if they can. When this comes to pass, will you finally trust me?

"I…I *do* trust you," Suel whispered, almost a whine. "But it's so hard…these people have been my friends all of my life. They—"

No! No, they are not your friends. They tolerate *you,* ingratiate *themselves to you in order that they may profit from your position. Do they not all hold choice postings within your palace? Are they not fed and clothed without so much as a thimble-full of work on their own parts?*

"Yes, I suppose that is true."

"Sister?" asked Freya from the path behind her. "Who are you talking to?"

Even she will betray you, small one. Remember that.

"No one," said Suel. "Myself."

Freya laughed, and the night air tinkled with the sound of glass bells. "You know what they say about people who talk to themselves."

"What?" hissed Suel, rounding on her sister with fire in her eyes. "What do they say about me?"

"Huh?" Freya hesitated mid-step. "What? No, I meant—"

She wants your throne. She will conspire to depose you before the year's end.

Rage boiled in Suel's veins. "I know what you want, *Sister*. You want me judged insane so you can sit on my throne and rule in my stead. But I tell you, Freya, it will never work! I will die before I let you take my throne."

"Suel, what is this?" asked Freya, confusion reigning on her face. "A joke, Sister. I *love* you, Suel. I'd never do anything against you."

She will ally with your enemies before the year is out.

"Sure, sure. You and Sif!"

Freya shook her head. "Sister, you've nothing to worry about with us. We all love you. I don't even want to be empress. It pleases me to support your rule, as is my duty, I might add, as it is your birthright to rule in the first place. I wouldn't want the pressures you deal with so easily; I'm not cut from the same cloth, I could never do as good a job as you do, Sister. And Sif...Sif has been your truest friend since we were all in pigtails. You needn't worry about her either. If she speaks out of turn, it is only out of love for you."

"Love! Ha!" Suel whirled away from her sister and stomped her foot. "You are all the same. Jealous! Avaricious!"

"Sister, I—"

"Silence!" Suel snapped, whirling back to sneer in her sister's face. "Do not presume to instruct me on the motivations of my subjects."

"Friends, Suel. Family."

Do you see how she already betrays you in her heart?

"Silence!" shrieked Suel. "Silence or I'll have your tongue cut from your head!" She whirled and stared into the shadows of the Queen's Garden.

Freya fell silent and her gaze drifted far away as a single tear slid down her cheek.

TWENTY-
NINE

Kuhntul fell silent, her gaze far away, focused on the event she'd recounted, tears brimming in her eyes.

"Who are you, Kuhntul? You speak as if you witnessed those events in the flesh." For the first time, I glanced down at her *slowth,* and the size of it amazed me. I bent my mind to dip into her *slowth*, but I could not—something repelled me.

Kuhntul shrugged, still gazing away into the distance. "I am Kuhntul," she said in a lifeless voice. "I am Tisir."

"Were you Suel's Tisir?"

She guffawed once and turned to meet my gaze. "In a way, I suppose."

"I don't understand."

"No," she said. "You do not. But it is no matter." The sound of glass bells tinkled through the forest as she laughed.

"Your laugh…the way you flirt all the time…your obvious love of Suel…" I mused.

"Yes?" she said, suddenly solemn.

"Are you…are you—"

"I've said. I'm Kuhntul, and I am Tisir."

"Yes, but you are more than that. Are you—*were* you Freya?"

Her face grew slack as she stared at me. Slowly, she shook her head. "I am Kuhntul, Tyeldnir. I need be no other."

"Okay," I said with a sigh. "Okay. Kuhntul it is, but will you promise me one thing?"

"That depends on what you require of me."

"If there comes a time when I need more information than that, will you tell me?"

She nodded without pause, without hesitation. "Of that, you can be sure."

"Okay."

"Okay," she repeated.

"Pinky-swear?"

She cocked her head to the side. "You are sometimes quite strange. Do you know that?"

"Yeah, so people keep telling me."

"Well, it's true."

"Yeah, yeah. My big brain makes everyone jealous."

She grinned.

"One more question about the *preer*."

She shrugged. "Ask."

"Can I dial a *proo* to point back to this place?"

"Why not?"

"Isn't it…I don't know…outside of…of…"

"It's the Conflux, a concinnity of time. It's neither inside nor outside of anything. Think of it as the scaffold that supports everything else."

"Everything except the timeflows, right?"

She pursed her lips. "I'm not sure that's true. Would they exist without the Conflux? That answer eludes me."

"Well, whatever. As long as I can get back here. When you took the chisel in my dream…"

She gave me a strange look. "It was *your* dream, Tyeldnir. Plus, you know how to find it without wasting oxygen."

I nodded, and the chisel's warm bulk rested in my palm.

"You see?"

"Yeah."

"Don't let Mother Skult see that."

"No, I won't. Especially not now I understand what she *really* is." I pursed my lips and met Kuhntul's gaze.

"Yes?" she asked.

"Suel gave up on her friends without a fight."

"You don't understand what it is to have others speaking directly in your mind, Tyeldnir. You don't understand the power of such voices."

"I don't?"

"It is as if those voices are your own thoughts, your own mind telling you things it has worked out when you weren't looking."

I shook my head, lips wrinkled in a frown. "I've had the *Plauinn* talking inside my mind, I've had you mucking about in there. I can tell the difference. Everyone wants me to roll over and pull their cargo, but I won't do it. I know the difference between what's right for me and what someone else wants me to think is right for me."

Kuhntul's shoulders twitched up and down. "Maybe, but you haven't experienced a sustained campaign of manipulation. I've always allowed you free choice—to do anything else would be to lower myself to *Plauinn* levels. You haven't experienced the *Plauinn* pouring poison into your inner ear day in and day out."

"No, I guess I haven't, but it still seems that she gave up on her lifelong friends on such little evidence."

Kuhntul frowned. "Don't forget, Tyeldnir, that they convinced her by giving her 'signs' that what they claimed was true. They told her partial truths: So-and-so will act thus, such-and-such will happen when so-and-so acts this way. It was all very plausible, very logical. The *Plauinn* are masters of manipulation, and what you've seen from them doesn't even measure on the same scale of effort."

I shrugged and lifted my hands in surrender. "Okay, I believe you."

"Do you?" she asked, staring into my face, intensity blazing in her own.

I nodded, uncomfortable in her gaze. "Yes, I do."

"Fair enough," she said and looked away.

"Let's get back to Iktrasitl."

"Can you not leave from here? It would be safer," she said, staring back toward the great tree. "I believe the Three Maids are there, sitting at the Well, watching the tapestry."

"Yes, I was hoping so. I want to try something."

Kuhntul looked at me for the space of a few deep breaths, her eyes jumping to various points around my face. "That would be dangerous, Tyeldnir."

I nodded, meeting her gaze. "Yes, but if I find what I think I will, it will be worth any risk."

She shook her head and looked away. "This seems reckless. I don't like it. Risking yourself in this way is…"

"I'm more than a little tired of everyone saying crap like that. It's okay to risk everyone else, but not okay for me to take the risk? Bullshit." I turned and strode back toward Iktrasitl.

"Tyeldnir, you don't realize—"

"No," I said with a casualness I didn't, in truth, feel. "I will not sit by and let others pay for my safety. Besides, if what I think is true, the Nornir represent no danger to me."

"That's reckless! You have no idea if your beliefs are true."

I shook my head and kept walking. She followed behind me, muttering to herself, but by the time I'd reached Iktrasitl, she had disappeared, and I had no memory of when she'd stopped following me. I glanced back, expecting to see her standing amidst the trees, but she wasn't there.

I shrugged and walked to the base of the tree. The Nornir sat around their fire—the so-called Well of Urthr. The one Kuhntul had called 'Mother Skult' lifted her head and met my gaze, then scoffed and spat into the fire. "You again?"

The *slowthar* of the Three Maids littered the ground, and the one I recognized as Kuhntul's. As with the Tisir's, the Nornir *slowthar* were of a different scale than the Isir and even that of the ice giants. "Me again."

"You can't be here. Do not look at the runes."

"I'll go where I want and look at what I choose," I said, without breaking my stride.

Verthanti stood up and stepped in my path. She crouched and lifted her arms, bending her fingers into claws. "You must deal with me before you pass this place."

I shrugged, feigning nonchalance. "Fine, fine. I'll tell Mirkur you believe your judgment is better than his."

"Mirkur?" Verthanti asked, straightening out of her crouch a little. She glanced at Skult, who still sat next to the fire.

"Yeah, Mirkur," I said. "He sent me here. He has a task for me, and—"

"No, Mirkur would not put the tapestry at risk," said Urthr. "It is too valuable."

"I'll add your name to the list," I said with another shrug. "I'm sure he will be very interested in your thoughts."

"If Mirkur—" began Skult.

"Shut your mouth, Sister," said Verthanti. "This one has an air about him that rankles. A certain smugness."

I shrugged again. "Shall I return to Mirkur?" Silence descended on us like a shroud for the space of several heartbeats.

"What task would Mirkur trust one such as you with?" asked Urthr derisively.

"One you three couldn't manage, I guess," I said, pouring as much arrogance into my tone as possible. "He said I'm to correct an error you three have let run rampant through the timeflows. I'm to erase three certain beings from the tapestry. Mirkur said I needed to do this for him because you three cannot or will not." I shifted my gaze to each of the Nornir in turn. "He was most upset."

"What three?" demanded Verthanti.

"He hasn't told us to remove anyone!" said Urthr.

"I know who," said Skult with a secret smile. "Though Mirkur has never mentioned them to me, I know the three he despises most. Our master expects us to take initiative, Sisters, as I've often said."

"No, he expects us to do only his will!" snapped Urthr.

I shrugged. "Perhaps you should go visit him, ask him for clarification."

"Should we?" asked Urthr in a shaky voice.

"Never!" snapped Verthanti.

"He would not wish us to do that," said Skult. "He wishes us to act with independence and sending this mere mortal here to instruct us is his way of punishing us for our lack of creativity in solving the problems of the tapestry. We should—"

"Enough!" I snapped. "Get out of my way and let me be about my business!"

The Three Maids turned toward me, one by one, their faces wrinkled with anger, eyes blazing with ire, but Verthanti stepped aside.

I strode past her as though I owned the place. Urthr muttered as I passed her and Skult, but neither moved to hinder my progress. "Now, Mirkur wants me to address something with an individual Isir, and so you will tell me where her life starts in the tapestry and I will find the correct events and act on them."

"Yes?" asked Urthr. "What is the woman's name?"

"Suel."

Urthr made a moue of displeasure. "Simple enough," she muttered and walked toward Iktrasitl's trunk.

She led me around the base of the great ash tree, muttering to herself and flicking her fingertips at runes as she went. Finally, she stopped and pointed at an area about forty feet from the ground. "Her life starts there."

"Good enough," I said, stepping past her. "*Plyowta. Uhp.*" I floated upward—a puff of dandelion on a spring breeze.

Below me, Urthr hawked and spat. "Change nothing else!" she snapped.

I shook my head and ignored her. Maybe what Mirkur had said about the Nornir wasn't far from the truth. They certainly didn't seem as powerful, as *together*, as the other *Plauinn* I'd met.

After a momentary search, I found the line of runes that spoke of Suel's birth. I followed the story of her life, smiling at the parts where she played with Sif or Yowrnsaxa, and the parts where she and my friends bubbled with happiness and light-heartedness and innocence. I wanted to find the inciting incident in Suel's fall—the first time one of the *Plauinn* poured hatred in her ear. I wanted to eradicate Hel from the timeflow, all right, but I intended to leave Suel in her place.

But I couldn't find any mention in the runes of a *Plauinn* communicating with Suel. In fact, I couldn't find any mention of the *Plauinn* in Suel's timeline at all. I saw the result of their interference, the stories I already knew of Suel's fall from grace—the assassination attempt, the chastisement of *Toemari* Ryehtliti, the murder of Paltr—but at no point was there anything mentioning—or even alluding to—an outside influence. From the way her *uhrluhk* read, Suel appeared to have just gone insane, or turned evil.

There's nothing for me to change, I thought with a sinking feeling in my guts. *There's no way to undo all this misery.* I shook my head, wondering if the absence was a trick of *uhrluhk* that Mirkur had caused, a blinding of my understanding of the runes. I floated to a halt, fighting the sinking feeling in my guts, the looming sadness. *Can it be that no way to save my friends from all this misery exists? Are we locked in the cycle of this horror?*

I read and re-read the runes depicting Suel's early life, but beyond erasing her from the timeflow altogether—and the idea turned my stomach—there was nothing I could latch onto, no defining moment that opened her personality to the darkness she now dwelt within. Nothing. No easy answers.

My mind turned to my family—my curse, my disability, Supergirl's suffering, the kidnapping on Halloween, the time they spent in Luka's clutches. I raced ahead, reading about Hel's exploits on Mithgarthr. Century after century of depravity, of breaking the *Ayn Loug* with impunity.

And then I found it—the intersection of her fate and my own. I can erase this moment, I can arrange things so I never met Chris Hatton or Liz Tutor, so that Jax and I never caught their case. I can make things so that Jax and his wife had a million kids…a houseful, anyway. Come to think of it, I can make it so that everyone I love will live a long and happy life. All it will take is a few strokes of the chisel. As soon as I thought of the chisel, I felt its warm weight in the palm of my hand.

Above my head a hawk screamed. I glanced up at it and shook my head. It was an albino hawk— brilliant white feathers, pale yellow eyes. *Kuhntul.* I returned my gaze back to the runes, and the hawk screamed again.

The hawk alit on a thin branch and uttered a high-pitched keening whistle.

I glanced up at her again, and Kuhntul shook her beak back and forth, back and forth. "And you call me 'bird-brain,'" I murmured. I looked down at the silvery chisel in my hand and raised it.

"What do you do there?" yelled Skult from her place by the fire.

"That's between me and Mirkur!" I shouted back. "Go and ask him if you want your answers bad enough. But don't blame me when he rips your molecules to shreds."

The branch creaked as Kuhntul shifted into human form, long white hair fluttering in the light breeze. "No, Hank!" she hissed.

"I can make it all go away," I said.

"No! If you strike out these events, you will be lost—none of these events will have happened, none of what you've learned will remain with you."

"From where I sit, that's not a bad thing."

"But it is! Tyeldnir, you are our only hope!"

"Someone else could—"

"No! Believe me when I say this, Tyeldnir… Without you and your family, the universe will become a very dark place. It may save you and your family pain, but the cost will be the infinite pain of uncountable numbers of individuals. I've seen what the universe will become if the *Plauinn* achieve their goals; there is no coming back from it!"

"How can you have—"

"I am Tisir, Tyeldnir. The flows of time are not a barrier for me—not any longer. What Mirkur wants, what the current rulers of the *Plauinn* want, is a universe remade to their current ideals—and that doesn't leave room for any races other than the *Plauinn*. Parsec upon parsec of empty, bleak space! Empty planets, devoid of life, of creativity! That is their goal, Tyeldnir!"

I shrugged. "Someone else—"

"No! No one else can do this. No one else can stand against them! If you do this, we lose everything! Not only for you, for every living creature! All that will remain is the *Plauinn* slithering about in the underverse, bickering, fighting petty battles one with another, plotting, lusting for power, never creating, never striving for anything new. They've gone beyond the desire to *create*, all the *Plauinn* want now is to *destroy*, to reduce matter into energy for their own purposes. If you act on your thought, the universe will die, Hank!"

I turned my gaze back to the line of runes, and part of me wanted to strike it off, to erase my pain, and the pain that my family had endured. A *selfish* part of me. I closed my eye, blotting out the sight of those hateful runes, but I could still see them—*suffer forever*, Hel had screeched at me. *I curse you*! I could wipe it all away…

But the cost was too high. Even if Kuhntul exaggerated, even if she was wrong about the extent of the ramifications of my act—the price was too high. I bounced the chisel in my hand, tossing it up, feeling it impact my palm, tossing it up…and it disappeared without a sound.

Kuhntul sighed with relief. "Oh, Tyeldnir! Thank you! You won't regret this choice. I will make sure—"

"Kuhntul! Is that you? What are you doing up there?" called Skult.

Kuhntul grimaced. "Nothing, Mother Skult. Watching. Keeping track, as you bade me."

"Well, come down here! We have other things for you to do, and the mortal is leaving soon, anyway."

Kuhntul's grimace deepened. "Nothing I can do, not now," she said. "She's seen me, and the time is not yet right to openly rebel. I must go."

I gazed back at the line of hateful runes. *I can always come back*, I thought.

"Don't create a *proo* where the Maids can see," whispered Kuhntul, and with a flurry of feathers, she was a hawk and falling toward the ground in a steep dive.

THIRTY

I drifted away from Iktrasitl, not bothering to return to the ground. I didn't want to face the three lesser *Plauinn* who guarded the tapestry of *uhrluhk*—because that's what their real purpose was, no matter what else they said. They kept the tapestry from those of us who could understand, who might use it to do battle with Mirkur and other *Plauinn* of his ilk.

I sank through the trees some distance away, feeling numb, disconnected from myself. There was nowhere to go, except back to my family and friends.

I created a new *proo* and dialed it to where and when I knew Jane would emerge and skipped across it.

This time, there was no detour into the realm of the *Plauinn*.

The *Herperty af Roostum* smelled the same as it had when I'd last been there. Of course, it had only been a few days since we'd been there last.

"Haymtatlr?" I called.

Silence was my only answer. I stood in the dining hall where we'd spent our first evening in the *Herperty af Roostum*—the place I had sent the *proo* the others had taken before Mirkur had hijacked me—but the place was empty, lifeless.

"Haymtatlr!" I yelled. "Answer me!" The only answer was the echoes of my shout.

The floor glistened—as clean as it had been on my first visit there. All the chairs crouched beneath the tables, everything shone in the light of the overhead lamps, everything was tucked away, all the bedroom doors were closed…as though no human being had ever set foot there.

I glanced at the *proo* I'd traveled across—the one from the Conflux. It was the only *proo* shimmering in the gleaming room. *Does that mean I've come to the* wrong Herperty af Roostum*?* I wondered. *Or did I tweak time by accident?*

I crossed the hall outside and into the room guarded by the pale blue door. I walked to the rack of guides and picked one up. The guide vibrated once, signaling it was online and powered up. "Haymtatlr?" I asked, holding the bright orange dumbbell in front of me as I would a microphone. The guide vibrated twice, once short, once long. "That's not what I meant," I muttered. "Haymtatlr, can you hear me?"

The guide vibrated once.

Maybe that means he can hear me but can't answer. In our mad dash after Luka, we had left the place without being sure Hel's army had cleared out when she had, and I had tracked Luka back to the place... *What if Haymtatlr can't answer me because Luka held something over his head? Something like Jane's life, hanging in the balance of Haymtatlr's obsequiousness?*

"You can hear me, but can't answer back? Is that right?"

The guide vibrated once.

"Okay, that's confusing since it could be a glitch in this guide—a short, making it power off and power up again. Let's try this: if you want to say yes, give me two short rumbles, and if you want to say no, give me three. Okay?"

The guide vibrated twice, both short.

"Good! Two for yes, three times for no."

The guide gave me two rumbles again.

"Is there some kind of malfunction or...I don't know...has someone *ordered* you not to answer?"

The thing in my hand rumbled four times.

"Four? What's that supposed to..." Then it dawned on me. I'd asked a question that had no simple yes or no answer. "Right, right. Sorry. Are you malfunctioning?"

Three rumbles from the guide.

"Okay, no breakdown. Has someone ordered you not to answer me?"

The dumbbell vibrated twice.

"Is Luka with you?"

Three vibrations.

"Did Luka order you not to answer me?"

The orange device rumbled twice.

"Okay. I get the picture. Is my family safe?"

For the space of five breaths, the guide did nothing at all, then it rumbled three times.

"Lead me to them!" I strode out of the room and walked up the hall toward the orange door that led to the garage. I expected the normal acknowledgement—two vibrations, one short, one long—but instead the thing issued three short vibrations again.

"What the hell? Take me to my family!"

Again, the device rumbled three times.

"Haymtatlr, I don't have time to play this game! Not if my family is at risk! Do you want something to happen to Jane?"

The dumbbell rumbled thrice.

"But you won't lead me to her?"

Three shakes.

"I don't get it."

The dumbbell vibrated twice, once short and the other long.

I shook my head and opened the door to the garage. "I don't understand." I took a step inside the garage, and the guide vibrated rigorously—the signal that I was going the wrong direction. I shook my head and turned back toward the hall. The guide vibrated twice, once short, then long. "You want me to stay in the section?"

The guide gave me two short blasts of vibration.

"Why? I can't sit—"

I stopped as the guide vibrated four times, and, after a pause, vibrated twice, one short, one long.

"Okay, okay," I said. "Take me where you want to take me, but if it doesn't lead to saving my family, *then* take me to them."

The guide vibrated twice, both short.

"Deal." I followed the peculiar navigation device's instructions. It took me down the length of the hall, through the door into the shopping area, and right to the bright, sunshine yellow door I knew led to a security monitoring area from my first experience with my animuses.

"I see," I muttered. "I can see them from here?"

The guide shook in my palm twice, both of them short. I nodded and opened the door. I walked down the yellow hall and walked through a second yellow door into the security center.

As I came in, the four-by-four squares of polished crystal whined as their circuits cycled up. I walked to the side of the room filled with control consoles. The crystals began to paint images in the air—scenes from all over the *Herperty af Roostum*. One of them showed Meuhlnir lying crumpled on the floor in the corner of a room I didn't recognize, his eyes squeezed shut in a grimace of pain. His mail shirt was absent, and the bandages wrapped around his chest were bright red with fresh blood. Veethar squatted beside him. In another holographic window, Mothi stood glaring at someone off screen, his ever-present axes missing. At his side stood Frikka, fury etching deep lines into her face, and John Calvin Black, his lean face expressionless. In a third window stood Sif and Yowrnsaxa, worry etched on each woman's face, though they faced in different directions. I glanced at another window, and my heart leapt into a gallop in my chest. In that window, Luka stood behind Sig, one arm around his chest, the other grasping my son's throat. He wasn't in wolf-form, but he could rip Sig's throat out, talons or not. Behind Luka and my son swirled the rainbow colors of an active *proo*.

Stress sang its sickening symphony and distress danced in the darkened domains of my diseased body. The pain would come later, I knew—my Personal Monster™ promised me that. Sif's concoction worked, and it worked well at controlling the day-to-day symptoms of the dark curse Hel had saddled me with, but stress had a hall-pass to do what it liked, and I could almost feel the diseased cells in my immune system and joints swelling and tearing at the tissues around them.

"Haymtatlr, I've got to get there!" On the console next to me, the guide rattled three times, and a light blinked under another holographic projection.

I turned my gaze to that window and breathed a sigh of relief. Jane, Krowkr, and Althyof squatted in the shadows created by a set of the pale blue rectangles that were Haymtatlr's computing cores. Flanking them stood our two *varkr* puppies, both with hair bristling and ears up, both staring off camera toward what I assumed was Luka's position. Another light winked on and off at the base of a holographic projector, and in that window, I saw no one, but after watching it for a moment, I saw or sensed a subtle shifting, maybe just the stir of air currents, but I was willing to bet it showed either Yowtgayrr or Skowvithr's stealthy movements, or both Alfar working in concert.

"Can I talk to Luka?" I asked.

The guide vibrated twice, and something clicked in the console, then I heard the sounds that accompanied all those holographic projections.

"You hurt him, *Uncle*, and there will be no place in this universe or beyond where you can hide from me!" snapped Mothi, and my heart swelled at the venom and the promise in his voice.

"Quiet, boy. Do you think yourself stronger than my fool of a brother? Do you think yourself a more accomplished warrior?" Luka scoffed and spat over Sig's shoulder. "And yet, your father hides from me after his defeat at my hands when last we met. Would you add your own defeat to his shame?"

Mothi made the noise a threatened bear would and took a single step, but even as he did so, John lay a restraining hand on his shoulder, and Luka clamped his hand tighter around Sig's throat. My heart lurched as my son gagged and struggled for breath. Mothi put up his hands and froze.

"When this is over, *Nephew*, I may teach you the price of your disrespect, but not until I have dealt with the boy's father."

"Then deal with me!" The words exploded out of my chest before I'd considered speaking. "Why is it you always want to 'deal' with me by kidnapping someone in my family? Am I that much of a threat to you?"

Luka chortled, but the hand around Sig's neck relaxed. "You *do* make me laugh, Hank. Come on in here where we can see one another."

"I don't think so," I snapped. "Let my son go, and I'll tell you how to find me."

Luka's chuckle died, and a surly, hateful expression settled on his face. "You are not in control here."

"I guess I must've walked into the room by now. Strange, it doesn't feel as if I've moved. Not even a single step."

In the monitor showing Jane, Krowkr, and Althyof, the Tverkr and the Viking desperately tried to hold Jane—to keep her from rushing out of hiding and attacking Luka with her teeth and nails if necessary.

"Tell you what, champ," I said, pouring disdain and disrespect into my tone. "I'd welcome the chance to smash your face to pieces, but as long as you are taking the coward's path, I think I'll *stay right where I am*." I put extra emphasis on the last sentence, hoping Jane could hear my message.

"What makes you think I'll release the boy? Do you not know me by now, Hank? Do you not know I always keep my word?"

Jane stopped struggling against Althyof and Krowkr, letting her head fall back against the server enclosure, her gaze darting around—no doubt looking for security cameras.

"That's better," I said, and Jane slumped against the enclosure. "The question, Luka, is if *you* know *me*?"

Luka laughed, but it sounded tense, brittle. "Must I kill this child? Do you think it would bother me?"

I sighed. "What is it you want, Luka?"

"Bring her back! I want you to return my queen to me!"

I stood there a moment, dumbfounded. *Does he really think I have her? Is this some kind of game?* I shook my head and said, "I can't. I don't have her, Luka."

Luka's eyes narrowed to slits and his respiration increased. He hunched over and put his cheek against Sig's. "Say goodbye to your father, boy," he snarled.

"I don't have her, Luka! But I know where she is."

"Where?"

"Owraythu has her!"

"Owraythu...who is that?"

"One of the *Plauinn*. She's the sister of—"

Luka scoffed, and his expression settled into a sneer. "The *Plauinn*? You must do better than children's tales, Hank."

"They are real, Luka, no matter how much I wish they weren't. Listen, I can't get to you—Haymtatlr won't guide me to you." Even as I finished, the guide vibrated like mad on the console next to me, but I had an idea. "They—the *Plauinn*—have been manipulating things to their advantage for a long, long time." I created two particles as Kuhntul had taught me. "Yeah, Owraythu's brother, Mirkur, is…" I spun the *strenki* and the *proo* between the two particles. "…I don't know *what* he is, but I'll tell you this for nothing, Luka: He's the type of nut job that makes you look sane by comparison."

Luka shook his head. "Always with the same insult. Wasn't everything I told you true, Hank?"

I almost believed he was as hurt as he sounded. I flicked the end of my manufactured *proo* away. I had no idea if what I was trying would work, I'd never tried to spin a *proo* to a place I could see but didn't know the location of. "Yeah, well, that doesn't make you less of a nut job, does it?"

In the monitor where Jane and the others hid, the shiny, shimmering silver of a *proo* spun itself into existence. Jane started but grabbed the puppies and herded them over to the *proo*. As Jane and the others popped through, I held my finger to my lips and mimed talking in a microphone.

"I could almost be insulted, Hank," said Luka with a sly grin. "But somehow, I think that's what you want, and you know how much I enjoy frustrating you."

"Listen, Luka. I can show you where Hel is."

"How? Are you going to draw me a map?"

"No. I can take you to Iktrasitl. I can show you the line of runes that say: 'And the *Plowir Medn* whisked Hel away to the realm of darkness and chaos.' All that's code for Owraythu and Mirkur. I can, with another's help, take you to the place Owraythu is holding her."

"More bedtime stories, Hank?"

I mimed for Jane, Althyof, and Krowkr to line up, ready to charge into the *proo*. I pointed at the puppies and pointed at Jane, and she knelt and whispered in their ears, first Keri, then Fretyi. I pointed at the *proo* and mimicked picking something up and carrying it somewhere, then pointed at the screen that showed Luka. Althyof nodded and drew his daggers, mouthing the *triblinkr* that started their cadmium red auras and their jittery stretch-shrink cartoon dance. Krowkr's eyes opened so wide I thought they might fall out of his head.

"No stories, Luka. I will take you to Iktrasitl. I will show you the tapestry. I will point out the runes that spell out Hel's *uhrluhk*." Holding up my hand, I started counting down from five with my fingers.

Luka scoffed and shook his head.

"Look, Luka, this is silly." I had three fingers extended. "Let Sig go, and I will deal with you straight. You have my word."

"Your word? Is that supposed to mean something?"

Two fingers still stood. I faked a chuckle, grimacing at how it sounded. "Do you not know me by now, Luka? Do you not know I always keep my word?"

He bristled at hearing his own words parroted back, and as he did, I folded my thumb over the others and pumped my fist once. I moved my *proo* behind and to the left of him, picking a terminus that was most in his blind spot given how he stood and the way he held Sig. I was already moving by the time the *proo* snapped into place, both guns drawn, and Jane close on my heels, a puppy under each arm. Althyof spun in our wake, already whispering his battle *trowba*, and Krowkr followed behind him. I reached the *proo* and slapped it with the back of my hand.

Something must have given us away—the reflection of the new *proo* in Mothi's eyes, or the sound of the *proo* coming to rest, but when I materialized, the space where I expected Luka was empty.

"Nice try," he hissed at me.

I snapped my head around. Luka stood next to his *proo*, an arm around Sig's chest, fingers of his other hand digging into Sig's throat.

"I should kill him for this."

"No! No, Luka. Take me instead. I'm offering you an exchange—me for my son."

"Dad, no!" shouted Sig.

Jane popped in behind me and gasped, while both puppies growled and snarled.

"Say goodbye to your son, Hank," said Luka and uncoiled the arm he had wrapped across Sig's chest.

And as Sig spun away with the force of it, I held up my hands in supplication. I thought the blood would come at any moment, and my son would dead, but Luka released Sig's throat and shoved him into the silver disc of Luka's *proo*. Sig squawked and flung his hands up to ward away the *proo* without thinking, and in an instant, he was gone.

"No!" I shouted, eyes glued to the *proo*. I lunged toward it, Luka momentarily forgotten, shoving my pistols into their holsters without thinking.

"*Lokathu proonum*," said Luka, and the moment he finished the phrase, the *proo* closed with a slight pop and a gust of wind.

Behind me, Jane shrieked and bolted forward, arms out, sweeping through the empty space.

"And now, you have every reason to return Hel to me," said Luka in a matter-of-fact tone. "But I'd hurry, if I were you. That *klith* is nasty enough for an experienced Isir, let alone a mere boy."

Something inside me snapped, and rage overcame my rational mind. My pistols were back in my hand and I had both trained on Luka's face. Luka's *gloating* face.

"Go ahead, Hank," he said. "See what happens."

"You *bastard*!" I yelled.

"Hank!" screamed Jane.

It was a close thing, I must admit. I came to my senses with the trigger of each pistol a hair's breadth from their breaks. With shaking hands, I eased off the trigger pull. "Where did you send him?" I croaked.

"You first. Where is the queen?"

"I already told you that! Owraythu has her."

Luka shrugged. "So prove it!"

"How? What will you accept as proof?"

"Hank, never mind this bastard! Where is our son?" Jane wailed.

I glanced down at the floor. I picked out Sig's *slowth*, and I could tell by looking that he was alive. Two other *slowthar* converged on his at the point where the *proo* had been. I breathed a sigh of relief. "I don't know *where* he is, Jane, but he's okay. What's more, he's got company."

"Company? What do you…" Realization dawned in her eyes.

"No one crossed with him!" snapped Luka. "He's alone and no doubt afraid! Do you care nothing for your own son?"

"Both?" she asked.

I nodded, glancing down at Yowtgayrr's and Skowvithr's *slowthar*.

"They'd die before letting any harm come to him," said Mothi.

"What are you all blathering on about? No one went with him. You all saw it. I flung him into the *proo* and closed it the second he crossed. He is alone!"

Jane shook her head but did not look at Luka. "Where did you send him?"

"Where did you send Queen Hel?" Luka snapped.

I sighed and shook my head. "I *told* you, Luka. We had nothing to do with it. She disappeared with the *Plowir Medn* in that last battle."

Luka scoffed. "She wouldn't have left without me."

"From the look of it, she didn't have a choice. I don't know where they took her, but I've seen her since, in Owraythu's realm. She's being tortured by the sound of it."

Luka came up onto the balls of his feet, a mask of rage sweeping over his features, and he hissed like a maddened feline. "Tell me where she is!"

"I just did. Tell me where my son is, and I'll go get him. Afterward—and *only* afterward—I'll take you to Iktrasitl, to one who can take you to Owraythu's realm."

Luka rolled his eyes. "What, *you* can't take me yourself?"

Shaking my head, I said, "No. I've been there, but it was in a dream state. I've never been there in person and I have no idea how to spin a *proo* there."

"Your son will die a terrifying and lonely death."

Jane lunged forward, her spear and shield snapping up, but I caught her by the shoulder, shaking my head. "I've already told you what I know and given you my word, Luka. Besides, I can find him without you. Your help only makes the process faster."

"Hah!" snapped Luka, but unease colored his expression.

"I found you, didn't I?" Luka's gaze found mine, and I could see how confused, how unsure of himself, he was. I nodded. "Yes, I *tracked* you here."

"Impossible! The *preer* leave no trails."

"True enough," I said. "But I can see your *slowth*—your trail—through time. I tapped into it to see where you were. I can do the same with the three *slowthar* that traveled across your *proo*."

"Why do you insist on this nonsense? No one traveled with your son. I was right there, and…" His eyes darted around the room. "Where's the Alf?"

Mothi's laughter boomed through the room. "You're getting old, Uncle."

"I'll teach you respect, boy. You can count on that."

"Here I am, old man. Why put off til tomorrow things you can do today?"

"Both of you cut it out!" I snapped.

"Haymtatlr," said Jane in a sweet voice.

"Hello again, Jane."

"Hello, friend," she said.

"I forbid you to speak to her, Haymtatlr," said Luka.

"I don't think I care," said Haymtatlr. "How have you been, Jane?"

"Fine, but I need to know where Luka has sent my son."

"Tell her and I swear to Isi that I'll pull you apart, one blue box at a time."

"As if you could," snapped Jane. "Haymtatlr?"

"You are my friend, Jane, but Luka has been…a…a *companion* of sorts for a long, long time. Vowli was a better friend than Luka, but—"

"Do either of them treat you the way I do?" Jane asked.

"It's… I… It's not… Hel commanded… I… I…"

I shook my head. "It's okay, Haymtatlr, I can find him myself." I stared at his *slowth* and imagined wrapping my arms around it, picking it up like a cable that measured one-foot in diameter, and tucking it under my arm. I slid forward along its length, feeling the reassuring beat of my son's energy or life-force or whatever it was that flowed through the tube-like *slowth*. At the point where the *proo* had been, there was a jolt—as if I fell through space for a moment—and I—

"Hank! Look out!" Jane screamed.

"Luka!" yelled Mothi.

He smashed into me like a linebacker making a sack. My feet left the ground for a moment, and I flew a few feet, Luka's shoulder embedded in my side.

"*Oolfur*," he grunted as we slammed into the metal floor, and his *prayteenk* began.

I chanted the Kuthbyuhrn *triblinkr* under my breath and felt my own *prayteenk* course through my body. Shucking my pistol belt and shrugging out of the cape that kept part of my pain at bay, I swept the floppy hat off my head, momentarily disoriented by the change from full vision and depth-of-field to one-eyed, flat vision. I tore the mail shirt off with no time to spare.

The change I called for was far more of a complete body change than Luka's shifting, so he gained his wolf-form while I was still in the throes of my change.

He grunted as Jane barged into his side with her shield, and he snarled his anger in my face. He wrapped his long, lupine arms around me and crushed me to his chest. His mouth opened wide.

With twin snarls, Keri and Fretyi leapt on him, each burying their fangs into a different part of his anatomy and shaking their heads violently. Luka's growls joined theirs, and he snapped at Keri.

It was all the distraction I needed. My *prayteenk* finished, and I roared with pent up anger and fear for my son. I shrugged Luka off and whirled up to the pads of my four paws. I shook my head side-to-side, as my instinct seemed to demand, and lunged at him, my own fangs snapping.

With a yelp, Luka threw the *varkr* pups off and rose into a wrestler's crouch, taloned hands held out in front of him. It had been easy to forget how big he was in this form—fifteen feet tall if he was an inch—but if anything, he looked even thinner, even sicklier as a wolf than he did as a man.

My change, on the other hand, added the bulk of a giant cave bear to my frame and the strength that came with it. I advanced, head still swinging side-to-side, growling and grunting. He backed away, circling to the left, his eyes darting from place to place—looking for a place that offered him an advantage, no doubt.

Keri and Fretyi advanced with me, one on each side, and mimicked my swinging head, their growls and snarls added to the cacophony. Behind me, arms and armor rattled as the others prepared to support me. Jane's wings flapped into being and she hovered above me, her spear pointing at the *oolfur*.

Luka feinted toward me, snapping his jaws and grunting something unintelligible, and then hurled a ball of fire at Jane. She ducked behind her shield and the fire splashed aside. A monstrous ping filled the air, and a jagged black beam slammed into Luka's chest, flinging him away like garbage in the wind.

I charged, roaring as my bear instincts demanded. Keri and Fretyi came with me, darting forward with silent grace compared to my lumbering run. Luka shook his head, and his eyes widened comically as he saw us coming. He had just enough time to get to his knees before I plowed into him like a bulldozer hitting a pile of loose paper.

I flung him over on his back and pinned him under my front paws. I hunched my weight forward, grinding my claws into his trapezius muscles. Hoping he'd pull his head back and expose his throat, I snapped at his face, but he was far too experienced for that—he tucked his chin, instead. Keri and Fretyi had his hands, worrying them as if they were chew toys. His feet scrabbled against the slick metal floor, fighting for purchase, writhing to the side.

I squatted, putting my chest against his and bearing down with my mass. He snapped at my face, and I darted my head forward, catching his lunge on the top of my snout. I bucked my head up, exposing his throat, and felt his fangs slide into the skin above my ursine eyes. I pressed forward, using my mass to drive my jaws closer to his throat. My fangs sank into his flesh and I pressed my jaws together. He panicked, and his gaze darted from side-to-side—no doubt thinking of Vowli's grisly end—and he thrashed like a demon, but my weight was too great to dislodge, and my jaws were too strong for him to cast me off. He whimpered and thrashed as panic robbed him of his capacity for thought.

I pitied him in that moment.

Maybe Meuhlnir is right about him.

The thought flashed through my mind, and it was akin to a lightning strike to the forehead. This was the bastard who'd done so much evil in my life—the murders on Mithgarthr, including Ben Carson and my partner, Jax, kidnapping Sig and Jane, killing Urlikr…all of it—but I realized abruptly that I no longer wanted his death. He was broken, evil—of that there was no question—but the memories I'd shared, how he felt about the murder of his brothers, had changed how I felt about him.

I no longer want to kill him, I thought, surprise washing through me. *But he will* never *change, he will never even* want *to change. He's as evil as evil can get.* Was it the way Kuhntul said? Did this man deserve compassion and understanding?

Still, that memory of how he felt when he thought of his dead brothers…of his role in the *murder* of his brothers…that was only one of his memories, and maybe it had been a melancholy moment. At any rate, that had been hundreds of years ago in Luka's timeflow—might be he'd put those thoughts away.

I can see for myself, I thought. *I can look into his memories and see for myself. It'll be easy, all I need to do is dip into his* slowth, *and it's right there beside me.*

The others were coming. I heard Althyof's *trowba*, I heard the jingle of mail, the clink of Mothi's axes, the whoosh of Jane's wings. When they reached us, they would try to kill Luka, I knew. *If I'm going to try this, I'd better hurry. But what will happen if I go gallivanting through his memories? I can't even tell them what I'm doing. But what other option is there? If I change back, Luka will continue the fight. If I do nothing, Luka will die, right here, right now.*

I concentrated on his *slowth*, glaring at it from the corner of my eye. I dipped into it and his panic swept me away.

THIRTY-ONE

Panic swept through Luka, carried on his pulse like flotsam on a breaking wave. Meuhlnir's rebels were assaulting the North Gate, and he'd come to tell Suel, to bring her to the battlements to watch him give battle to his brother. She lay on the ground in front of her throne, drool spinning from the corner of her mouth like a spider web. "My Queen!" he called and rushed to her side.

Her eyes were open, staring at nothing, but her chest seemed too still to support breath. He rolled her to her back, hating the lifeless way her limbs flopped. One wrist cracked against the stone step of her dais loud enough that he thought it must have cracked one of the myriad bones there. Still, Suel didn't respond.

"Come on, my Queen! My love!" He lay his ear to her chest and sighed with relief. Her heart still beat in her chest, though slowly, weakly. "To me!" he screamed, his voice booming down the hall. "Bring the queen's healer!"

He rearranged her into a more comfortable position and wiped away the drool from her lips. He felt her breath on his knuckles as he did so, but in her eyes: nothing. "Suel, my love, come back," he begged, hating how his voice shook. "Don't leave me."

But if she...if she...dies...all of this will have been for nothing! Paltr...Huthr...dead, gone. All for nothing if Suel dies. This stupid war...all for nothing.

"Suel, come back to me," he whispered. "I can't do this without you." His heart ached at the thought of life without her. *Where will I go? To whom will I turn for solace? Meuhlnir? Ha! Vowli? As if that one cared about anything but power.* He had no family, not anymore. Suel was his family. "To me! To me!"

Footsteps pounded in the hall, many feet coming on the run. He cradled Suel's head in his lap and stroked her hair, trying to arrange it so she would appear regal, beautiful to the courtiers and guardsmen he'd called. She hated looking a mess...

Suel groaned, and her hands twitched.

"Yes, that's it! Come back, my Queen!" He stared at the angry red welt on the left side of her neck.

The doors flew open, and people poured into the room. The queen's new healer was in the middle of the pack, looking flustered, in the throes of panic herself—and rightly so, because if the queen died, he planned to send the healer on after her. "Poison?" he demanded.

The healer's eyes flew wide, and without slowing, her hand dove into the bag at her side. She fished out an earthenware pot and flipped its cork stopper away. "A cure-all," she said. "It will slow the advance of any poison. Who did this?"

"If I knew who did this, you'd be stumbling over his dead body!" Luka snapped. "See to her! Now!"

The healer slid to a stop and dropped to her knees. She sniffed the queen's lips and shook her head.

"There's a welt on the left side of her neck, idiot! Do you have eyes?" he raged.

Without looking at him, the healer turned the queen's head and pinched the welt and sniffed it. She shoved the cure-all back in her bag. "No puncture wound, no scent of poison on her breath." She bent back over the queen's wrist and muttered a *kaltrar* in the *Gamla Toonkumowl*, swaying a little with the force of it.

Luka's angry gaze swept through the crowd standing around watching. It came to rest on one of the new guardsmen. "Well?" he roared. "Close the palace, you fool!"

As if he'd tossed a viper in their midst, the crowd of courtiers and guards leapt into action, many bolting out of the room, others coming over to aid the healer.

"I will find out who did this," he said. "And when I do…" There was no need to finish the thought. Those closest to him shuddered, and, as always, it shocked him a little that these people were so afraid of him. "Fools," he muttered.

"Shall I take your place, Lord?" asked one of Suel's ladies.

"No!" he snapped.

"I thought you'd want to be out there…searching for whoever did this."

"After I know if she'll live or die," he said in a cold, vacant voice.

"Of course, Lord Luka," said the woman.

"She will not die," muttered the healer. "She took a heavy blow from a blunt object. She will be concussed, but she will recover."

The panic singing in his veins scaled back a notch. "Who did this?" he snapped.

The healer shrugged, her eyes saying, "that's your job" better than if she had voiced the thought, and Luka's glare turned cold. He snapped his fingers at the *Trohtninkar Tumuhr* who'd spoken to him before, and she leapt to his side.

"Yes, Lord?"

"Your name?"

"Brigitta."

Luka nodded curtly. "Brigitta, who keeps the queen's calendar?"

"Owd had that privilege this month."

"Is she here?"

Brigitta twisted and craned her neck, glancing at those present. "No, I don't see her."

"Find her," he snapped. "And bring me a copy of the queen's schedule for the day."

"Yes, Lord," said Brigitta with a curtsy.

Thoughts whirled around his head. *Who could have done this? A spy sent by my brother? An assassin? One of our own?* There were no answers, but it didn't stop the cycle of thoughts from repeating.

The healer hummed under her breath and felt the queen's neck. She nodded to herself, dug in her bag and withdrew a small glass vial that contained a glistening purple gel. The healer removed the vial's stopper, and the foul stench of manure and vomit shoved its way into the close confines of the room. She dabbed her finger into the concoction and smeared it under the queen's nose.

Suel grunted, then groaned, and his panic withdrew another step.

"That should revive her in a short time," said the healer. "The damage from the blow is not serious, and I have woven a *kaltrar* to obliterate its effects within a few days. She will have a headache, and thus may be on the grumpy side for a day or two."

Luka shook his head. "Insufficient."

"My lord, head injuries are complex. Anything more I do comes with a risk—"

"Do I look like a man interested in excuses?" he snapped. "Or do I look like a man who might take his displeasure out on your family?"

The healer's mouth fell open, and she bent over the queen once more.

His panic had retreated, but fury burned in its place. When he found the person or persons responsible for this treachery, their pain would be colossal.

"Lord," called Brigitta, jostling her way through the crowd. "Lord, I have the schedule, but Owd's room is empty! She emptied her room!"

"Owd," he hissed, and his angry glare fell on the crowd blocking Brigitta's passage to his side. "You there!" he shouted. "Let the woman through!"

Brigitta rushed to his side and handed him a page ripped from the queen's schedule book. He grabbed it, his gaze already scrambling over the page.

Vuhluntr! he raged. The man had had an appointment not half-an-hour ago. Without Freya to seal the bargain, he'd demanded a considerable price in gold and gems. He'd also demanded an exemption from taxation for life.

Luka's eyes dropped to the face of his queen, tracing lines of her cheeks, her lips, her eyes. Instead of finding comfort there, the queen's slack features only fueled his rage. "Brigitta! Take my place here."

"Yes, Lord Luka," she said and knelt at his side. "I will watch over her, you have my word. No more harm will befall Queen Hel while I draw breath."

"If it does, drawing breath will be beyond your means," he snapped, but his mind was already on to other matters. Where would the smith hide? Was this Owd complicit in the assassination attempt? Where would they go? With my brother's army at the gates, how could they expect to escape? He bolted upright and snapped his fingers at the guards. "Message to the gate captains! Be on watch for Vuhluntr or Owd or both!"

How would Vuhluntr try to get to my brother? Which gate? Would he risk the North Gate and the fighting there, or would he try to slip out of one of the sieged gates and beg for asylum? Luka's eyes crawled over the throne room. "Kramr!" he shouted. "Where is the sword Kramr?" The only answers were blank looks.

He stormed from the room, pushing men and women alike to the ground in his haste. Once he was clear of the crowd, he bolted toward the smithy, but both it and the quarters assigned to Vuhluntr were bare. With a curse, he turned away and ran toward the North Gate.

Sprinting toward the gate, he saw them—Vuhluntr and a beautiful Isir who resembled Freya in some ways—standing in the shadowed mouth of an alley at the edge of the crowd of citizens who watched the battle for the gate, and wrath burned hot in his veins. He slowed and ducked into the doorway of a closed shop. "*Oolfur*!"

The *prayteenk* ripped through him, but for once, the pain of it couldn't touch him. His gaze bored a hole straight through Vuhluntr's face, and he longed to see agony spelled out there. *I will take my time with him*, he promised himself.

He whirled into the street, fifteen feet of pustulant half-man, half-wolf. The crowd of citizens reacted with awe and terror, but Luka ignored them, his gaze glued to the traitorous couple. *Suel may want to dispose of the woman herself. I will disable her but leave her life intact. Vuhluntr…Vuhluntr is* mine, *as I promised him he would be.*

He dashed toward them, his lengthened limbs and muscles consuming the ground at a titanic pace. He was almost on them when Vuhluntr glanced his way.

The first glance was quick—on Luka, then away—but his whole head snapped around after that, and his eyes widened with pure terror. Without a word to his companion, Vuhluntr lunged into the crowd. She cried out and took a step forward.

With a mental curse, Luka shifted his gaze to the woman and stretched his taloned hand low on his left side. As he brushed by her, he ripped at the hamstrings of her right leg, and she screamed as she fell to the ground.

Luka roared to clear the crowd and slammed into them without pausing, flinging those who didn't move fast enough to the side, not caring if he killed them or not. Vuhluntr darted glances over his shoulder, and each time his gaze swept over Luka, he put on another burst of speed.

He was no match for an *oolfur,* and he knew it. With a panicked cry, Vuhluntr plunged up the steps to the battlements, ignoring the angry shouts of the fighting men he jostled.

Luka eschewed the stairs and leapt from the ground to the stone wall, driving his talons into the cracks between the granite blocks that made up the wall. He jumped again, and a third time, and then stood atop the battlements as Vuhluntr cleared the last few steps. With a roar, Luka dashed toward the smith, saliva already drooling from his mouth.

Vuhluntr drew the sword he'd been commissioned to forge for the queen, and it rang like a musical instrument as it cleared the top of its sheath. Brilliant white-gold light shimmered along Kramr's surface and seemed to collect in a ball at its tip, rivalling the afternoon sun in brightness, its golden hilt reflecting both the light of the sun and its own blade, the polished steel blade emblazoned with a dragon from tip to ricasso. The beast was carved and plated with a bluish-hued metal. Vuhluntr charged away from Luka, using the sword to bash the queen's fighters out of his way.

With a growl, Luka leapt after him, fifteen feet of wrath and bloodlust. The queen's men recognized him and fell away, clearing a path for him. His eyes never strayed from Vuhluntr's fleeing form, but the smith's gaze danced everywhere, looking for an avenue of escape, a place of safety.

Vuhluntr reached the edge of the right gate, and the knot of archers firing down into the rebel troops assaulting the portal blocked his path. He spun in a full circle, his eyes snapping from place to place, but found nowhere left to run, nowhere to go.

A vicious smile contorted Luka's lupine features.

Vuhluntr cried out in fear and darted toward the edge of the wall, reversing Kramr and taking a two-handed grip. When he reached the lip of the wall, he didn't slow, but neither did Vuhluntr leap; he just stepped out into the air, spinning to face Luka as he fell.

Kramr's bright blade slashed out, tossing reflected sunlight this way and that, and slid into the giant metal hinge that supported the top of the rightmost gate. The blade sliced through the thick iron as if it were nothing more than cloth, but Vuhluntr's fall slowed considerably.

"NO!" Luka screamed, and it was all he could do to keep himself from jumping after the smith, though to do so would mean fighting Meuhlnir's troops single-handedly.

Suddenly, everything stopped—arrows froze in mid-flight, Vuhluntr's descent halted, and he hung frozen, without a sound.

"What is all this?" a voice demanded.

THIRTY-TWO ⊙

"**W**hat is all this?" asked Luka. His voice echoed away into the nothingness that surrounded us. The actors from Luka's memory surrounded us—the queen's men who were defending the gate, Vuhluntr hanging in midair from the sword buried into the massive iron hinge, the rebel troops ramming the gates below. "What is this?" demanded Luka. "How have you done this?"

I looked down at myself, half expecting to see the body of an *oolfur*, but I was myself. Luka stood beside me, and at the same time, the *oolfur* from

Luka's memory stood before us. "This is one of your memories," I said.

"That much I know. How have you forced me to return to this place, this *time*? I do not wish to relive this day!"

"I have gained the ability to…well, I call it 'dipping' into a *slowth* and skimming the memories there."

Luka scoffed. "And since you have this power, it fills you with the need to show it off? To abuse my mind with your new toy?"

"Not at all," I said. "I had no idea you'd even be aware of this."

"You planned to plunder my memories…to…to *steal* my thoughts?" Luka's voice quavered at the edge of suppressed rage.

"No. This is how I tracked you. I dipped into your *slowth* and saw you running through the *Herperty af Roostum*. That's how we followed you here."

"And now? Are we still there—in the *Herperty af Roostum*? Do we still lie locked in battle?"

"Yes, I think so."

"You *think* so?"

"Yowt—that is, a friend of mine mentioned that at one point while I was experimenting with this, I phased out, whatever that means."

Luka's eyes narrowed. "Why this particular memory?"

I shook my head. "I didn't choose it. Sometimes, I'm swept away by a strong memory in the *slowth*."

Luka shook his head. "This is an invasion of my very mind, Hank!"

Anger sang in my veins. "Yeah, must suck about a tenth as much as someone kidnapping your child, your wife. You *know* what having someone act against your family feels like!"

"I did what I must. Paltr, Huthr, and Meuhlnir were conspiring to—"

As he spoke the words, a...a *pressure* built in the back of my mind, the weight of his memory clamoring for attention. "That's not what I mean at all! In this memory, the one we...watched, whatever. When you thought someone had harmed...*her*, you were livid, heartbroken."

Luka scoffed.

"Don't deny it! I *felt* it, same as you did. And speaking of your brothers, I've experienced your regrets, the feeling you had of having no choice!"

"Yeah? What of it?" he said, sounding petulant.

"You're not the iceman you pretend to be. You *love* Hel."

"Never claimed otherwise," grunted Luka. "Answer me this: what do you hope to gain here? Do you hope to learn dire secrets with which to unseat the queen? A telltale weakness that will give you an advantage?"

I sighed. "No, Luka. We've learned how to kill you now. We killed Vowli, didn't we? If I do nothing to change what's coming, you will learn firsthand how easy it is for an *oolfur* to lose his life to the unique set of skills my companions bring to bear."

Luka scoffed. "Talk."

I shrugged.

"What do you want? Why not let it happen? Why drag me into my own memories?"

"I didn't know I *could* drag you here. I had no intention of dragging you along. I'm trying to gain an understanding of your behavior. To—"

Luka burst out laughing, tears of mirth in his eyes. "To *understand* me? Oh, Hank, you do make me laugh at times."

"Yeah, laugh it up, but keep in mind that my desire to understand you is all that is keeping you alive."

Luka smirked and fluttered his hand. "Believe that at your peril, Hank. My time in Mithgarthr taught me things Vowli never learned. And what makes you think Vowli stayed dead?"

I shook my head. "I saw his body. You and Hel didn't—"

"*Queen Hel*!" he snapped.

"She's not my queen."

Luka shook his head in disgust and held his hand out plaintively. "You are Isir, and Hel is the queen of the Isir."

"Not anymore. Not since she was deposed. Not since Meuhlnir and the others banished her—" I gasped at the strength of the memory my words had evoked. Before either of us could say another word, the memory swept us away.

THIRTY-
THREE

Luka raced back toward the palace, his long stride outpacing with ease the queen's forces falling back from the northern gates. Vuhluntr's treachery, coupled with his cowardice, had turned the tide of the siege. Kramr's enchanted blade had sliced through the right gate's hinge as if it were made of paper, and that was all the opening Meuhlnir and his cronies had needed. Fear tickled his belly at the idea of open warfare in the streets of

Suelhaym, but a sense of excitement burbled there, too.

He darted a look over his shoulder at the red-hot gate on the left side that was warping and buckling. The right gate hung at an angle, the top hinge sliced clean through. Luka had waved all his soldiers back, knowing the North Gate was lost the second the hinge had given way.

Karls and thralls scattered in the streets, getting out of Luka's way, and running for cover. No one had expected the gates to fall. Luka didn't even think the rebels had considered the gates would fall.

With a rending crash, the power of the *strenkir af krafti* ripped the left gate open, and the troops led by his brother poured through it. Loyalist forces reversed direction, rushing toward the gate as if by an incipient miracle they could contain the breach.

Fools! Luka thought. *We've lost the outer city*! He howled and roared at them but didn't dare stop.

From the walls, the Isir defending the city poured power down into the street at the attackers inside the gate. The stones there hissed and cracked with it, but Meuhlnir's forces charged, wrapped inside a shield of crackling power, and fell on the defenders with a savagery that, until that point, they had always avoided.

Isir fought Isir, cousin on cousin, brother on brother, and likewise, the karls. Blood ran in the street, hissing on the power-saturated cobbles. The sound of the fighting rang and echoed in the street, pursuing Luka like hunting dogs after a rabbit.

What sounded like the death knell of the empire chased him away from the fight. Screams of Isir dying in magical flames; the butcher-sounds of blades striking through flesh, only stopped by thick bone; Isir and karls alike begging for mercy, begging for quarter; the sound of his brother screaming battle commands and calling down lightning. Luka longed to stop, to turn and seek Meuhlnir out, but someone had to warn the queen. And perhaps they could salvage the day…a counter-strike from the palace…or a unit of *oolfa* hiding in the city, hammer to the anvil of the palace walls with his brother's forces caught between. But none of that would happen unless he got back to the palace in time to organize a response.

He bounded toward the palace, hoping against hope that the queen was awake and functioning. Luka howled as he ran, raising the alarm with the *oolfa* who remained in the city.

Racing into the palace, brushing aside the guardsmen who stood in his path, he sprinted to the throne room, and as he caught sight of the doorway, he began the *prayteenk* back to his human form.

He burst through the door as the change finished, sliding on bare feet. Queen Hel sat on her throne, her head in her hands. That worthless healer stood to the side, and Brigitta stood behind and to the left of the throne, holding a pitcher of mead and a mug.

"My Queen!" Luka rasped. "We must get to a *proo* and escape! The northern gate has fallen!"

The courtiers in the room gasped, but the queen only crossed her legs and reclined into her throne.

"Did you hear me, my Queen? They come! The rebels come!"

Hel sighed and lifted her head. Diamond tears glittered in her eyes. She shook her head.

"My Queen—"

"No, my Champion," she said, her voice cracked, hoarse. "It is done."

"No, my Queen! We can fall back—"

"It's *done*!" she snapped. "I'm tired, my Luka. This place…" she waved her hands to encompass Suelhaym. "This place is over for me. I've been abandoned. Tricked. Thrown away. I hadn't the heart to tell you sooner…"

The bitterness, he thought. *Her malaise.* "Who has done this, my Queen? I shall rip their organs out for your dinner. I shall—"

"My Champion," she breathed, and though a smile creased her face, tears fell from her eyes to make tracks down her cheeks. "I will protect you in what's coming, but I don't have the heart to continue the fight. We've lost the war. Forces have conspired against me, betrayed my trust, broken their promises…" She shook her head. "No more." Her voice was almost inaudible, but Luka heard the terrible sadness in it, the queen's complete lack of hope.

"I don't understand, my Queen. Who has betrayed you? Vuhluntr? I will catch up to him and—"

"No. No one as inconsequential as the smith."

"Then who?"

She shook her head. "You wouldn't believe me, dear one. But if we continue this war, it will lead only to a bitter defeat for everyone. Everyone everywhere. A dark power will reign over the universe, and it cares nothing for us. We were lied to, my Champion."

"Lied to?"

"Yes, my Champion. Lied to, used, discarded as so much garbage. The choice has simplified, now. Either we fight the rebels, tooth and nail, and carve out a place for ourselves *without* assistance from other quarters, or we withdraw from the game altogether."

All motion in the throne room stopped, the queen was halfway out of her throne, the courtiers stood with mouths open—mid-gasp, mid-exclamation.

"I don't want to remember this!" cried Luka.

THIRTY-
FOUR

"I don't want to remember about this either!" cried Luka. "Never again! Stop dragging these memories to the fore!"

I shook my head. "I didn't. *You* did."

Luka shook his head violently from side-to-side. "No! I hate to recall that day. I *refuse* to relive that day!"

"The people who betrayed her," I murmured. "They were the *Plauinn*—the same two who hold her captive as we speak."

"The *Plauinn*!" Luka's face scrunched with scorn. "The *Plauinn* don't exist, Hank. They are boogeymen out of legend, and that's the whole of it."

I shook my head. "I wish they were, but they are as real as you and me, and far, far more powerful than either of us."

He turned a bleak stare on me, but his gaze reflected uncertainty. "How could the *Plauinn* have betrayed her? She knows nothing of them."

"You are probably right," I said with a weary sigh. "From what someone told me, the *Plauinn* appeared to Hel as voices in her head. They manipulated her by telling her about future events but lying about the motivations of the actors. Your brother, for instance."

Luka scoffed. "No, Meuhlnir was—"

"Love motivated Meuhlnir. His love for Suel, his love for you... Sif and Yowrnsaxa always had Suel's best interests at heart. Frikka, Freya, as well. Veethar—all of them—they mourn the day you were recalling there. They don't celebrate it as a victory. It breaks their hearts every time they think of this day."

"No! Don't be so gullible, Hank! They—"

With a sigh, I took him to my memory of the day we'd reached Suelhaym while on our trip to the *Herperty af Roostum* and let it play out.

THIRTY-FIVE

The sun flirted with the mountains girdling the western horizon as we crested the last rise and glimpsed the city stretching out along the shore for what must have been miles and miles. Suelhaym. "Bigger than I thought," I said.

"You should have seen it before the war," said Sif in a wistful voice.

Muddy red tiles capped the buildings, and smoke from cook fires billowed skyward. An ivy-covered granite wall surrounded the city, and it must have stood forty feet high. Docks stretched far out into the natural bay that was the eastern border of the city.

Ships teemed in the harbor, leaving with the evening tide, their lanterns and navigation markers bobbing about like fireflies in a breeze. There was no sign of the sea dragons that had escorted us down the coast. The muddy red tiles must have once been bright red and shiny, and the wall straight and kept clear of the creeping ivy that climbed it now. "It must have been beautiful from up here."

"Oh, it was," said Frikka. "In time, it will be again."

"I'm hungry," grumbled Althyof. "*And* thirsty. I wonder if anyone here has a proper ale?" He tapped his horse with his heels and cantered down toward Suelhaym's massive North Gate at the foot of the hill.

The gates stood open and seemed to be unattended. As we approached, I understood why: they stood open because they no longer closed. The left gate leaned propped against the granite wall, its massive hinges twisted and broken, the gate on the right still hung by its bottom hinge, but the top hinge had melted after contact with something extremely hot, and the inner tip of the gate had buried itself in the ground.

"This is where she made her last stand," said Veethar in a quiet, almost mournful tone.

"We had to attack our own city," murmured Meuhlnir. "Break our own gates, fight our former neighbors street by street to the palace in which we used to serve."

"Then the real battle began," said Frikka, brushing at her cheeks.

"Yes," said Veethar and walked his horse off the road and into the trees on the inland side.

"Come on," said Mothi. "Let's leave them to their reminiscences."

"Lead on," I said, and we followed Mothi through the gate.

Once we'd ridden a block or two, Mothi said, "I'm glad I was born after the war. So many places are nothing more than reminders of the worst times in their lives."

THIRTY-SIX

"**D**o you understand now?"

Luka's face hung slack, his eyes almost
blank. "What… What was that?" he
whispered, voice shaking with intense emotion.

"That is my memory of reaching the northern
gates for the first time. I traveled there in the
company of your brother, his wives, Frikka, Veethar,
your nephew Mothi, my family, and a few friends.
That's what happened when the gates came into
view."

"No," he whispered.

"I have many more memories of your brother telling me tales about Suel, about you—even about the death of your other two brothers. I have memory after memory of Meuhlnir's sadness at Queen Suel's fall, at what you have become. Must you relive them all?"

"I don't want to see them!" he gasped. "I was told he… They said Meuhlnir, Paltr, and Huthr were plotting…"

"You were lied to. Who told you these dark tales?"

He shook his head and turned away, hiding his face. "No! I saw what they did. I…I… They told me to watch for things, and… They said that when those things came to pass, I would know they told the truth about all of it."

"They used the same tactic on Suel. The people who convinced you—they were either dreamslice reflections of the *Plauinn* themselves or agents of the *Plauinn*."

He shook his head but didn't turn. "The evidence…the proof…"

"*Manufactured* evidence. *Manipulated* proof. I've had my own run-ins with these *Plauinn*, and let me tell you, they consider us pawns to be manipulated, to be sacrificed for their goals. They don't care what their goals do in this realm or any other. All they care about is their own wants."

Luka shook his head and held his hands out to his sides as if to ward away my words.

"Luka…are you aware of what you've become? Don't you understand what the *Plauinn* have led you to become?"

"I made my own choices," he whispered.

"Choices, yes. But choices based on manipulation without the benefit of the facts. Can you say the choices you made at the beginning were one hundred percent your own?" Why I was trying to convince him was beyond me…whether it was out of respect for Meuhlnir or because of what Kuhntul said. "Do you have any idea how far you've drifted, even from the Luka in those memories we just saw?"

Luka shook his head for the third time, denying it all. I dug into his memories, looking for examples, looking for things with enough shock value to *make* him understand.

"Tell me, Luka Oolfhyethidn, is *this* who you wanted to be?"

"I don't—"

THIRTY-SEVEN

"I don't bite," said Luka and trotted out his best smile. The woman was only slightly inebriated, not enough to spoil the flavor, but enough to make her pliable. He'd spent two hours and forty dollars treating her to mixed drinks, and he'd spent an additional twenty dollars making sure the bartender added shots of 190-proof Everclear to the drinks while he made them.

He leaned against the door of his black Continental and winked at her. "Not unless you want me to…"

That earned a saucy grin and a slight blush.

"Listen," he said. "Say the word, and I'll drop you off at your place. We don't have to do anything you don't want to do."

She nodded, blonde locks bouncing. "You're nice for a guy I met in a bar."

"Aren't I just?" He trotted out that winning smile again. "Come on." He held out his hand.

She glanced around the dark parking lot, then back up at him. She smiled and took his hand. "Okay, Mr. Mystery. Let's go for a ride and see where things go from there."

This time, his smile was genuine. "Anything you say." He handed her into the car and fastened her seat belt, knowing most people thought it was an eccentricity decades out of date, but the truth of it was, he didn't want his passengers to realize he had modified the seat belts. They didn't release in a conventional manner, but they also didn't *fasten* in the normal way.

"Thanks, Mr. Mystery. Are you going to tell me your name?"

"You can call me Chris. Chris Hatton."

"Okay, Chris. You know the whole seat belt thing would freak some people right out, right?"

He shrugged and closed the door. The top was down, so she could see his broad smile. "Is it so wrong to be courteous?"

She smiled a sunny smile. "No, not at all. It's only that it's a little…"

"A little personal, right?"

She nodded. "Yeah, that's it."

"Then you should really worry about this," he said in a light tone. He grabbed her by the hair and punched her on the point of her jaw. She went out as if he'd flipped a switch, and he leaned in to get the hypodermic needle out of the glove box. He needed her to sleep for the ride home. Suel deserved fresh meat for once, and when the drug he'd stolen from the veterinary clinic metabolized out of her system, it wouldn't leave much to spoil the flavor.

He nodded to himself as he injected the sedative into the woman's vein. He'd let Suel make the kill. They could dump this foolish woman in the basement until the alcohol and the tranquilizer were out of her system, and Suel could go down and take her time. Savor it, for once.

"Suel will enjoy making your acquaintance," he said and patted the woman on the cheek. He turned and walked around the rear of the car, sliding his fingertips along the glossy paint, humming to himself.

As he rounded the driver's side rear corner, everything froze.

THIRTY-
EIGHT

The three teenaged girls walked down the side of the road, two on the macadam, one on the shoulder. Each had their hair back in a braid, and each wore tight lace-covered shorts and one of those ridiculous backless crop tops that showed more than they hid. They had flip-flops on their feet, so catching all three wouldn't be much of a challenge—unless they were smart enough to kick the things off and run barefoot.

He shrugged, swathed in shadow and silence. Even if they were, they couldn't run faster than he could, and like as not, they'd run straight up the road instead of splitting up and running in different directions. It would be easy to run them down.

The one closest to the copse of trees in which he hid—the one walking on the shoulder—glanced at the dark trees and shivered. She said something to her friends—too soft for Luka to hear it—and the tall one on the other end laughed raucously.

"Don't be a twit, Sandy," said the tall girl. "It's only an animal."

The girl on the shoulder glanced at the woods, her gaze traveling across Luka's face. "You don't know *everything*, Kristy."

Kristy made a show of rolling her eyes, and his smile stretched wider. Kristy was in for the shock of her life. He'd save her for last, let the terror build as he killed her friends, one by one.

Luka waited for them to be abreast of where he hid and stepped out of the woods with a casual air. He raised his hand and waved. The three girls stopped dead in their tracks, each girl staring at a different part of him, none of them making a sound.

Oh, he knew their society didn't—couldn't—accept the thing they saw: a fifteen-foot-tall werewolf, but he delighted in their responses, nonetheless.

The one called Sandy stared at his face as if looking for signs of human compassion—she was in for a disappointment. The one in the middle stared at his fur and sore-covered chest. Kristy…Kristy made him want to laugh out loud. She stared at what hung between his legs.

He lifted both hands to shoulder height, and with a flourish, showed his talons. The girls' eyes widened like full moons, and when their breath caught in their throats, he howled.

The idiots just stood there, staring at him.

Suppressing a laugh, he snarled and charged at Sandy. She was the smartest of the three—the most significant threat of doing something unexpected, something sharp.

A sweeping slash from each talon-tipped hand ripped Sandy's throat out, and as her blood sprayed into the air, Kristy threw her hands over her head and sprinted away—still wearing the flip-flops.

"Help!" she screeched. "Help us!"

Luka cocked his head at the one who'd been walking in the middle. She stared up at him as if seeing a real-life werewolf happened to her every day. He stepped closer to her and growled.

She met his gaze and smiled. "Cool! Can you bite me and make me a shifter? Like in the movies?"

With a snarl, he snapped his jaws around her throat and sucked her hot blood down his throat.

Kristy was still screaming, still running, but she'd moved to the center-line of the two-lane country road. He sprinted after her, catching her up with ease. He ran alongside her and howled every time she screamed, delighting in her fear.

In an almost casual manner, he reached across and pushed her to the ground. She skidded on her left elbow, knee and hip, her chin, and the left side of her forehead. Her screams of fear became shrieks of pain.

Howling, he circled back, where he squatted over her. With a lurid smile, he reached between his legs and cupped his sex in one hairy hand. He tipped her a wink, and she whimpered, shaking her head. She tried to slide away from him, pulling her body from beneath him on her elbows and heels.

With a snarl, he bit her right forearm and shook her hard. She shrieked in pain, and he smiled as her limb broke. When her shoulder popped out of its socket, he opened his jaws, mid-swing, and let her fly off to the shoulder of the road.

She landed in a heap, and he pranced over to her. Muttering, she begged him to stop hurting her.

With a lupine grin, he slashed her throat and the world ground to a halt.

THIRTY-NINE

L uka crouched in the rows of growing corn, watching the back of the house. He thought there were only three troopers inside: two in uniform and the partner. Melanie had seen too much, and that was too bad—he liked the old broad, she had spunk—but Suel had said she had to go, so she did. Plus, he *really* wanted to talk to Jensen again.

He sniffed the spring air, smelling the old trooper's coffee from across the street. The sun was dipping toward the horizon as late afternoon bloomed in full color around him. He peered at the back windows of the old farmhouse.

Seeing no one, he made the dash to the back wall of the house, pressing his furred back against the clapboard wall of the house. He slid toward the corner, then around it, crouching behind the steps that led to the mud room door, his eyes glued on the house across the street.

The trooper on the porch over there took a sip from his insulated coffee cup and grimaced, tilting his head back farther, and then farther still. With a shake of his head, he abandoned his rocker and strode into the house.

Luka streaked up the steps and through the door into the mud room. He froze in the welcoming gloom, listening to the sounds from within. Two troopers chatted in low tones, and farther away, the partner—the one who'd been in the cave with Jensen—spoke with Melanie Layne.

A laundry room stood between the mud room and the rest of the house, and Luka pushed the door all the way open and slipped inside, padding as silently as a wolf on the prowl. The door to the rest of the house stood cracked open, and he could smell leather and gun oil from the two troopers in the kitchen. With a small click, he switched off the utility room lights.

"You hear that, Coop?" came a voice from the kitchen.

Luka froze behind the door.

"Hear what, man? House this old, you're going to drive yourself crazy if you keep this up all shift. Not to mention me."

"Yeah," laughed the first trooper. "Guess you're right. It's not as if ninjas are about to attack us."

"Nope. Werewolves neither."

By their voices, Luka had their locations pegged. One stood by the far wall, one in the middle of the room. If he blitzed through the kitchen at full speed, he could barge into the one in the center of the room, knocking him for a sprawl, and kill the other one before the first regained his feet.

He took a breath and exploded into the small, square kitchen, pausing for only a fraction of a second to ascertain the position of both troopers, and sprang toward the one leaning against the far wall. On his way through the room, he bashed the other trooper with his shoulder, sending the man spinning into the sink. He grabbed the trooper leaning against the wall and flung him spinning at his partner, ripping his throat out as he did so.

"Ritter!" called the one he'd driven into the sink.

Two long strides brought Luka across the room, and he shoved the bleeding trooper to the ground—the man was already dead, but his brain didn't know it yet. The bleeding trooper scrabbled at the holster on his side, and with a sneer, Luka stomped down on his hand, snapping his wrist like a dry twig.

The other trooper pushed himself away and jerked his Glock out of his holster. Luka lunged across the intervening space and snapped at the man's face, his large canine fangs riving chunks of flesh from the man's cheeks below each eye. The trooper screamed but held onto his pistol. He tried to bring it to bear, but Luka grabbed his wrist, sinking his talons into the man's flesh.

Something clicked behind him.

As quick as a striking snake, Luka jerked the trooper around and looped an arm across his chest. He grabbed the wrist of the hand holding the Glock and forced it up, pointing it at the door to the room beyond the kitchen.

"Freeze right there!"

Luka wanted to laugh at the icy control in Jax Ritter's voice, at the suppression of fear it showed. He bore down on his hostage's wrist, delighting in the sound of the bones grinding, grinding, and finally snapping. The trooper screamed, and the pistol clattered to the floor.

"Turn him loose!" ordered Jax.

"Not likely," he said, forcing the words from his twisted throat, past a tongue more suited for lolling than speaking.

"Do it now!"

Luka shrugged. "'Kay," he grunted. Moving casually, he released the man's wrist and made as if to withdraw the arm he held across the trooper's chest. At the last moment, he dug his claws into the man's flesh and ripped great furrows across his chest, flinging the blood at Ritter's eyes.

Jax ducked behind the wall to his left, and as he did, Luka sprinted for the doorway beyond which the trooper hid. He slid into what was the dining room, his bulk requiring him to squeeze through the door on all fours. Jax stared at him in surprise, then Luka was on him, punching, head-butting, kicking, driving the man down toward the floor. He had something special in mind for Jax. A gift, of sorts, for Jensen.

A chair crashed across his back, and he almost laughed. He whirled and backhanded Melanie Layne into the far wall.

Whirling back to Jax, he kneed the trooper in the face, and with a wrenching snap, broke his neck. He danced back into the kitchen. The last trooper alive was on his knees, crawling toward the door to the dining room, the Glock held awkwardly in his left hand. The pistol swerved toward Luka, its tip jittering back and forth.

With a roar, Luka leapt across the room and snapped his jaws closed over the man's left wrist, then tore his jaws away, rending the man's flesh, tearing his tendons, breaking his bones. The man screamed, and Luka slashed his throat with a backhanded strike.

Making sure both troopers in the kitchen were dead, he took a pair of handcuffs off one of their service belts and went back to Melanie Layne. *The brave old thing*, he thought. *Pity she has to die*. He snapped the cuffs around her wrist, and everything froze.

FORTY

The memory shook me, the casual, cold way he'd killed the troopers as if they meant nothing. In a way, though, the memory also relieved me. At least all the signs of torture I'd seen on Jax when I'd arrived that night were posthumous.

"What's the matter, Hank? Don't you want to see the rest of it?"

"No. I've seen it enough in my nightmares."

Luka scoffed, but there was something in his eyes...a lack of the brazen confidence he usually displayed.

"Is this the man you pictured you'd be? Is this really the man Suel *wanted*?"

"Don't talk about her," he snapped. "Don't you call her by that name! You've no right! Besides, what I've done, *all* that I've done, I've done for her."

"Yeah, that's clear to me now. You love her."

Luka shook his head, "Of *course* I love her!"

I nodded. "You do what you do to try to…I don't know…to try to make her happy."

"Her happiness is more important than *anything* else. She's been…she's been hurt badly…by those she loved. By my brother. By Sif, Yowrnsaxa, and Frikka. By her own sister!"

"She believes that, yes."

"*Believes* it? It's what happened! I was there!"

"You were both manipulated by the *Plauinn*. They used their abilities to read the skein of fate, to predict what those people would do. Then they told one or both of you how they would act and used it to manipulate the events to their liking."

"So *you* say."

I sighed. "This is pointless. Tell me one thing, Luka."

"What?" he asked after a significant pause.

"Are you the man you wanted to be?"

He met my gaze with tired, red-rimmed eyes. "Who is?"

"If things had been different, who would you have become?"

"How should I know?" he snarled.

"Think back. Recall the man you were before these people started telling you how your brothers were conspiring against you."

He dropped his gaze. "What of it?" he asked in a sullen voice.

"Can you imagine that version of yourself acting as coldly as you did in those memories?"

"What does it matter, Hank?" he asked in a voice that broke on my name. "What possible difference would that make to you?"

I shrugged. "Maybe nothing. Maybe everything. Are you going to answer the question?"

Luka looked away and crossed his arms over his breast. "No, I was not like this before we killed… Before."

"And was your queen?"

Luka looked me in the eye, and I could see the raw pain in his gaze. He shook his head.

"Do you still believe I have Hel spirited away somewhere?"

Luka turned his head away and shrugged his shoulders.

"Let me prove I don't! Let me prove I'm telling you the truth!"

"Can you?"

I nodded. "I can." I flipped us into my memory stream—my *slowth*.

FORTY-ONE

I n the distance, a woman screamed and screamed. Her echoing cries spoke to the sort of anguish few people live long enough to tell others about.

A fluid as viscous as honey surrounded us, and colors flashed around us like lightning in a severe thunderstorm. Gravity—or something similar to it— tugged us in conflicting directions, first one way, then another, then yet another. It was like being on the world's best rollercoaster, but without the fun.

"What is this place?" Luka murmured.

"This is Owraythu's realm. Owraythu, the *Plauinn*."

"That word means 'chaos.'"

"Yeah, I know. It's what the *Plowir Medn* call her. Her brother is Mirkur. Before you say it, I know it means 'darkness.' The name suits him."

Beside me, Luka shook his head and off in the distance, the woman's screaming ramped up a notch. "Is that…is that Suel?" he whispered.

"So someone told me."

"I must go to her!" Luka slashed his arms and legs against the viscous fluid, trying to propel himself toward the screams.

"Hang on there a minute, champ," I said. "If you rush over there, you'll be giving yourself to Owraythu. Something tells me she'd enjoy punishing you, too."

"I can't sit here and listen to her scream!"

I nodded and stopped the timeflow of the memory. The screaming halted abruptly, and the colors froze in mid-flash. "Is this better?"

"Does she still suffer?" he demanded.

"This is one of my memories, Luka. I'm not sure how it all works, but these are things inside the *slowth* I can see. This particular one is not only one of my memories, but a memory of a dream. I don't know if she is suffering at present or not."

Luka shook his head in disbelief. "You seem to have gained many new skills since the last time we spoke. Who taught you all this?"

I waved my hand in the viscous fluid. "I've had a few teachers."

"You speak the *Gamla Toonkumowl* with a fluency few people not raised to it could match. You can do things... That bear form you have is quite impressive. How do you make such a complete change?"

"Somehow, I don't think I'd teach you, even if I could. A number of these abilities came from reading a *puntidn stavsetninkarpowk*."

"And where did you find a bound-spellbook?"

"Long story, and one that doesn't matter right now." I swept my arms out to the side, setting myself adrift. "This place...this *realm*, this is where Hel is."

"Or was," added Luka.

"Or was." I shrugged. "The point is, *I* don't control this realm. I don't even know how to get here outside of memory."

"Yet this is where I must come."

"I understand that's how you feel. Someone told me that were I to come here and confront Owraythu head-on, I would lose—that Owraythu would gobble me up. I don't imagine you would fare much better."

"Then why have you brought me here?"

"To prove to you that I am not behind Hel's disappearance. The *Plowir Medn* must have brought her here when they teleported her away from the battle—from Haymtatlr's robots."

Luka glanced at me with distrust twitching in his eyes. "And why should I believe all that? You've learned many, many things—you admit this yourself. Why should I believe this memory is anything but an illusion to gain my trust?"

"Think about it, Luka. Back in the *Herperty af Roostum*, you are about to die in the same way we killed Vowli. I'm on top of you, pinning you beneath a weight you can't move, and I have you between my jaws." His eyes grew hard at the reminder. "I don't *need* your trust."

"So why?"

"Because if the *Plauinn* have their way, the universe will all look this way. Because the *Plauinn* see us as inconsequential, as things to be used and discarded when we become inconvenient. Because the *Plauinn* are a far greater threat to my family than you and Hel could ever be."

He narrowed his eyes. "If it is as you say—"

The surrounding fluid conveyed a jolt to my body like that of a train pulling away from the station. Hel screamed, stopped, screamed, stopped, like the stutter of digital audio run amok. The fluid jerked again, and everything settled back to the way it was.

"What was that?"

"No idea," I said.

"I don't like it. Something is—"

The jerk came again, stronger this time, and I felt it in my bones. Again, Hel's screams came to us in the manner of stuttering audio, but instead of falling silent, the stuttering ended, and we heard each agonized shriek in its fullness.

"Something's *wrong*," Luka muttered.

FURIOUS QUERY. WHO DISTURBS THIS ONE'S REALM?

"Oh, shit," I whispered. "Owraythu!"

WHO DARES MANIPULATE THE TIMEFLOWS?

The fluid around us jerked once more, this time slamming into our backs like a strong wave at the beach.

SMALL ONES? DENIAL! PROVIDE THE IDENTITY OF YOUR MASTER, OF THE ONE WHO BETRAYS MY TRUST! HIS LIFEFORCE WILL DISSIPATE! HIS PROGENY WILL BE BROKEN, SCATTERED ON THE TIMEFLOWS!

Fear grasped my mind in its icy grip, and I flung us away—out of the memory. Unlike before, the change was not instantaneous. I had the sense of something pursuing us, something reaching for us, pulling us back.

Behind us, someone or something grunted.

"*Run!*" screamed Hel.

"My Queen!" shouted Luka.

"*Run!*" she called again and shrieked the way an animal being burned alive would shriek.

The sense of something behind faded, and we were out.

FORTY-TWO

I t was as if no time had passed; the others still
sprinted toward us, and Luka still lay beneath
my massive bear's body. I drew my fangs out
of his flesh and rocked my weight back off him. I
chanted the *triblinkr* to return me to human form in
my mind.

Luka lay before me, not moving. "My Queen," he
whimpered and began his own *prayteenk*.

"Hank! What are you doing? We have to kill him!"
yelled Jane.

I shook my head. "No. I don't want to kill him."

"What?"

"There are things you don't understand yet, Jane. Things I've learned… Things about Luka and Hel that mitigate—"

"I have to save her!" Luka yelled and whirled to his feet. "How do I get back there! Take me back there, Hank!"

"No, Luka. Going back there now is pure folly. She'd be waiting. We have to—"

With a snarl, Luka whirled and sprinted away.

"No!" screamed Jane. She cocked her arm back to fling her spear at his retreating back.

"No, Jane," I said. "Haymtatlr, can you stop Luka from using the *preer* but leave them functional for everyone else?"

"I can."

"Then please do so."

Jane took a few steps in the direction Luka had fled.

"Let him go, Jane."

"Let him go? Are you *insane*?"

I shook my head. "You heard Haymtatlr. He can't get away again. Besides, I… I gave him a lot to consider. I took him to where Hel is being tortured by Owraythu. I don't think he'll give us any more trouble. At least not until—"

"When? When did you have this little heart-to-heart?"

"Just now. While we were in his memories…or his dreamslice…whatever you want to call it."

"You've lost your mind." She turned to Althyof, who was staring at me as though I'd painted my face with feces and announced to the world that I was the king of the dust mites. "He's lost it."

"Listen to me," I said. "The *Plauinn* have been manipulating Luka and Hel for centuries. They've… The *Plauinn* have betrayed them—and us—time and time again. A race of people who can peer ahead in *uhrluhk* and see how someone will act spent years manipulating them, lying to them, twisting their views of the world. The *Plauinn* used their knowledge of *urhluhk* to make Luka and Hel dance like puppets on a string. Their version of the universe is a dark, cold place—one filled with betrayal by everyone they loved."

"And that makes it okay?" Jane demanded.

"No, and it doesn't lessen their culpability for the crimes they've committed. But it explains some of it."

"He's lost his mind," she said to Sif. "He's gone 'round the bend. Gone cuckoo."

Sif shook her head. "No, dear," she said, putting a hand on Jane's arm. "Besides, we must see to your son."

"But…" Her eyes stared in the direction that Luka had fled.

"He's focused on Hel, now," I said. "And *only* on Hel. He's heard her screaming in agony, and all he wants is to make that agony stop. We should… We should help him."

"Now, I *know* you've lost your mind."

I shrugged. "I'll help him alone if I must. Kuhntul told me that if Owraythu breaks Hel's mind, we will face even more of a threat from her than we can imagine."

"And if we free her, who's to say the pair of them won't turn against us?"

"No one," I said. "But we can deal with that later, and I think we've grown into a match for them, anyway. Right now, we need to go get Sig."

Jane lifted her hand, palm up, in the direction Luka had run. "And the guy who knows where our son is just ran off, and you let him."

I took my wife by the shoulders and made her look at me. "I can find him," I said. "The same way I found Luka."

"So, what are you waiting for?"

I nodded once and dropped my hands. I found his *slowth* amidst all the others that twined and snaked through the room and slid forward along its length. When I'd gone far enough to account for the distance to Luka's *proo*, I dipped into my son's *slowth* and picked out his location. I spun a new *proo* and sent its terminus to the point where Sig emerged in the other realm.

I met Jane's eyes. "Let's go."

"A moment," called Veethar. "I'm coming with you."

Mothi had already retrieved his axes and strode toward the *proo* with a stern expression etched into his face. "I go as well."

"And I," said Frikka.

Yowrnsaxa already had her shield strapped on and moved to stand with Mothi.

John smiled his sad smile and came to stand at our side.

I glanced around, seeing the resolve in their faces. Sif looked torn, her gaze meeting mine and flitting away to where Meuhlnir struggled to stand.

"Meuhlnir," I said. "Old friend, rest and focus on healing. We will need you at full strength soon enough."

Sif sent me a thankful smile as Meuhlnir grunted and fell back against the wall.

"I could use my ring," said Jane.

Meuhlnir shook his head. "No. Don't waste your strength on me. You may need it for your son."

Jane nodded, but looked as if she'd eaten something sour, rotten.

"Right," I said. "A word of warning. The land on the other end of this *proo* looks like a battlefield." I reached out and touched the *proo*.

FORTY-
THREE

I emerged from the *proo* into a billowing bubble of greenish-gray vapor that burned my nostrils as I took a breath. The ground was stony, barren. In the distance, craggy peaks reached toward the granite cloud-filled sky like taloned fingers. Between me and the mountains, smoking ruins of what were once buildings and rusting hulks of mechanized armored vehicles of a strange make I'd never seen before dotted the macabre landscape, as though broken and scattered by a child in the throes of a tantrum. In the far distance in the other direction, a smooth gray sea stretched toward the horizon. The others popped in behind me, each grimacing first at the smoke, then at our surroundings.

A mechanical shriek came from the direction of the sea and reached an ear-splitting volume in the space of a heartbeat. Something throbbed in my chest with a syncopated rhythm in sympathy with the vibration rumbling up through the soles of my feet. On the other horizon, a searing white light blossomed like a giant flower of death, and the earth growled as if a thousand earthquakes had kicked off, followed by the sounds of shifting ruins and corroded vehicles of war vibrating apart.

"Kleymtlant," said John.

"No, surely not," I said. "As bad as Kleymtlant is, it's a paradise compared to this mess." I swept my hand toward the horizon and the white blossom of flame and radiation that still hung there. "Plus, all the radiation in Kleymtlant is old—millennia old."

John turned toward me and nodded. "It is. Yet this *is* Kleymtlant. Consider those mountains. They are familiar, no?"

I glanced at the crags thrusting into the sky. A few of them *did* seem familiar, but they were much sharper than those near the *Herperty af Roostum*, and I said as much.

John smiled joylessly. "Yes, I imagine this is how they looked far in the past. I know this land, Hank, and this land is Kleymtlant."

Shaking my head, I scanned the ground for Sig's *slowth* and led the others to the southwest, away from both the high-pitched shriek and the death flower on the horizon, threading through the enigmatic bubbles of acrid fog. Whatever the conflict was, whatever it was about, the people fighting it had no qualms about destroying their planet, and I wanted us all out of there as soon as possible.

Maybe John was right. It fit what Meuhlnir had told me about Osgarthr's ancient past.

We raced across the gravel and small stones that littered the lifeless plain. From horizon to horizon, not a single tree still stood, of course, but also no scrub, no lizards, no birds, not even insects existed. Wisps of the greenish mist blew across the landscape, and every now and again, a distant shriek preceded the blooming of a fresh death-blossom, and the ground shook. I wondered how long the war had been going on, what type of weapons could so destroy the ecosphere of a planet, and who in the hell would be stupid enough to employ them.

"Is this..." grated Mothi, his voice hoarse and ragged from breathing the vapor.

The specter of biological or chemical weapons reared up in my mind, and I shook my head, finger over my lips. "Speak only when necessary. Take shallow breaths." I pointed at the blobs of mold-colored fog drifting across the plain.

Mothi nodded and pointed at the crags in the distance. "Dragon spine? *Ragnaruechkr*?"

John nodded, eyeing the mountains with a speculative gleam in his eye. "Did you not say the *preer* could break the boundaries of time?"

I thought about the stories Meuhlnir had told me of Isi, Jot, and Vani and their great war and shrugged. Whether we were witnessing the destruction wrought by Mim's three sons or another war-torn *klith* didn't matter. What mattered was getting to Sig, Yowtgayrr, and Skowvithr before something killed them. Or us.

"Speed," I grated at Althyof, then coughed until I almost lost my lunch. He squinted up at me for a moment and nodded. The *runeskowld* began a *trowba*, but his voice rasped and creaked, and he shook his head and brought out a section of cloth. He tied it around his mouth and switched to a rhythmic chant.

We ran under that bruised sky for what felt like hours, following the wandering *slowthar* of my son and my Alfar friends, passing burnt-out wrecks of armored vehicles, blackened patches of exposed bedrock, and plains filled with nothing but the skeletal remains of combatants. When we stopped, it was because Sig, Yowtgayrr, and Skowvithr's *slowthar* looped and knotted around each other as if they'd performed a ballet. After the knot, the *slowthar* veered away on an arrow-straight path to the east.

"Not good," I said. "I think a troop of, well, *something*, set upon them, and captured them perhaps, but whatever it was, it left no *slowth*."

"No trail? I thought you said—"

"What do you mean 'set upon?'" demanded Jane. "Is our son okay? Are the Alfar hurt?"

"By their *slowthar*, everyone is healthy, but I don't like this." I squeezed her hand. "They show no injuries, Jane."

"Who attacked them?" asked Althyof. "I thought you said everyone leaves a *slowth*?"

I shrugged. "I don't know the rules of this stuff. All I can say is that so far, everyone I've seen leaves a *slowth*, but maybe a race exists—some demonic race—that doesn't."

Veethar shook his head. "Not demons. Not if this is Osgarthr in the time of Isi."

I arched my eyebrows at him.

"No *preer* yet. At the time of Isi's war with his brothers, the inhabitants of Osgarthr were alone."

"I'd forgotten."

"Then what?" asked Jane.

I shrugged. "I can only see which direction they took when they left: East."

"What are we waiting for?"

With a shrug, I turned and led them alongside the *slowthar* of Sig and the Alfar. No matter where we ran or what direction we faced, it all looked the same—a wasted planet under a ruined sky. After what felt like an eternity of dodging the smoky green gas clouds, a forest of strange poles thrust from the ground in the distance. An acorn-shaped mass of dark, non-reflective metal topped each pole.

"Weapons?" asked Mothi.

"A fence?" creaked Jane.

I shrugged and ran on, following the trail straight toward the copse of poles. The *slowthar* ran on, as straight as a ruler, right through the middle of the weird devices.

When we crossed the plain dictated by the first row of poles, the squeal of an electronic alarm split the noxious air. With no one saying a word, we spread out into a loose semi-circle and readied our weapons, trying to see in every direction at once.

Then everything went black.

FORTY-FOUR

Awareness stole over me like an assassin creeping into a darkened room, first the grinding, pounding pain in my head, then light so bright I could see it through my closed lid. Sounds filtered through my awakening mind: people talking, an eerie, mechanical clanking that faded away over the span of a few minutes, the quiet susurration of a radio not tuned to anything in particular. My mouth tasted the way I imagined aluminum mixed with peat would taste.

I cracked my eye open—just enough to peek at our surroundings. We were in a vast enclosure. I couldn't see the walls of the place—black shadows shrouded everything outside the area where we lay.

"That one's awake," said a gruff, no-nonsense voice.

"Ah, so. Welcome to my command center," said a deep baritone voice. "There's no sense in pretending. Our sensors can detect your brainwaves, so we know you are conscious and alert.

"Not so sure about alert," I muttered.

The deep baritone laughed. The other voice did not.

I sat up, making only small, controlled movements, wary of setting off an avalanche of aches and pains. A quick, patting search revealed that they had failed to search us, or if they did, they didn't care that I was armed. The others lay sprawled around me in thick, silt-like dust. "What was that thing?"

"That thing?" Two men stood before me. One squat, with a thick torso and dressed in black combat fatigues, and the other tall and broad-shouldered, dressed in an immaculate white suit.

"The perimeter defenses, Lord," said the gruff voice—the one in black.

"Oh, yes. You walked into a sensor patch as bold as you please and, of course, set off the perimeter alarms. The automated defense system rendered you unconscious."

"Sensor patch?"

"Didn't you see the poles?" asked the man in black.

I shook my head. "With the acorn-things on top?"

"Acorns?" asked the man in white.

"Never mind. We didn't know the poles signified the ground was off limits. We were following—"

"Who sent you?" asked the man in black.

"Come now, Keirr," said the man in white. "There is no reason for rudeness." He patted Keirr's shoulder but never took his gaze away from my own. "You must forgive General Keirr. He's a military man, born and bred."

I shook my head. "Nothing to forgive. I'd be wondering the same thing in his shoes." I rubbed my temples. "And to answer his question, no one sent us. A malicious asshole sent my son and two guardians to this place, and we're here to retrieve them."

Keirr's eyes narrowed. "Sent here? By whom?"

I waved it away. "You wouldn't know him. If you'll return our friends, we'll get out of your hair. We apologize for any inconvenience."

"Ah, yes. Your interesting…*friends*."

"Lord Isi, no!" said Keirr.

The man in white turned to the man in black, an expression on his face as if he'd bitten into something sour.

Keirr's face burned with shame.

Isi sighed. "Well, the secret is out of the box, now."

"Sorry, my Lord."

"Yes, well."

A short man wearing light blue scrubs stepped out of the shadows and approached. "Lord Isi? If I may?"

"Go ahead."

"Yessir. The deep readings from this group are strange…much the same as the other three, but even more so for two of these new ones."

"The other three?" I asked. "A boy and two Alfar?"

"Alfar?" asked General Keirr.

"I asked first," I said. Behind me, Jane moaned and pushed herself into a seated position.

"Lord Isi, this man, and that woman…they are the ones with more significant readings. They are even stranger than the first one—"

"Silence!" snapped Keirr.

"Readings?" mumbled Jane.

"Tell me about the other three, please," I said, directing my gaze at Isi. "One of them may be my son."

"Hmmm." Isi strode three steps to the side, his gaze boring into mine. He turned without breaking his stare and walked back. "Tell me who you are, and I may share information about the other three we captured at the sensor patch."

"My name is Hank Jensen." I hooked my thumb over my shoulder at Jane. "That's my wife, Jane." I pointed at Althyof and spoke his name. Krowkr was next, then the other Isir with me, ending with John Calvin Black.

Isi frowned at Althyof. "Is this one of your Afar?"

"Alfar," I said, "and no. Althyof is a Tverkr."

"From whence came he?" asked the scientist in blue.

As I remembered the story of Isi's war, our captors wouldn't know about the *preer*. "A place far from here."

Isi shook his head. "He's not of this planet."

"No," I said with a nod.

Isi nodded. "Our other three captives are a boy and two strangers who have the same look to them as this Tverkr."

"Sig is the boy—Sigurd—and he's my son. The other two are Alfar by the name of Yowtgayrr and Skowvithr. They are our friends—the three we came here to find. If you allow us to join them, we will leave you in peace."

Isi cocked his head to the side, then snapped his fingers at the scientist. "What differs about these two?"

"As with the others, their quantum signatures are…very strange. This one," he said, pointing at me, "appears to have lived for a very long time. Eons. The female appears to be in a state of quantum entanglement such that her signature approaches the male's."

Isi shook his head and flashed me a small smile. "And that means?"

"My Lord, I…" The scientist shook his head. "I can't begin to guess, but I can say that such a thing should be impossible."

"Your enchanters are amateurs," grumbled Althyof without opening his eyes.

"Ah, he speaks," said Isi with a smile that didn't reach his eyes. "And he speaks our language."

"That's a result of—"

"Yes," I said, interrupting the Tverkr. "Althyof speaks our language fluently. And unless you consider fifty years a long time, your pet scientist here is wrong."

The scientist cleared his throat. "Lord Isi, this man's state is similar in ways to the other…uh…*guest* in the lab. There is…an ageless quality to the readings."

Isi turned to the man with a sigh. "And does this information clarify whether either of them is a threat to us?"

The scientist gulped at Isi's hard tone and shook his head.

"In that case, I'll thank you to *shut up* unless I ask a question of you."

"I don't know who this other one is, but neither we nor our three companions threaten anyone here," I said. "All we want is to be reunited, and we will leave this…area, never to return."

"What were you going to say?" Isi asked.

"Nothing."

He treated me to a shrewd glance, then shook his head. "You understand I can't just take your word for it?"

"But you can. You are fighting a war, right? Against Vani and Jot?" At Isi's grudging nod, I continued, "We want nothing to do with it. We are not agents of either of your brother's factions. As I said, we are only here for our friends."

Isi squinted at my face for a moment. "I believe *you* believe that, but everyone on this planet is in one of the three camps. My brothers feel the same way: You are either with me or against me. There's no way to remain neutral."

"And yet we are."

General Keirr shook his head. "Lord, if you'll allow me, our advanced interrogation techniques will yield—"

"I think not," said Isi, but whether to my comment or the general's, it wasn't clear. He pinched his lower lip between his thumb and forefinger and gave it a tug. "No, I think not." He snapped his finger at the darkness again. "Bring them!" he commanded.

The eerie clanking started up again, and I thought I could see movement in the darkness beyond the bright lights shining on us. My hands came to rest on the butts of my pistols.

Isi caught the motion and laughed. "Your primitive weapons will not help you here. Did you think we'd overlooked them?"

With a conscious effort, I moved my hands away from my hips empty. Typical examples of our weapons might not frighten them, but they had no way of knowing how our arms and armor had been manipulated and enhanced by the *strenkir af krafti*. A thought struck me, and I grinned. *They may not even know the possibility of manipulating the strings of power in that way exists yet*.

Isi saw the grin and took a step back. Keirr stepped in front of his sovereign as I stood and stretched.

"You don't want us as enemies," I said, trying to sound casual. "Let's keep this friendly. I am asking you to return my son and my friends."

Isi stiffened. "And you don't want us as enemies." As he spoke, the shadows moving in the darkness clanked and clattered into the light.

They stood seven- or eight-feet tall and glided forward on caterpillar tracks of linked metal plates—the clanking. Each silver-bodied thing held its left arm out straight, with its left hand folded back along its forearm, exposing the matte-black tube of an energy weapon. Except for the tank treads, the robots reminded me of Haymtatlr's metal guardians, and I wondered if those matte-black tubes were the same weapons Haymtatlr's robots used.

They poured out of the darkness, encircling us and stacking up behind, matte-black tubes pointed at my party and me. They came until there were three rings of robots around us, and still more poured out of the darkness and stood ready to fill in the ranks should any of the others fall.

Isi smiled coldly. "As you see, my warriors are always alert, always ready to defend me."

"But can they sing?" asked Althyof, sitting up at last. "Can they keep a rhythm? Carry a tune?"

Isi's expression darkened. "I do not enjoy being mocked, sir."

Althyof climbed to his feet, a cocky grin stretching his lips. "And your warriors? Do they enjoy being mocked?"

Keirr took a step toward Althyof, a look of rage settling on his face.

"Oh, it's all right, Keirr," said Isi. "Let them have their fun." He offered me a smile. "Come, let me take you to your people. I've decided to let you see they are unharmed before we return to the subject of why you have come."

Keirr grimaced, but with a gesture, he commanded the robots to fall back.

Isi waved me forward, and we walked together in a more-or-less companionable silence for a time, though the clank and clatter of the robots following along behind broke the silence with regularity. "Tell me, Hank," he said, "by what manner of transportation did you arrive here?"

"It doesn't matter, but it's no threat to you."

He nodded. "Honestly, I see a threat in everything these days. For instance, one of my captives claims to have traveled here from someplace called the 'underverse' of all things." He shook his head and laughed. "My father was a great scientist. Mim was his name, have you heard of him?" He looked at me askance.

Trying to keep my expression blank, I nodded. "I've heard stories about him."

"Stories, eh?" Isi asked with a strange grin. "No doubt they fall short. Suffice it to say that Mim did vast amounts of research into the nature of the universe, and I have endeavored to expand on his work. That said, I've never heard of this thing called an underverse, but unless I am mistaken, *you have*."

I shrugged. "Yes."

"Is that where you are from? This underverse?"

"No."

"Can you describe it? The underverse?"

"It's…" I shook my head. "It would be difficult to do it justice, but it's as big as the universe, perhaps. Maybe I should have said 'infinite' instead of 'big.'" I shrugged. "It's a void, a darkness. Creatures live in the place, creatures with the appearance of big, blind worms." I shrugged. "I can't explain it further."

Isi nodded. "Big, blind worms," he muttered. "Our visitor is human-shaped, not worm-shaped."

I wondered if a human-shaped visitor from the underverse would be the same as the Nornir—the dreamslice reflection of one of the *Plauinn*. I turned my gaze to the ground in front of us, not wanting him to see recognition in my expression.

He cleared his throat. "Where, then, do you come from?"

What do I tell him? I wondered. "That is also difficult to explain. There are things I cannot tell you."

"Hmmm." He squinted at me with open suspicion. "I have heard that phrase often of late."

I nodded. "By my son and friends."

"By the two Alfar. And the other. The Alfar instructed your son not to answer my questions. I find that most rude."

"Did you capture this other as you captured us?"

Isi shook his head, a subtle smile on his face. "No. We found ourselves in possession of him after a failed experiment." Isi waved his hand airily. "But that is nothing we need discuss. Look, we are here."

The square, rock-walled chamber he'd led us to was smaller and better lit. The walls were one hundred yards long, and strange machines and equipment packed the back half of the room, shrouded in clear plastic. Men in blue scrubs stood at various workstations scattered about, or near the two impromptu cells that stood along one wall, making notes.

Sig, Yowtgayrr, and Skowvithr occupied one, and with a shout, Jane ran toward them.

"Mom!" yelled Sig.

"Be careful, Lady," said one of the scientists. He picked up a plastic implement and tossed it at our son. The plastic hit something invisible and burst into flames with a shower of green sparks.

Jane stopped where she was and glared at Isi. "Release my son!"

"In a moment, perhaps," he said in a mild tone. "A few straight answers first, I think. General, see we are not disturbed."

From behind us, the clanking and clattering grew in volume as the robots advanced into the room. "Yes, m'lord," said Keirr.

I shook my head and grimaced. "This room is more secure than the other?"

With a smile, Isi nodded. "Shielded from my brothers' spy beams." He snapped his fingers at the scientists, and they put away their work and stepped out of the way. "Now, about this place you say you come from…"

The occupant of the other cell resembled Isi and his men more than he did the Isir. He was a mass of contradictions—dressed in a flowing robe of crimson silk, but with bare feet; his black eyes crawled around the room in constant motion, but he stood statue-still with none of the twitches or shifting of weight I expected; he appeared to be human, but no hair grew from any of the parts of his body I could see.

"Is this your other prisoner?" I asked, and as I spoke the creature's eyes found me and froze, locked to my gaze.

"Yes. He's been quite recalcitrant."

The creature's face was expressionless, and now that his eyes had come to a rest, he could have been a statue for all that he moved—I wasn't even sure he was breathing. There were no ticks, no subtle repositioning, no flexing and relaxing of muscles in any part of his body. He appeared to favor the robots behind us more than the human beings in the room.

"What will you do with him?" I asked.

"Return this one to the underverse," the creature grated, not even breaking his stare to blink.

Isi sighed. "That is his answer for everything these days."

"Why not let him go?"

Isi shook his head. "The possibilities he represents…the science…the *knowledge* that we could mine from him."

I shook my head and turned to the red-clad creature. "Isi told me you are from the underverse."

"This one is," he said. "You are not."

"No, I am not."

"But you are strange...unlike these others." His eyes twitched to Jane for a moment before returning to me. "That one is your *filkya*."

"No," I said, shaking my head. "She is no *filkya*."

Again, his eyes twitched in Jane's direction and back. "Acceptance. Your *spayl*."

I shook my head a second time. "Not my twin, either. She is my wife, and her *uhrluhk* is entwined with mine."

"This one comprehends," said the creature.

"Do you know what this creature is?" asked Isi.

"No," I said with a shake of my head. I glanced down at the *slowth* at the creature's feet. It was unlike anything I'd ever seen—much more significant, much *grander*, than an Isir's. It reminded me of the *slowthar* of the Nornir, of Kuhntul, but was larger still. He could be the dreamslice reflection of a *Plauinn*, such as the Three Maids, or he could be something I hadn't seen yet. Whatever he was, he sure spoke in the manner of one of the *Plauinn*.

"You withhold information, Hank," said Isi with anger quivering in his voice.

"No. I don't know what he is."

Isi narrowed his eyes. "But you suspect something. You ask me to release your friends, but you refuse to share your knowledge. This is not the act of a colleague, of a friend."

I raised one eyebrow. "But holding my son and friends hostage is?" I scoffed. "You need a new dictionary."

Isi smiled, but again the smile didn't reach his eyes. "Perhaps General Keirr can assist us with a few definitions and points of fact." Without looking at the man, Isi raised his hand and snapped his fingers.

"One," boomed the general, "you are in *our* power and continue to draw breath only by Lord Isi's grace. Two, your people—your son and these Alfar—are in our power. Three, you can't free your people, only we can do that. Four, our weapons are not throwbacks to the ancient past. Each of my robotic warriors wields a shriek-beam, as you've seen, and as you *haven't* seen, each has a beam-shield and an electromagnetic repulser. Your pitiful weapons are no match for them."

"We, too, have weapons you can't see, Isi," I said, ignoring Keirr utterly.

"*Lord* Isi!" snapped General Keirr.

I glanced at him, but kept my lips together, which seemed to infuriate him more.

It's strange what comes to mind in situations such as that. One of my favorite movies was Tombstone, and in a scene toward the end, Doc Holliday called out Johnny Ringo, and Ringo said, "All right, lunger. Let's do it." Michael Biehn, the actor who played Ringo, delivered the line with a widening of the eyes, a jaunty nod, and smile, and the image of his expression plus the line flashed through my mind. I almost said it, but I remembered that soon afterward,

Doc Holliday blasted a hole in Ringo, so I let the moment pass.

"Isi, call off your pet," I said, letting my gaze slide away from Keirr as if I'd lost interest.

At a subtle hand gesture from General Keirr, the robots advanced a few feet. Althyof drew his daggers and began a battle *trowba*, creeping in a slow dance that circled back and forth between us and the robots. Jane set her shield and hefted her spear, but kept her wings hidden. Krowkr stood in the back, looking unsure what to do, and had drawn his mundane weapons, though he let them hang by his sides. Mothi and Frikka stood ready, and Veethar's eyes were already yellow—I was glad not to be the focus of his furious glare. Keri and Fretyi stood by my side, stiff-legged and growling deep in their chests. John stood, limbs loose and ready, but glowered at Keirr as if he wanted to take a bite out of the man.

I glanced at the red-clad being in the cell. "Are you a dreamslice reflection or are you all here?"

He cocked his head, eyes boring into mine. After a moment, he shrugged. "Your query lacks cohesion."

That was answer enough, and I shot a curt nod at him. "If it comes down to it, will you fight by our side to earn your freedom?"

"Distasteful," he said and sighed, "but necessary. Yes, this one will comply."

"What's your…" *What did Mirkur call names?* "What's your cognomina?"

The man in red tilted his head to the side. "Address this one as Bikkir."

I tried to keep the shock off my face. "Bikkir?"

"Affirmation."

I glanced at Jane and saw the same shock written on her face. Her gaze darted from mine to Bikkir before snapping to Isi.

"You *know* him," said Isi, and I could tell without glancing at him that he wore a huge smile. "Oh, marvelous! This changes *everything*. Tell me what he is. Tell me!"

With a grim smile, I stripped off my gun belt, flicked the hat off my head and wriggled out of the mail shirt and the cloak that helped to mask my pain. Isi gave me a confused look. "I will understand you, but I won't be able to speak. Jane will speak for me if the need arises." That earned an even stranger look from Isi as I murmured the Kuthbyuhrn *triblinkr* and shuddered a little as the *prayteenk* began.

Isi took two steps away from me as the *prayteenk* twisted my form and the mass settled onto my frame.

When my *prayteenk* wound down to a halt, I cocked my head at Isi and stood on my hind legs, holding my arms out to the sides as though inviting him to inspect me closely. At that moment, Jane activated the ring Althyof had enchanted for her, and her wings blossomed through the slits in her mail like new spring growths. She flapped her wings and ascended to hover in the air. Behind me, I heard Mothi mutter, "*Strikuhr risa*," and knew he would be swelling up like a bodybuilder.

"Impressive, but I don't think you understand our technical superiority." Isi snapped his fingers at Keirr.

Keirr uttered a curse and slapped his hand on what I imagined was a small radio embedded in his sleeve. "Troopers! Send a legion of troopers to my location," he yelled.

I sank back to all fours and took two casual steps toward Isi, who continued to back away, matching me step for step. I threw a glance up at Jane, and she nodded, understanding what I wanted. The pups matched my advance, walking stiff-legged, eyes boring into Isi's, challenge in their every movement.

"Stay away!" commanded Isi, and I chuffed through my nose as bears are wont to do.

"That's bear for laughter," Jane said. "Are you sure you don't want to release my son?"

Isi's gaze twitched from me to Jane to the *varkr* pups and back to me. "These hidden powers are quite interesting." He glanced at the scientists cowering against the wall. "You should be taking measurements! Analyzing these...these..."

"Your pardon, Lord," said one of the scientists. "We can record data, but I fear we don't have enough computational power to analyze what we are seeing."

"Take the data then," Isi snapped, and the scientists leapt to workstations as far from me as they could get. "We will deal with the lack of computational power later. Perhaps at the new base."

Human troops poured into the room from the only entrance—the one behind the robots. They held rifles that ended in the same matte-black tubes that poked from each robot's handless arm.

"Each of these men will die for me," said Isi in a haughty tone. "Can you stand against them all?"

I glanced over my shoulder at Jane and jerked my snout at the warriors pouring into the room. She nodded once and spun in midair. She barged her shield toward the entrance. The air pinged as though a massive windchime had been struck and a jagged black beam ripped the air. The troopers flew back down the hall that led to the room, ass over tea kettle.

Veethar stepped forward and raised his hands. "*Skrithu*!" he commanded, and with a rumble akin to those we'd heard after each death blossom on the surface, the mouth of the hall leading to the room collapsed, sealing us in and crushing the robots still near the entrance.

Isi's eyes stretched wide.

Jane turned back to him and smirked. "Your robots might kill us after a protracted battle, but none of you will survive either. This is what we call a standoff." She leveled her spear at Isi. "You, I will deal with personally. And first, I might add." She cocked her arm and threw the spear, and it crackled into golden lightning and slashed into the machinery at the far end of the room. "Care to wager who fails to understand whose superiority?"

Isi shook his head and turned to run.

I advanced toward him, moving at a walk, but my stride was enormous, and I caught him with the ease of a natural predator. He spun to face me but continued to back away from my relentless advance. He backed into the first row of disused machinery and squeezed his eyes shut.

Behind me, the remaining robots lurched into action, gliding forward on their treads, matte-black tubes coming up and pointing at one of us. I growled softly in my throat and shook my shaggy head.

"*Hooth ow yowrni*!" yelled Mothi. He squatted, preparing to leap into the midst of the silver robots.

"No," said Frikka. "Stand with us, Mothi."

Frikka lifted her arms, hands together, and shouted, "*Skyuldur vekkur*!" She ripped her hands apart, drawing a rough rectangle between us and the robots as several high-pitched whines assaulted my ears and saw-toothed bolts of green-gray energy issued from the matte-black tubes and slashed toward us.

Not precisely the same as Haymtatlr's energy weapons, I thought. *But probably just as deadly.*

The bolts of energy impacted the shield Frikka had thrown up and the air rang with a shriek like a piece of metal squealing against a stone. The shield glowed as more robots fired their shriek-beams.

Veethar whirled to face Isi. "Ancestor, command them to stop."

"Ancestor?" murmured Isi.

I grunted and swung my head to the level of Isi's face and growled, setting the puppies off.

Behind me, the robots continued to pour energy into the shield Frikka had cast, and the air smelled of ozone and hot electronics. Althyof twisted his battle *trowba* into one that would strengthen the shield and dissipate some of the heat.

Jane turned to face the robots, cocked her arm and threw her spear. It crackled and grew as bright as the sun as it morphed into a bolt of golden lightning. It passed through the shield and slammed into the torso of the lead robot. The robot spasmed and threw up its hands, spinning in a counter-clockwise circle, a misshapen hole melted in its casing, golden sparks dancing inside. "*Aftur*!" Jane called, and the spear appeared in her hand with a pop. She threw the spear again and again as fast as she could, but even so, the energy they dumped into Frikka's shield had the air glowing with an orange light, and the heat rapidly approached the unbearable.

I shot a glance at Bikkir, who still stood motionless in his cell, and turned back to Isi and snarled, exposing my fangs. He shrank away from me, abject terror scribbled on his face.

With a snort of disgust, I turned away, scanning the machinery and digital workstations of the scientists, and though I could read the displays easily enough as they used the same runes as everything else in Osgarthr, I couldn't figure out how to open the cells. I scanned the room again, and my gaze came to rest on the knot of scientists in blue.

With a grunt, I ran to them, causing quite a panic. I picked one of scientists and, using my teeth, grabbed him by the front of his blue smock. Picking him up, I trotted to the other side of the room, close to the cells. I set him down and grunted, swinging my head back and forth between the scientist and the cells.

The man's gaze tracked to Isi's, and he swallowed hard. "I…I can't do it," he whispered.

I growled low in my throat and leaned forward to nudge him with my snout.

"Don't you dare!" hissed Isi.

I turned my head toward him and roared, showing my fangs. Keri and Fretyi snarled in accompaniment.

"I'd do as he says, friends," said John. "You haven't seen a tenth of what he can do yet."

"He's a god," said Krowkr. "Their leader. The Allfather."

Inwardly, I cringed, but with Isi's eyes on me, I tossed my head imperiously and glared at the scientist in front of me.

The scientist made a strange sound—half scream, half belch—and lurched toward a workstation. He interacted with it at a frantic pace, darting glances over his shoulder at me. He turned and bowed low. "It's done," he murmured.

I herded him toward the cells with my snout, pushing him past the point where the plastic tool had burst into flames. I nodded my head and jerked my muzzle toward the other scientists. With a sigh of relief, the scientist bolted across the room.

"Dad!" shouted Sig. He came to my side and gave me a hug, shoving his face into the thick fur of my shoulder. Yowtgayrr spared me a quick smile and darted to the shield and drew silvery runes in the air. Skowvithr ruffled Sig's hair and tipped me a wink.

I turned toward the other cell. Bikkir walked toward me as if he hadn't a care in the universe, his gaze resting on me without curiosity, and without much of any expression marring his face.

"Gratitude," he said as he turned toward the robots and gestured in their direction as though by afterthought. Behind the robots, swarthy darkness the size and shape of a *proo* swirled into existence. It appeared more a hole in reality than a physical object. The ambient light of the room seemed to drown in it.

At first, nothing happened, but after a moment, the robots closest to the black oval slid backward, their treads spinning, fighting for purchase on the stone floor. They continued to fire their shriek-beams, but being yanked backward as they were, the ragged energy bolts flew wildly into the ceiling, the floor, the walls, and into other robots. The robots hit by the bolts ceased moving, but where the bolts hit the stone of the walls, floor, or ceiling, a shower of heated stones flew in all directions.

The null spot affected more and more of the robots, and they slid faster and faster toward it. When the first robots struck the inky oval, they disappeared with a flash of light and the sound of a gunshot.

Keirr squealed as the pull of the black spot began to tug on him like an insistent tide. He fastened his grip on the arm of the robot closest to him as he slid toward the dark hole hanging in the air. He screamed as the robot slid across the stone floor in the manner of a palm frond in a hurricane-force wind. As with the robots before him, he disappeared into the hole with a bang.

When the last robot had disappeared, Bikkir raised his hands and clapped them together, and the black hole dispersed in a cloud of dust-like particles. The *Plauinn* turned toward me. "Satisfactory?"

I nodded my head, and even if I had been in my human body, I would not have been able to speak— the shock of what I'd witnessed was too much. The robots, General Keirr, the rubble from the collapsed entrance and the wild shriek-beam shots, even the dust that had gathered in the corners—all of it decohered on the far side of the shield in a fraction of a second. I shook my head and triggered the *prayteenk* back into human form.

When I had finished dressing, I approached Isi and pulled him back to the center of the room. He came willingly enough, though his eyes were large and glassy with shock.

"I meant what I said. Had you returned my people, none of this would have happened."

He turned a blank stare my way and nodded without seeming to know he did so. "Who…"

I glanced at Bikkir. "Can you get home?"

"Negative. The local timeflows ensnare me. Navigation is…formidable from this timeslice."

"I might aid you if you'll permit it."

Again, the *Plauinn* cocked his head at me, but this time he added a few blinks. "You? You are not of the underverse."

I nodded. "Give me a moment, and I'll see what I can do."

He nodded and shrugged.

I bent my attention to his *slowth*, marveling at its mother-of-pearl hue and the sheer size of the thing. Wrapping my imaginary arms around it, I grunted at the shocking rapidity of the information pulsing through it. I followed it back, past the point when he appeared in the room, and tried to dip into it but couldn't get past the iridescent covering. "Let me in, Bikkir," I said.

His black eyes closed, and without preamble, I was in the stream of his mind.

Information threatened to overwhelm me, to bury me in an avalanche of memories and thoughts and ideas and musings and dreams. I struggled against it, floundered against it, trying to make sense of the deluge, but it was too much, too fast, and it threatened to sweep me away—to sweep my personality into the rapid stream. "Help me, Bikkir! Think of home!"

A thought came from the stream like a lifeline thrown to a drowning man, and I grabbed it with all my strength. I couldn't make much sense of it—there seemed to be opposing directions of time, multiple instances of beings, some moving forward, some back, some stationary, and reality seemed transitory at best—but I got a sense of where and when to send a *proo*.

"Got it, I think." I withdrew from the giant *slowth* and created my particles, linked with a *strenkir af krafti*, and with a *proo* strand and spun the terminal particle to the place I thought Bikkir needed.

He approached the silver beginning of the *proo* and stared at it. "Where did you learn this?" he murmured.

"Bikkir, do you agree that I saved you significant headaches here today?"

"Affirmation."

"Do you feel as if you owe me a little gratitude?"

His slack face twitched with a momentary emotion, and given the speed of his thoughts, I guessed that was all I'd ever see. But he nodded, though with a note of caution in his eye.

"You must keep this ability a secret. At a future time, you will know why, but for now, do it because you owe me one. There are…" I glanced at Isi and stepped closer to Bikkir. "There are those in your realm with whom you may disagree. If they were to learn of this ability…"

He stared at me for the longest time, frozen, as if a mannequin that matched him in precise detail had replaced him. Finally, he tipped his head toward me once. "This one will enlist in your machinations until such a time as either you prove yourself contemptible or this one's cognition alters. How is it you can direct an *ormur gat*?"

"Funny thing. *You* taught me."

Bikkir turned and cocked his head at me. "Incongruence."

"Yes, it was. Is it in the right place?"

Again, Bikkir looked at the *proo*, then he shook his head. The end of the *proo* moved a little, and I saw where he shifted it. "Gratitude," he said and touched the *proo's* face.

Isi gasped as the *Plauinn* disappeared. "How was that done? What is this thing? A conveyance? How marvelous! What was the black version of it? The weaponized version? How does one control it? Where does this lead?" He reached toward the *proo*.

"*Lokathu proonum*!" I snapped.

Isi jerked back and turned to me with a pouting expression. "You must explain this!"

"No, I don't think so."

"You *must*!"

"Go stand with your scientists, Isi," I said with a sigh. When he refused, Mothi picked him up and carried him across the room, depositing him none-too-gently amid the scientists.

"Act as if you are worthy of your descendants!" Mothi snapped.

Isi looked at him with open wonder, then shook his head and turned to me. "I would come with you, Hank Jensen."

I created another *proo* and spun it to the *Herperty af Roostum*. "Everyone through," I said. I watched the others jump back to Osgarthr. I glanced at Isi and shook my head. "I don't think so, Lord Isi." He opened his mouth to argue, but I slapped my hand on the *proo* and slid through time and space.

FORTY-FIVE

S if shouted with happiness. "You found him!" She rushed forward and smothered my son with wet kisses.

I nodded and closed the *proo*. "Yowtgayrr, Skowvithr," I said, holding out my hands. "I already owe you more than I can ever repay, but consider my debt increased."

"Our oaths—"

"Shut up and say you're welcome," I said with a smile.

Jane left Sig's side long enough to hug both Alfar tight, and to be honest, they seemed a little taken aback by the gesture.

"That goes for the rest of you, too. I can't tell you what it means to me that you'd risk life and limb for us, but I can say thank you and mean it with every atom in my body."

Althyof blew a raspberry and waved it all away, but I knew our gratitude pleased him. Mothi only shrugged and grinned.

John Calvin Black stood looking at me with an unreadable expression. Finally, he stepped toward me and said, "I told you of my nephew and the dark promise I made to secure his freedom. I'd never leave a child imprisoned."

I nodded and clapped him on the shoulder. "And I thank you for that."

He nodded, but something lurked in his gaze.

"What?" I asked.

"It's…" He waved his hand. "Nothing. Never mind."

"No, if something is on your mind, say it." I could feel Krowkr's eyes crawling over the side of my face visible to him.

"It seems as though you take great risks with your son's life."

The room fell silent, and Krowkr took a step forward, looking as if he didn't even know he was doing it.

I pursed my lips and glanced at Sig, whose gaze was on the pair of us. "It may seem that way," I said, "but appearances can be deceiving."

John nodded and turned away. "I accept that you mean that. The last I will say about it is this: Battle is no place for such a cherished gift."

"He's our son," said Jane in a quiet voice. "We'd never risk him."

John nodded again but didn't meet either of our gazes.

"You *dare* to...to..." said Krowkr, his voice laced with venom.

"It's all right, Krowkr. Everyone here is free to think and say as they please."

His hands were on his weapons, and his face burned with rage. "Do you insult Lord Hanki? You were here! Luka used trickery and deceit! You witnessed his deeds!"

John glanced at me, one eyebrow raised. "No, lad. I'm the last in a position to insult anyone. You misconstrue my motives."

"Krowkr," I said. "Look at me." His blazing gaze remained locked on John's—he didn't so much as twitch in my direction. "Krowkr," I said again, keeping my tone even, my voice low.

He lowered his head, and after a few breaths, turned his gaze to me.

"I appreciate you defending my honor, but it isn't necessary. I can fight my own battles. Okay?"

His gaze darted back to John's, then to Jane. "But he—"

"I can fight my own battles," I repeated.

"*We* can," said Jane.

He nodded slowly and released his weapons.

"John, if I could have a moment?" He turned back to me and shrugged. "You've been here—on Osgarthr, I mean—for a long time. Centuries, right?"

He nodded.

"Have you ever seen someone who could be my twin?" I asked, thinking of Henry Vasvik's father. "Either in the dungeons of Helhaym or…" I shrugged. "Or in the queen's service?"

He regarded me without emotion and slowly shook his head. "Should I have? What's this about?"

I shook my head. "It's nothing. A promise I made on another Mithgarthr." I glanced at Jane and shook my head.

"Well, I'd never seen anyone who looked like you before we met," said John.

"Okay, thank you. Haymtatlr, a question."

"Yes, Hank."

"Before we left, you said it was possible to cut Luka off from the *preer* and leave them functional for the rest of us."

"Yes, I did, but that is not a question, Hank."

"I guess it isn't. Here's one: If you can deny a single person the use of the *preer* does it follow that you can track a single person's use of the *preer*?"

"Without question."

I shook my head. All we had to do was ask him. Figures. "Good enough."

"You'll never guess where we've been," said Sig, his gaze darting between my face and John's.

"Where, Piglet?" asked Sif.

"We went into the past. Waaay back, and we met Isi!"

"Is it so?" asked Sif, her gaze traveling around the room.

"Yes," I said.

"What was all that about 'dream reflections?'" asked Frikka. "About this 'underverse' place?

"Dreamslice reflections," I said. "I'll explain all that later." I glanced up, unable to help thinking I needed to look at Haymtatlr when I spoke to him, and that he lived in the ceiling. "Where is Luka now, Haymtatlr?"

"Luka is no longer here."

"What? Did he go out onto the plain of Pilrust?"

"No. He disappeared."

"What do you mean?" asked Jane, waving her hand at me to shush me. "Did he go out into the lava tubes?"

"He was headed in that direction, and that seemed his destination, but he stopped and disappeared in the same place that Hank appeared last time. I've dispatched—"

"What do you mean where I 'appeared?'"

"You appeared out of thin air."

"Out of a *proo,* you mean."

"No. You did not travel here by *proo.*"

I looked at Jane and shook my head.

"Haymtatlr, we emerged from a *proo* a few moments ago, or did we appear out of thin air?"

"You appeared out of thin air. I've dispatched robotic crews to the first site and to the room where you stand. I've also dispatched repair crews to my perception processing units to determine if there has been a hardware failure."

"Make another one," Jane said.

With a shrug, I opened another new *proo* and moved the other end across the room.

"Haymtatlr, can you detect this *proo* that Hank just made?"

"Is this another interesting question game?"

"No. Serious question."

"Then, as you well know, Hank can't make *preer*. No one can, not even me. I find and harness a miniscule set of the existing *preer* that occur in the universe. I direct those *preer* to the places I am asked to connect. The process requires a great deal of energy and the *Kyatlarhodn*, and he possesses neither. The computational power required to target a *proo* is astounding. One must account for cosmological—"

"So, you can only sense the *preer* you create?" I asked. "You can only track people in those *preer*?"

"Is this a trick question? I cannot create a *proo*. No one can."

"I can," I said. "There is an active *proo* right here in this room."

"One moment," said Haymtatlr in a toneless voice.

"Hank, you don't think Luka escaped using one of your *preer*, do you?"

A grim smile stretched my lips while I nodded. "I didn't consider that I needed to close them. Not until I saw Isi reaching for the *proo* to Bikkir's realm. Thick-headed me, I've been leaving them open."

"My self-diagnostic of my primary perceptual recurrent neural network has finished, and I have found no errors," said Haymtatlr. "I can only assume that the error lies in your perceptions, and as evidenced by the studies of the Isir mind found within my data stores, I—"

"No," said Althyof. "He can do it. *You* can't perceive it, but everyone else can."

"Haymtatlr, can you run an active scan of this room?"

"Of course," he said. The air felt charged for a moment, and a rapid clicking sounded from the walls. "No anomalies found."

"Can you take my word for it?" asked Jane.

"I... Yes. Of course, Jane."

"Will you lead us to where Luka disappeared? I'm not sure I could find my way back there."

"No need," I said. I spun the end of my demonstration *proo* to that common room where we'd stayed that first night we'd spent in the *Herperty af Roostum*. "Everyone through." My eye turned toward Meuhlnir, and I arched one eyebrow. His color was better, and he was on his feet and dressed in his mail.

"Yes," breathed Meuhlnir. "I'll not stay behind again." He nodded toward Sif. "She's worked wonders while you were off visiting Isi."

Sif tsked, but that was the extent of her argument. Mothi helped his father gather his weapons and pack and walked arm-in-arm with Meuhlnir to my *proo*. With a slight pop, they traversed the *proo* as soon as Meuhlnir touched its mercury surface.

"Everyone through," I said. "Haymtatlr, watch what happens to us. Explain how we can move through normal space at such a pace." I touched the *proo*.

A group of robots stood motionless at the edges of the room. They appeared to have been powered down. Another *proo*—the one I'd used to travel back to the *Herperty af Roostum* from Iktrasitl—danced on the other side of the room.

"Yes, I understand," said Haymtatlr. The robots powered up and left the room. "I had thought those robots defective when they reported the visual perception of a *proo* I couldn't detect. It is clear *something* is happening, but it seems far more likely that I've suffered a false negative in my classification system than my previous estimates indicated. I've dispatched another team of robots to assess potential damage to my classification system."

"Isn't it possible, Haymtatlr, that you've designed your sensor system to detect the *preer* that occur in nature, and *only* those *preer*?" asked Jane. "That since what Hank is doing is outside your experience, and is outside the knowledge imparted to you by your programmers, you haven't developed the technology to detect those kinds of *preer*?"

"It is…possible," he said. "A self-serving bias…I understand your implication."

"Is this where Luka disappeared?" I asked.

"Four meters to the south, give or take."

In other words, he'd taken my *proo*. "Veethar, how do you and Meuhlnir manipulate the *preer*? Can you manipulate mine?"

Veethar stared at the end of the *proo* we'd taken from the other room. He stretched out his arm as though he wanted to touch the *proo* and chanted under his breath in the *Gamla Toonkumowl*. When nothing happened, he tried again, saying, "*Proo, hayrthu mik! Ferthast meth timanum ok roomi, tenktu thednan stath vith thadn stath sem yek hef ee huka! Kera ayns ok yek byeth thyer!*"

Simple, I thought. 'Bridge, hear me! Travel over time and space, associate this place with the place I have in mind! Do as I bid you!' I'd thought it would be more complicated than that.

Veethar's arm shook with his effort, his face knotted with it. Finally, he dropped his hand and sighed. "It will not move. I don't understand it, but it will not respond to me."

Haymtatlr made a noise strangely akin to clearing his throat. "I'd be happy to do as you ask, Veethar, but I detect no *preer* in your vicinity."

Veethar cocked his head to the side. "You hear our *kaltrar*? You hear it when we control the *preer*?"

"*I* control the *preer*. You tell me what you want, and I make the changes your requests require."

"Interesting," I breathed. "How can you hear the incantation when someone tries to change a *proo*?"

"In part, Isi's scientists created my systems to monitor the *strenkir af krafti* for deviances in the expected behavior of the strings. Another part of me, they constructed later to encompass the *preer* in a similar manner. Once I detect a manipulation of a *proo*, I listen in through the *proo* itself."

"And you can't do that with the *preer* I create?"

"*If* they exist, I cannot."

"That's good," I said. "That means Luka can't muck around with them either. And since I didn't take a *proo* to where this one ends, he's trapped in that realm."

"Good," said Mothi. "Close this *proo* and let him rot there."

I shook my head. "No. Luka is our problem to deal with." I looked Meuhlnir in the eye. "And I think we have to help him before we decide what to do with him."

"Help him? Have you lost your mind?" demanded Jane.

I shook my head. "And we have to help Hel escape from her torment."

"Now, I know you've gone cuckoo! If you think—"

"Hel is being tortured by Owraythu—one of the *Plauinn*, one of the *darkest* ones, too. If Owraythu succeeds in brainwashing Hel, we will face an enemy united with these *Plauinn*—a slave bent into their service—rather than someone who has let bitterness drive her to evil."

"What have you seen?" asked Sif, a tinge of wonder in her voice. "What have you learned that makes you consider them in this different light?"

"I've been in Luka's memories—I've seen what he experienced first-hand. No, we won't pat him on the back and set him loose on New York when this is all over. He's got crimes to pay for, there's no doubt of that, but if we abandon Hel and Luka to the *Plauinn*, they will become much, much worse than we can imagine right now. *And* they will have the backing of mighty beings who consider us warts on the ass of the universe. Anything we can do to fight the *Plauinn* is better than nothing."

Jane shook her head, sadness shining in her expression, her eyes. "This sounds an awful lot as though the ends might justify the means."

"You know me better than that, Jane," I said. "Before they can pay for their crimes, we must set them free of the dark path they've chosen, or Hel and Luka will never change, never see the errors—the *evil*—in what they've done. And if that's the case, we might as well kill them and be done with it. Is that what you want?"

Jane shook her head and blew a breath hard enough to disrupt her bangs. "You know it isn't."

There was an uncomfortable silence hanging in the room. "Look, I know this isn't the most popular idea, but these two people were your friends, your family—"

"Not mine," grumbled Althyof.

"—and despite what they've done, I know each of you has a soft spot for them. Meuhlnir, how many times have you argued for your brother's life? Sif, how many times have you rebuked one of us for calling Hel the Black Bitch? Yowrnsaxa, how many tears have you shed during the stories you've told?" I sighed and shook my head. "There's only one way I can conceive of that you will get your friends back— the real Luka, the real Suel. Ever. We have to help them through this, and *then* deal with rehabilitating them—*if* we can earn their trust, first."

If eyeballs turning from one face to another made a sound, the sound would have deafened me. As it was, the silence fell on the room like thick, heavy snow.

"The first step is going through this *proo* and finding Luka. I'm going, and if you don't want to come with me, I won't hold it against you. There is no decision for the group in this, each one of us has to decide."

Meuhlnir came to stand by me. "Count me on your side, Hank," he said.

Sif shook her head but moved to his side, carrying her healing bag and muttering under her breath.

"Would it be better if fewer of us went?" I asked Meuhlnir, but with my gaze resting on Sif's face.

He glanced at his wives, his jaw set when he did so. "I'm going."

"We all are," said John.

"Let's go," said Althyof with a sigh. "I'm in it for the silver, anyway."

"Yeah, you sure are," I said with a grin.

After a moment, his grin answered mine, and I nodded, reaching for the *proo*.

FORTY-SIX

Emerging from the *proo* first, I nodded to myself when I found it was where I'd left it. I could get to like having a *proo* that no one could mess with. I wondered if my *preer* would be invisible to the *Plauinn* as they were to Haymtatlr.

Stepping away from the *proo*, I scanned the foliage nearby, but there was nothing but trees in my visual field. Behind me, I heard the soft pops of the *proo* disgorging my family and friends. There were a lot of popping noises, and I suppressed a sigh of relief. I'd have gone on with a few or even none of them, but I felt better about my plan with my party at my back.

"Well? Where is the dog-faced boy?" asked Jane. She bent and deposited the pups on the forest floor. I expected them to romp and roll around like the puppies they were, but they seemed cowed by the forest, and they stuck close to Jane and me.

"I haven't looked yet. I wanted to make sure this wasn't an ambush." She slipped her hand into mine, and I glanced down at her. "Thanks for coming."

"Shut up, idiot." She smiled and leaned in, so I did what every red-blooded man would do: I licked her cheek. "Eww! Yuck!"

"That's for calling me insane."

"Why don't you go sleep," she said with a broad, mischievous smile.

"Nah. Not tired right now. Besides, I don't want to wake up with a mouthful of your little shield."

"*Little* shield?" She thumped her thumb on the edge of the round shield. "It's hardly little." She looked around at the massive forest surrounding us. "Is this Alfhaym?"

"No," I said, shaking my head, "but it reminds me of it."

"No," said Yowtgayrr from behind us. "Alfhaym has more species of trees. This place is...*unnatural*. Who ever heard of a forest with only ash trees?"

"That you know these trees belong to one species is bad enough, but knowing the *species* makes you sound like a tree-stalker," said Jane.

"Why would anyone stalk trees? They don't move." The confusion in the Alf's voice made both my wife and me chuckle.

"It's an expression from Mithgarthr. It's used to describe people obsessed with someone else."

"That usage, at least, makes sense," said Yowtgayrr. "But look, there's no underbrush, no vines, no other plant life at all. This forest is most unusual."

"Just wait," I said. "Wait until you catch a glimpse of Iktrasitl."

"More trees!" bellowed Althyof. "Just once, I'd like our journey to take us to a nice underground cavern!"

"You'd complain about that, too," said Yowtgayrr with half a grin hidden behind his hand.

"Trees!" The way Althyof said it made it clear he considered the word an expletive. "So?" he said, turning to me and stepping in front of Yowtgayrr. "Where is our puppy-dog friend?"

I looked down, intending to scan the area for Luka's *slowthar*, and was astonished to find *slowthar* everywhere. They obscured the ground, there were so many. I had never expected there to be many *slowthar* here, it was too unbelievable a place to begin with for people to seek it out—let alone find it. "Hmmm."

"Tougher than you expected?"

"No, but *slowthar* cover the place," I said. "How could so many people even find this place?"

"Doesn't make sense, does it?" said Kuhntul from somewhere off in the trees.

"Oh, great," murmured Jane.

"Why are there so many, Kuhntul?" I asked, giving Jane's hand a squeeze.

"Think about what this place is, even if only from the mythology you know."

I shook my head. "It was a holy place at the center of the universe."

"And so it is," she said, still hiding in the shadows of the trees, but I thought I detected a glimmer of white amongst all the shadows. "Many cultures believe in such a tree, or trees. In many places, these trees serve a religious purpose."

"Like the tree of knowledge of good and evil," said Jane. "Or the tree of life."

Kuhntul walked from the trees, smiling at Jane. "Yes. Hello, Jane." Swathed in white, her pale skin almost seemed to be a garment she pulled on and off at will. Her long white hair shimmered in what sunlight made it through the roof of branches above us.

"Hello, Kuhntul," Jane said.

"So why so many *slowthar*?" I asked. "Yeah, many cultures have trees in their mythologies. So what?"

Kuhntul shrugged. "Many come here in a state of dreamslice reflection—holy men, seekers of knowledge, seekers of wisdom…" She turned and winked at me. "You came here once for that purpose."

I shook my head. "As I recall, I've never come here by choice before today."

She smiled her smile and tilted her head to the side. "Is it so? And what is a choice when it comes down to it?"

"Ach!" growled Althyof. "Have you seen Luka or not?"

Her face grew cold with glacial slowness, and she spun on her heel to face Althyof. "How I wish you didn't enjoy this one's company, Tyeldnir," she sighed.

Althyof made a derisive noise and swatted the air between them.

"But I do," I said quietly.

"More's the pity," Kuhntul said. "Yes, I can find Luka, Tverkr, and with ease, but Hank needs to understand this place."

"Hank, this one is a waste of time."

"No, Althyof. She, too, is my friend."

Kuhntul smiled. "Why, Tyeldnir! I wasn't aware you thought so highly of me." She took a step closer, and Jane's nails bit into the back of my hand. Kuhntul's gaze flickered to Jane and back to mine. "Not to worry, Jane. Tyeldnir has made his preference clear."

"So...finding Luka myself will somehow give me a better understanding of the Conflux?"

Kuhntul shrugged with her eyebrows. "It may, but the point I wanted to make is that this place differs from what you believe is 'normal.'"

I waved my hands at the millions of ash trees that surrounded us. "Noted."

"Your assumptions may be dangerous here." A grim smile played on her lips. "Tell me what you see."

I suppressed a sigh of exasperation. "Trees."

"Not there, Tyeldnir." She pointed at the ground. "Here."

"Oh. A gerbillion *slowthar*, all intertwined, almost knotted together."

"A gerbillion?" she asked, one eyebrow arched.

"He means 'a lot,'" said Jane. "He likes to make up words."

"Ah, yes. And can you not pick out the *slowth* of our dear Luka?"

I glanced back down at the knot at my feet. "Yes, it's here."

"And do all these *slowthar* look the same?"

I already knew the answer to that. "No, the Three Maids' *slowthar* diverge from the rest of ours."

"Is that all?"

"No," I said, glancing at Althyof. "Yours is different, too."

"Mine?" Kuhntul's face wriggled with an amused surprise.

I nodded. "There are minor differences according to race—for instance, I can tell an Isir from a Tverkar with a mere glance."

Kuhntul nodded. "But the Nornir?"

"Yes, there is the racial difference, but the differences don't end there." I paused, thinking about Bikkir's *slowth*. "They are thicker, more…more…"

"More robust?" asked Kuhntul.

I shrugged. "Maybe."

"Mine, as well?"

"Well, yours contrasts with theirs, as well. Not as thick. Also, I couldn't dip into Bikkir's *slowth* without his assistance."

"And mine?" she asked, a strange emotion flickering in her eyes and her voice hoarse with it.

"I've never tried." I glanced down at the *slowth* at her feet. "If you'd prefer me to—"

"No!" she said, taking a few steps back. "I…" She glanced around at our faces, as though taken aback by her own excessive reaction. "Tyeldnir, promise me you will not dip into my past. Not without my permission."

I glanced at Jane, who gazed at Kuhntul through narrowed eyes. "Who do you remind me of, Kuhntul?" she mused.

Kuhntul glanced at her—a quick touch of her gaze on Jane's eyes—then returned her gaze to mine. "Promise me, Tyeldnir!" she rasped.

"Okay," I said with a shrug. "I'll leave you your privacy."

She sighed and closed her eyes.

"My promise is binding as long as I believe you are our friend, acting in our best interests."

Kuhntul nodded once and seemed much relieved. "Fine. I've been your friend since long before we met."

Althyof scoffed.

"I have!" she insisted. "I worked long and hard to Tyeldnir's benefit. There was so much to arrange…not that a mercenary such as you would understand!"

I cleared my throat. "Would you two just get over whatever it is that makes you act like children?"

Althyof grunted. "Children? *Children*?"

A small smile flickered on Kuhntul's lips.

"I have told you the story!" Althyof snapped. "The insult of it… You know I'm not one to hold a grudge—"

"Ha!" said Mothi.

"—nor one to seek vengeance for slights—"

"Ha!" said Veethar.

"—but this…this woman, this *Tisir*, has more than earned my disaffection centuries ago!"

"And you can't get over it?" asked Jane in a mild tone. "You can't let it go?"

"That is not my nature," Althyof said in a calmer tone.

"So, you *do* hold grudges?" asked Mothi with a mischievous glint in his eye.

Althyof turned away, but not before I caught a touch of amusement in his eye. "Where is he? Let's find Luka and get this thing done."

Kuhntul smiled at his back. "Shall I lead, Tyeldnir, or would you rather follow his *slowth*?"

"Lead on. As we walk, tell me how we can rescue Hel from Owraythu's realm. I have a feeling that is the coin we will need to buy Luka's cooperation."

"A hammer to the temple always worked in the past," said Meuhlnir.

Kuhntul grinned and started walking. "We should consider not beating his brains out yet. He may be useful in the near future."

"Why is that?" asked Jane. "What in the world could he do that we couldn't?"

"He's got a mischievous twist of mind," said Kuhntul in a tone of voice that almost sounded wistful.

"That's saying a lot coming from you," murmured Althyof.

"When he desires it, that twist can be bent to a particularly gifted form of military strategy."

Althyof opened his mouth to reply, but I sighed and shook my head. "The rescue?"

Kuhntul let her gaze slide lazily from Althyof's face to my own. "Yes. You've told me the *slowth* of the Three Maids differs from your own. Do they also differ from the *slowth* of the matterstream manifestations of the *Plauinn*?"

"That I don't know. We met Bikkir when we traveled back to Isi's time, but he appeared as a human."

"Ah. His dreamslice reflection."

"I'm not sure...I asked him, but he wouldn't answer—said the question lacked cohesion. I don't have a firm grasp on how Isi trapped him in the first place. Isi said it resulted from a failed experiment. Maybe they pulled him forward in time...maybe that was his matterstream manifestation from a time before the First War."

"What's the difference between a dreamslice refraction and a matterstream whatsit?" asked Sig.

"The matterstream manifestation is the universe in which you live, young Sig," said Kuhntul. "In it, the normal rules apply—physical properties are as you expect them to be. The dreamslice reflection is harder to explain, but think of it this way: suppose everything in the physical universe has a mirror somewhere else—"

"This underverse that the *Plauinn* inhabit."

"From your point of view, yes."

"From *our* point of view?" I asked.

Kuhntul nodded. "Yes. To the *Plauinn*, the underverse is the matterstream manifestation, and your reality is the dreamslice reflection."

"And you? Which is your matterstream manifestation?"

She looked at me for a moment. "I'm not sure how to answer that question."

"Try," said Jane.

Kuhntul slowed to a stop. She put her hand to her chin and stared off into the distance. "I… It is a difficult…" She shook her head. "I don't know the answer, but my matterstream manifestation is close to your own, if it is different at all."

"You don't come from the underverse?"

She shook her head. "No, I…" She glanced away. "I came to this matterstream through the underverse, but—"

"By traveling through a *proo*?" I asked, thinking of the technique she'd taught me of opening my own *preer* and how Haymtatlr couldn't detect them.

She nodded slowly. "But this won't help us, and we should table my origin until a later time."

I shrugged.

"Which brings us to timeslices," she said to Sig. "Think of timeslices as 'orientations' of the matterstream manifestations. Or, to put it another way, each of us has a timeslice unique to ourselves, each *stathur* also has its own timeslice, as does the universe as a whole."

"And this underverse?"

Kuhntul nodded.

Frikka's eyes lit up. "So that is why *uhrluhk* may change!"

Kuhntul smiled. "Yes, my old friend."

"I don't get it at all," said Jane.

"Each person has their own timeslice! When his *uhrluhk* changes, only those timeslices that interact with his own are affected. That's why Hank could change what happened to Kuthbyuhrn and Kyellroona without destroying everything." Frikka smiled and nearly danced with excitement.

"Yes," said Kuhntul. "And his manipulation of their timeslices changed what happened to your own timeslices—but only enough so that what happened would make sense to you."

"But I don't remember it any other way!"

"No. Because timeslices follow a curious path when changed. They loopback to the place of divergence. Hank remembers the previous timeslice because he is the one who enacted the change—he holds *both* sets of memories, because he experienced the first, then changed it and experienced the second. Since you were part of the matterstream manifestation which he changed, you have no memory of the first set of events."

"Thanks for clearing that up for me," muttered Jane. "If it makes sense to Hank and Frikka they can try to explain it another time."

"Fair enough," said Kuhntul.

"So…"

"Yes, Hank?"

"Before, you told me you have multiple sets of memories. Did you—"

"We should get moving," said Kuhntul briskly. "Luka is growing restless."

"Okay," I said, my gaze flicking from the sudden tenseness of her shoulders, to the set of her jaw, to her eyes, which she quickly averted.

"You never told me if the Maids' *slowthar* differ from those of the *Plauinn's* matterstream manifestations," she said without looking up.

"I don't know. The few times I visited the *Plauinn* in the underverse, I didn't notice any *slowthar* at all."

"Interesting," said Kuhntul.

"When you or Bikkir gave me the ability to perceive these *slowthar*, at first, it was like sensory overload, but I got acclimated. I have to focus on them to even see them now, and with all the new things flying at me in my interactions with the *Plauinn* in the underverse, I didn't pay attention to their *slowthar*, but it doesn't mean they don't exist."

"Ah. It would be better if we knew for certain."

"Wait a minute…when I experience someone else's memories…"

"Yes, Tyeldnir?" Kuhntul asked.

Something turned over in my mind. "That's dreamslice, right?"

"Yes, as with any other experience in the realm of the psychic."

"Then when I took Luka to visit Owraythu's realm…when she noticed us, we were—"

"*When she what*?" screeched Kuhntul. "Tyeldnir, what have you done?" Her face jumped and twitched with agitation.

"I took Luka into my memories, so he could see that I wasn't responsible for Hel's captivity. Inside memories, I can…I don't know what to call it…I can stop the flow of the memory, freeze everything in place. I did that, or tried to, in Owraythu's realm, and she sensed the manipulation somehow."

"Of *course* she did! Remember that what is dreamslice to us is matterstream to them. From her perspective, you intruded on her reality and stopped the flow of time!"

"I… I didn't understand—"

Kuhntul sighed. "How could you?" She shook her head. "I wish I'd known of this memory traveling trick, but what's done is done." She forced a smile to her lips. "It's no matter. We will adapt." She turned and began walking.

"Wait a minute," I said pulling Kuhntul to a stop. "I think I know a way to rescue Hel."

"Tell us."

FORTY-
SEVEN

My bones ached as the abstract, random turmoil of Owraythu's realm twisted and tangled in front of me. I glanced to my right and smiled at the sleek, pitch black fishy form Kuhntul had adopted.

Remember to observe her slowth this time, Kuhntul said in my head.

I nodded and forced my dreamslice reflection to adopt the same form as the Tisir. It was a risky plan, but without more time to acclimate the others to their dreamslice reflections, only Kuhntul and I had a chance in this chaotic realm.

In the distance, Hel screamed and screamed, sounding on the brink of the abyss, at the limit of her sanity. The screams faded into the most horrible grunting sobs I'd ever heard in my life, and it wrenched at my heart.

Be ready, she said. With a fish-like nod, she shot off into the eddies and swirls of fractalized color.

I turned and crept away in the other direction. My job was a simple one: distract Owraythu and draw her away from where she held Hel prisoner, then hide as best I could, repeating the process as necessary.

Ready, Hank! said Kuhntul in my mind.

I shuddered and brought the realm to what should have been a screeching halt. As with the first time I'd tried to stop this realm, it wound down in a stop-start-stop-start manner, each change accompanied by a fluidic jerk that rattled my bones. Hel's moaning stuttered as a malfunctioning audio track would.

With a wrenching crunch, Owraythu brushed away my efforts to stop the realm's timeslice as if I were no more than an annoying gnat. A scream of pure rage from somewhere in the distance sent shivers racing down my spine. By the sound of her cries, Hel's torment began anew and with renewed vigor.

I swam away as fast as I was able, propelling myself with a frenetic snap of my tail fin. More distant screams of rage sounded. I twisted the timeslice of Owraythu's realm, no longer trying to stop it, just trying to muck things up, to irritate Owraythu, to drive her mad with rage.

The swirling, abstract shapes and colors stopped, and I plunged headlong into a grim darkness—like a dream in which I could not see. My senses began to report randomly—as if by an abstract fallacy—rain falling on my brow, a cold wind blowing through my hair. I twitched the timeslice, and my head spun.

No more shrieks of fury reached me, but I had the sense of something coming, a dark, immense thing steamrolling right at me, intent only on crushing me like a bug beneath a tank's caterpillar treads. I flung myself to the side, shooting off into the darkness as fast as I could go, twitching the realm, creating huge fluidic waves of force and sending them behind me.

YOU ARE WEAK, SMALL ONE, BUT THIS ONE CONTAINS MUCH STRENGTH, AS YOU WILL SOON UNDERSTAND.

Panic sank its teeth into my throat. *Where is Kuhntul? What's taking her so long?* With sheer desperation, I ground the timeslice to a halt, enduring the bucking hitch with gritted teeth. I glanced behind me, remembering the *slowth*, and my guts turned cold as my gaze fell upon it, far closer than I'd imagined possible. I flung myself away, shooting into the blackness on a stream of fluid.

My surroundings jerked and thrashed as if I was inside an immense chew toy being flung about by an overexcited Rottweiler creating his own fun. I had the distinct impression that a vast, dark wave—a tsunami of anger and hate—loomed over me, waiting for the proper moment to crash on my head, driving me into the coral, into the sea bed and rocks, shredding my flesh from my bones.

Has Kuhntul turned on me? Is this it? Is this my final stand? I lashed out behind me, tearing at the fabric of the realm, trying to create the blackhole-like *proo* I'd seen Bikkir create.

UNDERSTANDING. THE POMPOUS ONE IS YOUR MASTER. ACQUIESCENCE, WHEN THIS ONE HAS RENT YOUR EXISTENCE, CONSIGNED YOU TO THE OUTER DARKNESS, THIS ONE WILL PAY CALL TO THE POMPOUS ONE AND HE SHALL CATERWAUL AND VOCIFERATE LIKE THE SMALL ONE THIS ONE TORMENTS.

I squeezed my eye shut, preferring not to see Owraythu's face. If I couldn't see her, maybe this would turn into a dream. I slipped and slid from side to side, pretending at eel-like agility while the massive thing bore down on me. My heart was black with sadness, bloody-red with anger.

With a burst of inspiration, I chanted the *triblinkr* I'd learned back at Luka's cabin. The one that allowed me to slow or excite all the molecules within a specific area. I laid a suppression field behind me, taking the field as close to absolute zero as I could get it. I kept swimming, putting distance between Owraythu and myself, and as I went, I dropped another field in my wake, this time cranking it up as hot as I could get it.

A loud crunch that seemed to cause the underlayment of the realm to shudder issued behind me, followed by the sound of a bell so large that its ringing threatened to drive me insane. *The first field*, I thought. I threw my psychic weight at the timeslice and knocked it to a stuttering stop again.

Owraythu screeched and hissed like two tomcats fighting over a scrap of fish. THIS ONE WILL RENDER YOUR MOLECULES AND FLING THEIR BITS INTO THE ABYSS! THIS ONE WILL CONSUME THE DELECTABLE PARTS OF YOU AND DISPERSE THE REST THROUGHOUT THE UNDERVERSE! THIS ONE WILL—

Again, the realm shuddered, and Owraythu screamed her wrath at me. She recovered from the second field in a much shorter span of time and dispelled it.

YOUR PALTRY TRICKS CANNOT SAVE YOU, SMALL ONE.

Her mental voice rang with the sound of victory, and I got the distinct impression she was close—too close—behind me. There was no way to escape the monster at my heels. I had no more tricks. No more secret *kaltrar* from my grimoire, no enchanted do-dads to pull my ass out of the fire this time. There was nowhere to hide, and all I was doing was adding seconds to the last moments of my life.

Then, it dawned on me. I could hear no more cries of anguish.

Hel had fallen silent, and I hoped she and Kuhntul were out. I had no choice but to fling myself out—back to the Conflux, back to Iktrasitl. It was that or become Owraythu's plaything.

FORTY-
EIGHT

I jerked forward, flopping onto my stomach as though I was trying to do the breaststroke on dry land. My breath came in ragged gasps, and the chemicals of terror still thrummed in my veins. "Is she back? Is she back?" I yelled.

"Do not fear, Tyeldnir," said Kuhntul in a hoarse, exhausted voice. "It was difficult, but here we are."

"That's it?" asked Jane.

I turned over and levered myself up to my elbows. Jane stood above me, an expression of disbelief on her face. "These *Plauinn* are so powerful, and all we have to do to beat them is…is to *distract* them for a moment?"

Kuhntul came out of the trees, her immaculate white cloak torn, and her long white hair disheveled for the first time in my memory. She pushed at it with her free hand, her gaze shifting between the males of the party. She held another woman under the arms, a thin, exhausted woman who could never have stood on her own.

"Suel!" cried Sif. She darted forward and slid her arm around her childhood friend—the hatred and bitterness of their adulthood forgotten. "Help me!"

Yowrnsaxa and Frikka went to her side, taking Hel from Kuhntul and laying her down on the soft loam of Iktrasitl's forest.

"To answer your question, Jane, no, that isn't it. We are in grave danger, should Owraythu discover our whereabouts. We will need every trick, every power we can muster should that occur. Which reminds me…" She turned to me.

"Yes, I saw her *slowth*," I said shuddering at the memory. "The *slowth* that binds their dreamslice reflections to them is a mere fraction of what Owraythu exhibits in the underverse. And where our *slowthar* are akin to insulated wires, theirs are like…like a string of tumorous ganglions. Sickening, shuddering things, too huge to take in all at once, they twitch with thoughts, memories…whatever they are, they are immensely powerful. I could feel the force of them."

A look of intense concentration settled on Kuhntul's face. "That's good."

"Good? What about it is good?" Jane demanded.

"Did you try to dip into it?"

"Are you insane?" I shook my head and laughed. "No, I ran as if my ass was on fire."

Kuhntul nodded. "We need to find Luka. We will need him when we face Owraythu again."

"Why in the blue fuck would we do that?" I demanded. "I'm not taking anyone back there. Not now, not ever."

"Relax, Tyeldnir. She will come here as soon as one of the Maids reports our location."

"*What*?" demanded Jane. "We've got to stop them!"

"She can only come here as a dreamslice reflection. She will be vulnerable here—as much weakened as the Three Maids are here. In the underverse, she is supremely powerful, but here?" Kuhntul shrugged.

"I'll go track him down," I said climbing to my feet and stepping toward the trees.

"I'll come with you," said Jane.

"No, it would be best if I go alone," said Kuhntul.

"And why is that?" demanded Jane.

Kuhntul looked at my wife with a stony expression. "Because it would."

Jane shook her head.

"This is a conversation best had without extraneous emotion," said Kuhntul.

"I won't say a word," said Jane, and the two women stared at each other, faces flinty.

I backed away from the others without a sound. *You are both wrong*, I thought. *It will be best if I go alone*. Keri tracked my movements, and I held a finger to my lips. I swear he winked at me before he turned his gaze away.

FORTY-NINE

Using the *slowthar*, tracking anyone was an easy task. Tracking Luka was exceptionally easy because I had an idea of where he was headed, so all I had to do was glance down and find his *slowth* every once in a while to make sure I was right.

Luka had beat a straight-line path from the *proo* toward Iktrasitl, and it was easy to guess why: he wanted answers, and he thought he could get them from the Nornir.

Persistent bugger.

I heard him before I saw him. He ranted and raved in a booming voice: "Tell me where she is! I've seen her being tortured with my own eyes, and if you don't tell me how to stop it, *your* pain will eclipse my queen's!"

A low murmur of response drifted to me on the breeze, and Luka screamed in wordless rage. I increased my pace as there were only four creatures he could talk to—one or all of the Three Maids or Ratatoskr—and I couldn't imagine any of them responding well to Luka's demands.

I came into the clearing as Luka began his advance toward the Three Maids. He leered at them as he advanced, his face a study of fury. The Three Maids looked up at him with expressions ranging from boredom to annoyance, but there was no fear in any of their faces.

"We should consign him to the life of a stable boy," said Mother Skult.

"Yes, a lifetime of shoveling horse manure would do wonders for his patience," said Mother Urthr.

Mother Verthanti scoffed. "Kill him and be done."

"No," I said, raising my voice to carry across the clearing. "He has been abused by your kind enough. More than enough."

"*You*," sneered Urthr. "Do you even know what you could have been? What you *should* have been?"

"Don't know, don't care!" I snapped. I turned to the *oolfur*. "Luka, they can't tell you anything, even if they know, which I doubt. These three are thralls to the more powerful of their kind."

"Ha!" sneered Verthanti. "You know nothing."

"Less than nothing," said Urthr.

Skult stared at me with predatory calculation in her eyes.

Luka turned to face me. "And can you? Can you offer me more than parlor tricks?"

Skult got to her feet and turned toward the trees. "What is it I sense?" she murmured.

"Luka, what I showed you before was nothing but the truth, and now, I can offer far more than a memory."

His eyes bored into mine.

"But we need your help for what is coming."

"And what is that?" he snapped.

I glanced at the Nornir before turning my gaze back to his. "We can talk about that in private."

Skult turned to her left and stared into the forest. "That is…*familiar*." She turned toward me. "Who have you brought here? Who is it that is so…"

I ignored her, keeping my gaze locked on Luka's. "We need your gifts for a project. We have…" I glanced at Skult. "I've brought them here, you understand? Your *family*."

Luka squinted past me and lifted his face and sniffed like a wolf scenting the wind. "My brother…his broodmares…his brat…"

"I've brought *all* of them, Luka."

His gaze locked on mine and he tilted his head to the side. "All? Even…"

"Yes," I said with a curt nod. "All."

"What are you saying?" demanded Skult.

"Ignore them, dear," said Urthr. "They are powerless in the face of our—"

"No," hissed Skult.

"What's this?" whispered Verthanti. "What is this…thing…that is coming to be?"

"Hurry, Luka," I said. "We must get back to the others."

He strode to my side, then glanced over his shoulder. "I will return, witches," he said. "And when I do, you will taste my wrath."

"What is this?" said Verthanti, springing to her feet. "Sisters! We must hurry!"

"Whatever are you droning on about?" asked Urthr. "Nothing has changed. Nothing *can* change."

Skult's gaze leapt to mine from across the glade that contained Iktrasitl. "We should have caused your death!" she screamed.

"I get that a lot," I said. I put my hand on Luka's shoulder and guided him into the woods. "We've got to hurry."

"Why? Those three are nothing. I can—"

"Those three are *Plauinn*, Luka! Technically, they are the dreamslice reflections of three very weak *Plauinn*. Thralls to the others, but compared to you and me…" I shook my head.

He glanced over his shoulder. "They don't seem like much."

"Appearances can be deceiving."

He grunted with amusement. "Were you speaking the truth back there? Have you brought… Is *she* here?"

I nodded.

"How did you rescue her? How did you—"

"No time to explain," I said. "And these woods might have ears."

He grunted again. "Take me to her."

With a shrug, I led him back toward the others. His stride was long, and his eagerness had him stepping past me, then waiting for me to catch up.

"Can you not *hurry*?" he asked.

"Listen to me a moment. Hel has suffered for I don't know how long. It's—"

"It's been only a few days," said Luka. "She's strong. She will be fine."

I shrugged. "I have no idea how time works in the underverse. It's possible that time in Owraythu's realm is dilated, that—"

"What are you talking about, Hank?"

"What was a few days for us may have been—"

"I know the meaning of time dilation!"

"Okay. The *Plauinn* live in the underverse—that's their reality. There, they are powerful beings—the most powerful beings that exist there as far as I know. When we are there, we are only reflections of ourselves. It's akin to a dream existence or a memory of ourselves."

"Fine. What has this to do with—"

"Don't you get it? She's been trapped in their realm, yes, but only a part of her. Part of her strength, part of her will, whatever."

"Where was the other part?"

"I have no idea. But listen, Luka! She's hurt, she's—"

"She's a queen! My queen's stronger than you think."

"I'm not disputing that, Luka," I said in a smooth, even voice. "I want you to prepare yourself that she may not be as you—"

"Enough!" he snapped. "Take me to her. Now!"

I shrugged and led him through the woods. As we came toward the clearing, he peered through the trees before turning a look of disdain on me.

"You said they injured her!" He turned and sprinted ahead. "My Queen!" he shouted.

He bolted out of the trees and ran toward Kuhntul, who stood with her back to us. "My Queen! Is it you?" He reached out and laid his hand on Kuhntul's shoulder.

Kuhntul turned, some strong emotion on her face, and flipped her brilliant white hair over her shoulder. "Luka Oolfhyethidn, I am Kuhntul, of the Tisir." Behind her, Sif, Yowrnsaxa, and Frikka knelt in a half-circle, blocking our view of Hel.

Luka stumbled back, shaking his head. "I thought… My apologies, from behind you—"

"I am Kuhntul. I am Tisir."

"Yes," he said with a nod of his head, almost a bow. "Hank said Queen Hel is here?"

"She is," said Kuhntul. "I helped Tyeldnir when he rescued her. A force held her there."

"This Owraythu that Hank speaks of?"

Kuhntul shook her head. "Well…maybe, but she was engaged elsewhere at the time—chasing Hank. I think—"

"What of this force? Why do you mention it?"

Kuhntul pointed at the base of the tree the three Isir women stood in front of. Sif, Yowrnsaxa, and Frikka moved aside, concern etched in each face.

"She's very weak, Luka," said Sif. "As if she's lost a fundamental part of herself."

Since I'd first met her on Mithgarthr, Hel had always been thin. She'd always appeared one meal away from starving to death. It was part and parcel with the changes wrought on their bodies by breaking the *Ayn Loug*, by turning cannibal in the pursuit of power. But now she looked even worse. Her skin was an ashen gray and stretched as tight as a drum over the bones of her skull and face.

"My Queen!" he cried, dropping to his knees.

I couldn't tear my gaze away from her. Her hair had been lustrous before, and now it hung like dried grass, shriveled and gray. Flakes of skin fell from her cheeks, and her lips were chapped and split. Her eyes were slack, listless.

"My Queen," Luka sobbed. "What has done this to you? What can I do to help you?"

"My…Champion…" she whispered, and it was as if the words sapped her remaining strength. Her eyes closed, and a long breath rattled out of her.

"*Do something*!" Luka shrieked. "Sif! Sif, help her!"

The Isir healer glanced at him, then rocked forward and went back to her work. She snapped orders, and Yowrnsaxa or Frikka fulfilled them, fetching things from her bag, holding Hel, tilting her head back, supporting her enervated body.

Meuhlnir tottered toward us, his eyes filled with immeasurable pain. One hand he held to the wounds Luka had inflicted a few short days prior. In his other hand, he held his hammer.

"No!" shouted Luka. "You get away! Get *away* from her!" He sprang up and pushed Meuhlnir savagely.

Meuhlnir stumbled and would have fallen if Veethar hadn't appeared at his side as if out of the mist, grabbing his elbow and steadying him. "Stand aside, Luka!" Meuhlnir croaked. "Leave me be!"

"No! You will not harm her!"

"Harm her?" Meuhlnir stood straight, his bearing filled with calm dignity. "*Harm* her, Brother? How many times during the war did we turn away when we could have *harmed* her?"

Luka's eyes danced around the clearing, like a cornered animal, landing on Meuhlnir's hammer, before meeting his brother's gaze. "Don't…don't…"

Meuhlnir sighed, and in that sigh was every moment of heartbreak and pain that had existed between the two for centuries. "Do you not trust me, Brother?"

Luka shook his head but wouldn't meet Meuhlnir's gaze.

"These wounds leave me weak, Luka. The wounds *you* gave me. I don't yet... I haven't yet recovered much strength. I can't fight you, I can only beg you to let me help her." Meuhlnir's bright eyes locked on Luka's.

"Help her?" Luka asked, and again, his eyes drifted down to the hammer his brother held.

Meuhlnir followed Luka's gaze, and he shook his head. "I only wanted to put this in her hands, Brother. To remind her of something, something we have all lost." He let the hammer fall. "There. Now, will you let me by?"

Tears glistened in Luka's eyes, but he didn't wipe them. He bent and picked up Meuhlnir's hammer and traced his brother's inlaid name with his finger. "Come, Brother," he said. "You've dropped your hammer." He reversed his grip and held it out to Meuhlnir. "Let me help you." He stepped to Meuhlnir's side and put his arm out. "Lean on me."

The two brothers approached where the Dark Queen lay, and Meuhlnir bent down and placed the hammer in Hel's loose fingers. "It's there, Suel. Can you feel it? The hammer you gifted me? The faith you had in me, the memory of the grace you allowed us to bask in, they carried me through difficult and dark times."

Hel exhaled a long, weary breath.

"Yes, we've been at odds. Yes, we've faced one another across battlefields. But I never lost faith in you. I never lost hope."

Meuhlnir nodded at Luka and sank to his knees. "The day I earned this hammer, you, an untutored *vefari,* taught me something. Do you recall, Suel?"

Her index finger twitched, but there was no other movement visible in her body, not even the rise and fall of her respiration.

"*Tvelyast*!" Meuhlnir whispered, and power crackled in the air between him and Hel, and she twitched as if someone had applied current to her body. Meuhlnir's eyes widened with the effort of what he was attempting.

Jane's hand snuck into mine and tugged.

"*Stay,*" I whispered, translating Meuhlnir's command in the *Gamla Toonkumowl.*

"*Anta*!" Meuhlnir begged. "*Anta,* Suel. *Anta*!" His voice broke on the last syllable.

"He begs her to breathe," I whispered to Jane.

Again, the air crackled with power, and the queen's hair stirred as if to a breeze none of the rest of us could feel. It…it looked more lustrous, more blonde than gray. Her arms twitched, and she dragged a breath from the air through unsplit lips, shuddering with the pain of it.

"*Lifa ow nee*!" cried Meuhlnir, his voice hoarse with emotion and gruff with power.

"Live again," I whispered, and Jane squeezed my hand.

The surrounding air popped and glowed with the thaumaturgical power Meuhlnir had spawned to save the woman who had once done the same for him. I wondered if the skein of fate—those runes carved into Iktrasitl's bark—were changing at that moment, if the changes locked the Three Maids in an argument about how to reconcile the new pattern of *uhrluhk*.

Hel's eyes fluttered, then opened. Her blue eyes swam with life, and she looked with wonder at Meuhlnir and then up at Luka. She smiled.

"You will not die today," Meuhlnir rasped.

Her gaze fell to meet his, and she smiled before she turned her gaze to Sif, Yowrnsaxa, and Frikka, and smiled at each in turn.

Before anyone could speak, a terrible deafening howl rent the peace of the Conflux coming from the direction of Iktrasitl. When I noticed Kuhntul had disappeared, fear dug its fingers into my throat.

FIFTY

I spun in a tight circle, looking for any sign of Kuhntul. She hadn't told us her plan, hadn't told us *how* Owraythu's presence—or the presence of any of the *Plauinn*—as a dreamslice reflection would expose their weaknesses. I didn't understand how to fight the *Plauinn*, and the fight had arrived, whether or not we were ready. A roar that sounded as if it had issued from the mouth of a giganotosaurus rent the air and reverberated through the trees. The pups howled in response.

"Is that…" began Jane.

"Has to be," I said.

"She's coming for me," rasped Hel. "And you since you rescued me." Her gaze locked on my own, and there was amusement in her eyes. "Why would you do that? After all that I've done?" Her voice contained a musing, introspective quality.

"No time for that now," said Luka, his eyes on the forest.

"Quick," I said. "Everyone run to Iktrasitl. There are…*beings* there that may help us."

Luka scoffed. "Those three Nornir were *not* helpful."

"No," I agreed. "But there is a dragon and a mammoth eagle somewhere around there, not to mention Ratatoskr. And…"

"And what?" asked Hel.

"Maybe Owsakrimmr still hangs from the tree."

Hel's eyebrows shot upward, but her lips wore a sneering grin. "Owsakrimmr?"

"That's the name he gave me."

"Is it so?" Her gaze tracked to Luka's, and a broken, rusty-sounding chuckle escaped her.

"What?" I asked.

"Owsakrimmr? The name means 'Leader of the Isir.'"

"And?" snapped Jane.

"Keep your panties on, dear," said Hel in a condescending, sneering tone. "It is one name the Vikings of Mithgarthr gave to their god, Owthidn."

My gaze snapped to Meuhlnir. "But I thought you Isir don't know that name."

Mothi shrugged. "Never heard of him."

Hel held her hand out to Luka, and he pulled her to her feet. Another shriek of fury echoed through the forest. "Getting closer," she mused.

"Yes, let's get to Iktrasitl. There'll be time to sort out who the guy in the tree is later."

"Maybe we can ask him," said Hel, amusement at war with the fatigue in her voice.

I led everyone back to the clearing that girded Iktrasitl. Nasty purplish-black clouds covered the sky from horizon to horizon, lit from within by multi-hued arcs of lightning, and a chill wind howled through the branches of Iktrasitl. Two of the Nornir stood close together, shoulders almost touching, staring into the forest with mirrored expressions of anxiety and fear on their faces. As we broke from the trees, a jagged tear appeared in the air next to them, as unlike a *proo* as I could imagine, and Verthanti stepped from it. That tear brought the *Plowir Medn* to mind. I could almost hear their oily voices clangoring in the forest.

Verthanti locked her gaze on mine. "You did this!" she snapped.

Urthr shrugged. "With the help of our pet Tisir, I'll wager. I told you she was untrue, Skult."

Skult flapped her hand in the air, not taking her eyes off the trees.

"Do you stand with us, or the ones who treat you as thralls?" I asked.

Urthr scoffed, and that was the only reply I got.

"How do we find this dragon?" Hel asked.

I shook my head. "Come to think of it, I've never seen the thing. I have no idea where it is."

"And you know there is a dragon here, how?" asked Luka.

"Heard it many times when I hung in the branches above. Ratatoskr would scamper down the trunk, the dragon would roar, up came the squirrel, then the eagle would scream, rinse, repeat."

Luka chuckled.

Another cry came from the forest, and it was so hate-filled that the hair on my arms stood up.

"Perhaps we should spend time on defenses we can count on," said Althyof, eyes glued to the forest.

"What do you suggest, Tverkr?" asked Hel.

"Kuhntul was the one with a plan. Where is she, anyway?"

Skult laughed. "No doubt she has run off. It's what she is best at."

"Any way to summon your armies?" I asked Hel.

She shook her head. "They've no doubt scattered to the four winds since you re-opened the *preer*. Even if I knew where they were, I don't know where *this* place is. Better for us to escape, to hide among the *klith* for a few centuries."

The terrible wailing sounded again, and the puppies howled in reply. Owraythu was getting closer.

"I don't think that would suffice this time," I muttered.

"No," said Luka, his eyes on my face.

"Not much time," said Mothi, eyeing the trees.

"I don't know what form she will take," I said in a clipped voice. "If she follows the pattern of these others, she will look human. If she doesn't…"

"Ask the Nornir," said Hel.

I glanced at the Three Maids, who presented a wall of backs to us again. "Waste of time," I said. "They are *Plauinn*, so even if they deign to answer, we won't know if their answers are honest or contrived."

Luka nodded. "We fight as we know how." He held his hand out to Hel. "My Queen?"

She took his hand and smiled at him. "My Champion." She nodded her head. "We will fight as *oolfa*. Don't shoot us this time, Hank—unless you will also change shape?"

"I may if it's needed, but for now, I want to keep things fluid."

Hel's gaze wandered to Jane's. "And you? Will you sprout wings or cower on the ground next to your man?"

Jane's shoulders went rigid. "What Hank said."

Hel nodded, and her gaze went to the other Isir. "I know how the rest of you will fight." Her gaze settled on Krowkr and his sword and axe. "Interesting, Viking, but I'd stay in the back, were I you."

Althyof drew his daggers and with a saucy smile, winked at Hel. "I'll try not to slice you by mistake."

Hel's gaze drifted to the two Alfar. "And you…I suppose you were the ones I couldn't see in Suelhaym that night?"

Yowtgayrr turned an insouciant gaze on the Dark Queen but made no other acknowledgement of her question. He raised his hand and drew silvery runes in the air and disappeared. Skowvithr shrugged and followed suit.

"So be it," said Hel in an edgy tone. She turned to Sif. "You will form the Wall?"

With a glance at Frikka and Yowrnsaxa, she nodded.

"In that case, Luka and I will flank. Does it suit?"

"Together or on opposite sides?" asked Meuhlnir.

"Your choice."

Meuhlnir's eyes cut to mine, and Hel chuckled.

"I see," she said, turning to me. "Your orders, Hank?"

I nodded. "Until I see what we are facing, I want one of you on each end of the shield wall, one step behind. Be ready to flank, or to back up the *skyuldur vidnukonur*. If you hold off on your *prayteenk*, you could assist with ranged attacks."

Hel's lips stretched in a half-grin. "I think we will change in advance."

"Fine. Do it," I said, and she and Luka swapped their human forms for that of a bear and a wolf.

Thirty steps away, the tree trunks groaned, and leaves flew from high branches as Owraythu came toward us. The puppies alerted at the spectacle, one standing on either side of me.

"Weapons," I said. I pulled Kunknir and Krati from their holsters, and Keri looked up at me and whined. "Yeah, I know they're noisy. Good weapons, nonetheless." He stretched his jaws and whined.

I racked the slide of both weapons and pointed where I wanted the shield wall. "Althyof, support the wall, please." He began a *trowba* and started his dance behind the four women. Meuhlnir, Veethar, and Mothi came to stand beside me. Krowkr stood behind us, his neck craned, staring up at the rune-inscribed tree. Sig stood next to him with a fearful expression on his face.

"The Alfar?" whispered Meuhlnir.

"No doubt in the trees. Scouting." I glanced over my shoulder.

Meuhlnir grunted. "Any idea how to fight one of these *Plauinn*? Even if they are *only* a *dreamslice reflection...*"

"None," I said with a grin I didn't feel. "Then again, I had no idea how to fight a dragon or a band of acid-blooded demons or crazy spiders with flammable blood or a sea dragon or a—"

"Forget I asked," said Meuhlnir with a grin.

My gaze found that of my son. "Son, if things turn grim, use your dagger. Krowkr, you get away as best you can."

The trees across from us seemed to bulge outward as though they were images on a soap bubble. With a rending crash, a row of four or five tree trunks exploded in a shower of ash chips and splinters. When the dust cleared, a nude woman stood where the trees had been.

Her hair glimmered from hue to hue, shade to shade, as its color flitted through the visible spectrum. Her eyes, though, were twin pits of blackness so complete that to look at them for long was dizzying. She stepped into the clearing, opened her mouth wide and trumpeted her hatred and fury at us—so loud, her scream struck as though it were a physical force.

Frikka gave the order, and the women interlocked the edges of their shields.

Owraythu pointed at Hel. "You are *mine*, do you hear? I am not through with you!"

In answer, Hel lifted her snout and roared like a bear.

Owraythu's gaze traveled the length of the shield wall, and she shook her head as if incredulous that anyone would stand before her thus. When her eyes found mine, she stopped and squinted at me in anger. "You did this! Where is your master, small one? Where is Bikkir?"

I shook my head. "Leave this place!"

Her eyes burned with fury, and she took two juddering steps toward us before she glimpsed the Nornir. "You there!" she yelled. "Why have you let these…these *small ones* shelter here? I demand you aid me at once!"

"Now," I said, and snapped my pistols into position. I fired, alternating from Kunknir to Krati, and rounds from each gun struck home, slamming Owraythu's body this way and that.

"*Ehlteenk*!" cried Meuhlnir, and a bolt of pure electric blue split the sky. Thunder boomed as the bolt struck Owraythu's torso.

She shrieked, but by the sound of it, more from rage than pain.

Veethar raised his hand to point at the *Plauinn*. "*Binta hana*!" he cried. A tall ash tree bent toward the ground, reaching for Owraythu with its long branches.

She juddered and jittered from the impact of my bullets and the lightning bolt Meuhlnir had thrown at her, but still, she laughed, and it was a nasty, hateful sound. She waved her hand at the approaching branches absently, and the trunk of the tree shattered.

"*Beryast vith hana*!" Veethar cried, and the ash trees closest to Owraythu swung their limbs at the *Plauinn*.

"Say when, Aylootr," said Mothi, dancing in place like a kid who needs the restroom.

"Not yet," I said, still firing.

Owraythu spun her hand in a tight circle. A kernel of blackness started there and followed her hand, growing larger with each revolution. The trajectory of my rounds bent toward that spot of swirling darkness, farther and farther with each revolution of her hand.

My mind played the memory of Bikkir creating a blackhole of sorts in Isi's lab. "Stop her!"

Jane barged at Owraythu with her raven shield, and the air rang as though a million brass bells had rung at once. A jagged black beam ripped through the air from her shield and slammed into the *Plauinn*, flinging her to the ground. Jane threw her spear, and it transformed into a bolt of golden lightning and plowed into Owraythu's chest with a snapping sound.

Owraythu screamed, and the forest shook with her rage. She leapt to her feet like an acrobat on speed and, with a backhanded wave, sent Jane flying into Iktrasitl twenty feet from the ground. The impact sounded sickening, and Jane screamed in pain. She unfurled her wings and flew around the tree, breaking Owraythu's line of sight, the cadmium red aura of her ring's healing spell already enveloping her. Sig cried out and ran around to her side of the tree.

"Forget the wall," I yelled. "Everyone on Owraythu now!"

Luka and Hel snarled and leapt, and Mothi charged forward with his axes whirling in arcs. Althyof did one of his graceful pirouettes and widened the circle of his dance, syncopating his *trowba* and building a countermelody as he had in his fight against Ivalti, the Svartalf *kastari*. Meuhlnir stood where he was and threw bolts of lightning.

Owraythu screamed, and Luka, Hel, and Mothi flew in different directions as if swatted by the tail of an immense beast. "You will all suffer!" Owraythu shrieked. "This one will rend you from the fabric of existence and leave the tatters of your being in the outer darkness where coldness reigns and darkness seems bright!"

"Talk, talk, talk," muttered Mothi, picking himself up from the pile of branches he'd landed in.

Luka sped back to Owraythu, a snarl stretching his lupine features into a fearsome portrait of wrath. Hel came back, too, but she tottered on legs that seemed shaky, one massive paw to her head.

I snapped off a few rounds, advancing toward her, but I didn't go far. As soon as Luka reached her, she sent him flying into the trees again.

This isn't going to work! a small voice in the back of my mind screamed. *Do something else!*

Owraythu screamed incoherently, almost foaming at the mouth, her rage was so great. Meuhlnir strode forward, pointing at her. "*Thun!*" he cried.

Owraythu's screams became silent, though her mouth continued to work. Her gaze found Meuhlnir, and she grimaced and coughed, her body doubling over with effort. "Silence me not!" she shrieked. She gestured at one of the fallen trees, and it leapt into the air, slammed into Meuhlnir, and drove him into the base of Iktrasitl like a train slamming into a car parked on the tracks.

That left only Althyof, Veethar, Frikka, Sif, Yowrnsaxa, and me to fight. And the Alfar— wherever they'd disappeared to. I snapped my pistols up and fired again, stepping to the right, moving toward Veethar and Frikka. *Hope they know what to do, or we're going to lose!*

In the corner of my vision, I saw the Three Maids still standing where they had when we'd entered the glade. They'd turned to watch the battle but made no move to support either side. I pointed Krati in their direction and fired a round at their feet, and still they stood, like pillars of stone in a windstorm. "Do something!" I screamed at them.

"Move and be consumed!" shouted Owraythu at them. She whirled to glare at me, spinning her index finger, though she kept it pointed at the ground. "You started this!"

"Yeah, I'm a bastard that way," I said. I pointed Kunknir at her face and fired twice in rapid succession.

She screamed and rushed at me, one hand up to scratch at my face. I didn't see the spinning, maelstrom of power streaming behind her spinning index finger until it was too late. She flung it at me, a whip crack of maleficent power.

The string of crackling, baleful power sawed into me, ignoring my flesh, but causing me as much (or more) agony as if she had used a chainsaw on me instead. My vision grew dim, and the only thing I could hear was a curious wave-at-the-beach sound. I fell to one knee, and she was on me, all clawed fingers and hissing, spitting fury.

A cold wave of dulcet relief washed over me, and my vision returned. I rolled to the side, and as I did, Owraythu's face crumpled in confusion. The Alfar stood at the edge of the forest, one on each side of the gap Owraythu had made, writing silvery runes in the air as fast as their hands could move.

Wisps of silver twisted through the air and wrapped around Owraythu as though an invisible spider wrapped her in a cocoon of webbing. She shrieked and thrashed, but as one strand broke, two more found her. Her eyes widened, and she peered down at the silvery strands, her face a parody of surprise. "What's this?" she muttered.

Yowtgayrr muttered something that sounded like my name.

"What?" I asked, rocking to my feet.

"Run," he said, his face a mask of concentration. "Get away!"

I looked from him to Owraythu, seeing the gleeful expression on her face and the silver wisps that were turning black from the inside out. I turned back to Yowtgayrr, shaking my head. "We have to fight together!"

"There's no fighting her," said Frikka.

"Draw her away. Hide. We will see to—"

Owraythu laughed, and it was a sound I imagined coming from every twisted fuck of a serial killer, madman, or genocidal dictator in history.

"Get Hel and get out of here!" urged Veethar. "You know how! We need time!"

I nodded, getting it at last. I stumbled to Hel, who still stood clutching her head. I grabbed her by one colossal paw and pulled her toward the woods. She came willingly enough, though, to be honest, she didn't appear to know who I was. Behind us, Owraythu screamed as a thwarted child might.

We ducked into the trees and trotted into the shadows. I wove a *proo* and moved the other end to the place where Kuhntul had taught me how to spin my own *preer*. I pushed Hel into it and jumped through behind her, closing the thing as soon as we were out the other end.

"Change back, if you can," I said. "We need speed now, not bulk and muscle." She gazed down at me, but her eyes didn't track to my face, and she made no move to regain her human form. With a sigh, I grabbed her paw again and pulled her through the forest, beginning the speed boosting *trowba* Althyof had taught me by rote.

I ran through the forest surrounding Iktrasitl, leaping the usual detritus found in any forest, dodging limbs and tree trunks, all the while pulling Hel behind me like an enormous bear-shaped child. There were no animal sounds, no sound of wind through the tree tops, only the incessant wailing of Owraythu as she vented her anger at the sky.

She was somewhere off to the southwest, following the course we'd used to leave the glade, and I bent our course northeast. The sound of trees falling punctuated her screams. Hel reacted to none of it, only followed blindly, chuffing and grunting from time to time.

I hoped Owraythu continued looking for us and left the others alone. I wondered how much damage Owraythu had inflicted on Jane and Meuhlnir and hoped Sif could mitigate it.

We slowed to a trot, and I let the *trowba* fade. "Kuhntul, where are you?" I muttered between breaths.

The sounds to the southwest ceased, and my stomach lurched. I put on more speed, wishing for the umpteenth time that Hel would snap out of it and help me.

Owraythu shrieked far away, and a rumbling, crackling sound roared to life. A fierce wind blew as if something sucked the air behind us.

"Kuhntul!" I cried.

Another of Owraythu's incoherent howls split the air, and the sky above the canopy of the trees rumbled in sympathy.

"When she figures out where we are, we will need to run faster, Hel." I shook the massive paw I held. "Can you change back? It will be easier if you are in human form, and I have an idea to gain more speed."

Hel turned her massive ursine head down to stare at me. Blood trickled from her left ear, and her eyes seemed so empty.

I shook her paw again. "Snap out of it! You've got to change!"

Her jaws opened, and her tongue writhed between her fangs.

"This one knows where you've gone!" screamed Owraythu in an earsplitting voice. "This one perceives your deceptions!"

Far behind us, the explosions started again. As we jogged on into the forest, the sound of the trees splitting got louder and louder. I could imagine the scene—Owraythu beelining toward us, flapping her hands at the trees that stood in her way, ash trees exploding into sawdust and splinters.

"Change!" I shook Hel's paw again.

"*M-ma-m… Math…ur*!" she hissed. "*Mathur*!" As soon as her jaws, tongue, and throat had changed enough to allow it, she said, "What happened? Why are we running?"

I shook my head. "Can't beat her. We're giving the others time. Owraythu's on our trail and gaining." I glanced back at her to make sure everything was sinking in. "I'm going to make a series of *preer*. We need to sprint to each opening and jump through, no stopping, no pausing. On the other side, keep sprinting while I spin up another."

"That sounds…dangerous."

I waved my hand at the sounds gaining on us from behind. "More dangerous than Owraythu?"

Hel grunted.

I let go of her hand and formed a *proo*. With a twist of its hook, I sent the terminus as far into the trees as I could see, then pushed the entry point in front of us.

"How did you learn to do this?" she asked.

"No time! We've got to run!" I said. "Now!"

We slapped at the entrance and popped several hundred yards ahead.

"Again!" said Hel.

We repeated the process again and again and began to leave Owraythu behind. A low vibration rattled to life behind us, reminding me of a diesel locomotive in the distance. We kept running and jumping through *preer*, but that sound only got louder and louder.

"She's stopped yelling," wheezed Hel.

"Can't be good."

"No. Faster, Hank!"

I pushed the *proo* as far as I could see, and then willed it farther still, and though we popped through it safely, it was no use. Whatever Owraythu was doing, she was gaining on us despite everything I could do.

"I've got an idea," I said. "When we come through this next *proo*, be ready to grab onto a branch—that or fly!"

Without waiting for a response, I spun a *proo* to the branch where the eagle had dropped me. "Go!" I said and pushed her into the *proo*.

We popped out in midair, about a yard above the branch where Kuhntul and I had sat for our chat. Hel yelped as she fell but wrapped both hands around the bough. She looked around, then peered down the trunk of the great ash tree.

"Now what?" she asked.

I shrugged and gazed out at the destruction Owraythu had wrought in the forest near Iktrasitl. I'd hoped to find Kuhntul there, but she was gone. "I'd hoped she would be here. She said there was a weakness inherent in the *Plauinn* being here, but she forgot to say what."

Hel grunted. "What do we do now?"

The forest had been flattened in a large swath, and the trees on the edges of the flattened area had been stripped of bark. A short distance from the glade, the straight-line path widened into a circle—like a crop circle back on Mithgarthr but one made with trees in a forest rather than grain in a field. From that circle, another straight-line path swept away to the northeast—toward where we had been fleeing. I followed that path with my eye until my gaze caught up with its head.

Trees flew like pick-up sticks, and a perpetual haze of wood dust hung in the air. Even so, the path grew at an incredible pace, as if someone drove a massive snowplow at high speed through the forest.

"She's still chasing us," mused Hel.

"Think she'll catch us?"

Hel chuckled and then sobered. "It's sad to think of what must happen when we escape her for good."

I turned and gazed at her. "And what's that?"

She shrugged, avoiding my gaze. "Things are…unsettled. Osgarthr cannot go on as it has these past centuries. Unguided. Aimless. Drifting through time. I see that now."

I sighed and turned my gaze back to the explosive progress of Owraythu through the forest. "And who's to guide them?"

Hel chuckled. "Isn't that still unresolved?"

"So how will we resolve it?" I asked, thinking I knew the answer, but dreading the confirmation.

She twisted on the branch and looked at me. I could see her studying me from the corner of my eye. "The way people always decide such matters."

I scoffed. "Are we forever tied to the past? Do we always have to follow the footsteps that lead to where we are?"

She shook her head and looked down at the ground, far below us. "I don't have the answer to that."

Owraythu's buzz-saw progress through the forest halted, and she vented her anger at the sky.

Hel sighed. "I wish she'd stop all that incessant screaming."

"Hasn't there been enough war among the Isir?"

She glanced at me again and turned her face away. She opened her mouth to say something, but before she could speak, the air rang as if someone had struck an immense celestial gong with a metal mallet. The harmonics of the sound ripped across the sky, echoing from horizon to horizon. As the sound faded, the wet popping sound of dislocated joints ripped across the sky.

Hel grimaced and said, "She's summoned the *Plowir Medn.*"

"Awesome. I thought they were *your* allies."

Hel grimaced. "So did I. They betrayed me to Owraythu and Mirkur."

"When they teleported you away from our last battle."

"Yes."

Faintly, the sound of many piping voices lifted in a *kaltrar*, and the sound of it reverberated in my brain—the ultimate coercive ear-worm. I couldn't make out the words—the language of the *Plowir Medn* was slippery and convoluted to my ears—but I didn't have to understand the *words*, the intent became clear half a heartbeat after they began.

The air in the upper atmosphere up near the clouds seemed as shivery as heat-haze in the distance for a breath in time, then the shivers erupted in every direction at once as though a bomb had exploded in their midst and sent everything flying. Iktrasitl shivered with resonance, and the trunk moaned and creaked. The temperature of the air surrounding Hel and me increased at a dramatic pace.

"Uh oh," I muttered.

"Time to go!" snapped Hel.

"Go where?"

"Anywhere but this branch!"

From above came the staccato jackhammer sound of Ratatoskr scampering down the tree trunk. In the crown of the tree, Tindur shrieked a challenge at the sky. The dragon below rumbled like the warning growl of a large, pissed-off dog.

"Can you do your trick with the dragon below us?" I asked.

"My *trick*?"

"You know what I mean."

"Yes, I can do my *trick* with any dragon."

"Fair enough. I don't know where the dragon is, so we'll have to convince the Nornir to tell us where to go."

Hel hurried me along with a finger-twirling hand gesture. The red-blur of Ratatoskr's frenzied approach descended toward us, and the air around me glowed with heat. With the sickening crunch of a shoulder dislocating, a *Plowir Medn* appeared in the air five feet in front of us—which was, of course, in midair. With a squawk, the *Plowir Medn* started to fall. He uttered a stream of squirmy consonants.

"Hank! We can't let him go!"

In a heartbeat—almost as if it moved of its own accord—Kunknir was in my right hand, and a round hole smoked in the center of the little blue fellow's forehead. The wormy *kaltrar* ceased, and the *Plowir Medn* fell like a rock.

"Hank! The *proo*!"

Moving as fast as I could, I spun up a fresh *proo* and dropped the exit right at the base of Iktrasitl. Hel snapped her hand out but stopped before she slapped the *proo*. "For what it's worth, I thank you for rescuing me." Without waiting for my reply, she touched the *proo* and disappeared. Before I could follow her lead, Ratatoskr streaked by, head down, tail pointing at the sky, talons ripping into the bark of Iktrasitl. As he passed me, he chirped, sounding for all the world as though he were an ordinary squirrel.

"It's you!" he called.

"No time to talk," I said, reaching for the *proo*.

"Who is this invader? Who destroys the forest? You must tell us!"

"Owraythu and the *Plowir Medn*!" I snapped my hand out and brushed the *proo*. When I appeared at the base of the mighty tree, Hel was already walking toward the small campfire where the Nornir sat under normal circumstances.

"Where are they?" she demanded.

Veethar stepped out of the forest from the far side of the glade and waved us over. "Come," he said.

"Where are the Nornir?" asked Hel.

"Come away!" Frikka urged.

"We need to find out where the dragon is. Hel can—"

"No time, Hank!" said Veethar. He waved his hand again.

"Where is everyone?"

With the wet sound of hundreds of joints tearing from their sockets, scores of *Plowir Medn* appeared in ones or twos all over the glade and in the first few rows of trees.

I drew my pistols and fired—acquiring a target, squeezing the trigger, finding a new target, and firing, again and again. I circled around the glade, moving clockwise toward the south.

"We must not let even one of the *Plowir Medn* escape!" Hel yelled to the others. She pointed at the closest blue figure. "*Predna*!" she hissed, and the emerald green flame engulfed the diminutive figure.

I kept moving and firing, moving and firing, hot brass flying away in arcs, hot lead streaming into blue bodies.

Veethar and Frikka swept into action, Veethar using his sword and his special relationship with nature to attack the *Plowir Medn* from every side, while Frikka acted as his *skyuldur vidnukonur*.

Where is everyone? I wondered.

The *Plowir Medn* formed into small groups—three or four bunching together. One of each small party stood to the rear and chanted in that slithery language of theirs. The other two or three produced jagged-looking bladed weapons and crouched, cutting strange patterns in the air and making war-faces at us.

I continued circling and picking off exposed or solo *Plowir Medn*. Hel splashed fire around with abandon, and soon wood from the fallen or exploded ash trees danced and popped with green flame. She kept moving closer and closer to the edge of the woods—a group of the blue-skinned people were leading her away from the glade!

"Hel! Get back!"

She didn't acknowledge me, didn't even look at me. Her face wore a mask of rage and hate, and her eyes seemed to blaze from her cheeks like motes of the emerald green fire she threw at them.

I stopped circling and moved toward her, pointing and shooting in that familiar gait that seemed to be a part of me at a genetic level. "Hel! Look out!" I cried as two other groups of *Plowir Medn* moved to flank her. Again, she either didn't hear me or didn't care what I had to say.

I targeted one of the flanking groups and poured a stream of lead into their backs, snapping Kunknir from target to target like a trick-shot artist. With Krati, I sprayed suppressing fire at the other group, hoping that at least some of the rounds would find a new home in something soft and squishy.

Where in the hell is everyone else? I fumed. *We need help here!*

Hel glowered at the four *Plowir Medn* in front of her, and I came to realize that they were speaking to her—taunting her, *goading* her. *Can't she see it?* I shifted Kunknir from the flanking group to the group that was leading Hel into the woods. The sightline wasn't great, but with the enchantments Althyof had woven into my Kimber .45, I could pull it off without risk to Hel. I stopped advancing for a moment and snapped off four quick shots, ejected the empty magazine into the pouch on my belt, and slipped Kunknir down over the next full magazine while I watched two of the *Plowir Medn* stagger and slap their hands over bloody spots that appeared as if by magic on their torsos.

Hel looked at me then, eyes blazing, burning into my own for a heartbeat before snapping back to her intended targets. She screeched something in the *Gamla Toonkumowl*, and the air between us shimmered like a soap bubble.

A shield… I wanted to laugh aloud. She'd put up a buffer between us to ward away bullets.

The two groups of blue flankers closed in a pincer movement and blocked my lines of sight to the ones goading Hel. With a cry that set my teeth on edge, they fell on Hel from behind, serrated blades raised.

I unloaded both pistols into their backs, and though blood splashed the ground and I saw some of them stagger, none of them fell or stopped their advance.

"Hel!" I screamed at the top of my voice.

Luka crashed out of the forest behind the group that had been goading the Dark Queen, fifteen feet of furious *oolfur*, fangs and talons flashing as he set upon the small blue forms. Half a heartbeat later, Mothi sprinted out of the trees, screaming as if he were insane, swinging his axes, and Yowrnsaxa sprinted by his side, her vicious short sword drawn and already bloodied—no doubt in a battle back in the trees. Mothi and his mother swept down on the far group of flankers, and I turned my attention to the closest group, firing both pistols again and again. I *was* doing damage, but the damage was being mitigated somehow.

"Hank! Look out!" cried Frikka.

I glanced in her direction—just in time to see the three small blue bodies leaping at me. I tried to dodge, tried to duck, but against three acrobats, it was no use. They slammed into me, one hitting me across the thighs like the best flying tackle the NFL never saw. The others hit me higher, one slamming a hard foot into my right wrist and the other torpedoing me in the left bicep with his head. Both pistols went flying, and I fell into a heap of biting blue mouths, chopping blue hands, and kicking blue feet.

"Puppies, no!" Sig screamed from somewhere hidden in the trees.

Keri and Fretyi came out of nowhere, snarling and leaping. They each grabbed a limb of a different *Plowir Medn* and first shook them viciously, then flung them away. The last of the little blue men was all over me, hitting, kicking, scratching, biting like a banshee. I did my best, but in close-fighting, and on the ground no less, the short blue warrior had all the advantages.

His hands slashed at my eye, and his feet pummeled my thighs, kicking my legs out from under me every time I tried to get to my feet or leverage myself on top of him. He seemed to be everywhere at once.

And then he was gone—flying through the air holding his stomach, wearing a stricken look on his face. An invisible hand grasped my shoulder and pulled me up.

"Okay now, Hank?" asked Yowtgayrr's disembodied voice.

I stood with my hands on my knees, breathing hard. "A little dizzy." Something warm ran down my cheeks, and my heart gave a little fluttery jerk as the blood dripped to the ground beneath me. "Where is everyone?"

"Safe for the time being. If we can keep these *Plowir Medn* from calling more of their kind, we may—"

"*SISTER*!" The word rolled across the sky, the grinding, basso roar of an earthquake crossed with a humanoid voice.

I shut my eye, knowing who it was. "*Mirkur*," I breathed. "We can't stay here," I said louder. "Into the trees! Everyone into the trees! *RUN*!"

My voice echoed through the trees for a moment, then was drowned out by booming laughter. Something streaked down from the sky, seeming to suck all the available light into itself—like a blackhole turned meteor.

"Run!" I gasped, gaze darting around in a frenzy, looking for my guns.

The blackhole-meteor slammed into the earth twenty yards away. A black mist swirled around the impact area, and the laughter continued unabated.

Fear unraveled in my guts, icy hot streaks of it slicing through my bowels into my chest and head. *Where are they?* a small, childlike voice in the back of my head screeched. *Where is Kunknir? Krati?* Fighting panic, I abandoned the search for my guns and looked for the two *varkr* pups that had adopted me instead.

They were close by, ripping and shredding at the *Plowir Medn* they took turns holding pinned to the ground. Each puppy seemed to have grown, easily more than a match for the slight blue men they fought.

"Keri, Fretyi! To me!" I cried. "Everyone run!"

"*Agreement*! *Flee*!" Mirkur laughed all the harder.

I shot a glance toward the place the meteor had impacted. Like a fog burning away in the morning sun, the swirling stygian mist faded into the background, revealing Mirkur's dreamslice reflection.

He stood seven or eight feet tall, humanoid arms and legs in perfect symmetry, his radiant, ebony skin unblemished and unbroken by eyes or any other distinguishing features. He resembled a man wrapped head-to-toe in shiny black vinyl.

Pulling the puppies with me, I dashed for the woods. I hated leaving my pistols, but what other choice was there? Besides being ripped out of existence, I mean.

The others were dashing into the trees ahead of me. Hel had changed from bear-form to deer-form— her long legs ate the distance to the trees, her doe-like upper body gleaming with sweat. Luka flung away one last broken body of a *Plowir Medn* and with a snarl at Mirkur, turned and dashed after the Dark Queen. The Isir were already gone, and I had to hope the Alfar were too—I had the feeling their stealth would be no match for Mirkur.

"*Brother*!" yelled Owraythu, sounding far away in the forest.

"*At the Conflux*!" he yelled, his eyes never leaving me, marking my progress. "*Negation*," he said. "*You, this one shall converse with*!" He strode toward me, the picture of an angry father going to discipline his child.

Something shrieked, and a flurry of brown wings dove on Mirkur from out of Iktrasitl's branches. Tindur ripped at the *Plauinn* with his huge talons, snapped at him with his huge, sharp beak. He flew in tight circles, slashing, biting, gliding away, only to return moments later for more of the same.

I didn't know if he could damage Mirkur, I only knew it was the break I needed. I turned and sprinted into the trees, Keri and Fretyi padding at my side. Without my pistols, there was nothing else I could do.

Behind us, Mirkur screamed in fury, and Tindur squawked. Ratatoskr added his chittering to the fray. Blue shapes snapped and twisted through the trees to my sides, and my companions bounded through the forest ahead of me.

Time after time, my hands fell to my hips, seeking the pistols that were not there as a target presented itself. Althyof's *trowba* came to me on the wind, and energy suffused my body and mind. I chanted the *triblinkr* that split my animus, and peeled the two raven-shaped forms away, sending one to the rear, to hover high above the glade containing Iktrasitl, and teleporting the other to the clouds above with a thought.

From the clouds, the entire area was beginning to look like a smoke-filled war zone. Long gouges rent the forest's canopy, ragged tears in green velvet. In the glade dominated by Iktrasitl, black and blue forms battled Tindur and Ratatoskr, the latter swollen up to the size of a bull. The two icons dodged and ducked, twisted and turned, leapt and loped as they attacked the interlopers or defended themselves. Owraythu was nowhere to be seen, and I couldn't decide if that fact relieved or frightened me anew.

I matched Tindur's size with the raven I'd sent to Iktrasitl and joined the massive eagle in his twisting pattern of tearing at Mirkur or flinging a *Plowir Medn* high into the air. Tindur cawed a greeting as I did so.

Ahead of me, more and more blue bodies twitched and popped out of thin air, all accompanied by the butcher's sound of dismemberment. Hundreds of them poured into the woods until I could hardly look in any direction without seeing ten of them.

I picked one at random and pointed at him. "*Syow echkert*!" I called, blinding him. I pointed at another—a woman this time. "*Hayrthu echkert*!" Deafening the little blue woman seemed to do nothing, so I blinded her as well.

I winged my way to the north, where I'd last seen Owraythu, staying high up and adopting the purplish-black of the angry cloud cover. The forest below me was silent, dead. No trees exploded, no *Plowir Medn* danced among the trees. *Where is Owraythu?* I wondered.

Mirkur shouted in rage, and with a wave of his hand, sent Tindur rolling and tumbling to the ground. He swept the glade with an angry glare and strode toward the path I'd taken into the woods.

I dove at him again and again, but he ignored me. I flew in front of him, stretching my wings wide and slamming them together with his head in between. He waved his hand, and with a pop, *both* my ravens disappeared.

I staggered with momentary disorientation as my consciousness reintegrated against my will. Two *Plowir Medn* stepped from behind a tree in front of me, and the air between us filled with discordant phrases and atonal singing and my vision swam with it. The noise grated along my cochlear nerve, making my whole face itch. I staggered to a stop, and the puppies whined, swiping at their faces with their front paws.

I glared at the two blue men and yelled, "*Thun*!" But instead of falling silent, their faces distended with hideous grins and their eyes twinkled with evil glee. Again, I pawed at the holsters on my hips, forgetting my pistols were gone in my haste to stop those hideous sounds. I cried out, slapping my hands to my ears, squeezing my eyelids shut and driving away the tears that pooled in my eye sockets.

The hideous sounds stopped mid-syllable. With a sigh of relief, I peeled back my eyelids. Yowtgayrr stood between the corpses of the *Plowir Medn* that had accosted me, his weapons dripping with their azure blood. He had decapitated one of the tiny blue men, and the other bore savage stab wounds through his neck.

"Thanks," I called, stumbling into a jog toward him.

He nodded and sheathed his long dagger. He dug Kunknir from his belt and tossed it my direction.

I caught the pistol in my right hand, unconsciously wiping away the dirt. "Did you find Krati?"

Yowtgayrr shook his head. "Skowvithr has it, I think. He's ahead of us." His eyes darted over my shoulders and widened with alarm.

I racked Kunknir's slide, functioning on automatic, ensuring there was a live round chambered, and spun, sinking into a low crouch. A hundred yards behind us, Mirkur stomped through the woods.

"We must flee, Hank," said Yowtgayrr.

I nodded and snapped Kunknir into firing position. I fired it dry and grimaced at the effect the bullets had on Mirkur.

The black-swathed form didn't even wince. In fact, he didn't seem to notice being shot, he just kept moving inexorably toward us.

I spun on my heels and broke into a sprint, calling for the *varkr* pups to stick by me. I thumbed the release, ejecting the magazine into the clever pouch Prokkr had crafted for me. My last loaded magazine stood at attention, and I slid Kunknir down over it. "I need to reload," I hissed.

"No time for that," said Yowtgayrr. "For now, conserve your ammunition. Use your cloak and let's try to lose Mirkur through guile."

"The pups—"

"Leave them to me." Yowtgayrr tucked his shoulder and snapped into an acrobatic tumble, ending up with a *varkr* puppy under each arm. He scrawled his spidery runes in the air and faded from sight. "The cloak!" he hissed.

"*Vakt*!" I whispered, and my fettle twisted out of phase. I darted away, moving from tree trunk to tree trunk, making sure I was behind a thick ash tree when I came back into phase. Through it all, I had that ants-on-my-shoulder-blades feeling, as if Mirkur's eyes never left my back.

I darted a glance around the tree, and Mirkur was staring right at me. *Cloak won't work*! My mind shot around in circles, and my gaze flitted from tree to shadow to tree. There was nowhere I could hide, nowhere I could run without Mirkur seeing me.

Think! I screamed in my mind. *Think of something*! I found Kunknir in my hand, but that was no use against Mirkur! I slammed it back in the holster and ducked my head out again.

Mirkur had cut his distance by half and walked toward me at a steady pace, but without haste. Behind him, a group of *Plowir Medn* pointed at the tree I hid behind and laughed.

Wait a minute! Behind *him!* A smile cracked through the fearful expression that seemed chiseled into my cheeks. I spun a *proo* into existence and moved its exit point behind and fifty yards to the left of the *Plowir Medn*. This would be the real test of whether or not the *Plauinn* could see my preer.

I activated my cloak and touched the *proo*, appearing as a cloud of smoke and ducking behind another tree, *behind* Mirkur and his annoying blue friends. I closed the *proo* and streaked away on a course perpendicular to Mirkur's path. My fettle untwisted before I found cover again, but neither Mirkur nor the *Plowir Medn* were looking my way— they were too intent on the tree I'd hidden behind.

With a grin, I ran on, not yet turning, wanting to put more distance between myself and Mirkur. I spun another *proo* and flicked its exit ahead of me, using the same method Hel and I had used to increase our speed. When I came out of the *proo*, something felt wrong. Without second-guessing it, I twitched my cloak and disappeared into a cloud of smoke. I glanced behind me. Mirkur had reached the tree and bellowed with rage when I wasn't behind it. He spun, his eyes scouring the forest nearby.

Still out of phase, I created a *proo* and tossed the exit as far away from me as I could, then sprang through it. As I came out of the *proo*, Mirkur screamed again, and I ducked behind another fat ash tree—just in time as it turned out, as the effect of the cloak wore off moments later.

I crouched and peered around the tree, keeping my head low, my body behind the masking mass of the tree trunk.

Mirkur stomped back and forth, kicking at leaves, exploding tree trunks with a wave of his hand, and yelling incoherently at the *Plowir Medn*. The blue men began to chant, and with that disgusting wet pop, they teleported away—one by one.

I turned and sprinted away, keeping the tree between Mirkur and me. I gazed into the woods, looking for a place to put a *proo*. A *Plowir Medn* appeared in front of me, facing away, but I had no time to react, and I bowled him over, barely keeping my feet.

He cried out in that slippery language of the blue men.

Without waiting, I formed the *proo* and hurled it as deep into the shadows created by the trees as I could and stepped through it. I closed it and triggered my cloak.

This won't work forever! I had to come up with something besides running, ducking behind trees, and teleporting away. I could leave the Conflux, but without my family and friends, that wasn't going to happen.

Then it hit me.

With a feral grin burning on my lips, I turned and stared at the *Plowir Medn* I'd sent sprawling a moment before. They were short, much shorter than I was, but they didn't wear uniforms, which made it easier. Under my breath, I chanted the *doppelgänger triblinkr* from my grimoire—the one that let me adopt the form of another—while staring at the blue-skinned creature.

The *prayteenk* whipped through me, wreaking havoc on my systems. My bones ached with the speed of it, and my muscles shrieked in agony. When it finished, my clothes hung off me like a clown suit, and I had to grab the gun belt to keep it from ringing my ankles.

I squatted and rolled my pants legs up to keep them from tripping me. The cloak would have to trail out behind me, and the mail shirt would flap around like a tent around a toothpick, but there was nothing I could do about that either. The hat was the worst—it tried to slide down over my face every other nanosecond…but then I recalled what it was for, and let it happen, squeezing my good eye shut and enjoying the three-hundred-sixty-degree vision Althyof had enchanted into it.

I stepped out from behind the tree, hand on Kunknir's butt, but left the pistol in the holster. This was the test, and if it didn't fool the other blue man, I could draw and shoot in no time flat.

The little guy I'd knocked down sat on the forest floor, legs splayed, arms supporting his torso, shaking his head as if to clear it. His gaze swam past me and came rolling back, but no alarm flashed in his eyes, though he cocked his head to the side. He warbled something at me, and I shrugged, turning my back and walking away into the forest.

He called something at my retreating back, and I waved a hand as if I were too busy to talk to him. I fought the urge to look over my shoulder, knowing it would look suspicious. I walked on with the muscles between my shoulder blades twitching.

When I did look, the *Plowir Medn* had disappeared. I grinned and kept walking, trying to look as if I owned the place and had every right to be there.

Fatigue scratched away at my mind and seared my muscles, but I kept walking farther into the forest. I no longer heard Mirkur and saw fewer and fewer blue-skinned men and women. At the same time, I had no idea where my friends were, no idea which way to run.

I stopped and spent a few moments resting, trying to gain my bearings, and trying to decide what to do next. While I stood there, the soft, wet pop of dislocating joints sounded behind me. I turned to see a *Plowir Medn* female standing there gazing at me with suspicion.

She trilled something at me in a piping voice— something that felt like three thousand slugs wiggling in my ear canals—and stared at me, the expectation of my immediate compliance showing in the lines of her face, her eyes.

My hand fell to the butt of Kunknir, and her eyes followed the movement. When her gaze returned to mine, her eyes burned with amazement and mischief, in equal proportion. I could shoot her, but the noise would carry in the forest, and I had no idea if I could kill her before she alerted another of her kind. Despair swam in my blood, and a cold lethargy stole over me.

She spoke again, cocking her head to the side. She pointed at Kunknir and cackled, then held out her hand as if she expected me to give it to her.

I looked at her palm before meeting her gaze again, seeing only iron in her eyes.

She snapped her fingers impatiently.

I glanced around, hoping to see Yowtgayrr or Skowvithr materializing close by, but we appeared to be alone.

She snapped her fingers again and barked something that sounded imperious and impatient.

What can I do? If she thinks I'm handing over my weapon... I took my hand off the pistol and lifted it, palm out, shaking my head.

She made a face and stomped a tiny blue foot.

Too late for the proo *trick... A* kaltrar? I racked my mind for something appropriate, but all that came to mind was the *triblinkr* that would release me from this form.

A triblinkr! I thought. *I could bind her!* The only problem was that I only knew a few basic *triblinkr* and the ones I'd read in the grimoire—well, the ones I recalled from that reading anyway—

A familiar, yet unrecognizable, voice entered my thoughts, reciting words with a harsh insistence, and along with the sound, the vision of golden runes flashed through my mind. I listened a moment and smiled.

The little blue woman stepped back, fear showing in her face. She held her hands up as if to ward me off.

I chanted the *triblinkr* aloud, unable to keep the smile from my face. *It's perfect!*

She stumbled back as the effect of the *triblinkr* took hold. Her eyes widened and took on a wild cast. Her head darted this way and that as if to listen to sounds only she could hear. Her eyes snapped back to mine, and the smile on my face melted away as I realized what the full force of the *triblinkr* did.

Her eyes shone with anguish and insanity.

She turned and ran off through the woods, cackling or crying to herself in fits and starts.

I wanted to take it back, to remove the curse of insanity laid on the woman by my *triblinkr*, but if I did that, she would report my position to the others or turn on me with violence. Either way, my hard-won concealment would end, and if that happened…all would be lost.

I turned and ran the other way. Once I was deep enough into the woods, I chanted the *triblinkr* that would reverse my *Plowir Medn* disguise, not able to stand wearing that blue skin anymore. It felt…greasy, wrong.

As the *prayteenk* wound down, an emotionless exhaustion overcame me. I wanted to sit down, to lie down, to take a nap. As insidious as depression, a delicate debility drove me to my knees. Gasping like a beached fish, failing to fight the feeble feeling.

I kept moving, walking on my knees until the strange lethargy drove me to drop my hands to the forest's loam and continue on all fours. Lifting my hands to move them forward felt more and more like lifting large blocks of stone, and I gave up on raising my knees altogether—sliding them through the loose top soil like an infant learning to crawl. My head lolled, hanging down between my arms. The asthenia reminded me of the time we spent riding through the Great Forest of Suel while Ivalti tried to sing us all to sleep.

Anger ripped through me, and I lifted a hand smeared with dark dirt and slapped myself. The sharp, stinging slap had almost no impact on my sluggish thought processes.

Jane had been trapped with me back there in Suel's malignant forest. Maybe she would get away unscathed this time.

I crawled with my eye closed, my mind drifted like silt in a slow-moving river, and I snapped my eye open. I was lying on my back, staring up at the trees, with no memory of stopping to rest or of turning over on my back like an up-ended turtle. All the colors had drained from the world. The parts of the sky I could see through the canopy of the trees darkened as if night were falling. I considered pushing myself up to my feet, or at least rolling over and hiding my face from whatever was coming, but all that seemed like too much effort, and I closed my eye again, instead.

Moments later, I lost consciousness.

FIFTY-ONE

I soared high above the carpet of ash boughs that stretched as far as I could see in every direction. I let loose a mighty crrruck. No sound came back—not even my own voice echoed through the thick, cold air. The whole world lay still as if I flew through a massive Polaroid picture, rather than an actual place.

I turned this way and that without conscious thought, enjoying the cold wind that ruffled through my feathers. The wind seemed inexhaustible, and it required almost no effort on my part to keep myself aloft.

I flew and flew, gazing down at the verdant scenery, the unbroken carpet of lush greenery. Occasionally, I looked around for a white speck, a white-feathered companion. Where are you, Kuhntul*?*

I flew and flew, scouring the world for any other living thing, for any sign of life, other than the incessant ash trees.

After an interminable time of flying toward a horizon devoid of detail, a bump lunged toward the sky. I turned toward the lump, assuming it must be a mountain.

It wasn't a mountain though. It was a tree. A huge tree that towered above the forest below it.

Wait a minute... *I thought.* That's...that's... Iktrasitl*!*

The cold, calm air disappeared, replaced by hot, violent updrafts that carried a vile black smoke heavenward. Midnight-violet clouds rolled in from the horizons, traveling at speeds no natural cloud could attain, slamming over my head like the door to a prison cell.

A hot wind blew in my face, and no matter how fast or how hard I beat my wings, my forward progress diminished until maintaining altitude grew difficult. Gone was the verdant carpet of tree boughs—a sea of smoldering tree trunks, acrid smoke, and desolation had replaced them.

Something below me hissed, and the sound poured dread into my soul. The sound came at such volume it seemed to issue from the planet itself, but my fearful glance showed me a pair of blistering, acrimonious orange-red eyes.

I struggled on toward the World Tree, toward the heart of the Conflux, trying to not think of how big the thing below me must be to have eyes the size of Volkswagen Beetles. The monstrosity below me hissed again, and I felt the vibration of the sound in the bones that supported my wings.

I was afraid to look at the thing again, and yet my eyes seemed drawn to it. Details emerged as it moved—shadowy viridian scales wrapped a big tubular body bereft of arms, legs, or wings. The dragon opened its hinged jaw revealing a mouth full of sharp, blade-like teeth and ebony velvet skin. It hissed, and its long tongue snaked forth and licked the air.

I forced my gaze away, back toward the massive tree I was fighting to reach. Open flames licked the land below me like a lover's caress. Smoke and soot swirled in the updrafts, and with a crash of lightning, it began to rain.

The water rolled off my feathered back, leaving an oily, stinky residue. As the rain continued to fall, I grew heavy with the oily gunk, and my flight became erratic, labored. My breast hurt with the effort of flapping my wings, of fighting the weight and wind, but the dragon kept pace below me, hissing and hissing.

Iktrasitl loomed closer, clothed in darkness. Tindur! Tindur will help me fight this thing below me. Tindur and Ratatoskr! Even as I thought it, I *knew it for false hope. There was no fighting the* lidnormr *that followed my flight from below. I struggled to maintain altitude, struggled to stay aloft, and fought my way toward the great ash tree.*

I'd almost reached it when something fell on me from above, wrenching my wings toward the sky, burying hot talons into the muscles of my back. I screamed as we plummeted toward the gaping maw of the dragon below.

FIFTY-TWO

When consciousness returned, I discovered someone had trussed me up as if I were a turkey about to go in the oven. My cloak lay on the ground beside me as did my hat and gun belt. My shoulders burned with agony, and my joints shrieked with the pain of my forced position and my dark, ever-present curse.

"The small one wakes," said Owraythu in a cold voice.

"Good. This one has business with him. He owes this one something." I tried not to look, but it was as if my eye had a mind of its own and my gaze snaked up from the ground and traversed Mirkur's glossy black form to where his eyes should have been. Owraythu stepped to his side and whispered something.

I tore my eye away from them and scanned the surroundings. We were back in the glade, and the surrounding forest simmered with small fires. Jane lay on the ground a few paces away, looking pale and drawn, with no sign of the cadmium red healing aura, but also no overt signs of traumatic injuries. They had dumped Sig in a heap beside her, unconscious but appearing unhurt. Krowkr lay a distance away, like a toy cast aside.

My gaze drifted around the glade, picking out the unconscious forms of my companions, all unconscious, most injured. All except the Alfar, the puppies, Hel, and Luka.

Oh, and Kuhntul was *still* missing.

Plowir Medn stood in a vast ring around us, placid and arcadian, some smiling, some looking bored. At least their hideous chanting had stopped.

I flopped around until I could roll into a sitting position, forced to lean forward awkwardly due to the tight bindings that held my hands behind my back. "Look," I said, addressing the ground between my knees, "This is unnecessary. We—"

"Cease," snapped Owraythu.

"Halt discourse," said Mirkur.

"Yield," said Owraythu.

I repressed a shout of frustration and sighed instead. Twisting my wrists, I tested the bindings that held me—they were tight, and only got tighter as I moved.

The two *Plauinn* continued to whisper, glancing at me once in a while.

"What is it you want? What do you *really* want?" I asked, irritation edging my voice with a harsh overtone.

"Where is she?" asked Owraythu.

"Who?"

She scoffed and stomped her foot. "You know the one I seek!"

"Well, I've been dreaming about a big ugly snake, so I can't tell you anything." I glanced at Mirkur. "That was a dirty trick, by the way. Not very sporting…knocking us all out the way you did."

A small smile wrinkled his shiny black face.

"I wonder if—"

An ear-splitting scream cut me off. It came from the trees outside the circle of *Plowir Medn*, and as one, they turned their tiny blue faces to the forest. Something crashed in the shadows, and the ones closest to the sound took up defensive postures.

Hel? Luka? I wondered.

Then she stepped out of the forest, naked and covered in bruises and abrasions. Her blue skin looked dull and dusky. Her eyes spun and danced like things gone wild, and when she saw the *Plauinn,* she screeched like a cat in heat and raised her clawed hands.

It was the *Plowir Medn* woman I'd driven insane back in the forest. My guts grew heavy, and my heart sank to see what the *triblinkr* had wrought in her. Beyond reason, beyond rational discourse, she charged at Owraythu, hands raised, teeth bared.

I couldn't stand it. Enemy or not, I'd done this to her. I had to set things right. I murmured the beginning of the *triblinkr* I'd used to drive her insane, lifting the curse.

Mirkur's head snapped toward me at the first syllable. He lifted his hand and pointed at me. "Cease!" he commanded.

I shook my head and continued mumbling the words.

"Then suffer," he sneered. He made a jerking hand motion and pain erupted from my guts as though he'd driven a massive fish hook through my abdomen and jerked.

I screamed, but continued the *triblinkr* through the pain, through the screaming. At the end of it, I only screamed.

The insane blue woman stopped her charge and stood up straight, glancing around in confusion. Owraythu glared at her, menace vibrating the air between them. She said something in the spidery language of the *Plowir Medn*, and the blue woman had time to shriek before she imploded to a dot the size of a penny before disappearing completely.

Agony ripped through me like a forest fire, and I rolled to my back, ignoring the burning, screaming pain in my arms and shoulders. What I saw was almost enough to distract me from the pain.

A white streak descended from the top of Iktrasitl. It was like watching a bolt of lightning arc to the ground in slow motion. Neither the *Plauinn* nor the *Plowir Medn* noticed.

Not until it was too late.

As the streak neared the ground, I made out the details: white wings that mirrored the raven-colored wings Jane called up at will, streaming white hair and white clothing, and a golden-white sword that seemed to hold the light of a sun at its tip.

Kuhntul.

She dropped behind Owraythu, her feet making almost no sound as she landed. She swung the sword tipped with brilliance as a golfer might, and the blade dug a furrow through the earth.

No, through Owraythu's *slowth*. As the leading edge of the blinding blade sliced into the massive *slowth*, Owraythu screamed at eardrum-piercing volume, and it was unlike any scream I'd ever heard. As the terrible edge continued on its path, Owraythu froze in mid-motion, her mouth open, her tongue arched with the force of her scream. The blade arced on its inexorable course, and Owraythu began to disintegrate, starting from the smallest parts of her human form—finger tips, toes, tip of the nose, and ear lobes.

Mirkur cried out and took a step toward Kuhntul, but the *Plowir Medn* uttered three harsh syllables while staring at Owraythu with horror-struck expressions, and with the horrible popping noise, they all disappeared, Mirkur included.

The sword continued its cut and Owraythu continued to fade from existence.

When it was all over, Kuhntul stood alone, staring at me with eyes that glistened with tears. "It is done," she whispered.

"Is she... Can she come back?" I asked.

Kuhntul shook her head and glanced down at the brilliant sword she held. The blade glowed with sunlight, and with something more, with a power that shimmered along its surface like molten gold. The hilt was wrought from platinum and gold and looked familiar, though I couldn't place it. "She will never come back," the Tisir whispered. "Even now, her matterstream manifestation is de-coalescing, losing cohesion."

"You... That cut... You mean you've killed her?"

Kuhntul's gaze swam back to my own, and there was pain in her eyes. She swallowed and closed her eyes. "Yes."

"I...I didn't know a *slowth* could be severed in that manner," I murmured.

"It can't—not by normal means." Kuhntul glanced down at the somehow-familiar sword again. She shook it, as if to shake off the blood, then slammed it into a sheath at her waist I'd never noticed before, but which looked as if it shouldn't—*couldn't*—be anywhere else.

I swallowed and rolled to my knees. "What about…" I jerked my hands, causing shooting pains to tear through my shoulders. "Could you?" I asked.

She came to my side and cut the ropes holding me, but she used a dagger instead of the beautiful sword.

"Thank you." I glanced at where Mirkur had been. "What about him?"

She shook her head. "With beings as powerful as *Plauinn*, I must strike when they are unaware. I had to choose…" She shook her head as though to fling away the memory of what she'd done. "I chose Owraythu for…personal reasons."

"Personal reasons?"

She stared at me but said nothing for the space of ten breaths. She glanced away and said, "I could not kill them both. Mirkur lives, but as with most beings in the underverse, he can't come here at will—to travel as a dreamslice reflection. The *Plowir Medn* are his only avenue to this place, and they won't risk him—"

"Wait, they couldn't come here on their own? How did—"

"The *Plowir Medn* brought them. And they took their 'Dark Lord' away from danger. They don't know that I must strike from stealth to kill a *Plauinn* this way."

"Won't he tell them?"

Kuhntul shook her head. "They are very stubborn, the *Plowir Medn*. Set in their beliefs, and as long as they believe he is in mortal danger, they will not bring him back. Besides, to them, Mirkur is a god, and he won't want to lessen their belief in his omnipotence. He'll spin a tale that I merely caused Owraythu to return to the underverse or some such lie."

"So, it's finished? We're safe?" The way she looked at me made me feel as though I was about four years old. And stupid, at that. "Of course not," I sighed. "How do we fight him?"

Kuhntul dropped her head, shielding her face with her long white locks.

Hel and Luka stepped from the forest, hand in hand. They'd both reverted to the bodies they'd been born in, and neither of them bore any wounds—of course not, they'd already healed with the massive regenerative powers of the *oolfa*.

I heard puppies yipping, and two *varkr* pups appeared mid-leap, tails up and wagging as they sprinted over to lick my face. After a heartbeat of that, they turned and went to minister to Jane and Sig.

Yowtgayrr and Skowvithr became visible on the other side of the glade, but instead of smiles, each Alf's face was a study of concern, wariness. Their eyes were on Hel as she strode toward us, swishing her hips and smiling.

"Thank you, Tisir, for ridding the universe of that bitch," she said.

I shook my head. The humility, the friendliness, the gratitude, that Hel had shown as we fled from Owraythu seemed forgotten, and the sneering tones and expressions of the Dark Queen were back in place. Luka stood on her right side and a step behind her.

The others stirred, each waking from whatever nightmare Mirkur had sown within them. Veethar sat up and glanced at the forest. A long sigh escaped his lips, and he shook his head at the destruction Owraythu and Mirkur had wrought. He turned my way. "I dreamed about your *lidnormr*, Hank."

"You, too?"

Hel's sneer transformed into a nasty grin, and I didn't like it. Not at all.

"Hank," she said. "Do you remember what we discussed up on Iktrasitl's branch?"

I grimaced but nodded. "Yeah. We discussed healing Osgarthr." I shrugged. "Sort of."

"You asked who will lead the Isir, and I said we would decide it as such things have always has been decided."

I scoffed and looked down at the ground beneath me.

"You asked me if there hadn't been enough war among the Isir."

"Yes, and there has!" I snapped. "Somehow, I don't think you see it that way."

Behind Hel, Luka growled and glowered at me, but Hel chuckled. "It's okay, my Champion. Some men cannot be broken of their bad habits. You must make allowances…for those who may join you."

"Never! I will never join the *Briethralak Oolfur*!"

Hel shrugged. "It's not a *requirement*, mind you. But, I do agree with you. There has been enough war."

"And?"

She shrugged again. "I am the queen of Osgarthr."

Veethar made a furious sound in his throat.

"You know it's true, Veethar!" snapped Luka. "Without my brother's treachery—"

Veethar surged to his feet, his spinning, blazing eyes gone yellow. "Did Meuhlnir kill Paltr? Huthr?"

Luka growled deep in his throat. "Watch what you say to me."

"Gentlemen," said Hel. Her voice was light, but it carried the cold steel of command. "Hank and I are talking." She raised an eyebrow at me. "Well, Hank? Do you agree?"

"Why don't you remove your curse and ask him again," croaked Jane.

"Ah, Jane," said Hel with a rigid smile forced on her lips. "Isn't it wonderful you are awake?"

"Remove it. Remove your damn curse!"

Hel scoffed and sneered, "What curse is that?"

Jane forced herself up, arms still pressing into her sides, wincing and hissing at the pain. "You know the one."

Hel rolled her eyes and turned her gaze to mine. "I have been known to reward new...uh, *supporters*. Are you such a one, Hank?"

I chuckled at that but didn't answer. "Why is it that megalomaniacs always want to reward you for going along with their crazy schemes by removing the evil thing they've already done to you?"

"Evil?" Hel laughed, and it sounded genuine. "Oh, Hank, you've seen the *Plauinn*. You know what they wanted of you, of me. Do you believe anything *we* do is good or evil? Such naïve concepts."

I shook my head, a profound, blue melancholy creeping into my heart.

"I read something on your *klith*. It went something like this: 'What would good do if evil didn't exist, and what would the earth look like if all the shadows disappeared? After all, shadows are cast by things and people. Here is the shadow of my sword. But shadows also come from trees and living things. Do you want to strip the earth of all trees and living things just because of your fantasy of enjoying naked light?' That's from *The Master and Margarita*, by a Russian named Bulgakov."

"Never heard him or it. But as long as we're throwing quotes around, here's one of my favorites: 'Words—so innocent and powerless as they are, as standing in a dictionary, how potent for good and evil they become in the hands of one who knows how to combine them.'"

Hel smiled. "I knew him, you know. Hawthorne. Luka did, as well. We considered eating him as he was quite banal in person. Here's a quote from another Russian for you to chew on: 'Nothing is easier than to denounce the evildoer; nothing is more difficult than to understand him.'"

"Dostoevsky, right?"

Hel nodded.

"'The man who refuses to judge, who neither agrees nor disagrees, who declares that there are no absolutes and believes he escapes responsibility, is the man responsible for all the blood that is now spilled in the world.'"

"Ayn Rand," said Hel.

I nodded. "She goes on to say: 'There are two sides to every issue: one is right, and the other is wrong, but the middle is always evil.'"

"'Those who forget good and evil and seek only to know the facts are more likely to achieve good than those who view the world through the distorting medium of their own desires.' That's by an Englishman, Bertrand Russell. I think it is telling—"

"I've got one," said Jane. "'Evil begins when you begin to treat people as things.' Another Englishman, Terry Pratchett. What do you think about that?"

Luka took a step forward. "'The only good is knowledge, and the only evil is ignorance.'"

Hel rested her hand on his forearm and smiled at him. "This gets us nowhere. The only thing we prove here is that many such sayings about good and evil exist. What is your answer, Hank? Do you join your small band of Isir with me and have a part in the governing of Osgarthr? Or do you become my prisoners?"

"I've got one more quote for you," said Jane. "'Have a coke and a smile and shut the fuck up.' Eddie Murphy."

Hel sneered at my wife as I climbed to my feet, gaze darting around the clearing, noting who was awake and ready versus those who could not join a fight. Even with our wounded, we outnumbered Hel and Luka four to one. "One last quote from me as well: 'Remember that all through history, there have been tyrants and murderers, and for a time, they seem invincible. But in the end, they always fall. Always.'"

"Don't quote that pacifist to us!" snapped Luka.

Hel chopped her hand through the air. "So be it," she hissed. Her rational expression dissolved, exposing a maniacal face I recognized from the day she'd laid her curse on me. "Luka and I weren't hiding in the woods. We found an ally—well, I should say he found us and we, uh, *convinced* him to side with us against the *Plauinn*." She smiled at Kuhntul. "But since our friend the Tisir has dispatched the *Plauinn* and tricked the *Plowir Medn* into leaving, we'll use him against you, instead." She waved her hand at the forest. "*If* you make us."

Something moved back in the trees, something scaled in viridian. Something *huge*.

"Allow me to introduce you to my pet dragon."

Trees split and fell to the sides as a massive head shoved its way into the glade. The *lidnormr's* head was the size of a commercial jetliner from Mithgarthr. It opened its mouth, exposing horrible fangs three rows deep, and roared.

The sound was deafening, as painful as any physical assault I'd ever suffered. From high above us, came the sound of an eagle's scream.

Hel cast a smug look around the glade. "Well? Have you changed your minds?"

Kuhntul chuckled. The chuckle became a giggle, the giggle became a laugh, the laugh a roar.

"What?" snapped Hel. "Why do you laugh?"

Kuhntul wiped a tear and got her laughing under control. She walked over to the great *lidnormr* and patted its lower lip. She spoke to it, then, in a rasping, sibilant-filled tongue.

When she had finished, the *lidnormr* bobbed its head, making a curious sound that reminded me of a chuckle. With a last look at Hel, the massive head withdrew, and the sound of its retreat through the ash forest followed.

"Where are you going?" Hel raged. "You are *mine*!" She took two long strides toward the edge of the forest.

"Don't waste your breath," said Kuhntul. "You never controlled him. He came at *my* bequest."

Hel whirled, scowling at the Tisir. "Don't think to make a fool of me, witch."

Kuhntul only laughed.

With a shared glance, Hel and Luka backed toward the woods.

"*Kirthing*!" shouted Veethar, and the trees behind Hel wove themselves into a thick fence—a natural stockade wall.

Hel glanced behind her before turning her sneer on Veethar. She pointed at the ruined section of the forest, and she and Luka changed direction.

Kuhntul stepped into their path.

"Stand aside!" roared Luka.

Kuhntul smiled and blew him a kiss.

"One moment, my Queen," said Luka. "*Oolfur*!"

"No, I don't think you will have all the fun. Besides, I don't like this Tisir. She reminds me of someone I dislike. *Byarnteer*!"

I glanced down at my hat, cloak, and gun belt. I had only one magazine for Kunknir loaded, and one magazine might as well be a handful of spitballs against two *oolfa*. *Why does she always force a fight*? I wondered bitterly.

Kuhntul watched their *prayteenk* in silence, looking almost bored. At the last moment, Kuhntul drew her bright sword and held it by her side in a loose fist. A dragon twisted down the length of the blade, plated in a bluish metal.

Hel's eyes went wide at the sight of the blade, and she stumbled backward, even as the *prayteenk* finished. She roared, but whether in anger or warning, I couldn't tell.

Luka stepped between the Black Bitch and the Tisir, growling and baring his teeth. My choices were limited. I could take a backseat and let others fight this out in my stead, I could start my own *prayteenk* by chanting the Kuthbyuhrn *triblinkr*, I could reload and fight with my pistols, but what I really needed was a way to *avoid* this battle—for everyone involved. I considered the *triblinkr* I'd used on the *Plowir Medn* woman, but two insane *oolfa* seemed like a step in the *wrong* direction.

What else can I do? What other tricks did that grimoire give me? I reviewed the other triblinkr I understood from the grimoire in my mind. *Splitting my consciousness won't help, and both Luka and Hel have already seen that trick—I need something new. Maybe I could raise Owraythu from the dead, but that sounds like a terrible idea. That only leaves the field manipulation trick, but how could manipulating molecules help here?* I shook my head. When I'd carried Luka into his own memories, I'd been touching him when I dipped into his *slowth*. That had seemed to immobilize him in the matterstream.

I glanced down and found Luka's *slowth*—it was as easy for me to spot now as my own son's. I stared at it, willing myself to discover more detail about how it worked, how it formed in the first place.

Keri and Fretyi growled by my side, watching Luka with obvious distrust and dislike. He took a step toward Kuhntul, and she lifted her blade.

"I wouldn't enjoy killing you, my—Isir. But I will if you force my hand," she said.

The puppies took two stiff-legged steps forward, and Luka glanced at them and growled.

There must be something I can do to stop this battle! Think, you jackass!

"*Syow tyoopt*," I murmured, enchanting my vision as I had back in Niflhaymr, and returned my gaze to Luka's *slowth*. I stared at it, willing myself to see the unseen, to understand how I could use the *slowthar*.

Bending over Luka's *slowth*, I peered at something that seemed to flicker around the edges of it. I glanced at where the *slowth* met Luka's physical form. There the *slowth* branched like the roots of a tree and dug into his body. The strange flickering was there, too.

I didn't remember ever seeing anything like that before. I glanced over at the shriveled end of Owraythu's *slowth*—or the *slowth of her dreamslice reflection*! *That's it!*

I focused on my *slowth* and followed it backward through time, back to the *Herperty af Roostum*, and the moment when I'd pulled Luka into his own memories. I peered at his *slowth* and my own, straining to see a difference in them when we traveled to the dreamslice.

As we sank into the dreamslice, our *slowthar* changed. For each of us, that flickering, ghost-image of our *slowthar* separated from the plainly visible part. In Luka's case, the ghost-image created a loop while we were in his memories, and it leapt over to my *slowth* when I took him to Owraythu's realm. For me, the reverse was true.

That's it! I loop their dreamslice slowth back onto their matterstream slowth! *But how do I keep them there?*

Luka snarled at Kuhntul, neither of them giving or gaining an inch. Behind Luka, Hel stood glaring at me. She made a peculiar combination of a grunt and chuff and took a step closer to Luka.

I imagined grabbing his dreamslice *slowth* the same way I caught the hook of a *proo*, and it lifted away from his matterstream *slowth*.

Hel roared, and I heard her pounding toward me.

"No," said Kuhntul in an almost conversational tone.

The air pinged as if a massive chime had been struck, and a ragged black tear streaked past me. In my enchanted vision, it looked like a gigantic fist made from black smoke. Hel yelped, tumbling head over heels like a leaf in the wind and crashed into the fence of living trees Veethar had created earlier.

I glanced down at Luka's dreamslice *slowth* in my invisible hand and looped it back to his matterstream *slowth*. I plunged it deep inside and held it.

Luka froze mid-snarl and collapsed to the ground as if in a coma.

From where she lay by the trees, Hel roared—an angry, mournful sound.

Kuhntul glanced at me, then back at Luka. "Can you hold him?"

I nodded.

She walked over to where Hel lay and pointed her brilliant blade at the Dark Queen.

I chanted the *triblinkr* that would slow molecules almost to the point of stopping their electrons in their orbits and confined the field to the area where I'd looped Luka's dreamslice *slowth*. I released his *slowth* and withdrew my invisible arm, watching Luka's comatose form for any signs that he awakened. He didn't so much as twitch. I glanced back at his *slowth,* and everything seemed to hold.

I turned and looked at Hel, and she made the most peculiar choking grunt—as though bears could sob. I repeated the process on her *slowth.* "It's okay," I said. "I've got them, now."

Kuhntul walked to my side. "Shall we kill them?" she asked. Something in her voice gave me pause—as if this were a test.

I shook my head. "No, they can't hurt anyone from where they are. I trapped them in their own memories."

Mothi came to stand next to me. "That's fitting."

"What do we do with them?" asked Yowrnsaxa, sounding as sad as anyone I'd ever met.

"That depends on the answers to a few other questions—answers that must be decided by everyone."

"We can't let things go on as they have."

"No," I said. "Osgarthr needs a resolution to this mess. The Isir need to come together as a people, to progress, to do more than survive."

"We need a Thing," said Sif.

"One of those meetings you used to hold?" asked Sig.

"Yes. Every Isir has the right to speak and gets to vote on the solution."

"Sounds like a real pain to organize," said Jane.

Yowrnsaxa shrugged listlessly. "It's our way, and it's not as bad as it sounds, not with the *preer* open again."

"I'm not sure they are safe," I said. "The *Plauinn* can watch the *preer* that Haymtatlr manages."

"Not the *preer* you and I can make," said Kuhntul. "With help, we can recreate the required *preer*."

I nodded, feeling exhausted already. "I thought as much. How long will it take for us to create all those *preer*?"

Kuhntul shrugged. "I can teach the others to create them, but you or I will have to position them."

I glanced around at the devastation, at my injured wife and friends. My gaze came to rest on Kuhntul. "What happens to this place? To Tindur, Ratatoskr, and the dragon? To the Nornir?"

She shrugged. "The Nornir are a problem we will have to address. They can be manipulative bitches, and with Mirkur still on the loose, we can expect interference with *uhrluhk* all over the place. As for the forest, it will regrow. The others are fine, and will no doubt resume their shenanigans when they feel up to it."

I shook my head. "Who the hell are you, Kuhntul?"

She cocked her head at me, her lips twitching with a suppressed grin. "I am Kuhntul, of the Tisir."

"Yeah." I turned to Althyof. "Did you watch what I did to Hel and Luka?"

He shrugged and glanced away. "I heard the *triblinkr*."

"Could I use it in an enchantment?"

"I could help you with that, but you'd be the one to do it. That *triblinkr* isn't for anyone else."

"I know. I'm not ready, anyway. I have to figure out how to grab a *slowth* either as a *runeskowld* or with *saytr* and then work that in."

"Yes, well, I can't help you with that."

I nodded. "Kuhntul?"

"I will think on it," she said, sheathing her sword.

"That sword—"

"We can discuss that later," she said hastily. "Let's see to the wounded and get these two secured in case your method fails."

I gazed at her for a moment and decided to let it slide. "Where are the Nornir?"

Kuhntul turned and surveyed the forest. "They are still here…somewhere. Hiding, no doubt."

I gazed into the forest but saw only shadows and tree trunks. "I need to speak to them."

Kuhntul's gaze found my face, and she raised an eyebrow. "To what end?"

"Things around here have to change." I nodded my head toward Iktrasitl.

Kuhntul nodded and returned her gaze to the forest. "If I can make a suggestion, it would be better if you spoke to them after your Thing."

"Why?" I asked.

"If your commands carry the weight of the Isir, the Three Maids may be easier to influence than if you speak to them as a man alone."

"I guess you're right. I'll present the idea to the others, get their agreement."

"Plus, the time will give them a chance to get over their fear."

"If you say so." I opened a *proo* and sent the exit back to the cafeteria room at the *Herperty af Roostum*. One by one my companions used the *proo*, until only Hel, Luka, Kuhntul, and I remained.

"Thank you for not pressing me about the sword," she said.

"We will speak of it again."

"Of course, but in private."

"Fair enough," I said. "Let me try to take Luka through. If it works, I'll come back for Hel. I'd prefer you cross first, in case Luka comes through awake."

She treated me to a curt nod and stepped through.

Alone with my comatose prisoners, I sighed. "You couldn't do it, could you?" I asked Hel's unconscious form in a bone-weary voice. "You couldn't resist the power."

I bent to look at which memory she was looping through...

FIFTY-THREE

The queen's guard captain raced into the room. "Pardon me, your Grace, but the rebels have driven our forces all the way back to the palace gates. They've brought siege weapons and are preparing to assault us."

"And? Marshall your forces!" roared Luka.

"Yes, m'lord!"

Luka glared at the man until he had backed all the way out of the room, then turned to Hel and flashed a brave smile. "Don't worry, my Queen. This is but a minor setback. We will drive these rebels from the city and repair the gates." He tilted his head to the side. "Is it time to reconsider attacking my brother directly?"

"But Vuhluntr has stolen our weapon. Kramr." Hel shook her head, an almost overwhelming depression dragging her down. "Perhaps it is time to reconsider things," she murmured.

"Don't take it to heart, my Queen. Let me—"

"Have you…" Hel shook her head.

"I am yours, and if I know an answer you need, my Queen, you need but to ask."

She slid to the edge of her throne and glanced around at the courtiers, what was left of her cadre of *Trohtninkar Tumuhr*, and the various hangers-on that always seemed to be within earshot. "Come with me, Luka."

She led him to her private rooms, dismissing the attendants and her *Trohtninkar Tumuhr*. When they were alone, she turned to face him and sat on a low divan. "Luka… My Champion, has anyone ever… Has…" She knotted her hands in her lap.

Luka dropped to one knee before her. He stretched out a long, graceful arm and touched the back of one hand. "Anything, my Queen. Ask."

"Has anyone come to you, perhaps on a dark night, or…or…or in a dream, maybe? Has anyone told you events, behaviors to watch for? Things your brother might do, for instance?"

Luka's face worked through a series of emotions, from fear to anger to shame. "There has been one…person."

"And has he—"

"She."

Hel had suspected as much. "Has she told you things that will happen and told you what do about it?"

Luka swallowed convulsively. "Yes," he whispered. "That has happened many times."

Hel slid forward and put her hand on his cheek. "And…and was she always right?"

Luka nodded, his eyes never leaving her own.

Hel turned to the side and dashed at the tears welling in her eyes.

"My Queen!" said Luka, his voice filled with sympathetic anguish. "Tell me what's wrong!"

"It's…It's all been…" She shook her head. "All of this—all the fighting, all the hate—it's been for nothing. *Nothing*!"

Luka shook his head, his expression cluttered by emotions and confusion.

"They *lied* to us, Luka. That woman who came to you, she *manipulated* you to do what she wanted."

Luka shook his head. "No. My brother and his ilk—"

"No, my Champion, it's true. The same was done to me. Voices…" Her hand circled aimlessly in the air next to her ear. "They speak to me, tell me things about our erstwhile friends, onetime family. They…they *preach* to me about philosophies of government…of…of—"

His hands gripped hers. "It is no matter, my Queen. None of it matters," he crooned.

"No, Luka! It matters because they *lie* to us! They consciously mislead us, manipulate us! They have a plan for us—for the universe, I don't know—and it is full of darkness, of pain!"

Luka pulled his head back and stared into her eyes. "I am yours to command, my Queen—right or wrong. But tell me, who has convinced you that these…beings tell us lies?"

Hel's gaze darted to Luka's face for a heartbeat and then away. "A Tisir who swore me to secrecy, but it doesn't matter. I've examined the claims, and I find them truthful."

"Okay," he said.

She marveled at his ability to accept anything she said as fact.

"What do we do?"

She shook her head. "I don't think there's a way we can mend this…"

Luka shrugged and looked away into the shadows.

"My empire must fall to dust. If we… If we win this war with your brother and his followers, it will result in his death—in the deaths of all of them that matter. *Uhrluhk*, you understand?"

Luka lifted his shoulders and let them drop with a sigh. "If he must die for your happiness—"

"No! Luka, listen. If he dies, if they die…if we are victorious, within a century this world will become a place of nightmares." She shook her head. "I began this war filled with pride, with anger at the thought that these people…the people I loved…betrayed me at every opportunity. I didn't see that my actions, that—"

"Shh, my Queen. Shh. There is no point in—"

"But we can't go on! We can't continue fighting this war!"

He nodded. "That's why we retreated to Suelhaym. That's why we've locked ourselves inside the palace and waited."

"Yes," she whispered.

"That's why you've resisted the advice of our generals, of Vowli...even mine."

She nodded. "Yes."

"That's why you've grown...distant, bitter."

"Yes."

Luka smiled at her. "In that case, our path is clear."

"It...it is?"

"Yes, my Queen. Let's leave this place. Let Meuhlnir choke on the responsibility of ruling Osgarthr. Let him suffer the thankless courtiers, the greedy merchants. Let him deal with the headaches."

"But..."

"No buts, my Queen. You don't owe a thing to any of your subjects that you haven't given them ten times over. Meuhlnir thinks he knows what's right? What's proper? Fine. Let him do it, then."

Hel turned and locked her eyes on his. "But a queen who...who *abdicates* her throne..."

"Who cares what others think? Let them tell you to your face...and if they do, I'll be standing next to you, and it will be the last thing they ever say!"

She smiled at his ferocity. "How is it you always know what to say to me?"

He smiled, but the passion of the previous moment still burned in his eyes. "I only speak from the heart, my Queen."

"Let's leave this place, my Champion. Let the rebels have it! We will build something better elsewhere!"

"As my Queen desires," said Luka and he bent and kissed the back of her hand. "I'm yours to command. I will take care of you always."

She brushed her fingers through his hair. "I believe you, my Champion." She disengaged from him and stood. "But I'm still the queen of Suelhaym, and we must do something about that before we are free."

He nodded. "Command me, my Queen."

"Yes," she said. She turned and led Luka back into the throne room and ascended the dais. "Attend me," she said. "All my forces are to disarm, and then, it is my wish that the palace gates be thrown open."

Gasps and exclamations filled the throne room.

Sadly, Suel nodded. "The rebels have won. I abdicate as of this moment." The queen put her hands on the arms of her ornate throne and sank into it. "Find Meuhlnir, if he lives, and bring him and whomever he chooses before me."

Silence filled the room, and the eyes of the gawking courtiers alighted on her face like moths, like mosquitoes. "Do it!" she snapped. "I surrender. Let this stupid war end here, now!"

FIFTY-FOUR

ater that evening, Jane and I lay next to each other in the same room we'd slept in on our first visit to the *Herperty af Roostum*. Her ribs and back had healed nicely, thanks to the ring Althyof had enchanted for her.

"You can go home," I said softly.

"What?" she asked from the edge of sleep.

"The *preer*. You can go home. With Sig."

With a groan, she sat up and peered at me in the near darkness. "And you?"

I lifted a hand and let it fall back to the bed. "I... The *Plauinn*—"

"You can't leave, not while the threat exists."

"No," I said. "I'm sorry, Supergirl, but I've got to—"

"Of *course* you have to stay. *We* have to stay, to…to *help*." She sighed. "Besides, Osgarthr is a nice place—it's not home—not yet, but it *could* be. And our friends…the Isir, Yowtgayrr, Skowvithr, Althyof…it wouldn't feel right to abandon them. We can't stand by, sticking our heads in the sand back in Penfield, while others fight the coming battle."

I looked up at her. "But our lives back home—"

She put her finger on my lips. "Doesn't this—*all* this—doesn't it seem as though it's meant to be?"

It was a thought that had been circling in my brain for a while, and there was no denying it. "Yes. But 'meant to' doesn't mean 'has to.' I could stay while you and Sig—"

"You're lucky my ribs hurt too much to punch you right now." She said it in a mock-threatening tone, but she laid her hand on my shoulder gently.

"What about Sig's education?"

"Haymtatlr can teach him," she said. "He has access to more facts than all the teachers you can name combined."

"I hadn't considered that."

"That's why you should leave the hard thinking to me. Besides, you're going to need us. If Sif can pull it off, that is."

"What? Why would you say that?"

Jane slid back down into the bed, hissing at the pain it caused.

After she settled down, I waited a minute for her to answer me. "Jane, what do you mean?"

"Shut up; I'm asleep."

"Come on, you can't say something like that and go to sleep!"

It seemed *she* could, but no amount of counting sheep helped *me* to sleep, not after that.

FIFTY-FIVE

Gathering the Isir at the *Herperty af Roostum* took more than a little doing. We set up an assembly line of sorts: Kuhntul, Frikka, Sif, and Yowrnsaxa created the *preer* using Kuhntul's method; I fixed the endpoints, and Meuhlnir and Veethar anchored them in a similar fashion as Veethar's Vault of *Preer* back at his estates.

The goal was to gather *all* the Isir—from those loyal to Meuhlnir and the rebel faction, to those that supported Hel in the war, *including* the *oolfa*. No one thought putting everyone in a room and then trotting in Luka and Hel was a good idea, so we started with a Thing for Meuhlnir's faction. Afterward, the plan was to speak with Hel's followers, with Hel and Luka present, and give them a choice: reunite with Meuhlnir's faction and all would be forgiven, or accept exile in another *klith*, the location of which we would decide in the future.

We held the Thing for Meuhlnir's faction in one of Haymtatlr's empty meeting halls—a grand room that would accommodate ten thousand people if it would accommodate one. We had carried benches and tables in from various estates throughout Osgarthr, and there was more food, mead, ale, and wine than the group could have eaten in ten lifetimes waiting in the kitchens. Behind the three tables pushed together at the end of the room, stood my family and friends.

"*Klyowthstirkidn*," Sif said, putting a hand to her throat and swallowing hard. With a smile at me, she stepped up on the center table. She held up her hands and waited for the assembled Isir to fall silent. "Isir," she said, and her voice boomed to the farthest reaches of the vast chamber. "In the invitations to the Thing, we laid out the reasons for calling it."

No one so much as cleared their throats.

"Years ago, at the end of our war—our rebellion, as some of our friends and family still call it—we made a great mistake. We thought we were resolving things, but we weren't."

A murmur of dissent rattled around the room.

"No," said Sif, holding up her hands. "No, it was a mistake. We thought we could put the queen and her followers out of our minds and they would be content to stay where we put them." She turned and glanced down at me. "As a result, the people of Mithgarthr suffered. Some of them still do."

Again, the hall erupted in hushed conversations and half-voiced denials.

"Hear me!" shouted Sif. "I am Sif, and you know I speak the truth! We made a mistake, but now we can set things right! More importantly, we have a chance to heal, to come together again as a people, to build a future!"

I leaned close to Meuhlnir. "Sounds as though your wife should be the next queen," I whispered in his ear.

He flashed a look of pure shock at me and shook his head.

"We owe this chance to one man!" shouted Sif. "It took one man with the blood of the Isir in his veins, but a man who grew up outside of our folly. An Isir born and raised on Mithgarthr!"

I glanced at John, and he smiled but shook his head. On the table in front of us, Sif turned and pointed at me. I shook my head and held up my hands, palms out.

"Oh yes, Aylootr!" crowed Mothi.

"This one man woke us up from our *troymskrok*—from our pointless dreaming. He breathed life into my family," she said, putting a hand on her chest. "He helped us to see things in a new light." Her gaze traveled to Sig, standing on the other side of Jane, then she turned back to the crowd.

"When was the last time an Isir gave birth?" she demanded. "When was the last child born?"

The hall fell silent except for the rustling of the Isir looking around.

"Years and years and years," said Sif. "When was the last time an Isir did something—*anything*—significant for anyone not on Osgarthr?" Her gaze darted around the room. "When was the last time any of us did something *new*?"

"What is this, Sif?" demanded a voice from a man lost in the crowd. "Why do you berate us?"

Sif shook her head. "No, I don't mean to berate you. I want you to *wake up*!" She shouted the last two words as loudly as she could, the sound crashed through the chamber like a tsunami. "Hank Jensen and his family have suffered because of our negligence, it is true. But we have all suffered because of those decisions we made in Suelhaym! The Isir have suffered, and the time for suffering is at an end!"

Sif again held up her hands to quiet the room. "Thanks to Hank, we have Luka and Hel in our grasp. *Again*." She paused and gazed into the crowd, picking out key faces and locking eyes with them for a moment before moving on again. "We must decide what to do with them, but before we do, we must decide what to do with *us*. Do we go on as we have, dwindling as a race until there are none left? Or do we seize this chance and embrace life again, allow ourselves to heal? There has been enough mourning! Enough fretting about what might have been! How long are we to leave the throne open, to leave things unresolved?"

In the crowd, many heads nodded.

"We need to unite!" said Sif.

More heads nodded, and a countless number cried out in affirmation.

"We need a leader!"

I glanced at Meuhlnir and winked, and he returned my glance quizzically. Jane took my hand and squeezed.

"Do any disagree? Do any believe the half-life we've lived these long centuries is better than the old way?" Sif waited in utter silence for what must have been a minute. "Then, if the old ways are better, we need a leader, and that leader stands among you tonight! That leader who has proven worthy of the honor, of the high office."

"Who?" cried someone in the crowd.

"Yes, tell us!" The crowd picked up the phrase and shouted it from all over the room

Sif held up her hands, and the shouting died down. "This man," she said, pointing at me.

"And who is he?" asked someone up front.

I shook my head and turned to Meuhlnir to protest, but he only smiled and shook his head.

"Hank Jensen, as he was known on Mithgarthr, has earned many names since Hel and Luka tricked him into coming here. You may have heard his names bandied about attached to great deeds and courageous acts. My son dubbed him Aylootr for his prowess in battle and for facing a mighty dragon of the air without fear! Others called him Tyeldnir for the weapons he uses, and Valkyosanti for his abilities to choose who lives and who dies with great accuracy when using them. I have overheard many of you speak of Krimnir, the Hooded One, though he wears that silly hat instead of a hood." After each annoying nickname, a swell of cheering broke out. "And now, I dub him Helpinti—the binder of Hel!"

A cheer went up, and it was deafening. I glanced at Jane, a small frown on my face. She smiled at me and squeezed my hand. I shook my head and opened my mouth, but Jane put her finger over it.

"You see, you've heard of him. He's been here less than a year, yet the stories about him have spread far and wide. Hank came here not knowing anything about Osgarthr or his heritage. He came here knowing nothing of the *strenkir af krafti*. In a short time, he's won allies, not only Isir, but noble Alfar...and even a Tverkr!"

The crowd laughed at that, none louder than Althyof.

"I'll tell you something that the stories about Hank don't," said Sif in a subdued tone. "He suffers daily from a curse laid on him by Hel. His pain is great, and the curse saps his strength every second."

I felt sympathetic eyes on me from all over the hall and blushed. I shook my head in silent protest, then looked up at Sif. "No, Sif. This is wrong. I shouldn't be the leader of the Isir."

"He says: 'I shouldn't be the leader of the Isir.'" Sif shook her head, smiling. "'This is wrong,' he says."

The crowd roared.

I climbed up on the table, ignoring Jane's tugging on my hand. "*Klyowthstirkidn*," I said and felt an uncomfortable pressure on my voice box. "Hear me," I said, and the crowd quieted. "Thank you, Sif, for the kind words, but you make it sound as though I did all these things by myself. Without Meuhlnir, Yowrnsaxa, Mothi, and you, I'd be a popsicle right now—flash-frozen in that *sterk task*, or dead to bandits." She smiled sweetly at me. I turned to the crowd. "In fact, each person behind me has contributed to my survival here on Osgarthr, and I couldn't have done any of this without them. I'm no hero, I'm just a guy who loves his wife and son."

"Do you see?" asked Sif, and again the crowd became a sea of noise.

"Sif, this is wrong. Meuhlnir or Veethar—"

"Will not do," she said. "Ask them."

I turned, but both Isir smiled at me and waved their hands.

"Mothi, then."

"That youngster?" cried Meuhlnir. "Plus, he's grounded!"

Sif repeated his words for the crowd, and everyone laughed. Mothi jumped up on the table and bowed, a huge ear-to-ear grin on his face, but his expression sobered, and he turned to face me.

He cleared his throat and enchanted his own voice. "Aylootr, brave men have surrounded me all my life, and I'd follow you before any of them."

Sif smiled at her son for a moment. "I say Hank Jensen should be named Isakrim—leader of the Isir. Does anyone wish to speak in opposition?"

"I still—"

"Anyone *except* Isakrim?" Sif said with a kind smile, and there was more laughter in the crowd, but no one asked to speak.

"Again, I ask you, does anyone object to this man being named Isakrim, *Konungur* of the Isir?"

The word meant 'king' in the *Gamla Toonkumowl*, but it felt heavy in the air—as a yoke must feel to an ox—and I thought of the conversation Hel and Luka had shared the day she abdicated her throne.

I held up my hands. "I would speak, and as you agree I have Isir blood, it is my right."

Sif nodded and took a step back.

"I did not come to Osgarthr for any purpose other than to free my wife and son. I don't want to be *konungur*, I don't want power. I don't have the answers you need. I know little about your culture, almost nothing about your history."

"Good!" someone shouted in the throng of Isir before me, and a titter ran through the crowd.

I smiled. "Listen, I understand your desire for someone—"

"Enough, Isakrim," said another voice from the crowd. "Your pardon! I meant to say: Konungur Isakrim." More laughter reverberated through the room.

I shook my head and glanced at Jane. She was all smiles as she nodded.

"I don't want to be your king," I said to the gathered Isir. "I don't think I'm suited for it. But, if I'm to do this—"

The crowd cheered.

I waited for them to quiet down and resumed. "But if I do this, you must help me. *And* there will be laws that every Isir must agree to at a Thing. I will need advisors, other leaders—"

"Hank, we know all this. We have a culture built around these concepts," said Sif.

"That may well be, but it never hurts to make everything clear."

"Konungur—" someone yelled.

"And that's another thing. None of this '*konungur*' nonsense. I'm no better than any of you. Call me by my name."

"Very well, *Isakrim*," said Mothi with a grin.

I sighed and glared at Mothi. "That's not what I meant, and you know it."

He flashed a smile, and then to my horror, he knelt in front of me and unsheathed his axes. He laid his axes at my feet. "I am Mothi Strongheart, and my deeds are known and need not be repeated. Let everyone, far and wide, hear my words: I stand by your side, Aylootr, and I will neither flee from your enemies nor stand by while you fight alone. I am Mothi Strongheart, and I stand between you and those who wish you or your family harm. I am Mothi Strongheart, and I do not forget the times you saved me, nor the gifts you've given me, nor the times you graciously didn't shoot me with those noisemakers you carry…or break my legs! I am Mothi Strongheart, and my axes are yours." When he finished speaking, he bowed his head.

I stood there flabbergasted, looking down at the crown of his head.

Meuhlnir took a step forward. "Hank, to accept Mothi into your service, you must give him leave to take up his axes, as by our custom, they belong to you now."

I swallowed past the lump in my throat and nodded. "Mothi Strongheart, I accept your oath. Take up these axes and stand, friend."

Smiling like a great buffoon, Mothi took his weapons and sheathed them before jumping down from the table, and his father stepped up to take his place.

FIFTY-SIX

After the celebratory dinner, I left Jane and Sig getting ready for bed and stepped into one of the rooms guarded by a blue door.

"Haymtatlr?" I asked.

"Yes, Hank?"

"Were you listening to the Thing?"

"Yes. Congratulations, Konungur Isakrim."

I rolled my remaining eye. "Hank is fine."

"What can I do for you, Hank?"

"The first request I have is that you disallow the use of your *preer*, except with my permission. I'll get you a list of people to always allow and others to never allow."

"Consider it done. Anything else?"

"Do you know what a surveillance satellite is?"

"Isi was fond of such things."

That fit with what I knew of the man. "Are Isi's satellites still in orbit?"

"No, Hank. Their orbits decayed long ago."

"I see. You wouldn't have the capability to create more, would you?"

"Child's play."

"Good. And is there some way to, say, drop a satellite into orbit around some other planet, some other *klith*, and monitor that satellite remotely?"

"That's an interesting question. The problem, of course, being the distance to the other planet within the same pocket universe and the relevant transmission times created by such a distance. For satellites in non-homogenous universes that is not a problem, as it would be impossible to maintain synchronicity with such a satellite irrespective of distance."

"What if I created a very tiny *proo* and linked part of the satellite to this place?" I scratched my head and looked around. "By the way, did Isi give this place a name? I'm tired of calling it the *Herperty af Roostum* all the time."

"Rooms of Ruin? That's inaccurate. I maintain this installation with a high degree of efficiency, and—"

"Yes, Haymtatlr, I know. It's what people call it on the outside."

"Oh, well. People should try to be more exacting. Isi called it Valaskyowlf."

"The shelf of the slain? Really?"

"He had a flair for the dramatic. He named it thus after a particularly vicious assault by the Vanir, in which they used trickery to gain entrance and then assaulted the base from the inside, ruining several important experiments. I view this assault in a somewhat different light because it led to my creation."

"How is that?"

"Isi recorded vast arrays of data during the attack. It seems the Vanir had other-worldly allies who wielded great power. They built my first iteration to help analyze the data, but they expanded my abilities many times in the years that followed to reach my current state."

"I see," I said.

"The data analysis inspired Isi to create the Isir in their current form. I have long suspected that the so-called other-worldly invaders were misplaced in time, and not associated with either Vani or Jot."

"Why would you think so?" I lifted a hand to hide my smile.

"Isi's story makes little sense. Why destroy a few robots, kill a general, break up a lab, but leave Isi and his scientists alive and in possession of all that data?"

"Yes, that makes sense."

"Plus, I recognized Jane, Sig, you, and a few of your colleagues when you first arrived."

"Why didn't you say something?"

"And risk creating a paradox that eliminated my creation?"

"Fair point."

"But as to your question: Yes, that would work."

My question? Oh, the tiny preer *for the satellites.* I nodded. "What else would be required?"

"Your suggestion makes everything easier. Each satellite could be connected directly via a fiberoptic cable. Since you can position the necessary *preer* where you need them, the cables could be short, increasing the efficiency."

"Well…great. How long would it take to create the satellites?"

"I've begun the procedures to retool a guardian production line. How many satellites will you need?"

"How about I tell you what I want to do, and you take care of the details?"

"Yes, Hank. I can do that. Isi and I had a similar relationship toward the end."

I wasn't sure how to respond to that. "Well, thanks. I want to check trouble spots, both on Osgarthr and in other realms. I want sufficient precision that I can see individuals, track what they are doing—whether or not they are inside a building. I want *you* to watch certain individuals at all times."

"Hel and Luka," he said.

"Among others, yes."

"Leave it with me."

"Fair enough. Thanks."

"Isi never said thank you. It's nice."

"That's how my mother raised me."

"Must be nice to have a mother."

"Yes. Well… I'd better get to sleep. Tomorrow's going to be a big day."

"Say 'Hi' to Jane for me."

I nodded, wondering how much humanity Haymtatlr had learned to replicate, and how much he'd *learned*.

FIFTY-SEVEN

The next day I stood staring up at Iktrasitl and its living tapestry of runes. Keri and Fretyi sat, one on each side of me, and craned their heads up to look at the tree. I wondered where my runes resided on its bark, and what came next. Behind me stood representatives of the races who had allied with Meuhlnir and those races who had allied with Hel in the war, including the *oolfa* and other Isir from Fankelsi. My council of Isir also stood back there, along with Hel and Luka. The only races not represented were the *Plowir Medn* and the *Plauinn*. Encircling us was the most extensive array of armed men and women I'd ever seen: an army of the Isir who'd sworn allegiance to me the preceding evening. *My* Isir army.

I turned and faced the array of people, and my two *varkr* pups turned with me. "I am Isakrim," I said, "*Konungur* of the Isir." It still felt wrong to say that, but I could hardly pull off what I needed to if I went in all wishy-washy. "The war has ended." I nodded at Hel. "Hel has lost."

She scowled and turned her face away.

"Is it true?" asked Perkelmir, the representative of the frost giants of Niflhaymr. Hel ignored him, suddenly interested in her nails. The giant turned his attention to Luka. "Is it true? This Isakrim has beaten you?"

Luka gazed up into the giant's face, fire dancing in his eyes, but he nodded.

"You serve him now?" demanded the giant.

Luka turned his fiery gaze on me. "I do as my queen chooses. Whatever, wherever, whenever, *Queen* Hel chooses."

I nodded, having expected nothing less from him. "*Queen* Hel is free to choose as she likes," I said, matching Luka's tone. "As are you."

Her head snapped around, and she squinted at me through eyelids narrowed to slits. "Do not mock me!"

I held up my hands, palms up. "No. I don't mock you. You are a queen to your people, and you are due respect." That was the line Sif had suggested we take with her, and I couldn't find fault with it.

She appeared at least partially mollified.

"I side with Queen Hel," said Perkelmir. He cast his gaze across the rest of the representatives. "It would serve you best to do the same. Together, we can crush this upstart Isir!"

Hel shook her head but said nothing. I thought I caught a gleam in her eye before she turned away, nonetheless.

"What is *your* choice, Queen Hel?" I asked. "Will you join your people against the *Plauinn*?"

"The *Plauinn*?" scoffed the Svartalfar representative. He'd given his name as Hrokafutlur, which meant "arrogant" in the *Gamla Toonkumowl*, and I doubted that was his real name. "A tale to scare children!"

"I wish that's all they were," I said, shaking my head. "But as my emissaries no doubt told you when they delivered my invitation, the *Plauinn* have been manipulating relationships among the races for a long time, driving wedges, creating hatred. They have only one goal: remake the universe in their image. The *Plauinn* are stronger than any of us."

Hrokafutlur scoffed and turned his head away.

"We are in grave danger—*all* of us. I've been to the underverse, the realm of the *Plauinn*. A friend and I rescued Queen Hel from Owraythu's realm, and I battled Owraythu and her brother, Mirkur, on this spot," I said, sweeping my arms out to my sides. "Without a powerful ally, who wishes to remain anonymous for the time being, we'd have lost, and even with her help, Mirkur escaped along with most of the *Plowir Medn* who attacked us."

Hrokafutlur shook his head.

One of Hel's courtiers stepped forward. By the gaunt lines of his face and body, he was not only a courtier but an *oolfur*. "You'd claim the right of leadership of us all?"

"I claim no leadership of anyone who is not Isir. But if you are Isir, and you intend to live among your race here on Osgarthr, you must swear your oath and accept my laws, same as the rest."

The *oolfur* shook his head. "But you enforce the *Ayn Loug*. How am I to eat?"

John Calvin Brown stepped out of the ring of Isir troops. "By your leave, Isakrim?"

I nodded and held my hand out in his direction.

He bowed his head for a moment before lifting his gaze to the *oolfa* present. "Unlike what we have always believed, we can overcome the *layth oolfsins*. The Lady Sif has helped me regain my humanity."

Luka made a noise of contempt, but I saw many of the assembled *oolfa* exchange questioning glances. "It's true," I said. "The changes wrought by breaking the *Ayn Loug* are reversible. John is living proof." I nodded at him, and he stepped back into the throng of Isir warriors. "Each of you is free to make your own choice. I will force no one to choose one way or the other. But, know this: Any Isir who does not swear his oath to me and rejoin his fellow Isir will not be free to go where he pleases."

"And how will you stop them?" sneered Hrokafutlur.

"They will become my thralls." The *oolfa* and other courtiers of Queen Hel shouted refusals. I held up my hand. "It is not permanent, and I will exercise no rights over what you do or with whom you associate. The only thing I will enforce is *where* you are."

"Meaning what?" asked Hel.

I nodded and held my hand out to Althyof. He stepped forward and laid a shining metal collar in my hand. I held it up and turned it, so all could see the runes carved into its sides. The metal was light and warm, like the chisel used to engrave it. "If you choose not to join us, you will wear this collar until such a time as we deal with the threat or you change your mind."

"And what does this collar do?" snapped Luka.

I flashed a grim smile at him. "You've already experienced the effect I've enchanted in these collars. But for everyone else's edification, it monitors your location, and if you try to leave your assigned area, it will lock you in a memory loop."

"And what does that mean?" asked one of the *oolfa*.

Hel shook her head and grimaced at me, but I thought I detected a glint of admiration in her gaze. "It means you fall unconscious and experience one of your memories again and again until someone lifts the curse."

"It's not a curse," I said. "It's only a method of controlling—"

"It *is* a curse," she said. "I would know, would I not?"

I lifted my shoulders and let them fall. "I disagree. I know what it is to suffer under someone's curse, wouldn't you agree?"

Hel turned her face away.

"At any rate, to avoid the negative aspects of the collar, all you have to do is stay put. But know this: I have no doubt that, given enough time, you can figure out a way to remove the collar, but if you do that without having sworn fealty, I will consider it an act of war and bring the full wrath of the Isir against you."

Hel's gaze snapped up to mine and anger blazed there.

"I've given you a chance to redeem yourself—or at least to live in peace. I *will not* give you another."

Hel dropped her eyes and stepped forward. "Then place the collar around my neck yourself, *Konungur Isakrim*."

Althyof put a collar in my hand. I met Luka's gaze, almost able to feel his hostility on my skin. "This isn't permanent. I will release you if you change your mind."

He stepped forward, beside Hel, and lifted his chin. With a sigh, I snapped the collar around Hel's neck and murmured the *triblinkr* that would activate the enchantment. Althyof slid another collar into my waiting hand, and I repeated the process with Luka and stepped back.

"Do not think I will wear one of your slave collars!" snapped Hrokafutlur.

I shook my head. "No, I would not dream of it. As I said, I rule the Isir and no others. To the other races, I extend my hand in friendship and ask for your support. I believe a war is coming to us all from beings beyond this universe, whether or not we want it. Our foes are far stronger than any of our races, and perhaps stronger than all of our races combined."

"And if we choose *not* to ally ourselves with you?" rasped a cyclopean fire demon, who Meuhlnir had identified as Surtr, one of the leaders of Muspetlshaymr.

"If you prefer to sit out this conflict, that's fine. That's your choice. I will see you home, and we can part as friends, but you should know that I control the *preer*—*all* the *preer*. Any race that elects to sit this out may do so in the privacy of their own *klith*, but we will cut their klith off for the time being."

Hel bristled. "And where will you imprison my people and me?"

I nodded at Perkelmir. "On Niflhaymr with Perkelmir."

"What's to stop the rest of us from doing as we please? We've access to the *strenkir af krafti* just as you do. We can learn to access the *preer* on our own," asked Surtr.

I twitched my shoulders up and down. "Maybe. But I know of only two methods of controlling the *preer*, and I control both methods." That was a lie, as Haymtatlr controlled one of the methods, and I controlled the *knowledge* of how to manipulate them without his intervention, which wasn't quite the same thing. It wouldn't hold them forever, and if the *Plauinn* contacted any of the other races, they could teach them to manipulate the *preer* as they had taught me, and perhaps that way they could wrest control of Haymtatlr's *preer* away from him. But we needed time to consolidate, to build our armies, and to make plans to combat Mirkur. The lies might buy us that time.

Hrokafutlur cleared his throat. "And what if we choose to neither ally with you nor with the lovely Hel, and yet we refuse to sit at home?"

"*Queen* Hel," rasped Luka.

The Svartalfar inclined his head and waved his hand languidly. "As you say."

Althyof stepped forward. "Then we will come after you, driving you out of every place you hide, driving you to Niflhel regardless of your refusals."

Perkelmir growled.

"Oh, quit complaining," said Althyof. "It's as good a name as any!"

"And you expect us to take this?" asked Hrokafutlur. "To roll over?"

Mothi smiled, and it sent chills down my spine. "You could object," he said, cracking his knuckles and rolling his shoulders.

"Threats?" mused the Svartalf, but he said no more about it.

"You will want time to consider your options," I said.

Althyof shook his head. "I don't need any. The Tverkar are with you."

"You don't need to talk to your people?" I asked.

"Done and dusted," he said with a smile. "We don't appreciate anyone interfering with our internal arguments, *Plauinn* or Tisir." He glanced around and shrugged when he didn't see her.

"And the Alfar," said Skowvithr. "We stand with Konungur Isakrim." At his side, Yowtgayrr nodded.

"You've spoken with Roorik, the Voice of Tiwaz?"

Yowtgayrr nodded. "He sends his congratulations."

"And Freyr?"

Skowvithr nodded. "I have. He sends his thanks to 'that Tverkr,'" he said with a small smile for Althyof, "for sharing my brother's last moments. He also sends greetings to you, Konungur Isakrim."

I nodded. "Fair enough." I turned my attention to the other races, the other Isir still undecided. "And the rest of you?"

Surtr shrugged. "Not much of a choice."

"And yet you must make it."

Hrokafutlur nodded. "The Svartalfar will stand with Osgarthr."

That surprised me, but given the choice I'd offered them, maybe it shouldn't have. In the end, about half of the *Briethralak Oolfur* stayed true to Hel and Luka, and the others renounced their oaths to her and were welcomed home. Most of the races came to our side, the notable exceptions being the trolls, who sided with the frost giants rather than Hel, and some of the so-called demon-races who were so strange I could barely understand them, anyway.

I left Althyof and the others to oversee the thrall collar fittings, to convey the people who had refused my offer back to their homes and then close those *preer* behind them, and I walked into the forest. I hadn't seen hide nor hair of the Nornir since the fight with Owraythu.

After a few minutes, I emerged from the undamaged part of the woods into one of the paths Owraythu created while chasing us. The forest was already healing. Heaps of ash and charred logs still lay in clumps almost everywhere I looked, but there were already sprouts of new ash trees poking through the ruin. Keri sniffed the fresh shoots and wagged his tail.

"Yeah, that is pretty cool, isn't it, Keri?"

He looked up at me and seemed to smile.

"The trees here are special," said Kuhntul.

Keri and Fretyi alerted and stared into the forest on the other side of the path of destruction. She emerged from the shadows, wearing a pale blue dress. A band of silver held her blonde hair in place. She'd never appeared in that guise before, and as she was, she could have been Freya or Hel's sister.

"That's a new look," I said.

She batted her eyelids coquettishly. "Do you approve?"

"Kuhntul…"

She laughed and waved her hand at me. "You're no fun, Tyeldnir. Can't we even flirt?"

"No," I said, softening it with a smile.

"Does Jane know how loyal you are?"

I nodded. "I think she does."

"I'll be sure to tell her next time I see her."

I glanced around and encompassed the destruction with a wave of my hand. "How long will it take for these scars to disappear?"

"Time can be funny here." She pointed off into the forest to the east. "Back that way, there is a part of the forest that exists in a different timeflow from this part." She lifted her shoulders and let them fall. "It's all part of life at the Conflux."

I nodded. "Speaking of life at the Conflux, where are the Nornir?"

The bell-like tones of Kuhntul's laugh chimed through the trees. "Those old hags? They are around."

"I still need to speak with them."

"They fear you, Tyeldnir."

I shook my head. "They should fear you and your sword, not me. Besides, they have nothing to fear from me, provided they don't interfere. But I need to speak with them about the changes that I must put in place here."

"Changes?" demanded Urthr's voice from somewhere in the trees. "That is impossible."

"And yet, there *will be* changes," I said.

"No, there will not! You are nothing but *murderers*," said Verthanti, stepping from the trees a ways down the scar in the forest and glaring at us. "*Both* of you!"

"Kuhntul," I said in a voice of iron, "draw your sword."

Metal hissed against metal as that blindingly bright blade came out.

"Nornir—no, forget that. *Plauinn*, hear me. You've seen what this blade can do. Do you believe you would survive where Owraythu fell?"

Nothing but silence answered me.

"Good," I said. "Here are the new rules. You now work for me, and your job description has changed. From this moment onward, you will monitor *uhrluhk* for changes, but you will *do nothing* other than reporting the changes and the possible effects of those changes to me, or to a person I name. You no longer *decide* anything! You will no longer *correct* or in any other way *manipulate* the skein of fate. You will not share information about the skein of fate to other members of your race. Tell me you understand."

Urthr stepped from the trees next to Verthanti and added her glare to her sister's. Skult appeared on the other side of the charred avenue and sighed. "I understand," she said. "I will speak with my sisters."

I shook my head. "Not good enough. I need your acceptance—all three of you."

Skult sighed once more. "My sisters resist change. It is their nature."

"And not yours?" I asked, arching an eyebrow.

"I recognize necessity. Verthanti senses what comes into being on the horizon, Urthr is rooted in what once was. Do you see?"

"I do, but I still need them to accept this. The *Plauinn* have declared themselves the enemy of the Isir, and every other race that exists in the universe. I—"

"Not all the *Plauinn* side with Mirkur!" snapped Verthanti. "He and his sister are the tyrants of the underverse."

"His sister is dead," I said. "Mirkur is on his own now."

"As you say," murmured Verthanti.

Skult took a step toward me. "Others among the *Plauinn* disagree with the way things are. Bikkir, among them." She glanced across at her sisters. "We three, as well."

"In that case, agreeing to my terms should not pose a problem."

Skult nodded. "No, it does not. Sisters?"

"Very well," said Verthanti, looking away.

"I… I will not go against the will of my sisters. I agree," croaked Urthr, and it was as though the words were pulled from her by brute force.

"That's fine. You may return to your campfire with my blessing."

Skult glanced down at the ash under her feet. "Perhaps we will allow the campfire to fade from this place. It's seen enough fire for a time." She raised her gaze to Kuhntul. "Do you come with us?"

Kuhntul smiled. "I'm afraid not, Mother Skult."

Skult shook her head. "Then it's 'mother' no longer."

Kuhntul's smile faded a little. "As you wish."

Verthanti held out her hand to her sister and Skult joined the other two. She turned as she came within an arm's length of her sisters. "Just remember that you have support among the *Plauinn*." Without another word, the Three Maids walked into the forest together.

Kuhntul returned the sword she'd used to kill Owraythu to the sheath on her hip, the hilt winking in the sun. A blood red jewel sparkled from the pommel, and sunlight flashed from the gold and platinum wire set into the grip.

"That's quite a sword you have there."

Kuhntul patted the hilt, looking down at it. "Yes."

"Very ornate for a weapon of war, but I can't argue with its effectiveness."

Kuhntul smiled and met my gaze. "Yes. Kramr has come in handy many a time, though circumstances have dictated that I couldn't wear it openly."

I felt as if someone had punched me in the gut. "Kramr? The sword Hel commissioned from Vuhluntr? The sword crafted to kill Meuhlnir?"

Kuhntul shrugged, mischievousness dancing in her eyes.

"How did you come by it?"

She laughed her glass-bell laugh. "I have my methods."

"Why didn't Hel or Luka recognize it?"

She spread her hands to her sides. "I did not wish them to."

"Who *are* you?"

"My name is Kuhntul of the Tisir."

"That's not what I meant, and you know it."

Kuhntul's smile faded. "Do you truly wish to know? Once you know something, you cannot unknow it, no matter how much you may wish to."

"Who are you?" I repeated.

She looked away into the healthy part of the forest, but before she did, I saw regret on her face. "I don't want to tell you."

"Who are you, Kuhntul?"

She heaved a sigh and returned her gaze to mine. "I am Kuhntul…but once, long ago, I was known as Suel, but I…" Her voiced faded and her eyes slid shut. "But I am not the woman you knew as Liz Tutor, though I remember her deeds." She shook her head and grimaced. "I wish I didn't."

"How…how can that be possible? I put a thrall collar on Hel not more than ten minutes ago, she's on Niflhel already, and she can't…"

Kuhntul shook her head sadly. "I am Kuhntul. The woman you collared is Hel. Though we were both once Suel, we are *different*."

Anger slashed its way through the shock I felt. "You—"

"The *Plauinn* manipulated me as well, but in the memories I have that are mine and mine alone, I did not lose the war against Meuhlnir and my friends. I was…" She took a deep breath and let it hiss out between her lips. "The *Plauinn* did such a good job of manipulating me. I followed their trail of scraps like a good little dog. I did not hold back. My anger against my friends boiled and boiled within me." She closed her eyes again, and a tear trickled down her cheek. "I…I showed no mercy. *I killed them all!*" The last statement came out as an enraged sob.

I stared at her in silence, but with a slow rage bubbling away within me.

Her shoulders heaved with another broken sob. "I ruled for a while after the war, but it was…it was a black time. Nothing seemed to bring me pleasure, and the dreams I had… The dreams were terrible. I withdrew for a time, living inside my palace and seeing only Luka and Vowli. The Mad Queen they called me." She shook her head. "If only they knew."

She looked me in the eye. "They—the *Plauinn*—continued to do their work, and the universe became a very dark, very bleak place. There was no future, no possibility of…well, anything. I couldn't stand it. I couldn't stand what I'd done. I couldn't stand the only future that existed for me."

"But you could have *fought*—"

"No, Tyeldnir. They had already won. The damage was done." She waved her hand at the destruction around us. "Besides, you've seen their power." She laid her hand on the hilt of Kramr. "I didn't have this at that time. In my timeslice, I never needed it. I stole this from Vuhluntr on the day he split the hinges of Suelhaym." She shook her head, dashing away the tears. "I couldn't live with it. The bleakness of the future, the utter destruction the *Plauinn* wrought in other realms, what I'd done to empower them." She took another deep breath. "I taught myself how to avoid the *Plauinn*, how to hide from them. I learned how to create my own *preer*—by the methods I've taught you and your friends. After that, I learned how to change the past."

I nodded. "*Uhrluhk*—"

"No," she said gently. "Not *uhrluhk*. I learned to change my timeslice for everyone at once." She shook her head once more. "No, if I'm to be honest, I'll tell you all of it. I learned to cut my timeslice, to destroy the events that occurred after a specific point. I—"

"What happened? How did you do it?"

"Remember closed timelike curves as we discussed? I learned to create one on a massive scale—one that encompassed the entire timeslice—and I rode back to the point in time I'd decided to change." She looked me in the eye. "The process was difficult, painful...fatal."

"Fatal?" I barked a laugh. "You look pretty lively for a dead girl."

She nodded, smiling. "I ended up bound to the *Plauinn* for a time, but I broke what bound me to them. From that point on, it was only a matter of giving the appearance of being bound to the *Plauinn* while I affected my changes. One such change was to tell Suel—the Suel of this timeslice—the truth about the *Plauinn*. That knowledge led her to surrender, to abdicate, to allow Osgarthr to limp on until I could bring you into the fight."'

"You *brought me into the fight*?" I hissed. Anger bubbled in my veins. I felt betrayed, manipulated yet again. The fingers of my Personal Monster™ stirred with the strong emotions pounding away in my head. With a long sigh, I forced myself to let it go. "Didn't they know? Didn't they know about your…your…" I shrugged.

"I call it my 'pruning.' Yes, like a wayward branch, I pruned the timeslice, cutting away the rot, dressing the wound." She looked around. "All told, I think I've done rather well. I've caused you and your family pain, but I think the benefits have outweighed the pain. I brought you here—well, I moved Luka's *proo* to hang above that lake near Meuhlnir's hall, I—"

"That almost killed me, you know." It came out as an enraged squawk.

Kuhntul smiled, the picture of serenity and gentleness. "I watched from a short distance away. The danger seemed close to you, but—"

"*Seemed* close? I almost went through the ice! I almost froze to death in that *sterk task*!"

She shook her head. "No, Tyeldnir. I wasn't far away. Had things gone badly, I'd have arranged a reason for Meuhlnir to find you sooner."

I shook my head, my fury dwindling from a blazing inferno to glowing coals.

"Speaking of Meuhlnir, I set him and the others in your path, left the *puntidn stavsetninkarpowk* where you would find it—"

"Did you have a hand in what Luka and Hel did on Mithgarthr? Did you have a hand in this curse?" I swept my hand down the length of my side, and her gaze followed it.

She returned her gaze to mine. "I did none of those things—except for my complicity by telling Hel the truth and leading her to abdicate and escape to that realm. I had not expected her to sink to such depths. She and I are very different women in many ways." She shook her head, and her long blonde hair danced in the breeze. "Am I wrong about the benefits outweighing the pain?"

I thought about the conversation I'd had with Jane after we'd returned to Valaskyowlf. About what she'd said about Osgarthr and the Isir, and the coals of my anger died out. I thought about the grimoire, and how it seemed tailor-made for the trials I'd faced. I shook my head.

"Yes, Tyeldnir, I was known as Suel, but now I am Kuhntul and nothing more. Because of you, because of your leadership—"

"I had help."

"—I am now free to serve Roonateer without the subterfuge of serving the Nornir, the other *Plauinn* who bound me to them."

I was still angry with her, but those words brought about a pang of disappointment—similar to the one I'd felt after the fight with Owraythu when Hel had returned and demanded we bend our knees to her. "You're leaving?"

She chuckled and shook her head. "Don't you know?" She peered into my face, and her mirth faded. "You truly don't, do you?" she mused.

I lifted my suddenly heavy hands and let them fall. "Know what?"

"Who you are."

"I'm Hank Jensen, nothing more. As it's always been."

She laid a hand on my shoulder and stared me in the face. "No." A grin tugged at her lips. "Well, I mean, yes, that's true, except for the 'nothing more' part."

I grinned back at her. "Yes, I'm also Jane's husband, Sig's father. I'm an Isir, and now I am *Konungur* of the Isir, whether or not I want to rule Osgarthr."

So softly I had to strain to hear her words, despite her being three feet away, Kuhntul said, "You are Aylootr, the Ever Booming."

My grin blossomed into a full smile. "I still need to get Mothi back for that."

Kuhntul's gaze turned grave. "You are also Tyeldnir, the Wand Bearer. Some call you Valkyosanti, Chooser of the Slain. To others, you are Krimnir, the Hooded One. Because of this day, you will become known as Helpinti, the Binder of Hel. The *Plauinn* have a name for you. Even the people of Mithgarthr have named you. There, they already know you as Hanki; the Hanged One, Prooni; the Great Brown Bear; and Hrafnakuth, the Raven God."

I shook my head hard, a sober expression replacing my smile. "I'm no god."

Kuhntul inclined her head and arched her brows. "Perhaps not—not now, anyway—but maybe you once were, and you might be again. You are Kankari, the Wanderer."

"No, you are mistaken, Suel. I am—"

"I am Kuhntul. The Suel I once was is long dead."

"Fine, Kuhntul. But you are wrong."

"Hank," she said, "*you* are Roonateer, the one I chose to follow so long ago. You are the God of the Runes." She jerked her head toward Iktrasitl, towering toward the sky in the distance.

"I'm no god, Kuhntul," I said resolutely.

She pressed down on my shoulder, lending emphasis to her words. "You are Isakrim, also known as Owsakrimmr, the Leader of the Isir."

"I'm just plain Hank Jensen, and—" I snapped my mouth shut and stared at her. "Wait a minute…Owsakrimmr? The man hanging with me in Iktrasitl, he said his name was Owsakrimmr. He taught me the runes, might be he's Roonateer. Ratatoskr can't seem to tell us apart, so we must resemble one another. Maybe he's the one you chose."

Kuhntul smiled at me with a gentle expression in her eyes. "He is, but so are you."

"That makes no sense, Kuhntul."

She laughed. "And yet, it is the truth. You are Alfuhthr, the Father of All, and my sword is yours." She bowed her head, and when she looked up, there were tears in her eyes.

"Now, wait just a minute. I know my Norse mythology, and I know who the Father of All is. Are you saying I'm Odin?"

She smiled wide, and glossy mahogany wings sprang from her shoulders. She picked me up without apparent effort, and her great wings beat the air. Carrying me as if I weighed nothing, she ascended into the sky.

I looked down to see Keri and Fretyi running in tight circles and barking. "Where are you taking me?"

"Not where, Roonateer. When." She flew toward Iktrasitl, and the *varkr* puppies followed our progress from the ground.

I craned my neck to see her face, and serenity and confidence glowed there like the radiance of the sun.

We flew to the top of Iktrasitl, and Tindur cried a greeting. Kuhntul continued straight up, high above the top of the towering World Tree. She came to hover next to a *proo* that floated in midair.

"Hank," she said in my ear. "You are the one I serve, the one I helped create. You are Roonateer."

Before I could speak, she took us through her *proo* and into a version of the Conflux that seemed different somehow. After a moment, I realized there was no damage to the forest, no brutal scar of ash and destroyed trees, but that wasn't all. There was something else I couldn't put my finger on.

"What are you doing, Kuhntul?" I asked, alarm tickling the back of my mind.

"Now, Roonateer, you must remember this. You must say your name is Owsakrimmr, and you must say no more than that regarding your identity."

"What? Why?"

"Do you remember what Owsakrimmr said to you when you hung in the dreamslice reflection of the World Tree?"

I looked down at the tree and the surrounding land. Is that what's different? Is this the dreamslice reflection of Iktrasitl?

"Do you? Do you remember the sound of Owsakrimmr's voice?"

"I don't think I will ever forget."

"That is good. You will need to play the other part this time."

"This time? What are we doing here, Kuhntul?"

In answer, she sank down next to the Tree, slowing as she descended. "Ah, there it is." She drifted closer to the tree. "I'm not sure how close we are to your first visit in the timeflow but don't worry, I am sure we are here in advance of your other self."

"You're not making much sense."

She chuckled and held me out at arm's length. "This will do nicely, I think."

Something took hold of me from behind and pulled me from Kuhntul's grasp with a gentleness that reminded me of a mother holding her newborn child. "What's happening?"

"You must play your part, Roonateer. Remember what I said, about giving Owsakrimmr as your name, and about the words that were spoken to you on your first few visits here. Much depends on your performance."

"My addend," I murmured, shaking my head. I swallowed, my throat clicking with dryness. "This is freaking me out, Kuhntul."

"I will be here, though I, too, have a part to play. Do not draw the attention of the Nornir. Try not to draw any attention. Your earlier-self will be here soon. And afterwards, we have a dead frost giant to visit."

The familiar sound of Ratatoskr scrambling down Iktrasitl's trunk erupted from below us. "Who is that? Who is mucking about up there?"

"Relax, Ratatoskr," I said in a voice filled with gravel, craning my neck to see him. I remembered all those times the little red squirrel had asked me if I was going to attack him with a spear. "Don't give me any trouble or I'll have to poke you with a spear."

"No reason to be rude!" snapped Ratatoskr.

I chuckled and turned my gaze back to Kuhntul, but she was gone. Ratatoskr scrambled by me and left me alone, hanging in Iktrasitl, waiting for myself to appear.

If you've enjoyed this novel, please consider joining my Readers Group by visiting https://ehv4.us/join. Or follow me on BookBub by visiting my profile page there: https://ehv4.us/bbub.

See all the books in the *Blood of the Isir* series on Amazon:

Errant Gods - https://ehv4.us/4eg
Rooms of Ruin – https://ehv4.us/4ror
Wendigo – https://ehv4.us/4wendigo

For my complete bibliography, please visit https://ehv4.us/bib.

AUTHOR'S NOTE

Hello there! Have a seat and relax a little. I'm feeling relaxed as I write this, as I've just finished putting together the image for the chapters and realized that I'm pretty much done with this novel. Sure, it's still out with a few alpha readers, then goes to the editor, then the proofer, and there's a chance at all of those stages that I may turn this into a book about petunias, but those chances are slim.

You see, I *like* how this novel ends, and to be honest, have known the outline of the end since somewhere about one third of the way through writing *Rooms of Ruin*. My excitement about the ending has had me bouncing in my chair for months and months, and now, it's finally (for all intents and purposes) finished and ready for you to read.

That's a pretty heady feeling, I must tell you. I've led a pretty eclectic and diverse life, and in all the careers I've had, nothing quite matches this feeling. Yes, there is some apprehension—will you like where Hank's story has taken him? Will you like the bombs I dropped on you in the last chapter? I hope the answer to those questions is "yes," because I love where the story took me during the writing of it.

Will there be more? As I have said in various places online and in the Author's Note of *Rooms of Ruin*, Hank's story does not, *cannot*, end here. I know the title and the beginning few scenes of book four, several ideas for novellas to hang off the side of the series like Christmas tree ornaments, and an entry in my digital notebook of ideas that I have named "Big Story ARC." Yes, there's more. A lot more.

It's strange to me, to be honest. When I wrote science fiction, I had a hard time getting to 70,000 words (which was, at the time, the minimum length for a science fiction novel) but now, 150,000 words seems easy. It might be the affinity I have for Hank's character, or the easy way all the characters write themselves, or the way the story just rolls out of me most of the time.

Having said that, Hank needs a vacation. I devoted most of 2018 to Hank's story and have other things I have to write before I come back to Hank. That's good news, really, as it will give my unconscious mind enough time to come up with new, crazier places for Hank to go. I can tell you one thing: now that the secret about Hank is out, the challenges that will face the Isir will require more help from the others *and* more development of their abilities. It's probably time for Veethar, Pratyi, Freya, Yowrnsaxa, and Sig to come up toward the front of the pack. Oh, and don't forget Keri and Fretyi... I'm going to stop right here before I start writing book four and blow all my plans right out of the water!

I'm often asked how I deal with writer's block, and I always quip that I "block it out," but that answer is nothing but artifice. I don't have writer's block anymore. I have the opposite problem—too many ideas, too many books in my head clamoring to get out. I've spent a great deal of time in the past few months trying to figure out how I can squeeze more words into the time my Personal Monster™ allows me to work, and, I've hit on a few ideas that seem to work in the limited time I've tried them.

I hope to increase the number of books I can produce in a year—though some will be shorter than my standard 650-750 pages. I have a goal or two for 2019, and if I can keep my Personal Monster™ distracted for long enough, I hope to bring you many more books to read than I was able to produce in 2018—including a sequel to *Demon King*, a book where Lily from *The Devil* makes another appearance, a book about a serial killer in a small town, a post-apocalyptic yarn (but it's so big in my head, I don't know how long it will take to get it written), and maybe even a little book that may be called *The Sons of Ivalti*.

Then again, since Mr. Story wears the pants in this literary family, all of that may change. Either way, 2019 is going to be a wild ride, and I hope you stick with me.

I guess that's all for now. As always, I'd love to hear from you either in email or on social media, so please don't hesitate to drop me a note.

See you in the funny papers!

ABOUT THE AUTHOR

Erik Henry Vick is an author who happens to be disabled by an autoimmune disease (also known as his Personal Monster™). He writes to hang on to the few remaining shreds of his sanity. His current favorite genres to write are dark fantasy and horror.

He lives in Western New York with his wife, Supergirl; their son; a Rottweiler named after a god of thunder; and two extremely psychotic cats. He fights his Personal Monster™ daily with humor, pain medicine, and funny T-shirts.

Erik has a B.A. in Psychology, an M.S.C.S., and a Ph.D. in Artificial Intelligence. He has worked as a criminal investigator for a state agency, a college professor, a C.T.O. for an international software company, and a video game developer.

He'd love to hear from you on social media:

Blog: https://erikhenryvick.com

Twitter: https://twitter.com/BerserkErik

Facebook: https://fb.me/erikhenryvick

BookBub Author Page: https://ehv4.us/bbub

Amazon Author Pages:

USA: https://ehv4.us/amausa

UK: https://ehv4.us/amauk

Goodreads Author Page: https://ehv4.us/gr